SAKTHI

SAKTHI

By Misha Hussain

Bluemoose

Copyright © Misha Hussain 2022

First published in 2022 by
Bluemoose Books Ltd
25 Sackville Street
Hebden Bridge
West Yorkshire
HX7 7DJ

www.bluemoosebooks.com

British Library Cataloguing-in-Publication data
A catalogue record for this book is available from the British Library

Hardback 978-1-910422-94-6
Paperback 978-1-910422-95-3

Printed and bound in the UK by Short Run Press

For Mir, Sjakie & Juniper

Author's notes

On 21 February 1952, Bengali-speaking students were shot dead and wounded in Dhaka for protesting the exclusion of their language in state affairs, which were predominantly conducted in Urdu. It was the start of the Bangla Language Movement, the first in a long series of events that would eventually lead to the independence of Bangladesh 20 years later. Today, that day is recognised by the United Nations as International Mother Language Day.

Language, wherever you live in the world, is an integral part of identity politics, and is sadly used to undermine and disenfranchise populations. In England, we see how non-standard dialects are regarded as inferior, or unintelligent, e.g., Manc, Scouse, Brummie or even the fast-evolving multi-ethnic London English (MLE), when in fact they are rich with local vocabulary and grammatical idiosyncrasies.

In this book, I want to celebrate languages and indeed dialects, so the story contains quite a few unfamiliar words. I've tried to smooth the reading process with footnotes and a glossary for words that may be too difficult to find online. This is controversial in some literary quarters, a hangover from the post-colonial period, but for me, having to check a dictionary every five minutes pulls the reader out of the narrative dream.

SAKTHI'S JOURNAL

১. MUTTON BIRYANI

Meghna

I smiled all the way through my mam's funeral, and if it wasn't for the rain masquerading as tears, the mourners might've thought I were callous, or half mad. I was neither, just glad another woman was free of the shackles of life, and men. I'll come clean: in our tradition I shouldn't have even been there. It's men who carry the body to the grave, a man who leads the prayer, and men who do the burial; as if women are too fragile to deal with the grief of death, despite enduring the agony of birth. But Meghna was stronger than any of the men who put her in the ground.

It was a squally day in Shaleton, sky a thousand dirty Brillo pads. The hearse pulled up alongside a messy, flooded part of the cemetery, where simple markers lay so close together, you'd think it were chock-a-block in the afterlife. Only a handful of people showed up, hardly enough to get the coffin out, so Father asked some randoms visiting the next grave but one to be pallbearers.

"Who died?" they asked.

"Sakthi's mother," someone replied.

The imam leading the service was a tubby little man. His wife fed him well, too well. His plain white tunic stuck to his belly in the wet, showing rolls of fat that questioned his piety. A rough, dark spot dominated his forehead where it had struck the Earth five times a day, every day for the last God knows how many years. His beard, dyed orange with henna, flapped in the breeze. He let his arms drop to his side, looked towards the east and began the *janaza* funeral prayer.

"Allahu Akbar," he said, and launched into a passage in Arabic with an off-putting Northern twang. Nobody had a clue what he was on about, but they still followed his actions regardless.

His words weren't welcome in my brain. Every nerve and synapse were jammed with memories, some sweet, mostly bitter. Pressing my eyelids tight, I remembered washing her body hours before, top to bottom, left to right, as is custom. Above the neckline, she seemed peaceful. Her jet-black hair pleated and tied in a bun, her eyes tranquil. I traced the ridge of her slender nose, across the cleft in her chin, and down her neck to her chest. Here, her smooth brown skin became rough and discoloured, the ribs a patchwork of blue and black. Running my fingers over the bruises, I could hear the screams again. The coroner said she'd died quickly, and without pain, but nothing could've been further from the truth. Every day alive inflicted a new flesh wound until she bled out like a sacrificial lamb.

The men stood shoulder to shoulder in a neat line behind the imam. They lifted their hands until their thumbs touched their earlobes and then folded them in front of their paunches. When the prayer finished, they turned their heads to the right and then to the left to send their blessings to the Noble Writers, angels who sat on either shoulder recording their good and bad deeds.

The men brushed their palms over their faces. Father took the body out from the coffin with the help of Akaash, our only male relative in the country. The imam nodded, and they lowered her into the grave making sure her head faced towards Mecca.

How I wished I could lie beside her. To be her light as the last rays of sun were blotted out. To keep her warm when the hard winter frost spread through the ground. And, when enough time had passed, when the creeping ivy had wrapped its fingers round her headstone, and the weeds had swamped her grave, to have a word with the bugs that crawled around underground and say, no, leave her be. Here lies a great woman, a mother, and a friend.

Father picked up a spade and thrust it into a heap of topsoil. But before he could throw it in, I burst through the line, grabbed a handful of earth and threw it over her body.

"It's your fault she's dead," said Father, wrenching me back into place.

I broke free and ran, I ran as fast as my little Bengali legs could carry me, away from this charade. Near the gates, police officers cordoned off several graves that had been defaced. Nazi swastikas in red paint loomed large across the headstones. The fetid stench of beer and urine made me retch. I covered my face with my orna[1] and made for the exit where Mrs Finch, our elderly neighbour, sat in her wheelchair. She crossed herself one last time. When she'd said her goodbyes to Meghna, she squeezed my hand and I pushed her back up the hill.

Rain, always with the rain up north. In between the showers, the smell of chips and vinegar wafted across the narrow streets and reminded Mrs Finch of a bygone era. Back then, she said, Shaleton sat at the heart of the industrial revolution. Blue-collar workers toiled long, hard hours in the textile factories and down the mines. Life was tough, but there were jobs and food enough on the table.

"Even the canaries had work," said Mrs Finch, as we approached the covered market in the town centre.

"Canaries?" I said, playing along.

"Down the coal mine," she said, with a wry smile. Mrs Finch twitched her nose as she often does before going off on one about Britain's lost glory.

"What happened, Mrs Finch?" I said.

1   A light Bengali scarf.

"Foreigners," she grumbled, waving her walking stick at some brown face that happened to be walking by. "Not you, chuck."

"No, of course not," I said, looking around.

Round our way the terraces buzz with women in black burkas and salwar kamiz, their placky bags packed with calabash gourds, taro root and bitter melons from the local Asian store. And in the evenings, the tang of chicken bhuna, fried tilapia and curried ladies' fingers engulfs the streets as tired shop keepers in kurtas with rumbling bellies follow their noses home, hug their children, pray, eat, and fall asleep in front of the telly.

We went along the main road and Mrs Finch pointed out where pound shops, fast food outlets and bookies have replaced artisanal stores. And where the baker used to hand out alms every Sunday, now homeless lovers huddle together in the cold. By their feet, a hand-written notice begging for loose change, some grub or just dignity. Those abandoned by love turned to Special Brew and song. They bellowed at us as we passed through the central square, for which they got a tenner! Seemed quite generous, but I guess you don't take it with you.

"Cheers, Mrs Finch," they called out, beaming. Despite the destitution, she remained optimistic. Shaleton has been told it can have its cake and eat it too.

We crossed the street at the Mill Road junction, which acts as the frontier between the Asian and white communities. The Mill Crew patrol everything above the pelican crossing. The older ones were drinking on the garden walls as we walked by, hiding their cigarettes as soon as they saw Mrs Finch. But the youngsters carried on pulling skids and wheelies on their mountain bikes, knocking over dustbins. Below the traffic lights belongs to the equally menacing Black Paws, teetotal on religious grounds, but stoners through and through. They see white girls as whores and Asian girls as property. Some days I don't know which is worse.

I turned the key and helped Mrs Finch in through our front door. The house reeks of curry when you come in from outside.

Over the years, the cumin has seeped into the sitting room carpet, the curtains, and the sofa. In the kitchen, the worktop is stained with turmeric, the wall behind the cooker mottled with specks of sunflower oil. I opened the fridge. No homemade lassi, no creamy dhoy,[2] no tubs of red-hot shutki borta,[3] comfort food for the Bengali housewife. Empty! Slowly, the relief at the cemetery ebbed away. In the back yard, a train of Meghna's saris fluttered on the washing line. I went outside and buried my face deep in the muslin, soaked from the morning downpour. Meghna has gone, and nothing can ever bring her back.

In the evening, some women from the neighbourhood came over with mutton biryani, sabji and dhal to feed the funeral-goers. Dadhi, my paternal grandmother, met them in her ghost-white sari, grey hair drenched in coconut oil and tied in a tight ponytail. Since moving in with us, she has taken it upon herself to be my chaperone. So whenever I step out of line, I get a discreet but painful pinch on my forearm.

I sat by Mrs Finch, perched on her wheelchair picking out the red meat she could neither chew nor digest. I gave her a running commentary on events like I was David Attenborough narrating Planet Earth.

"The males have been seated in a separate room from the females in case they are unable to control their natural urge to copulate," I said.

"Oh, you little devil, you!" she said.

"In the corner sits the imam, reeling off pearls of wisdom in between mouthfuls of curry. To his right, his deputy, Father, legs folded, back straight, ready to obey any command.

2 Bengali milk-based dessert.
3 Spicy paste made of dried fish.

"To his left, Dastgir, a.k.a. Dast. The leader of the Black Paws. He has swapped his Manchester United cap for a prayer hat and is trying his hardest to reconcile the Hadith with his ASBO."

Mrs Finch listened to my narration and corrected my grammar with the usual passive-aggressiveness she adopts when her beloved mother tongue is under siege. Whenever she gets a chance, she complains bitterly about the ruin of the English language. Today she raged about the demise of the semi-colon, the triviality of which on such a day made me chuckle.

Dadhi glared at me across the table. She disapproved of something: the way I crossed my legs in front of elders or spoke too loud; the way my hair fell loose on my shoulders or my blue eye shadow; my very existence perhaps. Thankfully, she was too far away to pinch me.

"Who are the couple in the doorway? They are with neither the men nor the women," said Mrs Finch.

"That's Trina, my cousin, and her husband Akaash," I said.

"I don't see them here much."

"No, they live in Manchester," I said, as Trina wrapped a shawl around her head and approached Father.

Uncle, do you need help with the shinni⁴? she said in Bangla.

"*Na, help lagbe na.* There won't be a shinni," said Father, looking away.

Kenno, why not? said Trina.

"Because it's *bid'ah*, un-Islamic," the imam said, tapping the Qur'an in his hand.

We are Bengalis, are we to forget our culture? said Trina.

The venom was in the query, not the volume or the tone of her voice. Nobody questions their elders, let alone the imam. The room went quiet. Even the women gossiping about how so-and-so's daughter had run off with a white boy waited for the answer, but it never came.

---

4 Get-together 40 days after a funeral for the wider community and those who couldn't attend the funeral.

Thik ache, that's fine. *Khuda hafiz*,* she said, bidding Father farewell.

"*Allah hafiz*," Father said, swapping the Persian name for God to an Arabic one.

The imam smiled.

Trina came over to give me a hug and then left the house with Akaash. Mrs Finch took this as her cue, so a little before Maghrib[5] prayers she asked me to fold up her wheelchair and pass her the walking stick.

"You're allowed to mourn, chuck. Jokes will only help so much," she said, holding my forearm.

"I'll be alright," I replied, and pressed my lips tight.

After she'd left, I followed the women upstairs to count prayer beads. We rocked back and forth, repeating God's name until I fell into a hypnotic trance. I started hallucinating. Opposite, the clock wheeled backwards faster and faster till the hands became a blur. The walls closed in. The chanting grew louder and angrier, until at one point the women all turned in on me.

Amongst them, a shadowy figure who hadn't finished eating. Meghna! Her shoulders sagged under some invisible weight, her hands were bloody. On her lap was a plate of biryani, a spoonful of dhal and a beating human heart. She dipped it in lime pickle, tore out fat chunks with her golden teeth and washed it down with lassi. With every bite I felt this sharp pain in my chest. I scrunched up my eyes, but she was still there, vivid, inescapable, etched into my eyelids with indelible guilt.

Death happens to others; the deceased don't have to mourn their loss. It's the rest of us who are doomed to live with the burden of unanswerable questions and the third conditional. If only this, if only that. *If* clauses will be the end of me. Could I have saved her? Was Father right?

I share a room with Dadhi. Late in the night when the old bat was snoring away, I crept downstairs to the kitchen. I took out

5   The evening prayer, at sunset.

12

my journal from the back of the spice cupboard, made myself a cup of tea and sat down at the kitchen table. In the early hours, the moon shone its frozen rays on the back alleys where stray cats rummaged through litter bins. In its light, I turned to my first entry just over two years ago and pored over the pages searching for morsels, hanging on every jot and tittle that brought me closer to understanding Meghna's death.

TWO YEARS AGO

२. CHICKEN TIKKA MASALA

By airmail

Today was my birthday, not that anyone should care. I mean, why would they? Around fourteen years ago, an unremarkable sperm impregnated an unremarkable egg resulting in an unremarkable pronoun. Me. The direct object of all verbs hateful.

We don't do birthdays in our house. No pressies, no visits from friends, not even a song. Father went all religious on us a while back when the imam at the local mosque changed. Since then, any protests only got me a bollocking, reminding me how Rohingya infants are drowning out at sea and Syrian children are being bombed in the desert. You should be happy I don't leave you to starve in a gutter in Dhaka and that you have a first-rate education, he says. That's my perpetual present, for which I can never be grateful enough.

Only spice helps lift the mood at times like this, mind-boggling, dizzying levels of chilli. So, when Father went to work this morning, me and Meghna chopped up some green mango, roasted a few cloves of garlic on the gas stove, crushed a handful of dried Tientsin peppers with our fingertips and mixed it all together with salt and fresh coriander leaves. Oh. My. God. I'm salivating just writing about it. So tangy! And the heat. Meghna was hopping from one foot to the other like she was walking on burning coals. I leant up against the fridge and chugged down cartons of ice-cold lassi just to numb my tongue. A couple of times our eyes met, tears streaming, and we creased ourselves before going back to our chosen method of firefighting. It only lasted a moment, the pain, but long enough to make us feel alive again.

When Father came home before the evening shift, he put the pre-paid card in the lecky meter, set the groceries down on the floor and slumped on the kitchen chair.

"Sakthi, put the bazar[6] away," he said.

"*Jee*, Abba."

"And make me a cup of cha, I could do with some liquid wisdom," he said, massaging his temples with his thumb and forefingers.

"*Jee*, Abba," I said, this time in a robotic voice.

Meghna covered her smile with the pallu[7] of her sari, jabbed me in the ribs, then turned around and pretended to do the dishes. I stuck the shutki[8] in the freezer before it stank out the house and then made the masala for the tea. Above, the strip light flickered a full minute before bathing the room in a harsh glare, revealing every crack in the paint, every patch of mould. The garish light made Father look hard, fifty-two years old with a solid jaw and dark, stony eyes.

A letter lay on the kitchen table, all damp and moth-eaten round the edges like its country of origin. The mail is nearly always about cash: Shumon's got to bribe the teacher or he'll flunk college; Ripon has to pay off his debt or the goons will kneecap him. Every South Asian family has scroungers living off rellies abroad, so I thought nothing of it. He picked it up and felt the texture, smelled the dirt. Then he held it up to the light to judge if it was worth opening straight away. In the living room, a small clock on the mantelpiece chimed five times and started to play the adhan.[9] He put the letter back down and got ready for the Asr[10] prayers.

Father passed Meghna in the doorway, turning sideways so their bodies wouldn't touch. He moves through the house

---

6   The shopping.
7   The loose end of a sari usually draped over the shoulder.
8   Dried fish.
9   Call to prayer.
10 The late afternoon prayer.

like the dead. And if it wasn't for the creaky door hinges or the rickety staircase, you'd never notice him till he was right up close. Mostly though he keeps to himself, imprisoned by some dark secret that twists his features so even gallant flickers of happiness cower in the shadows of his scowl. But Meghna stands tall despite the lack of thanks, of love. People aren't born with sadness in their hearts, she says, it has to be learned.

After dinner, Meghna took Dadhi up to bed, I cleared the plates and Father opened the envelope. Inside, a photo of a man and a short letter handwritten in Bengali, which I couldn't read for the life of me. He mouthed the words, a weird habit he'd got from reciting the Qur'an. After a while, he stood up and paced around the kitchen, one hand clutching the letter, the other stroking his beard, foraging for inspiration – the cha clearly worked.

"Sakthi, it's your birthday."

"*Jee*, Abba."

"Time you got your first sari," he said, folding the letter up and putting it into his wallet like it was a cheque.

And what about the restaurant? said Meghna in Bengali, raising her eyebrows as she came back into the kitchen.

"Dastgir can cover," said Father, who nearly always spoke in English.

"Oh Abba, can I get a blue 'un? I wanna be like Amma," I said.

"We can do much better! We can make you like a princess, one who enchanted the fiercest Moghul warriors with their beauty and charm," he said. I lost all self-control, wrapped my arms around his neck and kissed him on the cheek like he'd offered me the moon. Meghna was hurt by his snide remarks, but she shrugged them off with her usual grace.

The sari shop was an explosion of colour, like two rainbows had had a fight over a packet of Skittles. I danced around the mannequins, skipping from one to the next. They stood there, lips puckered, and noses pierced, wrists and ankles adorned with bangles. I jutted my hips out, displaying my midriff and an attitude that oozed out of the Bollywood stars on the cable channels. Meghna cracked up, and then got lost in the bales of cloth: silks from Beijing, georgette from Calcutta, all printed with the latest designs and embroidery.

Father was smiling ear to ear.

"Pick something, Sakthi," he said, giving the shopkeeper a nod.

"Oh, can I?" I said and ran over to the teal saris embroidered with silver. How pretty they'd look with a mustard blouse and shiny sandals. But the man behind the counter gave a nod back to Father and showed me to the reds.[11]

Meghna's face darkened like a storm cloud over the Ganges. The more I giggled in the fitting room, the tighter she knitted her brow.

So, you want to be a princess? she said, dragging the comb kicking and screaming through my hair.

"*Nje* Amma, like in 'em tales ya used to read us, with all 'em wonderful clothes, and jewels," I said, flinching with pain when the teeth caught one of the knots and jarred my head backwards.

Thik ache. Just remember even beautiful, rich, and intelligent princesses are still only women,* she said. What did she mean by that? She can be so cynical sometimes, it does my nut in.

I stood in front of the mirror whilst Meghna unfolded the clothes. My breasts have been feeling tender lately and one is growing a little faster than the other, so when I slipped the blouse on, the left side appeared a little loose. The sari wrapped round my waist about ten times. Meghna secured it using a

11 Traditional colour of wedding saris.

safety pin as I still don't have the figure for the material to hang naturally off my hips. Last of all, she put on this heavy gold chain that entirely covered the bare skin between my neck and my breasts.

As soon as I had the outfit on I ran over to Father who was chatting with the salesman. His face beamed when he saw me.

"There, what did I tell you, like a princess," he said.

"Thank you, Abba," I said, cheeks red. I dared not look back at Meghna to seek her approval. Father sat me down on a wooden stage almost drowning in fabric as he took out his smartphone to take some photos.

"Don't look so happy!" he said.

"But, in't princesses meant to be happy?"

"In all your fairy tales, have you ever known a princess to be happy who is not married to a handsome prince? Cinderella, Sleeping Beauty, Rapunzel?" he said, his arm around my shoulders.

"Why'd I need a prince when I've got Amma, 'n' Mrs Fin—"

"Yes yes yes, now do as you're told," he snapped.

I looked down at the floor, folded my legs to the side and supported my weight on one hand. I tried, God knows I did, to keep a straight face, but a little smirk kept creeping in, which annoyed Father no end. When he finished taking the pics, he ordered me back to the changing room.

"But, in't we gonna buy it?" I said.

"*Na*, take it off before you ruin it," he growled.

"*Jee*, Abba." I walked back towards Meghna, who looked at Father with suspicion. She held me in her arms and pressed my head against her chest. Her heart raced, her breath fast and shallow.

"Oh, what are you two looking so gloomy for, we'll get one for a better price when we go to Bangladesh in the winter."

"Bangladesh?!" we said, but with different tones.

Dadhi was fast asleep by the time we got back from the shops. In the sitting room, Meghna switched on the telly and cranked up the volume on the Bangla channel. Whatever she wanted to say, it wasn't meant for my ears. I perched at the top of the stairs, craning my neck an extra few inches so I could listen in to the conversation.

That letter, was it about... said Meghna, voice trembling.

"Better to keep things in the community," said Father.

Silence. Awkward, frustrating. The TV blared out about the war crimes committed in 1971 during Bangladesh's independence struggle, and the thousands of women that had been raped by the Pakistan Army.

He was a mean child, he failed school, she said.

"He'll work for free, he'll be loyal," he replied.

More silence. Painful, maddening. Father knew how to weaponise his reticence. I could hear Meghna rearrange the objects on the fireplace in muted rage, placing them down in their new positions with dramatic firmness.

Ish, can't we wait a few more yea—

"If you had given me a son!"

But your daughter could—

"The shame!"

I beg you; she hasn't started her... she's still a little girl.

My periods? I crept downstairs, avoiding the steps that might give me away, pushed my hair behind my ears and leaned flat against the door.

Imagine being ripped from the bosom of your mother, taken away from everyone you love—

Smack! I jolted my head back. Smack! Again, and a faint whimper. The room started spinning. I could stop it, I should stop it, said a voice rattling around my head, but it'd only make things worse like the last time. Father stopped sending money back to Meghna's family in Bangladesh and they didn't eat for almost a week. Anyway, that's what I convinced myself, but if truth be told I was plain terrified. I put my ear against the door again.

That imam, what's he offering to you now, salvation? said Meghna, her voice hardening.

This time I felt the slap like his thick hands had struck my own cheeks, the sting, the heat as blood rushes into the capillaries and the skin swells, red and raw, leaving a relief of his fingers. I placed my palm on the door half to steady myself, half to reach out to Meghna through the wooden panels.

"As soon as she's... ready. And not a word about the letter, or I'll—"

Accha, thik ache, not a word, said Meghna, agreeing to his demands.

The telly went off and I bolted back to my original listening post and waited for them to come out. Sleeping Beauty, Rapunzel, Cinderella, they were not unhappy because they didn't have a prince, they were unhappy because they were trapped, by a curse, a dragon, or an evil stepmother. Is that to be my fate too? The door opened and Meghna walked into the kitchen, her safe zone. I contrived to come down for a drink of water and passed Father on the stairs rubbing his knuckles.

Meghna leant her head over the sink and splashed water across her face. She took a glass from the dish rack. She trembled so much she could barely lift it to her lips, which were cut and bruised. I walked over to the phone and picked it up, but she shook her head – the shame it would bring on the family. The roots of our culture twisted themselves around her neck. The blood on her lips made my stomach turn. I could taste the bile at the top of my throat. She passed me the water then turned round, slid her back down the cabinet and buried her head in her hands. I put my arm through hers, rested my head on her shoulders and sat by her on the cold, hard floor. She didn't say a word, nor shed a tear.

Wild rice

"Meg, shut those windows, I can't enjoy the hyacinths because of that ghastly curry smell coming out of your kitchen."

Mrs Finch's shrill voice made an entry well before her geriatric frame hobbled round the corner. She banged her walking stick against the pane and peered over the sill. Meghna was organising all her spices in pre-measured quantities, following Delia Smith's recipe for the perfect chicken tikka masala – that quintessential British dish. It was her way of assimilating in the light of last week's toad-in-the-hole.

"Shared values, shared tastes," Meghna said in her broken English as she unlocked the backdoor.

"What possible values can you coolies teach us?" said Mrs Finch, in her charming colonial-speak, before turning to me. "Your mum's a lost cause, but you, we'll make a Brit out of you yet, Sakthi."

"But I am British," I protested. She hmphed, rested her stick on the table edge and sat down.

"What's wrong? Your face looks like Mark Rothko's Untitled (Black on Gray)," she said.

"It's nothing," I said.

Mrs Finch was wearing a bottle green skirt that came down past her knees, a white blouse and a tartan shawl. Her hair is white, worn in a bob. Her eyes are blue, intelligent, penetrating, but ultimately blind. She needs thick lensed glasses to see anything further than the tip of her nose, which is sharp-ridged and pointy like a sundial.

"Oh my, that's a nice souvenir," she said, squinting at Meghna through her specs. "Heathcliff's been at it again, has he?"

This was lost on Meghna, who walked over to the fridge and took out a vial of insulin. She drew up the contents into a syringe, pushed her sari aside and plunged the needle into the fat above her hip without a wince.

"Tea, Mrs Finch?" she said, disposing of the needle in the sharps bin. She put a chopping board in my hands and gave me two large onions to slice exactly as Delia Aunty had instructed.

"Now, if there's one thing you Indians know how to do, it's to make a good cuppa," she replied, twitching her nose.

Mrs Finch and her compliments! They come with this quaint, disarming racism that touches you like a child saying a word wrong. And her prejudice isn't restricted to Muslims and Jews, Asians and Africans, but to anyone who hails from outside the circular waterways of the Rochdale, Ashton and Huddersfield canals. Meghna chuckled behind her pallu whenever she heard such a comment. In the end, people are like wild rice, even the coarsest grains soften, it just takes more patience, she says.

Meghna took a pan out of the oven and put it on the stove. She poured in half a pint of milk, ripped open three bags of PG Tips and chucked in a few cloves and cardamom seeds. The mixture simmered for a couple of minutes before she served it with a quarter plate of sandesh[12].

"Doesn't this remind you of home?" said Mrs Finch. This is our home, I thought, as I mixed the spices with the onions and fried them in some oil. Meghna smiled. The two ladies sat in silence side by side. After a good while had passed, enough time that even awkwardness had outstayed its welcome, Meghna called me over.

"*Ghurnijhara*... my house," she said, and made a flattening gesture with her hands before asking me to translate.

---

12 A type of Indian sweet.

"*Ghurnijhara*? Is that a food processor?" I said, putting together the words *ghur* which means spin and *jhara* which means to shake.

Na, moina. Accha, it's like a food processor, but bigger," she said.

"Huh? Like a food processor, but bigger? I'm sorry Mrs Finch, I don't know what that means." I said.

"*Bonnya*," Meghna tried again, searching for simpler language that I might be able to understand, but I couldn't. We only ever talk about cooking and tidying the house, so even though I know what a ladle or a dustpan is, I haven't a clue how to say simple stuff not related to child slavery.

Mrs Finch frowned, offering up words herself whenever Meghna got stuck. At times, I thought she was guessing, but she has a remarkable knack for working out the meaning of Bengali words, which endears her to Meghna.

"Cyclone. Your home was flattened by a cyclone?" Mrs Finch said finally, first a little too enthusiastically, and then with a touch more compassion when she realized she'd got it right. Her little face lit up like it does when she guesses the key word that links all the others in a cryptic crossword.

Meghna poured her tea from the cup onto the saucer and sipped it straight from the dish. Mrs Finch pursed her lips and asked for a fork to eat the sandesh, and then listened attentively to Meghna's story. The women chatted and ate sweets until they hit a linguistic impasse neither charades nor food could overcome. Mrs Finch sipped the rest of her tea and went home.

Upstairs, Father was on the phone to Bangladesh, shouting down the line as if he was connected by a piece of string and two polystyrene cups. When the floorboards above us started creaking, I took the tikka masala off the flame and set it to one side. Meghna got out the food she had made the night before from the oven and heated it up on the stove.

Sakthi's Abba, come, dinner is ready, she shouted up from the bottom of the stairs, and then asked me to set the plates. On the dinner table lay a brochure for a new private, Islamic school – Mycombe Girls. The front cover was a couple of students, fully clad in burkas, reading the Qur'an with the undulating English countryside as a backdrop.

"Who's this for, Amma?" I said, putting it to one side.

Don't worry, your abba can't afford to send you to a place like that, she said.

Father walked into the kitchen in a crisp, white shirt and a shiny, slim fit suit he had bought in the autumn sales. He wore a gold-plated watch and black, laceless shoes he could easily slip on and off before going into the mosque. The strength of the attar overpowered the fenugreek and hing seeping from the cupboards as well as the cumin and coriander bubbling away in pots on the stove.

He sat down at the table, laid out to feed a king. Bengalis don't skimp on matters relating to the stomach. To his right were shallow-fried circles of aubergine, spiced with turmeric, cumin, and chilli. To the left, fish stewed in a tangy, jujube-based sauce. In front, a large bowl of orange split lentils with a sprinkling of freshly cut coriander. Meghna served Father rice, scented with bay leaves, straight from the pot, as there was no more space to put another dish.

Dadhi shuffled into the kitchen, dressed in white, smelling of shite. She had those thick-lensed, plastic glasses you get for free on the NHS that made her look like one of the Minions.

"Moina,[13] help your dadhi sit down," said Meghna

Give me a quarter plate and some water, said the old wretch, taking out her teeth and setting them down on the dinner table.

"*Jee*, Dadhi."

---

13 A type of starling, the myna, found in South Asia. Affectionate name for a child.

She spat out the supari and paan[14] she'd been chewing for the last hour. She tilted her head back and gurgled the water, some of which leaked out the corners of her mouth and stained her white sari bright red. I made her up a plate, picking out all the fish bones.

"*Bismillahi rahmani rahim*," said Father in thanks to God before the two started eating.

Meghna and I served ourselves, added a handful of green chillies and joined them. We ate in silence for a while and after the initial pangs of hunger had gone, I asked Father about Bangladesh.

"What's it like over there, Abba?"

Father took a spoonful of dhal and mixed in the rice. He separated out neat balls with his fingers, lifted it into his mouth and took a bite of some lemon rind. With his index finger he swept up the remainder of the sauce before Meghna cleared his plate.

"From our veranda in the village, you can see the sun setting on the horizon, its red disk reflected on the paddy fields," he said.

"What 'bout tigers like, in't it dangerous?" I said.

"Tigers are where your amma is from. But pythons, well, they have a tendency to hide under beds and behind curtains."

Stop scaring her, Meghna said with a smile.

Those were precious moments when Father remembered who he was. But after a while he remembered where he was, the intolerable present, and he fell silent again.

Are we going to Bangladesh? said Dadhi.

Jee, Amma,* Father said, lowering his eyes and looking at the fried aubergine in search of answers deep within its spongy fibres.

Shorom nai?! How can you show your face there again?* said Dadhi.

14 Betel nuts and leaves chewed on the sub-continent.

What did she mean by that? I looked at Meghna in the same way Father looked at the aubergine, but she shrugged and took a big bite out of a Naga chilli pepper. Father reddened. A bead of sweat trickled down the side of his face, landing on the lapel of his suit with a deafening plod. He looked at his watch, loosened his tie and collar to help his breathing, which became shorter and faster, then looked at his watch again. He wanted to rub his left sleeve with his right hand, a nervous tic, but it was covered in curry. In a panic he hurried out of the house without washing his hands.

Sakthi, bring me a bowl of hot water and lemon so I can wash my hands. Meghna, make me some supari and paan, Dadhi barked. She got out of her chair and hobbled back to the lounge.

Thik ache Amma, I'll bring it right over, said Meghna.

I washed the dishes whilst Meghna put all the curries back in the oven. I wanted to prod her again about what Dadhi said, she looked like she knew, but before I could ask she leant up against the cooker, bent double to relieve the pain in her abdomen.

Na! she cried, smacking the hob with the bottom of her fist.

"Amma, you alright?" I said, helping her to lie down on the kitchen floor.

It's nothing, moina, she replied with a grimace.

They're trying for a second, despite all the doctor's warnings. Father wants help running the restaurant, and a son is the best investment for his old age. Why can't I run the restaurant like Meghna said? It's not how I see my future, but still, something irks me in that I'm not allowed to do it just because I'm a girl.

When the pain had passed, Meghna got up and took a spoon out of the utensils drawer, closed her eyes, and had a taste of the tikka masala we'd made earlier.

Y' Allah, mishti na te gur, it's so sweet! she said, slipping the curry into a tiffin box with some plain, boiled rice and naan bread. *Taratari, quick, take this over to Mrs Finch. Tell her it's Burmese-style chicken marinated in Ceylonese yoghurt.*

I looked at her in disbelief. It was like nothing had happened. Like she hadn't been beaten the night before, like she hadn't just miscarried. Same old Meghna – beautiful ship above the water, hull breached below.

"A favourite of the *Raja*, right?" I played along, for which I got a smile and a kiss on the forehead.

We didn't speak about Father.

Next door, Mrs Finch was sitting in a faded, high-backed armchair. I put the food down on the kitchen table and opened all the latches for her. Sunday evenings at her house are the best, snug by the log fire that burns even in the summer. She owns this mahoosive collection of books, which I can read on one proviso, that I read them aloud (she's losing her eyesight). It's Mrs Finch I have to thank for my English, and Mrs Finch who tells me to be a proud Shaletonite.

"They'll use it against you, the way you talk, so practice your English with me. But never let them tell you it's wrong, you hear me?" she said one day, all teared up after reading Elizabeth Gaskell. God, what is it in the way she writes that makes you feel the dirt under her character's fingernails, that makes you root for them so bad? I wonder what she would make of the way we live, how she would write my story? Anyway, as Mrs Finch would say, I digress.

"Sakthi, is that you? Now, pull up a chair by the fire and let me see that beautiful chocolate face of yours," she said. I remembered what Meghna told me about wild rice and smiled. I sat down next to her on a pile of old almanacs that made for a perfect stool.

"He wasn't always like that, your father," she said.

"What do you mean, Mrs Finch?" I replied.

"Oh come, stop playing silly beggars now!" she said, craning her neck to look for something on the dining table. My chest began to swell, and my head felt like it was going to burst. It was a little out of the blue, though I guess the Spanish inquisition was on its way when she saw Meghna's face all battered the way it was the other day. Father hadn't done that before, never to the extent that he left bruises.

"Meghna reckons the imam has got to him," I said, wiping away a tear. I wanted to tell her about the letter, but I couldn't. It was almost like if I said the words, they'd come true (a self-fulfilling prophecy if you believe in that stuff). Besides, Father has threatened to marry me off a million times before, but it never comes to anything.

"Fetch me that package would you chuck?" she said.

Mrs Finch unclipped a pen from her blouse, wrote a message on a small gift card and attached it to said package, all the time talking about my father.

"He was a friendly chap when he first arrived in Shaleton in those flares, and long hair," she said.

"Father, in flares? Long hair?" I said.

"Hard to believe when you see him now on Fridays, muddling along in that daft prayer hat and that frock that goes down to his ankles."

"You can say that again."

"He lived in the house you're in now with a dozen other coolies. One by one, they each got married and left till it was just your father, and his new bride – your mum. He worked long hours down the Wilmslow Road till he could buy the house off his friends and start his own business."

"Oh yeah?"

"He was so proud that day when he opened the doors to the restaurant. Big, beaming smile, made you feel all warm inside. They were happy for quite some years, your mum and dad, but then as your mother says he met that imam. The rest is history. Of course, you won't remember anything as you were only yea high," she said, hands palm down, hovering around waist height.

I tried to picture him like Mrs Finch described. At first, I found it hard to imagine he could ever have been that person, but now I think about it, every so often he does or says something that gives away who he really is, pure opens up his heart. Like earlier today when he cracked that joke about the pythons; the way Meghna looked at him, that connection, it's just a flicker, but enough to make you think there's still something there. It's the closest they'll ever get to holding hands in front of me, let alone kiss. Have they kissed? Did they kiss when they conceived me? I'm starting to believe they did, despite everything. Perhaps that's why Meghna keeps saying that sadness has to be learned, she knew Father as a different person. So, who was that man? If I could just figure out a way to get into his head.

Mrs Finch let out a huge sigh, usually the sign that she had finished doing something arduous, in this case tying a bow.

"Happy birthday, chuck," she said, giving me the package.

"But it isn't my birthday," I said.

"It's belated, chuck."

"Be-what?"

"Late, dear," she said, with an exaggerated cough, meaning I had to write it down in my vocab book.

Inside was a beautiful, leather-bound notebook with velvety sheets. On the front cover a small inscription read: 'Memories for romantics, memoirs for poets.'

"Aww, thanks Mrs Finch," I said.

"Now, there's something that goes with it. A quill," she said.

"Is this to tickle people?" I said, holding up the feather.

"No dear, to write," she said.

"Are you serious? It'll take yonks with this," I said, trying not to sound ungrateful.

"Precisely, so every word you do write, you will mean. Words are cheap these days, this will teach you their value," she said, taking out a small pot of black ink.

"But I've never written anything before," I said.

"You'll learn. If Mary Shelley could pen Frankenstein at the age of eighteen, you can very well jot down a few words," she replied.

"But..."

"What are you scared of, Sakthi?"

"That I won't be able to do it Mrs Finch, that everyone will laugh."

"Write like nobody is reading, chuck."

"Then why do it at all?"

"For the simple pleasure of creating a beautiful sentence," she said, holding my hand.

Well, what can you say to that? Some people go to the ends of the earth looking for nirvana, but for Mrs Finch, everything she needs can be found in the twenty-six letters of the alphabet. I gave her a big hug, taking care not to break any of those century-old bones. I set the journal to one side and picked up *Jane Eyre*.

"Do you ever read *modern* fiction?" I asked her, before taking out some baking paper that served as a bookmark.

"Yes, I quite like Kipling," she said, in such a way that I couldn't make out if she was dead serious or just winding me up. "Now, where did we finish?" she said.

"Helen Burns had just pegged it," I said, to get my own back on her.

"Try to sound a little moved!" she said, closing her eyes in anticipation. I cleared my throat and began to read.

"'elen 'ad jus'—"

"E-nun-ci-ate, dear! You sound like a diphthong having a stroke. Give these flappy things on the side of my head a chance!"

By the time I'd finished the first chapter, Mrs Finch had conked out on her armchair. I emptied out the water and the kitbits from the cat tray, refilled it and placed it back by her feet. Felix had died a few months ago now, after a good ten years, but she still fed him. I rekindled the dying fire so it would be burning when she woke and I slipped out.

Outside, the long summer evening brought the streets to life. On days like this there is something charming about the shabby old town. In front of our house the girls played kerby, while the boys sat on the garden wall acting all cool and grown up. Meghna was hanging out the washing in the back. Inside, Dadhi was watching the anniversary of India's independence on the telly, some documentary on the Bangla Channel about Khudiram Bose.[15] I saw a tear, but I didn't stop to ask. I rushed to the bedroom and took out my new notebook. After a few practice runs, I got the quill, dipped it in the silky ink and made my first entry, leaving a few pages at the front to jot down the madness of my birthday. I could feel the resistance of the rough pulp on the nib; it felt old-fashioned, like a craft. It felt magical.

15 One of the first martyrs of India's independence.

My own Rothko

The ginnel joining the back alley to the main road is just long enough to roll my ankle length skirt up above the knees, so before I get out the other end, I've transformed into my alter-ego, like Superman in the telephone booth. At the bus stop the boys were slouching about, their shirts untucked and trousers loose around the waist so everyone could see their trendy boxers. The girls strutted around showing off their bare white thighs and padded bras under semi-transparent blouses. But, like true Brits, both sexes were buttoned up at the collar with a tie.

The Mill Crew started to notice me a few weeks ago, and they whistled at me today. I could feel their gazes on my neck, and down my back to my toes. My body wields some exotic power over their rowdiness. I blushed when I walked by and thanked God for the dark brown skin that hid my mortification. A few of them have grown well tall over the past year. But others waited for their growth spurts, and the gang looked daft when they stood next to each other.

One of smaller lads, Tone he calls himself, came over. He had these chonging white trainers on and his rucksack slung over one shoulder. Pasty white, all skin and bones. I wouldn't say he's good looking, but he's got these puppy dog eyes and a constellation of freckles around his nose and cheeks that make him look quite cute. He speaks with a broad local accent, but unlike the rest he hasn't picked up the Gallagher swagger.

"Ya reyt, Sack-tea?" he said, tucking his shirt in.

"Shock-thi," I said, for the gazillionth time.

"Mind if I walk to school with ya?"

What he lacked in size, he made up for in boldness, and where the harder boys were frightened out of their wits, he at least had the balls to speak to the opposite sex. It wasn't the first time we walked to school together. Most of the time, he plods along in silence with his headphones in his ears. I don't mind. I appreciate the time to think away from the drone of the telly at home, which switches between the Bangla Channel and Islam TV. But today he was feeling chatty.

"D'ya watch match, England-Bangladesh?" he said.

"Bangladesh plays football?" I said.

"Nah man, cricket!" he said, taking his headphones out of his ears. I tried my hardest to look bored, but no luck. I fiddled with my skirt to stop it sliding down and untucked my shirt to cover the folds I'd made along the waist. Tone lit up a rollie.

"Shakib Al Hasan, pure class, almost got his ton, 'n' his super scoop shot, mint like," he said, shaking his head in wonder.

"What ya bangin' on 'bout, you?"

"Han't ya seen it? It's all over Facebook 'n' Instagram."

"I don't 'ave a mobile phone."

"How come?" he said, taken aback, like I'd told him I didn't have a belly button.

"Me father, he won't let us 'ave one," I said.

Tone took a drag and then let out the smoke in a long, exaggerated breath. He did that when he was, as he likes to put it, 'processing'. I'm gagging to try one. The other day he opened a pack of cherry-flavoured tobacco he'd filched from his dad and it smelled gorgeous. Only Father would go apeshit if he ever found out.

"Right. Anyways, I thought you'd be rootin' for t' Tigers."

"Why would I? I'm British."

"Dad reckons it in't right t'expect foreigners to support England over their ethnic team coz there in't no 'British' cricket team."

"Me ethnic team?" I said, raising my eyebrows.

37

"Well, ya know, coz you're like a Paki 'n' all," he said taking another drag.

"Argh, I can't be mithered with all this," I said, and stomped off ahead. A crushing pain came and went in my abdomen.

"What've I said now?" he shouted after me. I ducked into the corner shop to calm down and buy some asteroid belts. When I came out, I found Tone sat on a bench, scraping dog dirt off the bottom of his shoes with a twig.

"Soz Sakthi, I in't tryin' to be racist or owt. What it is, right, folks are sayin' immigrants should be more patriotic. Just in cricket it don't make no sense."

"Right?" I said, stretching out the vowel.

"See, my family is from Glasgow, so I'm for Scotland when they play England. So why can't you be for Bangladesh?"

"Yeah, s'pose."

"Dad says real Britishness is in our self-defecatin' sense o' humour, and everyone should be asked to mock 'emselves to be let into the country," he said. I burst into laughter, at the idea people might shit on themselves rather than do a citizenship test. Perhaps it really would bring down immigration.

"Self-deprecatin'," I said.

"Why, what did I say?" he said.

"Self-defecatin'."

"Well, like, we could call it a shitizenship test," he said. I like a guy with a quick wit, so I forgave him for his out-and-out stupidity earlier and offered him some sweets to make up.

"Nah thanks, got chuddy," he said, and plugged his headphones back in.

When we reached the school gates, I saw Mr Belton, our short, stocky headmaster, measuring skirts with a yardstick to make sure they were no higher than two inches below the knee. It's what God would've wanted, I could imagine him saying. Nearby, a long line of girls, some sorry looking but most pissed off, had been sent for a walk around the rugby pitch to rediscover

38

their modesty and return their hemlines to the right height. I too joined the disgraced adolescents.

St John's Church of England comprehensive is on the outskirts of Shaleton, perched up on a hill high above the town. On clear days you get stunning views of the southern Pennines – and when the wind blows, the ripe smell of cow dung from the neighbouring farms. As I rolled my skirt down, the countryside, lush and green, was framed picture-perfect between the rugby posts. It was then, as I walked along the dead ball line, that a warm trickle ran down my leg. The girl behind me noticed a dark mark on my skirt, and this worked its way round until it got to my best mate Kelly, who was in front of me. She took me to one side.

"Nice one, better late than never," she said.

"Yes! No! Fuck! Fuck! Of all the places," I said, mortified.

"D'ya need any help?" she said, taking a tampon out of her bag.

"Nah, I wanna go home," I said.

Mr Belton squirmed when I explained to him what had happened. Without looking up, he told me to get changed and be back for the next period. No pun intended; he isn't the humorous kind.

Back home, Meghna was in the bathroom hand washing Dadhi's soiled bed sheets. Father forbade her to use the machine so he could save on the lecky bill before our big trip to Bangladesh in the winter. I walked up the stairs like a penguin, thighs together, and called her as soon as I reached the landing.

"Amma," I shouted, "It's 'appenin.'"

What's happening? Why aren't you at school? she said, as she opened the bathroom door.

"I'm 'avin' me per—"

The blood drained from Meghna's face. She placed her hand over my mouth and pulled me inside.

Shh, Dadhi, she whispered.

"So?" I whispered back, not quite sure why we were whispering. I know we come from a conservative culture, but surely Dadhi knows about menstruation. Meghna opened the medicine cabinet. On the top shelf hidden from view, an object of shame, was a box of sanitary towels. She took a pair of undies from the washing rack and told me to sit down on the toilet.

I ripped off a sheet of paper and pressed between my legs. The tissue soaked up the vibrant red, filling me with fear and excitement. A Rothko of my own – 'Blood on bog roll, 2014' – I imagined the caption would read. I took the lota and cleaned myself.

Now, you know how to do this? she said, holding out a huge sanitary towel that could double as a parachute for elves.

"But Amma, why can I not use tampons?" I protested.

Because we don't put things in there! she replied, a little taken aback.

"The girls at school, they use 'em. Kelly says ya can get thin 'uns," I said, but she ignored me. I put the damn thing over the seat of my underwear, folding the sides over as they'd shown us at school. I pulled them up, washed my hands and recoiled in shock when I opened the door.

Dadhi! You scared the... never mind, how did you get up here on your own? Why didn't you shout for me? I said.

Meghna hid my bloody knickers in the folds of her sari. I helped Dadhi to the bedroom and followed Meghna downstairs into the kitchen where she washed them in the sink.

Sakthi, daughter, promise me you'll never tell Dadhi about your periods, she said.

"Why Amma?"

Promise, Sakthi.

"Whatever," I said, and left in time to make the second lesson.

I walked back to school, taking the longer, picturesque route along the public bridleways. I wondered why Meghna told me to hide my periods from Dadhi. Was it somehow related to what she'd had a fight with Father about that time I heard them in the living room? I should ask her, but Meghna is strangely protective of Father and keeps those things close to her chest.

Then I got to thinking about the everyday practicalities that come with 'bleedin' out your fanny' as Kelly describes it. How long is this going to last? Will I get the same pains that Meghna gets? What the hell am I going to call it? All the girls at school have ways of describing their periods. And how am I going to do any sports wearing Meghna's sanitary towels? Towels, that's an apt word, given how big they are. But it's the word sanitary that kept bouncing round my head. Why is it we bundle being on the blob – ugh, I hate that expression – in the same bracket as taking a dump, like it's dirty, like it has anything to do with sanitation? I mean, I'm not going to start rolling around in my own menstrual blood like, but there's an argument to be made here.

R.I.P.

I woke up this morning with a huge grin across my face. I didn't expect it would have such a big effect on me, my periods coming, but it's like I've found a long-lost friend. I slept with my hand between my legs and dreamed the sweetest dreams. I had my first period! Did I say that already? I can't wait to shave my legs and buy my own bras. I'm becoming a woman, my body an hourglass, every drop of blood like every grain of sand, unique and perfect.

Dadhi was still snoring away, so I retrieved a borrowed copy of *Just 17* from under the mattress and read until the alarm went off at a quarter to eight. After the shower, I sat down in front of the dressing table to pluck my eyebrows. Meghna came in with what looked like bed sheets. She let the material slip through her fingers. Her eyes, surprisingly hard, met mine.

"You in't bein' serious?" I said.

It's not so bad, she said.

"I in't wearin' that, Amma. I'll look like one of the fanatics out of Mycombe Girls. They'll laugh at us in school, like they laugh at all the other Muslim girls."

They're just words, Sakthi.

I tried to ignore her, put on some blusher, and went to turn over the month on the Islamic calendar. Anything but deal with this insanity, but she wouldn't budge.

At least try it on, said Meghna, holding it out in front of her like it was a spanking new ball gown for a jihadi homecoming queen.

"But Amma, you in't even religious," I said, repulsed at the thought that I might walk around the streets of Shaleton looking like a fundamentalist, as if being brown isn't hard enough.

For me, please, she asked, tilting her head.

"Gi's it here," I said, snatching it from her hands.

I dragged the woven prison over my head and let it slide down my body till the fabric almost touched the floor. The cotton was suffocating. I felt my breath on my face. The smell of garlic was at first a surprise, but then repulsive as it hung trapped inside. A trickle of sweat formed on my temples. I closed my eyes and opened them. Through the mesh I could only see ahead, like a shire horse, blinkered into following the 'straight and narrow' road to God's good grace. On the wall hung a framed poster with the text of the Last Sermon. Father had torn down all my pull-outs of indie rock bands and footballers long ago.

"There, I've tried it," I said.

I opened the drawer to get my school uniform out, but it was empty. I thought I was losing my mind. I pulled the entire drawer out, the one below and the one below that till they were all piled up on the floor. I looked inside the dresser. I walked over to the wardrobe where I hung all my dresses and my salwar kamiz. Empty!

"Where are all me clothes?" I said. Dadhi had woken up from all the noise and Meghna went over to help her sit up on the bed. She put her specs on and then went back to the door and stood there arms folded, sari pulled over her head.

"Amma, where are all me clothes?" I asked again, louder, as you do.

Accha, Sakthi, listen, I've given them away,* she said.

"Given 'em away? Who to?"

Nje, to a charity shop*

"Why d'ya do that?" I said, frantically searching the room, under the bed, behind the door. I pushed my way past Meghna and turned her bedroom upside down looking for something, anything. She'd chucked the damn lot, keeping only a bunch of loose-fitting clothes.

*Sakthi, moina, stop. Stop!" she said grabbing my shoulders.

"Don't call me moina!" I said, and she covered her face with her arms, thinking I was about to punch her. "Which one? Which shop?"

Come, I'll make some nice shutki borta to—

"Yer as bad as he is, ya know that? Ya deserve each other," I said, some pathetic attempt at a barb, but it bounced right off her.

It's blue. I thought you said you liked blue? she said.

"I like blue. It's got nowt to do with... what ya doin' now?" I said, as Meghna took my school uniform out of the wash basket and put it into a carrier bag.

Well, you don't need these anymore.

"Yeah, I do."

I grabbed the skirt in her hands and tugged at it, but she held firm. It ripped, right along one of the long pleats. I fell back on the bed, head in hands. That skirt, that bloody skirt that makes me look like Mrs Finch's chaperone from the nineteenth century, I'd take that any day over this flaming burka.

Why are you so upset? You don't have to brush your hair or put any make up on. Nobody will notice you, isn't that what you want? You can just study so you can be a lawyer, go to Oxford, she said.

"Why do I 'ave to wear a burka?" I said.

You're growing older now, boys are looking, she said, turning to Dadhi for support. The old wretch nodded.

What'll the Mill Crew do when they see this? I'll never hear the end of it. And what about Tone, would he still want to walk to school with me if I were covered in sheets? I looked at her, gobsmacked. How is it that she can swan around in her sari flashing her skin and then have the nerve to stand there and tell me I have to cover up head to toe? My whole life I've been

44

told not to dress like those English sluts, and now I am being told not to dress like a Bengali one.

"Well, what 'bout you?" I said, pointing to her sari, hanging beautifully over her shoulder, and displaying her dark brown waist.

Oh, I'm practically a grandmother, she said.

"You're thirty, Amma!"

Most women have had four children by my age.

"Well, it in't fair."

I picked up one of her saris that I'd chucked on the floor. I felt the soft georgette, the gorgeous embroidery. Some darkness I'd never felt before came over me. I eased my nails between the delicate fibres of the material and worked them apart till there was a hole big enough to fit my two fingers. I started with a quick, small tear. What is it about the sound of ripping cloth that's so soothing?

Sakthi, moina, stop. Please, that's the one my abba...

I clenched my fists around a wad of material in each hand and slowly spread my arms apart till I'd torn the sari in two. A teardrop. Finally, I got her where it hurts. You don't grow up in a house like this without developing a mean streak. It's pure survival. I looked in the mirror. The loose cloth removed all the lines and shapes distinguishing me as a woman, at least they would in a couple of years' time.

"I hate you," I screamed, and ran off to lock myself in the bathroom.

I took out her sanitary towels from the cabinet, cut them all up into minuscule pieces with her nail scissors and then threw them out the window, letting the breeze carry them off and scatter them all over the back gardens. It was snowing Lil-lets in Shaleton, and the absurdity of it all made me smile, if only for a moment.

How can she do this to me, her own daughter, I thought. She knows better than anyone what it's like to be trapped, married off aged God-knows-how-young to someone she doesn't know and told she has to 'learn to love' him. One tear, that's all I got, one measly tear, and that's only when I ripped up her precious sari. No wonder Father has to raise his hand to get a reaction out of her. She didn't even bat an eyelid when she saw me crawling around looking for my clothes like some H&M junkie. God, all I ever wanted is to fit in, to be normal, unnoticed. Well, now I've got my wish, except, there's a big difference between being unnoticed, and being in-fucking-visible. Might as well be dead.

I took the nail scissors and made a scratch along my wrists and then sat down curled up under the sink to see what happened. A small red ridge appeared along the line, tender to touch. I closed my eyes and caressed it till I fell asleep.

The Bismillah

Over the last few weeks, Father has splashed out so much on pressies for our visit to Bangladesh he can't pay the gas bill. The energy company has sent a bunch of love letters. First in frigid, black print, and then in passionate red, demanding the arrears be paid in full. And now, they've cut off the supply and threatened legal action. We spend the days cold and hungry, afraid to open the door in case we get jumped by the bailiffs. And Meghna can't use the stove, so in the evenings I creep out the back to pick up food past its use-by-date from The Bismillah – Father's restaurant.

The Bismillah was renamed under the guidance of our beloved imam. I overheard Father tell Meghna it was some rebranding exercise to comfort her as she had chosen the old Bengali name, *Kusbhoi* – meaning fragrance. But to be honest, I think he wanted to replace it with an Arabic word, in this case *bismillah*, whatever that means. That's just how it is with him these days with all the Wahhabi brainwashing on the satellite channels. Inside the restaurant, purple wallpaper and Perspex chandeliers try to recreate the atmosphere of a Sultan's palace but fail. The white tablecloths are ironed but splotched, the crockery clean but cracked, and the cutlery stainless but unpolished.

Saturday, ugh! Some rowdy football lads had taken it on themselves to rearrange all the tables as if they owned the place and were egging each other on to try the phall. An older couple next to them had already got their food, and they were piling the dhal on top of the chicken korma on top of the saag aloo and mixing it all up. Why do people do that? How are you meant to taste the individual dishes if you just bang everything together? And eating your rice with a fork. Use a bloody spoon you dimwits! It drives me nuts. At the front, a man in beige chinos held hands with his wife opposite, her wrists covered with colourful bangles. They ignored the ruckus and waited patiently for the perfect reproduction of their time in India. I hoped I didn't have to see their disappointment.

Dast from the Black Paws, who had agreed to take care of the business while we were away in Bangladesh, stood behind the counter folding two-for-one flyers. I gave him my salaam and climbed up onto one of the bar stools.

"*Accha*, is it true the pub next door is nickin' all our customers?" I said.

"*Haan*, yeah. They're offerin' authentic British curry 'n' pint for £7.95," said Dast, shaking his head.

"Authentic? Yeah right, they reckon."

"I know *yaar*, the cheek. Chef's some Neo-Nazi man. And we don't stand a chance against 'em since the boss man in't servin' booze no more, thanks to that bleedin' imam. No one wants to come in 'ere."

"In't he?"

"Says it's hypocritical-like, to build a mosque back home in Bangladesh with money made sellin' haram."

"I heard 'bout mosque. What's that all about? Meghna says they don't even need another, but Father's 'avin' none of it."

"I in't got a clue *yaar*, but almost all profits go there like, so there in't any dosh to buy new tablecloths an' what 'ave ya."

"Han't ya said owt to him?"

"*Haan*, but he in't hearin' nobody."

"Sounds 'bout right."

"Nah, he's alright your ol' man, heart of gold. He took us in, din't he? Anyway, what's with the burka?"

"Meghna, she's chucked all me clothes. Says boys are lookin', so now I've gotta wear this bloody thing all the time."

"*Accha?* All yer clothes?" he said. "That makes no sense."

"*Nje*, the lot. Don't ask why, I dunno, I in't talkin' to her."

"Don't sound like Meghna Aunty, that," he said, shaking his head and pouring me a glass of mango juice. "And I know tons of girls who wear burkas, but they can wear what they want underneath. Y'ave to bring The Knowledge, *pitchhi*[16]."

"So that's what I said to her like, but she's gone doolally. Tellin' ya, I'm livin' with Dr Jekyll and Mr Hyde."

"Well, it suits ya, really brings out yer... erm... fingernails?

Dast, Dast. What can I write about him? He's a bit rough round the edges, but he brushes up well in a shirt and tie. And he makes me laugh. He failed school with flying colours and spends most of his time pretending to be a gangster. His old man died of a stroke not long ago, and now as the eldest son, it falls to him to look after the family. But Father has a soft spot for him because of his loyalty to his mam. So, when she came begging one day asking him to help keep her son off the streets, he gave him a job.

"So, who's that *gora* you're 'angin' out with?" said Dast, using the pejorative Urdu word to describe white boys.

"Who, Tone?" I said.

"Tone? Kinda name's that?" he said, raising one of his bushy eyebrows humorously.

"Short for Anthony."

"Short by name, short by nature, innit? D'ya like him then?" he said, pouring out eight glasses of Indian tonic water to half-full, and adding a slice of lime into each one.

"Who's askin'?"

"He won't protect ya, *yaar*? Need brawn round these parts."

"Well, he's pretty high up in't Mill Crew."

"*Theek*, coz his ol' man gives all gang knocked-off food from his veg stall in't covered market," said Dast. "What, din't he tell ya? Not so 'high up'... Dunno what ya see in him."

16 Shorty.

"Honesty, humility, honour... I could go on."

"You been readin' H section of dictionary again, 'an't ya?"

"He's alright is Tone, leave him be."

"So ya do like him!" he said, stroking his cleanly shaven chin with his rough hands, covered with cuts and grazes.

"*Na*, man. I don't."

"Why ya defendin' him then?"

The football boys whistled, and Dast went over to serve them with the tonic water. When he'd gone through the swinging doors to place the order, the boys topped up their glasses on the sly with four fingers of gin. Dast must've known, but he ignored it.

"Anyways, till they get 'emselves a tandoor chef next door, we'll be right makin' money off takeaways," said Dast, returning to the bar.

"A tandoor chef?"

"We in't servin' fish 'n' chips with Manchester caviar. Even Gordon Ramsay couldn't cut it int' back."

He took me into the kitchen, frenetic like inside one of the mills in *North and South*. The boys were simmering onions and carrots with ginger, garlic, and turmeric to make the base sauce. One of them dolloped a ladle of this orangey gravy into a pan of boiling ghee.

"Add red peppers 'n' green chillies, you get a jalfrezi. Add yoghurt, garam masala 'n' almonds, you get a pasanda, *samaj ayi*, you get it?" he shouted over the sound of the clattering pots and pans. I always wondered what those words meant. I've been living in a Bengali home for well over a decade, but I only tasted a chicken tikka masala for the first time the other day!

"And this, this 'ere is the tandoor!" he said, pointing at the cylindrical object, guarded by a chubby chap with two massive skewers. Beads of sweat rolled off his eyebrows, furrowed in the heat of the great big oven.

"That there's the difference between us 'n' them chancers next door. Now, watch this. Mr Shah," he said, nodding at the chef.

"What's he doin'?" I asked.

Do you understand Bengali? said Mr Shah, lowering his bare hands into the depths of the oven, splatting two lumps of dough against the inside of the tandoor. I nodded. We were in a kitchen after all, this was my territory.

The tandoor is coated with spinach, mustard oil, jaggery, eggs, turmeric, and salt. Spinach helps dough stick, salt adds flavour, mustard oil and jaggery gives the bread a shine, he said.

He wiped his forehead and took a couple of metal naan hooks in his hands. With one hook he scraped the bread off the tandoor and pushed it on to the other. He set them to one side and then chucked half a dozen skewers of chicken into the burning charcoal. When they were done, he slid off a piece for me.

Delicious. Tender and smoky, I said.

Only in a tandoor, he said, rolling his sleeves up with pride. His arms were trophies to the years of experience, pain, in learning how to use the oven. He got one mark from when he was a lad, he said, taking the mince off a red-hot skewer. The meat fell away and the skewer left a hefty scar along the fate line on his palm.

Why did you leave? I asked him. Dast raised one of his eyebrows till it was halfway round the back of his head and, for a second, I wanted to curl up and die from embarrassment. Who was I to ask him such a personal question, the immigration police?

I have two daughters, about your age. I want to send them to college, he said with a smile.

Couldn't you find work back home? I said.

Nje, but the pay is terrible, and my salary would not be enough to support the girls, especially when you think about paying bribes to lecturers and session jams.

Session jams?

*When universities close because of political violence. Students have to wait months before the courses start again.

Sometimes you can leave university two-three years after you should.*

Accha, so what would happen if you weren't working here?*

I would have to find a husband for them, he said, matter-of-factedly? Is that even a word? Anyway, how harsh is that? It's not even their fault. I reckon you could exponentially increase the attainment levels of the girls in St John's if you threatened them with the prospect of an arranged marriage.

Do you wish you had a son? I said, remembering what Father had said to Meghna that night the letter arrived.

Sons bring their own problems, he said, tapping Dast on the back of the head as he tried to filch a piece of sheesh kebab.

I walked to within a few feet of the tandoor, the heat made my face dance behind the mesh of the burka. I pictured the fires of hell. Meghna is convinced there's a special place reserved just for her down there for failing to pray five times a day. Would it be as hot as this, or hotter? Does it matter after a certain degree?

500°C, said Mr Shah.

How have you not got more scars? I said.

You need thick skin, for sure. Want to try?

"*Jee-na*, Father says it's a job for men."

"D'ya listen to everythin' yer father says?" said Dast and put the skewers in my hand before walking back into the service area. I had a go but bombed. I gave Mr Shah back the skewers with a piece of naan shredded and burnt on the end. He flicked it off and into the bin around ten feet away.

First time, you're my lucky charm, he said.

If only I could be Father's lucky charm. He wanted a son so bad to help with the business, but he got me: a stubborn little girl more interested in Tagore than tandoori. He loves me, I'm sure he does somewhere deep down inside. I felt it when I was younger, when he'd walk home from the restaurant through the pouring rain, saving his bus fare just so I could have some fish 'n' chips for tea. Sounds daft when I put it down in my journal, but it felt exotic, because all we ever had at home was curry.

I want to feel loved like that again, and more, I want to love him back. But it's the way he goes on with Meghna that I can't get over. It's not her fault she can't have any more children. My birth was complicated. She'd just turned sixteen, and after the emergency surgery the doctors said another pregnancy would risk her own life. But it doesn't stop Father from trying, and Meghna keeps on miscarrying. I caught her the other day burying a box of kitchen matches with bundles of tissue inside. It seems no matter how many times she's done it, it never gets any easier, her tears watering the tiny grave.

Dast came into the kitchen and snapped me out of my little daydream, placing a stack of dishes in my hands.

"Make yourself useful, *pitchhi*," he said, winked at me and pointed to the sink before disappearing to the front of the house again. Mr Shah took the plates out of my hands and gave them to one of the younger lads to clean.

Don't you want to work as a waiter? I asked him.

Na beti, my skin isn't that thick,* he said, giving me the curry he'd whacked together.

Dast was printing out the Z-read on the till – apparently that's what tells you all the money you've made that day – so I let myself out. One of the footballers was chundering on the front window while his friends laughed and fell about him. It was parky out, so I put my hood up and hopped on the first bus home down the hill. I got a few stares, including from the drunk wolfing down chips drowned in malt vinegar. Curry has a strange effect on the public. When they want it, it's to die for, but when they don't, it's the most repugnant smell on Earth.

On the back seat, nice and cosy with the heat and hum of the engine, I thought about Mr Shah's girls. What are their lives like in Bangladesh? Have they had their periods, and did they complain about wearing pads? What do they want to be when they finish school? How would they feel about not being able to choose when to marry, and perhaps even who? I felt sorry that he couldn't watch them grow up, and that he had to make such a big sacrifice. Father uses that word a lot, sacrifice, but he wields it like a sword, ordering us around the place. Mr Shah holds it up like a candle, flickering with Virtue's grace.

I got home to a dozen suitcases all lined up along the entry hall, each weighed, locked, and secured in cellophane. On a shelf, a book that Mrs Finch gave me to read whilst away, our plane tickets to Bangladesh and our burgundy passports. I opened Meghna's, the photo taken almost a decade ago. Her hair tied back in a tight ponytail, her eyes vibrant. She looked defiant, feisty. How times have changed.

৩. PANTHA BHAT

Londonis

The suitcases on the carousel at Shahjalal International Airport were bursting at the seams, a bit like their owners. The fat trunks were interspersed with all kinds of stuff including fifty-inch flat screens, thousand-watt microwaves and the odd plastic jerrycan filled with holy water from Mecca. The cases came out in dribs and drabs, some with locks broken, others with gaping holes where the handlers had put a pocket-knife through the casing. One man had his kids running up and down the hall as their luggage appeared simultaneously on multiple conveyor belts.

Rich or poor, man or woman, it's a lottery how long you wait for your bags, said one man trying to cheer up his fellow travellers.

If you get them at all, added another, who even received some applause.

"It's the most democratic place in the whole country," Father joked, drawing the biggest laughter of all.

A massive orange-and-black striped banner runs along the top of passport control with the words, 'Bangladesh. Visit before the tourists come.' I looked round the room; the tourists never came. Around us stood locals, the new rich, tanned and fattened, sand still in their shoes from the beaches in Thailand. Looking at them disapprovingly, austere toga-clad men coming back late from Hajj. Sharp-suited businessmen on internal flights checked their mobile phones, and in the shadows, skinny migrants in jeans and baseball caps waiting on their life's possessions, returning after years of hard graft in the Gulf. Father could place them all.

Then there was us. We looked the same, but here on the banks of the Old Ganges we weren't Bangladeshi or British. We were Londonis,[17] a strange breed, shunned by the natives for losing our culture, yet preyed upon with pseudo-platitudes for our 'esterling'. And they could place us just as easily by our confident walk, our designer saris and suits, and our bling, bling, bling. And by the way we spoke with an English twang to the Sylheti dialect of the Bangla language.

I was struggling with the suitcases in arrivals, so an elderly man offered to help.

Dhonobad, thank you, I said.

British, madam? he said.

Jee, Uncle, how do you know? I asked.

Accha, we Bangalis, we don't say thank you, we remember good deeds with our hearts, he said, placing his palm on his chest. Meghna gave him a 20 taka note for his troubles.

"Thank you please," he said and walked away happy as Larry.

"I could've done it myself, Amma," I said.

Thik ache, don't worry. He's poor, he doesn't want to beg, so he's offering you whatever service he can, she said.

Outside, without the security and control of the airport guards it became a free-for-all, with everyone offering to help in whatever small way they could, all for a little baksheesh.[18]

Oh, Londoni bhai, where are you going? shouted the taxi drivers, sensing a large tip as we came out the exit with four trolleys full of luggage.

In the nine-hour flight from Heathrow, Father had found a swagger to go with his sense of humour. He waved off the chancers and waited patiently for the privately hired van in the parking lot to pull up in front. We got in, me and Father in the

17 A term used by Bangladeshis to describe the British diaspora.
18 A tip.

front seats and Meghna and Dadhi in the back – I still hadn't forgiven her for the burka and chucking all my clothes.

Slamalaikum sir, would you like to go to the house or the masjid[19] first, sir?* the driver asked, as we started out for Dholbari, the village where Father was born in the Sylhet Division.

**Wa'alaikum as-salam*, to the masjid,* replied Father.

The van sped off but then in fifty metres came to an abrupt stop. A long line of vehicles as far as the eye could see, rickshaws, baby taxis, cars, buses, trucks jostled for space on the tarmac. Young children, some no taller than my waist, walked amongst the black diesel fumes, flogging water in placky bags. And then came the beggars, tapping on the windows and putting their hands out for money. Many had been crippled, Father explained, by criminal gangs who wanted to play on people's guilt. The driver accelerated ten metres before anyone else could sneak in front of him and then came to a grinding halt again.

Once we were out of Dhaka, the traffic cleared, and the countryside opened up. On one side, boats were swishing along the river, dipping and swaying in the gentle current, the boatmen frantically baling out bucketloads of water to keep the beauties afloat. On the other side, rice and mustard fields stretched on for miles upon miles until their golden colours melted across a pristine blue horizon, untainted by a single cloud. 'Amar Sonar Bangla,'[20] wrote Tagore. Meghna still hums the national anthem every morning at seven when she's making the breakfast, a habit from her school days. It's a song about love, beauty, one's kinship with the land. Wouldn't it be nice if the English anthem had that, and not some old rivalry with the Scots, or blind loyalty to the Queen?

19 A mosque.
20 Bangladesh national anthem written by Nobel Laureate Rabindranath Tagore.

As the sun gained height and strength in the hemanta[21] sky, my burka became suffocating and stuck to my skin (old Tagore seems to have forgotten the debilitating heat and humidity).

Driver-sahib, how far is it?* I asked.

*Madam, about four hours, madam, *insha'Allah,** he said.

Four hours! It's so hot, is there air conditioning? I said, loosening my burka as much as possible.

Madam, bideshis[22] use a/c, madam. We Bangalis, we like the country breeze, he said, rolling down the windows.

There's that pronoun again I thought: 'we', so what does that make me? In England all I ever hear on the streets of Shaleton is 'go home Paki', but now I am 'home', it's clear that I don't even belong here. So, where am I from? Who am I? I put my head down and nodded off on Father's shoulder.

When I awoke the car was pulling up outside the mosque with three domes and three arched entrances that glimmered in the sunshine. Father got out the van and took off his shoes. A small, bearded man, the architect judging by his worried look, gave his salaam. They walked across the sandy courtyard, dotted with mango trees to protect worshippers from the beating sun. I followed them, jumping from one of Father's footprints to another.

"On the left side of the masjid is a walled graveyard covering an area of around half a bigha[23] of land, on the right a small madrassa," said the architect in English, showing Father the plan.

"Very good," said Father.

"The main, rectangular prayer hall holds around two hundred people. It has two further entrances, one each on the north

21 One of the six seasons in Bangladesh – November and December.
22 A foreigner.
23 A measurement of land – roughly half an acre.

and south walls, that allow a breeze to cross the concourse of worshippers," he said, bobbing proudly up and down on his heels.

It must've cost Father a packet. He touched the bricks with the palms of his hands, eyes closed in silent prayer. I stood back in awe, but something didn't quite add up. God, I thought, would be chuffed to bits with a converted terraced house for a mosque like the ones in Shaleton. This feels like much more... like atonement.

Across the river sits a pastel-coloured mansion built by a British-Bengali expat in the old colonial style, surrounded by a lemon orchard and a high, boundary wall with broken glass along the top. The house looks down on a shanti settlement built on stilts over the water as well as Father's masjid opposite. It shimmered in the soft, afternoon glow, the reflection rippling hypnotically in the water.

"*Dekho-saiya obosta*, look. The roads are broken, there's no running water in the village, but they build their mansions, unashamed of the poverty all around," said Father.

"Allah will be their judge, *bhaisab*," the architect replied.

Inside the masjid is a different picture. Wires hang loose from the light fixtures and water drips through cracks in the ceiling, leaving pools on the cement floor. The walls are bare. Only the mihrab, from where the imam leads the prayers, has been completed, its octagonal niche covered in mosaic with floral motifs and gold-laced Arabic inscription. Father looked around the mosque shaking his head.

"Where did all the money go?" he finally said. The architect, unable to accuse Father's family of corruption, started an anecdote.

"*Bhaisab*,[24] before independence there were two brothers separated at birth, Karim in Sylhet and Bilal in Karachi," he said, and paused for permission to continue.

24 Endearment meaning brother.

Father granted it.

"*Accha*, one day Karim decided to track down his long-lost brother. When he found him, he was amazed by the size of his house," said the architect, leaning up against the minbar.

"'You work for the government, how did you manage all this?' Karim asked Bilal.

"'See that bridge over there? Ten percent,' said Bilal, tapping his pocket."

Father raised his right eyebrow.

"The next year, Bilal visited Karim in Sylhet to see he was living in an even grander house, with servants and cars," said the architect.

"'You too have a government job, how did you afford this?' asked Bilal.

"'You see that bridge over the Shurma?' said Karim.

"'No, what bridge?' replied Bilal.

"'Exactly,' said Karim, and tapped his pocket."

Father acknowledged the architect's point and the two men walked out in silence.

"*Accha, bhaisab*, one other... sensitive... issue. We normally name mosques after a Pir, or someone esteemed, not a living...* started the architect, but wisely decided not to finish his sentence upon looking at Father's face.

Outside the gates in the shade of a banyan tree, beggars from the slum turned up when they caught wind a Londoni was in town. A decrepit old man came up to Father in a wheelchair made from the top half of a damaged office chair secured to a wheelbarrow. He put out his scrawny arms, his eyes dry, his smile a slave to misfortune. Father dug deep into his pocket and gave the man a bunch of loose change.

Du'a khoroin zeno, he said, asking the cripple to pray for him.

May Allah forgive your sins, he replied. Father rubbed his left shirt sleeve and got back into the van before a rowdy group of hijras[25] who had been loitering outside the mosque gates got to him.

Zao, let's go home,* he ordered the driver.

When we finally got to the house in the early evening the whole crew came out to greet us. Aunties and uncles, cousins I never knew I had, there must've been a hundred people in the courtyard. An old man came forward – the village elder I presumed from watching all those natoks[26] with Meghna. I knelt down to touch his feet and give my salaam, as is custom in Bengali culture, but the man recoiled with such horror he kicked me in the face and knocked me flat on my arse.

Na'udhubillah, that's a Hindu tradition!* he spat.

As salam-u alaikum. Forgive her Uncle; she's young,* said Meghna, helping me up off the ground.

I'd heard them talk about this on Islam TV back home, how Islam practiced in the east was not true Islam, but Islam polluted with local cultures. That was plain to see here, where the villagers still wear beads round their arms and their babies have black marks on their foreheads to keep the evil spirits away – old habits die hard, I guess.

The servants heaved the suitcases into the sitting room. And after tea and biscuits, Father opened them with a big smile and handed out the gifts. Apple watches for the men, jewellery for the women, clothes for the infants. For a second, I was happy for him, handing out pressies like Santa. All those nights slaving away in the restaurant, and now finally some just rewards. But then I remembered that this is where our money went. All those school trips we couldn't afford, all those laddered tights that

25 (South Asia) A person whose birth sex is male but who identifies as female or as neither male nor female.

26 A Bengali TV drama, or theatre production

couldn't be replaced, all those nights without lecky and gas, all that hiding from the TV license inspector. This here is the cost of saving face, and if anyone expressed any sign of gratitude, he told them to stop, that this is the least he could do, because everything in 'London', where the streets are paved with gold, is just hunky-dory.

Shumon, who I recognised from the family album, came in from the courtyard. Father had already wired him a large sum of money to pay off his debt, but now he wanted a proper present. Father took out a bunch of designer shirts.

"Shumon, choose one," he said. He took two and left without a word of thanks.

Meghna was sitting on a tool[27] talking to her sisters-in-law, and I was just glad to have found a seat underneath a fan. A young woman around twenty years old walked in holding a tray of fruit and cold water pumped straight from the village well (which Father had paid for too). Meghna swore by the metallic taste of groundwater and preferred it to bottled mineral water. When the tray was empty, the woman called over to me and beckoned me to follow her out onto the veranda.

"*Amar naam Trina*, my name Trina. I your cousin," she said, laughing out loud. A bright coloured bird sitting in a cage hanging from the ceiling copied her verbatim, grammatical errors and all.

"I am Sakthi. What is that?" I said, slowly, giving her the verb and tense she'd need to answer the question, as I'd heard Mrs Finch do with Meghna in Shaleton.

"That is moina bird," she said.

"That is what Amma calls me... moina," I said.

"*Nje*, it sings all day long," she said.

"*Ki shundor*, it's beautiful," I said.

"*Cholo*, let's go somewhere quiet," she said, grabbing a lantern. She put her arm through mine and led me into the courtyard,

---

27 Colloquial Bangla for the English word stool.

where the sand slipping into my sandals still felt warm from the baking sun.

"Trina, right?" I said.

Nje, your father has two sisters...*

"Boro Chachi, and Soto Chachi.[28]"

Nje, I am your Soto Chachi's only daughter,* she said.

By the entrance gate, a few village boys had tied a dragonfly by its tail to a pole and were watching it fly round in circles trying to escape. Trina whacked them round the head and released the poor creature back into the rural darkness. Black, proper pitch black like I've never seen. My eyes took ages to get used to it. I could taste it, feel it wrap its tender arms around me. The stars lit narrow, coconut-strewn paths for rickshawalas working late into the night, pulling passengers, timber, livestock, whatever their legs could pedal. Fireflies traced their way across the foliage and the sound of croaking frogs in the nearby fushkonis[29] increased and decreased in waves as the night brought a much-needed coolness.

Take your sandals off, she said. *It's so nice to feel the coconut fibres tickle the bottom of your feet.*

Jee-na Trina Apa. Are there not pythons?* I asked.

Arre, pythons don't bite silly... they ambush you and then squeeze you to death before they swallow you whole,* she said, waited a few seconds to see me freeze with terror, and then burst into an even bigger fit of laughter than before.

"*Ish*, don't do that," I said, digging her with my elbow. *Where are we going?*

To the house at the top of the hill, she said.

"Who's there?" I said, undoing the straps, placing my naked feet on the earth.

"Not who," she said, cryptically. "Now close your eyes. *Bishash koro*, trust me."

28 Elder paternal aunt, and younger paternal aunt.
29 Small village ponds.

She led me down a sandy path and then precariously along the narrow muddy banks that keep the water in the paddy fields, which I almost fell in a million times, and finally up some slippy steps made from banana trees. I'd never experienced life through the souls, yes, the souls of my feet. So, at one point I started to blubber like someone who's been given back their sight. The next small stretch was long grass, then sand again, and then the familiar cold hard floor of a veranda. As we went round the back of the house a gorgeous breeze ran through the folds of my burka, and I let out a sigh of relief.

You can take it off, she said. I didn't need a second invitation. The way things work in our culture, if an older sibling or a cousin says you can do something, you're sorted, it's all on them.

Don't worry, you're safe here, she said, helping me lift it over my head just as a teardrop rolled down my cheek. *Ya Allah, what's wrong?*

"Nothing, everything is perfect. *Accha*, it is a long story, but I have not felt anything for such a long time, and then when I took my sandals off, I got overcome with emotion. Stupid, ignore me, I am talking rubbish."

Na Sakthi, you're not. I understand, she said.

I studied her face when she closed her eyes as the breeze rustled through her hair. She looks just like me. Dark brown eyes, long black hair tied in a plait, wonky teeth, and a large nose. And she could have been me too, it's all a matter of chance. Would she want what I have? Would she exchange growing up in Bangladesh, surrounded by her own culture, her family and friends, her language, for growing up in England, and the North? Swap the village boys torturing insects for the Black Paws, or the Mill Crew? I couldn't wait to ask her and see Bangladesh through her eyes.

"I can show you the world," she started singing, grabbing a prayer mat and using it as Aladin's magic carpet. Oh my, she is going to hell for that, I thought. Meghna reckons there's this thin wire the breadth of a human hair that stretches across a pit of snakes and spiders. And when we die, everyone has to walk along it to reach Allah on the other side. But of course, if you're a sinner, well, just imagine. I took my chances with the creepy-crawlies and joined in a whole list of classics before it was time to go home for supper. What is it with Disney by the way? Pocahontas, Aladdin, Frozen, The Little Mermaid. Seems wherever you live in the world, even under the sea, young girls are trapped by their loving fathers. Trina says I should give them my diary, sell them my story.

Accha, Sakthi. If we are going to be friends, then we need to talk to each other using tui,* said Trina, as we made our way down the hill. Bengali has three ways to say you. One formal, and two informal, one of which is only used with children and close friends – tui. I mean, how cool is that? A whole grammatical conjugation just for your besties!

"Abba will drop a bollock if he hears me say *tui*!" I said.

"Drop a bollock?" she said.

"Get angry."

Thik ache, leave your abba to me.*

As we walked back, the rice stalks swayed in the breeze, bowing their heads like eager servants, waiting upon a nation. Trina practised her English with me, or rather, on me. It was surprisingly cold, and the darwans[30] on night duty were wrapped up in scarves and hats as if they were in the harsh grip of an arctic winter. They sat guard by their little campfires, chatting, brewing cups of tea. High above them was Sagittarius arching his mighty bow, the same stars I saw in Shaleton, and despite my hang-up with the pronoun earlier, somehow it felt like home.

30 House guards.

A red passport

In the village, the day starts at stupid o'clock in the morning. After the Fajr[31] prayer, me and Meghna went to the kitchen to help the servants who'd been hard at work since the rooster crowed, quite literally. At the back of the windowless room, a young woman dressed in a plain kamiz was bent double descaling a large fish with a da[32]. Another girl was putting wood on the fire, fanning the flames with a newspaper. Together, we toiled over boiling broths whilst smoke billowed out from underneath great big metal baltis and handis.[33]

Boro Chachi came in barking orders and if things weren't done good enough, or fast enough, the servants got a proper ear bending, again, quite literally. I saw enough fear in their eyes that would make Oliver Twist think twice before asking for more gruel. Please, sir, can I... d'ya know what, forget about it.

Ya Maboud! Look at these chillies! Rip them down the middle so the seeds come out or the korma will just taste of yoghurt and ghee! And how many times have I told you to stir the dhal or it will stick to the bottom? Get up! Get up before I smack your bottom red,* said Boro Chachi.

Arre, give her a rest, she's only ten years old,* said Soto Chachi, holding the girl around the shoulders.

You're such a bleeding heart. I took this girl from her mother's hands on the streets out of compassion and look at my reward... she just mopes around the house all day, she said,

31 The morning prayer, between dawn and sunrise.
32 A cutting instrument secured to the ground with the foot.
33 Large cooking pots.

giving the girl a whack on the head with the pakha[34] she'd been using to fan herself.

She'll learn, said Meghna, giving me a wink.

Oh, sit down and let the girls do the cooking, said Boro Chachi.

Thik ache, bhabbi, I like it. It reminds me of home, said Meghna with a smile.

I love it when she talks about Bangladesh, Meghna. The raw relationship her family has with the land, and most of all the river. For the river is both a provider and a taker. It gives life, yet at times, and at random, it takes life away, like it had her mother's back in the days when she was no older than me. And her eyes always light up when she talks about food. It's such an art with her, the way she prepares it, painstakingly grinding her own spices, mixing them by taste. Makes me think about those outdoor museums in England where they recreate how people used to live. Thousands of years of experience passed down mothers to daughters.

I wondered why the Bismillah and all those other restaurants in Brick Lane and down the Wilmslow Road have men running the kitchen, when in our culture, it's women who are the keepers of culinary knowledge? I asked Meghna, but she and the others laughed so long and hard it took a good while for them to collect themselves.

Ish, moina, you're killing me. Why do you think your abba eats at home? said Meghna, and the laughing fit started all over.

At around eight in the morning, when the day's cooking was done, I washed the smoke out of my skin and hair with cold water from the well. The bathroom door didn't shut, and Dadhi peeked through the gap to watch me bathe. I didn't think anything of it, she's a bit weird like that, but even Meghna was shocked to see her rummaging through my dirty laundry basket.

34 A handheld fan made of straw.

After bathing, I put in a tampon, the novelty of which still hasn't worn off. I mean, like, it's a fucking godsend. Meghna insists on sanitary towels, but they do my head in, so I bought a pack of Tampax before the flight to Bangladesh. I hid them deep in my handbag as if they were cigarettes, and every time I use one, I feel this sense of rebellion like I'm smirting outside the gates of heaven.

When I got back to the kitchen, Meghna was preparing a tray with tea, gulab jamun[35] and parathas for Father and some visitors that had come over from the neighbouring village. But then she dropped everything when a woman walked through the door. Meghna ran up to her, crouched down and touched the woman's feet. The woman bent down and pulled Meghna back up and the two hugged for an aeon.

Where is Sakthi? she said, and I too bent down to give my salaam, more out of instinct than anything else.

This is my elder sister – Padma, said Meghna, and put the tea tray in my hand. *We'll chat later, now run, taratari, take this over to your father in the sitting room before he beats us all.*

Servants and masters alike, sharing this one common aspect of life – their sex – LOL'd uncontrollably. In the end, it's just like Meghna said in the sari shop, the bottom line is that we are still only women.

I made my way across the courtyard, weaving in and out of the washing on the lines and up a short flight of steps to the main living quarters, taking care not to spill a single drop onto the saucers. Behind an old wooden door, I could hear the reporter on the news channel talking about Martyr's Day. Decades ago, the reporter explained, the Pakistani Army massacred hundreds of Bengali intellectuals just two days before the end of the civil war to stop the fledgling nation from prospering.

35 Bengali sweets.

They should be thanking us for protecting Islam, but instead we're being treated like criminals, said a voice I instantly recognised to be that of the village elder.

Meghna told me all about him after he kicked me to the floor the other day. He'd fought on the Pakistan side of the civil war in 1971. Towards the end, just before the Indian Army intervened on the side of Bangladesh, and defeat was certain, he lined up a group of Bengali men under the instructions of his commanding officer and executed them point blank – something he boasted of freely with blatant disregard for the law.

It was impossible to tell apart Indian sympathisers from men loyal to Pakistan. The Hindus amongst them were so used to living side by side with Muslims that they knew all our traditions, he said.

Aitcha, so what did you do? asked a voice I didn't recognise.

I made them drop their trousers, and if they weren't circumcised, I put a bullet in their heads and killed them like dogs, he said.

And what about the Muslims, did you let them go?

If they were sympathetic to the Indian cause, they met the same fate.

Masha'Allah, said the man.

My hands trembled, shaking the teacups on the tray. What a monster! Who could do such a thing? Let alone talk about it. I wanted to turn around and run but my feet were glued to the floor. The chatter stopped for a while before it picked up on a previously unfinished conversation.

Aitcha, where were we? Everything can be arranged as soon as she is ready. Now, shall we agree the... said the village elder.

"I can't give gold or cash you understand, but your son will have a lal passport[36] and a ten percent stake in my business as part of the *jatuk*," said Father, in English as usual.

"Ten par cent little," said the other man.

---

36 A British passport.

"*Khouwkka*, tell me. What do you propose?" said Father.

"Tarty par cent, minimam," he said.

"*Jee-na bhai*, that's too much!"

Didn't you say we could see her? That will help with the negotiation, said the village elder.

The talking stopped, and the clapping of loosely fitting sandals came towards me. The door swung open, and Father stood there filling the frame with his broad shoulders.

"There you are, let's not keep these men waiting. I've been telling them how you make a fine cup of cha," he said.

The room is the spit of our lounge in Shaleton. An oversized settee is pushed up against the wall, taking up much of the space, and a glass-covered wicker coffee table stands in the middle. On the wall opposite the door is a large, framed picture of the Kaaba[37], which hangs amongst a clutter of decorative ceramic plates. Two ceiling fans spun at full speed, blowing the men's panjabis[38] so the material danced around their knees. I set the tray down and served the three men.

Bho, sit, the village elder said. Father nodded. I sat on the edge of one of the ginormous armchairs that still had the plastic wrapping from the showroom to stop it from collecting dust. Knees together, feet high up off the floor, I listened attentively, ready, and willing to engage.

"*Ma*, can you remove your veil for a moment?" said Father.

"But Abba—" I said.

"Just briefly," he insisted with an underlying threat of violence.

I slowly lifted the veil and folded it back over my head. God, how things change. A few months ago, I would've gladly ripped it off and chucked the bloody thing in the dustbin, but now it felt like stripping. Might as well bring in a wrecking ball and let me go all Miley Cyrus on them. Ugh!

---

37 A building at the centre of Islam's most important mosque, the Masjid al-Haram in Mecca, Saudi Arabia.

38 South Asian men's dress consisting of tunic and loose trousers.

Oh, what beauty! And can you cook? said the unfamiliar voice, which belonged to a man a little older than my father.

"*Jee* Uncle, Meghna taught me, sorry, Amma showed me from when I was very young, my favourite is shutki bor—"

And do you pray? asked the village elder.

"She prays with her mother," said Father, on my behalf.

Masha'Allah. What would you like to be when you grow up?* asked the man, lighting up a bidi[39]. I wondered what would happen if I asked for a toke? That would set the cat amongst the pigeons, for sure.

"A lawyer," I replied, inhaling a deep breath of the smoke.

Tik asse, that's a very noble profession but is it suitable for a woman?* said the village elder, and before I could get my tuppence worth in on women's rights, I could see the men were talking at me, but not to me.

And when she gets married and has children, how will she cook, clean, look after the family? said the man.

Aasholei, it's true. Young girls of this generation have such wild fantasies,* replied the village elder, slurping his tea.

Here we go again... must've been here a million times. I put the veil back and waited to be dismissed. The men swapped between Sylheti and broken English, and after a while their voices faded, replaced by the hypnotic whirring of the fans. Finally, the old man spoke to me.

"That was fantastic... how they say in Ingalend... cuppa, isn't it? You will make a fine wife," he said, placing his teacup on the saucer and sliding the tray towards me.

And I'm glad to see you wearing a burka, but don't forget to look after your figure, said the other man. *Some of our women use that as an excuse to cook and eat as much as they want, caring not a jot about their husbands.*

---

39 A cigarette made from cheap tobacco wrapped in a coarse leaf.

I nodded obediently and headed back to the kitchen repeating under my breath a word I heard whilst waiting outside the room. Jatuk. What did that mean?

We spent the whole day inside avoiding the skin-darkening sun, and when the evening finally arrived, the women all breathed a sigh of relief and sat out on the veranda chewing supari and paan. But I found Meghna and Padma Aunty in the kitchen, eating out of metal plates and drinking red-tinged well water in the light of a paraffin lamp. You'd never know they were sisters, if it wasn't for the way they both dip their Naga chillies in the salt, bite off an unflinchingly large chunk, and then take a bite of Bengali lemon rind (it's not the same as English lemon; much more fragrant) with every handful of food. And they did all this in perfect synchrony, mirroring each other's actions and mannerisms like the moina on the veranda.

Padma is thin. Meghna calls her a stick of bamboo. But there's something about her, the way she carries herself or the way she talks, that makes her seem strong. She speaks Bengali like the actresses in those films from Calcutta's Golden Age that Meghna watches on repeat on Bangla TV. And with nothing else to stimulate the senses, it was then that I realised what a beautiful language it is that we speak. All those soft sounds; Padma Aunty said there are five letter Ss in Bangla. Five! And over a hundred joint letters, all combining seemingly impossible consonants. Mrs Finch would be in the seven heavens.

The sisters took turns in making small balls of rice and fish and feeding each other, giggling all the time like they had somehow been transported back to their village through the hard floor and the smoke. What love, what happiness they must have left behind to follow their own fates? Then, Meghna sprang to her feet and took a glass jar out of the almari[40].

Is that... Padma Aunty began.

*Shall I open it, *didi*?* said Meghna, and the two of them dipped their paws into the achar, eyes sparkling enough to light up the darkness.

Meghna, do you remember that time when Amma caught us? said Padma Aunty, and Meghna took a sharp breath, put the palm of her hand on her heart and looked up to the ceiling.

What happened? I asked.

*Amma, your nani[41], had spent the whole summer drying mangoes and satkora on the roof to make achars and pickles for the winter. And everyone for miles around knew that she made the best achars in Kushtia. *Ish, eto moja*, to die for. But one year they were so tasty, that every night when she went to sleep, we'd open the jar and have some,* said Padma Aunty.

One day Abba had received a marriage offer, but despite his protests, Amma insisted on inviting the suitor, some government man from Jessore, whose party stuffed their face with all the fish that Abba had caught that day. Halfway through the meal, the man says that he had heard she makes the best achar in the whole Division. And she proudly nodded and went to get the jar.

Only the jar was empty, Meghna intervened, unable to hold back.

Naaaaa! So, what did she do?* I asked.

Ish, your nani was quite the woman. Strict! And cunning. *Accha*, do you remember Meghna? She smelled the fingers of everyone in the household to find out who was guilty, starting with the servants. We panicked and rushed off to wash our hands with soap and water,* said Padma Aunty.

But everyone eats achar with their hands. I said, taking some from the jar.

40 A metal wardrobe/cupboard that is not fixed to the wall.
41 Maternal grandmother.

So, your nani, after going through the entire household pointed straight in our direction, she said.

But how did she know, Padma Aunty?!

We had washed our hands so well with soap that Meghna had even taken her skin off with the scour. Look, she still has the scar. So, our hands were the only ones that smelled of anything but achar.

Ki paglami, what stupidity! We pretty much had a sign above our heads saying guilty! said Meghna, and they both rolled around the floor in stitches. Meghna even knocked over one of the lamps and almost set her sari on fire.

Ish, Sakthi moina, I wish you could have met her, said Meghna.

You were telling Mrs Finch about the floods, what happened? I said.

Didi, you tell her, it's too heavy for me, said Meghna.

I brought them a bowl of warm water and soap as a joke, so they could wash their hands while I cleaned the dishes as they had sent all the servants away for the night. Padma Aunty then took me into her arms and squeezed me tight. One of those hugs you would only ever let your mum give you.

In Bangladesh, we say that an Aunty is as good as a mother, she said, looking at Meghna for agreement. *Accha, Meghna, why are you making this poor girl wear a burka? You never wore one! And in the kitchen, what man comes in here?*

Meghna shook her head discreetly and made a shh shape with her lips, but it was too late. Padma Aunty had already started to take it off, and then she gave me a Bengali kiss – that's when they (normally aunties) put their nose on your cheek and then inhale sharply through the nostrils like you do when you've got a cold. Absolutely disgusting! But then again, if I think about it, fair to say no more disgusting then one of those wet kisses you get from an English aunt.

Ya, ki shundor! You look just like her, your nani, she said, which filled me with this inexplicable pride. I mean, why would you be proud because you look like somebody, not dress, or behave, but just look like? Meghna gave us both a cup of tea and set down a quarter plate of sugary biscuits on the floor.

What came next can't really be described as coherent speech. Padma Aunty spoke mostly through questions to God, and Meghna wept in silence, telling her sister to stop when the memories became too painful, and then immediately after asking her to carry on. It was odd to see Meghna cry, and it reminded me of that solitary tear in Shaleton. When I realised the sari I had torn up that day perhaps belonged to her mother, I wanted to kick myself. How could I have been so fucking evil, so bloody reckless? Anyway, I managed to salvage some kind of a story from the emotional wreckage.

They come from a family of six, with four girls who are all named after rivers in Bangladesh. Padma is the oldest, then Meghna a couple of years younger, then there is quite a large gap due to 'Allah's will', and then two more daughters in quick succession, Surma and Kushiyara. Nani was a believer that her girls, like the rivers, would provide happiness and prosperity everywhere they flowed through.

But it was a riverbank bursting during a cyclone that completely changed their lives. The floods destroyed everyone's houses and crops. Nana[42] and Nani worked day and night to rebuild and provide for the children, and Nani grew weak due to the high price of food on the local market. People were selling everything they owned, Nani sold her marriage jewellery, just for a bag of rice and lentils. They had nothing left, and finally, when she fell ill, they didn't have the money to see a doctor or pay for the meds. She died of Typhoid fever later that year.

The sisters comforted each other and dried their tears on their pallus. Padma Aunty took a sip of tea, drew a deep breath, and then continued with a bit more fluency.

42 Maternal grandfather.

Abba was left alone with four girls and he couldn't bear to re-marry, such was his love for Amma. He too had grown weak, so there was no option but for your mother and I to go and find work in the garment factories in Dhaka and send money home. she said.

At the very last minute, a letter appeared that some Londoni wanted to marry a 'simple, honest, and kind' girl, and Meghna agreed to meet your father on the basis that he provided help for our aging Abba and our two younger sisters. Abba tried to convince her that he could take care of himself, Surma and Kushiyara, but Meghna had made up her mind. He regrets giving her that letter to this day, she said.

"You got married to save yer father, yer sisters from goin' 'ungry?" I said to Meghna, my lips quivering. "And ya never told me in all these years!"

This is my burden, moina, not yours, replied Meghna.

The rain beat a melancholic rhythm on the tin roof. Meghna scooped out the old rice from the day before and placed it in a large bowl. She added four fingers of water until there was an inch more than the level of rice and then placed a piece of fabric over the top and tied it down with string. She took the bowl and placed it outside on a stool on the veranda to ferment overnight.

Amma, I said. *What does *jatuk* mean?*

*Jatuk? You mean *zhautuk*?* Meghna said.

*Abba said he can't afford the *zhautuk*, and that maybe he could pay with a *lal* passport instead,* I said.

Lal passport[43]!* Meghna replied, looking at her sister.

What is it, Amma?

Zhautuk means dowry, Sakthi,* Padma Aunty said.

I leant with my back against the wall and slid down to the floor. The letter, and now this secret meeting. So, it's going ahead, I thought, this time it's for real. I wanted to scream, but my throat tightened. I hit myself, banging my head with my

43 A British passport.

knuckles, and then thumping my chest, my legs, fists tightly clenched, anywhere I could cause pain, feel pain. Nothing worked. Meghna held me tight against her bosom to stop my arms swinging and Padma Aunty got me a glass of water and a wet gamcha[44] to place over my forehead. They laid me down on the floor and fanned me until I could speak.

Sakthi, moina, drink, drink my little bird, said Meghna.

I want to be alone, Amma, I said.

Accha, cholo, we'll take you to your bed—

Na, leave me here, please, I said. Meghna protested, but Padma Aunty led her away and they walked out into the rain, across the courtyard to the bedrooms.

After they left, I sat out on the steps of the kitchen veranda gazing at the night sky. On the balcony ledge, Boro Chachi had left out the sarta[45]. I picked it up, the blade glistening in the moonlight. I played with it, placing a finger between the sharp and the blunt side of the nutcracker, squeezing the handles together and making little grooves in the skin. After a while, I opened it up wide and ran it softly along my wrists, tracing the previous mark. Once, twice, and on the third run I pressed the blade deeper and made a cut across my forearm. It hurt like hell, and I bit my sleeve to muffle the scream. Blood! Oh God, the blood. I hurried back into the kitchen and wrapped the gamcha tightly around. Finally, I could feel my heart pounding against my ribs. I looked at the stars and took a deep breath of the cold, night air.

---

44 A traditional thin, coarse cotton towel, often with a checked design, found in South Asia.
45 A nutcracker with an extremely sharp edge and a blunt side specifically designed for cutting betel nuts.

The cattle shed

On the morning of Vijoy Dibos[46], Trina came round the house dressed in a dark green sari and a red blouse for the Victory Day celebrations. Her eyelashes were done long, and the light mascara really brought out her dark brown pupils. On her ears were small gold studs and hanging from her neck a simple gold chain that exaggerated its length. Her hair was done up at the back in a tight, braided bun, and at the front everything was kept in place with an elegant hairband. I on the other hand was green with envy, and red with anger.

Shall I dress you up? said Trina.

Don't tease me! Amma will kill me if she sees me in a sari, I said.

If you stay indoors where I can see you, said Dadhi, sitting up in bed.

With Dadhi's get-out-of-jail-free card I whipped off the burka and we started fishing around in Meghna's suitcase. Trina pulled out a mustard blouse that fitted snugger than I thought it would, just above the belly button. And over a plain white petticoat she wrapped a dark blue sari that sat precariously on my hips. She held my hand in hers to spin me around, and she must've noticed the cut, so she slipped off the bangles from her left hand and split them equally across my wrists to cover the mark.

There... sisters, she said, with an affectionate smile.

What do you think? I said, giving her a twirl.

"You look too beautiful," said Trina.

46 Victory Day, 16 December.

You look ready, said Dadhi, knowingly, and Trina quickly put a chador[47] over my shoulders.

Meghna came in from the kitchen. When she saw me in the sari she chased me around the bedroom, shaking the frying pan in her hand and making absurd threats of violence.

Sakthi, take it off at once! she said in a loud whisper.

"*Na*, Amma," I said, running around the room.

Arre, googoo dekho, fad dekho na, she said.

"What does that mean?" I said.

You see the dove, but not the trick? translated Trina, laughing her head off.

Eh? I said.

"She's dropped a bollock!" she clarified. *Did I say it right?* But now was not the time to delve into the finer subtleties of the English language.

Take it off, Sakthi! repeated Meghna, out of breath.

"*Na!* And I don't care if ya hit us!" I yelled back.

Sakthi! said Meghna.

"I in't goin' out on Victory Day dressed like a black ghost when all other girls are wearin' lovely saris, it in't fair. This is my culture, in't that what ya wanted like, for us to be Bengali?"

Moina, please, listen to your loving Amma, take that sari off and put your burka back on, said Meghna.

I stopped running, disarmed by her tenderness. But when she got close enough, she grabbed my wrist and I grimaced. I squirmed free. She begged me once again to change, I refused and ran out of the door with Trina. On the way out, I opened the bird cage on the veranda and watched the moina fly off and sit on the branches of a nearby banana tree. And then we jumped onto a passing rickshaw, giggling like schoolgirls, and ordered the wallah[48] to take us to the mela.

47 A large cloth worn as a combination head covering, veil, and shawl
    usually by Muslim women.
48 A driver.

The road weaves through the tea estates, a sea of green speckled with the colourful kamizes of the pickers, nipping the youngest leaves from the tips and throwing them into this great big basket upon their backs. The countryside looks different when it isn't framed by the rectangular aperture of a burka. It feels different too. The warm wind caressing my neck, rushing past my tummy, the sound of my sari fluttering in the breeze. This was my Titanic moment.

"I'm the king of the world," I screamed as I stood up on the rickshaw, arms wide like Jack whatever-his-surname-is.

"Oh, Rose," Trina played along.

"*Accha*, I don't see why Amma won't let me wear a sari," I said, sitting down and holding on to the back of the bicycle seat to steady myself as the rickshaw bombed down the road with little care for oncoming traffic.

"Because he protecting you, Meghna Aunty," said Trina.

"From men?" I said.

"*Na*, I think from Dadhi," she said. *When I was getting you dressed, she looked at you in a strange way and then said that you looked 'ready'.*

"What did she mean by that?" I said.

I guess for marriage. The burka was covering your shape, so she couldn't see that you had matured.

That's why she was looking through my dirty underwear as well, I said.

Nje, maybe Meghna Aunty knew, said Trina with a shrug.

"God damn it, why didn't you tell me!"

I didn't know that's why you were in a burka. I thought it was because of Uncle, until now. And when I realised, I put the chador on you straight away. Dukkito, Sakthi, I'm really sorry, she said.

I am such an idiot... But what about you? How come you aren't getting married off? I said. Trina had a worried look on her face.

"Me? I thought you knew," she said.

"Knew what?" I said.

"I am getting married in a month, that is why your father bought so many gifts, as a kind of dowry."

Zhautuk? I heard Father say that word the other day.*

Nje, zhautuk. It's the money that a bride's family gives to the groom's family to take their daughter. Think of it like a maintenance grant.*

The pieces were slowly coming together, Meghna's thoughtfulness, my stubbornness. The men in the lounge that I served tea to, they weren't asking me questions out of politeness, they were testing my naivety to see how easily I could be moulded to conform with traditional values. I'm a Londoni after all, perhaps my western education would get in the way of the duties of a good Bengali wife. Amma had my back all along.

"So, who is he, your *damand*[49]?" I said.

"I do not know, I have never met him," she said.

"Then why don't you run away?" I said.

"*Kenno*, what for? I am going to England. Big Ben, double decker buses. It is a dream, I will be like you, like Meghna Aunty," she said.

"But you do not know him. What if he is mean? And don't say it is in the hands of Allah, that it is your fate," I said.

Thik ache, I understand your point. He might be mean, but then, so might someone I've known for years. Having a love marriage doesn't guarantee your happiness. Besides, my parents chose him, and I trust in their judgment, she said.

"But you do not love him!" I protested, more to myself than to Trina.

"I will learn to love him," she replied with equal force.

How can this girl that seems so out there even think like that, I thought. But we'd just met, and I didn't want to fall out with my only friend in Bangladesh. There's a whole month ahead and she's the only sane person for miles around.

49 A groom.

And what does he do? I asked, conciliatory in tone.

He's a businessman. He runs a chauffeur service in Manchester. His company has driven many famous people all around the country, like Maradona, she said. Maradona, I thought. Sounds iffy. But I let it pass.

The rickshaw pelted down the road, jumping violently over the potholes. I clung on to the rickshawala's seat for dear life. The tips of my fingers lightly brushed his muscular buttocks as he sat back down. The folds of his longi[50] rhythmically caressed my hands as his legs pushed up and down on the pedals. But despite the mortal embarrassment, my hands remained glued to the seat.

Harder, harder, harder, Trina teased.

The rickshawala, sensing a generous tip, worked hard to climb up the hill. Beads of sweat rolled down his neck and soaked his shirt till we could see his shoulder blades, the muscles on his back working away underneath. His longi was pulled above his knees and his calves glistened in the sunlight. When he got to the top he sat down, his chest heaved, and we free rolled down towards the town square.

Joi Bangla, victory Bangla, I screamed to everyone as the rickshaw hurtled past.

Joi Bangabhondhu[51], they replied.

We gave the rickshawala a healthy tip for being such a good sport and made our way to the main square. A gigantic red and green flag fluttered lethargically above the town hall whilst the public announcement system blared out Bengali liberation songs. In the centre, women and girls sat patiently on the roots of an

---

50 Bengali men's sarong.
51 Sheikh Mujibur Rahman, the founder of the nation.

old banyan tree, waiting for their husbands, brothers, fathers and occasionally, lovers, to come back with dhoy phuskas[52] and mango lassi from the stalls that had set up around the edges.

Trina ordered snacks as I soaked up the atmosphere. The sounds were a wall of noise at first hard to decipher, but after a while I could make out every crotchet and quaver all clamouring to be heard. Oh, and the smells, they changed between the diesel of passing buses, the stench of rotting garbage and fried street food.

Trina put a plastic bag full of pastries in my hand.

"Mmm, *bari moja*, what are they?" I said.

Shingaras,[53] said Trina.

Mouth awash with piping hot vegetables and spices, I marvelled at the life and energy in such a small village.

This is not the Bangladesh I see on the television, I said.

Not everything is so wonderful, said Trina, pointing to a couple of men in wife-beaters and longis scratching their sweaty balls and gobbing on the street.

Ugh, that's disgusting!

And then one of the men walked over to the stall where Trina had bought the shingaras and carried on serving the unsuspecting public.

It's an acquired taste, said Trina with a devilish grin.

We walked through the square past a wooden Ferris wheel with four carriages full of children being driven by one man, a bit like an ox would turn grain mills way back when. In one of the stalls, they were selling the Bangladesh cricket shirt, green and red with the tiger roaring in the top left.

"Let me, it's a gift, a *sriti*, to remind you of our Victory Day,* said Trina.

"*Na*, really, it's too much," I said.

"It is nothing. What size you are?* she said.

---

52 A pastry.

53 A pyramid shaped pastry filled with spicy meat, potatoes and vegetables.

L, I said, trying to picture Tone. I don't know why he popped into my head right then, perhaps all that chat about super scoop shots stuck.

Large? That's about four sizes too big for you, isn't it? How will you show off your figure? she said.

"No different to a burka," I said.

Trina laughed and gave the shopkeeper the hard-negotiated fee that had started at four times the local selling price on account of the fact that I am a Londoni. But by the end Trina had filled him with so many compliments that he had no other choice but to come down on the price.

Chol, let's go. There's someone I'd like you to meet, but it's our little secret, you promise you not to tell a soul? she said. I nodded. Trina took my hand and led me to a tea stall overlooking a small lake.

"Best cha in all Dholbari," she said, pulling up two rickety stools.

"Liquid wisdom," said the chaiwala, Jyothi, a young man who must be at most twenty-five years old. He has a thick head of hair, square chin and a large, broken nose with a personality and story all of its own.

That's funny, my abba says exactly the same thing, I said.

I got it from my amma, he said, smiling as he set down two glass cups on a metal tray.

Jyothi is pale and thin. Through his sweat-drenched shirt I could see he's been dealt a bad hand. But his smile and laughter are infectious. He had us in stitches with his stories, which he told with the timing of a stand-up comedian. I could see why Trina wanted me to meet him.

What's that you're making? I asked.

You never tasted seven-layered tea? said Trina, as the chaiwala carefully put a spoonful of tea into a glass of sugary water, waited for half a minute and then poured a mixture of tea and condensed milk down the side of the glass.

So, where is your amma? Such a tea lover surely belongs at a tea stall? I said, while he continued with his party trick.

She died when I was a little boy, he replied.

*Oh, *dukkito*, I'm sorry Jyothi bhai. I didn't think—*

It was a long time ago.

May I ask, how did she die? said Trina.

"Love," he said, matter-of-fact.

"Love?" This should be interesting, I thought to myself.

Aitcha, that's what the hijras say. When she was young, about your age, she fell for this Muslim boy. Apparently, he had a film camera, the only one in the village, so everyone used to invite him to their weddings to record them. So, he took my amma along, and she would film the bride, and he the groom.

They spent a lot of time together riding around the tea gardens on this old Honda. One thing led to another, and she got pregnant. When her father demanded the boy convert and take his daughter's hand in marriage to save the family from shame, his mother refused unless she converted from Hinduism to Islam.

God, I see, and—

Hold on. You have to see this bit, said Trina, and pointed at the glass. After about a minute, the mixture separated into a dusky rainbow of tea. Jyothi coughed heavily into his arm and excused himself for a while to recover with a glass of water. *Each layer has its own colour, temperature, and flavour.*

Ki shundor, I said.

Jyothi returned and continued his story.

Aitcha, so, the boy begged his mother, and my mother her father, to accept the other, but neither budged. The boy got whipped in public for his sins, my grandad made sure of that before he kicked his daughter out of the house with a small packet of money so she could support herself,* he said.

Ish, people!* I said. *And she opened a tea stall.*

So here we are, Shefali's Cha he said.

I think I'll have that cup of tea now if you don't mind, I said, and tried to bend my head around what I just heard. Your own father kicking you out of the house because you got pregnant. Happens all the time, apparently.

Accha, Jyoti bhai, forgive me, but you still haven't really said how she died from love,* I said.

She kept this photo of my abba under her pillow – wild hair, sunglasses, those American jeans that go wide at the bottom. She kissed it every night before she went to sleep. And then one day I woke up to find her dead, perfectly dressed, with the picture held close to her bosom, he said.

I wanted to comfort him, to tell him everything was going to be alright, but I feared I might have been about a decade late with that sentiment. I drank the tea and put the cup down on the tray. In my head it didn't make any sense. Why would she be perfectly dressed if she suddenly died in her bed? In any case, I didn't have time to dwell on it too long as the hijras I saw harassing people outside Father's mosque rocked up, pointing at their watches, and shouting at Jyothi.

"What's happening?" I asked.

"I don't know. *Chol*, let's get out of here," said Trina.

"*Na*, wait. I want to make sure he's OK," I said.

One woman, the leader of this mob, took out some pills from her handbag and gave them to Jyothi in exchange for a few hundred takas. He washed them down with a cup of tea in front of all to see. The hijras went off singing and dancing, begging passing folk for alms, threatening them with curses if they refused.

Ish, I left my handbag at home, do you have some *taka* Trina?* I said.

Na, don't worry. This one is on me,* said Jyothi.

Dhonobad, Jyoti bhai. *Abar dekha hobe*, we'll meet again,* I said.

"Oelcome. Good bye bye," he replied. So cute! We thanked him and set off back to the village square where we stayed the rest of the day hopping from stall to stall and watching jatra[54] plays.

54 Bengali folk-theatre.

By the late afternoon, the crowd had mainly become young men as the women and girls had gone home to prepare dinner. When we got back to the place where the rickshawala had dropped us off, I felt a tug on my pallu. I turned around to see a teenage boy, dazed and confused, lying flat on his back. Trina had given him some tough love.

It was nothing, Trina, he just pulled my sari, I said, offering my hand to the boy, but he was so ashamed he got up on his own and quickly lost himself in the throng of revellers.

Give them an inch, Sakthi, they'll take a mile, she said.

Dusk falls fast near the equator. Trina suggested we head back before the mosquitoes came out – she wasn't just talking about the insects I gathered – so we took a rickshaw home. As we got close to the house, I felt sick to my stomach at the trouble that lay in store for me. I wished I could stay out all night, till the temperature had cooled, as well as Meghna's temper. I was so sorry, she deserved so much better than that, than me.

When we got back the place was dead, with only the moina bird muttering something in his cage (evidently captivity is better than the wild). I found our bedroom turned upside down, and had it not been for my jewellery and passport, which lay untouched on the dressing table, I would've thought we'd been robbed. Stranger still, in Meghna's room, an empty vial of insulin and a used syringe, unclipped, lay on the dressing table – she never forgets to dispose of the needle.

Where is everyone? said Trina.

I don't know, I said.

The kitchen too was quiet apart from a young servant girl sat all on her tod fanning the flames under a handi. She pointed with her head towards the sitting room. I walked across the eerily quiet courtyard and slowly opened the door to the lounge to find the room packed with everyone from the village. In the middle, was Father. To my horror, he was holding Meghna up by her hair, her knees an inch above the ground so the only support for her weight were the tips of her toes. Next to him stood the village elder, and Dadhi who was waving around a pack of tampons. She must've found them in my handbag. My heart was racing.

Haramjadi, how long have you been hiding Sakthi's periods?* said Dadhi.

Maf kore dao, Amma,* said Meghna, pleading for forgiveness.

You must beat a disobedient wife, said the elder.

Father hesitated when he saw me. For a split second, I saw a flicker of the goodness, that he knew what he was about to do was wrong. And then it was gone. He slapped Meghna as hard as he could and let her fall to her hands and knees.

Are you a man? Then strike her like a man, or your daughter will grow up the same. The shame she will bring on our family. We'll never get any of our girls married! said Dadhi, pointing at Trina, who was hiding behind her mum.

Ya Maboud! She made a mistake, we should forgive her,* said Soto Chachi, holding her daughter tight.

Arre beta, have you forgotten the shame you brought on this family as a child?* Dadhi said to Father. The village elder nodded in agreement, Father stood there, shoulders shaking, jaws clenched.

"Stop!" I screamed. I pushed through the crowd to help Meghna to her feet, but Father's forearm hit my stomach so hard that I lay winded on the ground, unable to move. Ringside, I watched as he lifted one foot off the ground and unbuckled his sandal. Grasping it tightly, he whacked her across the face. Then he rolled up his panjabi sleeves, stiffened his fingers into a board and beat her to a pulp. When he finished, she collapsed on the ground. The room fell silent. The ladies from the kitchen hid behind their saris, should they be next for going against the will of their husbands. Only the geckos on the wall continued their clicking, as if nature obliged them to register some form of protest at what had happened.

Father took off his belt and Meghna crawled over to cover me with her body.

Leave the child, she's learned her lesson, said the elder.

You said you'd make a man of him, Amma, instead you made a monster, said Soto Chachi, glaring at Dadhi.

Father stood above us.

"This in't you, Abba," I said.

"Get up," Father ordered Meghna.

"Yer kind, gentle, yer funny," I said, weeping.

"There's no room for you under this roof," he said to Meghna.

"Generous, thoughtful, lovin'," I said louder, but the words kept bouncing off him. He took Meghna by the scruff of the neck, dragged her to the front door and chucked her out of the house.

"Please, Abba. She's yer wife!" I said, kissing his feet for forgiveness.

"Get away," he said, kicking out like I was a dog at his heels.

"I'm beggin', Abba, please, I'll marry whoever ya want," I said.

"That's not even for discussion," he said.

Accha, at least let her stay in the shed, said Soto Chachi, placing a key in my hand and hurrying me out the door before Father could stop me. I ran outside to pick Meghna up off the ground. The door slammed behind us, and the bolts went across.

The shed is a good fifty yards from the main house complex, next to the cesspit. My bare feet had already been bitten by mosquitos before we made it to the door, which was locked with a chain to stop the cows from escaping. The smell of dung was overwhelming with flies buzzing around everywhere. The moon shone in through a large gap at the top and lit up the inside just enough for us to make our way around.

In the corner were two large cows that were being fattened up for Trina's wedding. I crept up behind them and filched some of the straw they were lying on to make a bed. It was cold, the wet kind that gets into your bones, so I took off my sari and placed it over Meghna as a cover before going to fill up the plastic shingara bag I had kept from the mela. I never in a million years imagined I'd be recycling it for this.

I lifted the lever of the well to pump the water but stopped at the top. It was Father who paid to dig the borehole, and have it installed, and it annoyed me that we had to depend on his charity despite everything he'd done to us tonight. What a bastard! And what is this mystery, I thought, this shame that he has brought upon the family? What could possibly have been so bad to have changed him from the loving person that I remember growing up as a child to the monster that Mrs Finch saw emerging after he'd met the imam? I desperately want to believe he is good inside, and to find that good, but tonight will take some getting over.

When I got back Meghna was delirious, having a proper gabble with God. I pricked a small hole in the bag with my hair clip so she could take a sip, but no sooner had I lifted it to her mouth, she fainted.

"Amma? Amma!" I shouted, shaking her by her arms. Her head wobbled loosely on her shoulders, she could barely speak.

Pantha... pantha, she said.

I ran over to the house and pounded the front door. Nobody answered, nobody dared. The windows were open. Through the mosquito netting I could see the women sat in the bedroom counting prayer beads, but Trina and Soto Chachi were nowhere to be found.

*Dadhi, *sahajjo koren*, help, she's passed out. Dadhi!* I said. But the louder I screamed, the louder they repeated the name of God. The men were still in the sitting room. I begged them for help, but even the village elder seemed scared. Father ignored me, poured everyone a cup of tea and passed around a tray of biscuits.

I went to the kitchen, but it was locked.

I rushed back to the shed to find Meghna shaking. She reached out for something in front of her and pushed it, a door or gate of some sort, and then smiled. And then it occurred to me, the insulin, the empty syringe, her blood sugar-level must've plummeted without something to eat.

Outside, not a mango or jackfruit hung from the naked trees, the season having long passed with the monsoons. I legged it to the roadside to fetch help, and by pure chance bumped into Jyothi on a rickshaw going back home to the slum across from the mosque.

I told him what had happened. He jumped off, took out a small tub from the compartment under the passenger seat and hurried after me back to the shed. Meghna was mouthing words again, but barely any sound came out. He put his ear up to her mouth.

Pantha bhat, he said, and looked at me as if he wanted me to do something.

Pantha bhat? I replied.

"Rice! Old… rice," he said. *Soaked in water. The servants leave it out overnight.*

I dashed to the kitchen veranda and brought back the pot Meghna had left out a couple of days ago. Jyothi took a handful, crushed it in his fingertips, added some gur[55] from his tub and held it to Meghna's lips. I raced off to refill the placky bag with water, and by the time I got back she had come round again. She reached for his face with her dainty little fingers, softly tracing a line down the ridge of his nose and caressing his cheek with her thumb.

So, you are Shefali's little boy? she said, looking tenderly into his eyes.

Jee, Aunty. Did you know my mother? he replied.

She gave you a beautiful name, said Meghna, thanked him for his help and pulled her pallu over her face. Before he

55 Jaggery.

left, Jyothi lent us a blanket he carried with him for those cold winter nights and offered to run any errands. I walked with him over the sandy courtyard and out to the front gates. How come Meghna knew who he was? I was dazed, confused, and now didn't seem like the time to bombard her with a thousand questions.

When I got back Meghna was well out of it. I held her tight and wrapped the blanket around the both of us. Is this what has been going on behind closed doors in Shaleton, I thought? All those screams, all those groans. She never had a choice of who to marry, and worse, she had no way out. And now it seems no matter how hard I work at school, no matter how well I do, I will end up like her. If that's the case, then what's the fucking point?

8. KITCHURI

A cup of tea

Mrs Finch was in the armchair where I left her a month ago and if she hadn't sniffled, I'd have thought she were dead. Her lounge has that velvety wallpaper with scarlet prints of the fleur-de-lis. A simple glass chandelier hangs from the ceiling. And in the corner a fancy mousetrap, baited with gourmet cheese, is set to spring on any murine companions. One side of the room is covered in fiction. Opposite, in between the door for the kitchen and another door, always locked, stands a grandfather clock. A cheerful fire burned next to her and on the tea table was a copy of the Telegraph, with a front-page splash on 'Mycombe Girls: A very English Madrasa?'.

"Shall I make us a brew, Mrs Finch?" I said.

"Kettle's warm, chuck," she replied.

She's ancient, Mrs Finch. Meghna jokes she may be older than the train station, but she still looks graceful. She always wears elegant clothes and never any jewellery, except a silver band on her ring finger and a bronze key that dangles around her wrinkly neck, day and night. She was hunched over something tiny in her hands.

"So, how was it?" she said, without looking up.

"The holiday? It was—"

"No, the book. The book I gave you to read on your holiday. Inspiration for your own journal?" she said.

"I couldn't finish it, to be honest," I said, shuffling my feet.

"Oh?" she said, drawing a magnifying glass closer to the object and away again.

"The way the writer talks about the subcontinent, it just didn't, well, to cut a long story short, it's racist, Mrs Finch," I said.

"How so?" she said.

"Well, he talks about Indians like they're savages," I said.

"Indeed," she said.

"I come from a civilisation that's thousands of years old, perhaps much older than Western civilisation, and here's this guy that thinks he's more cultured, more sophisticated and that we're like barbarians. It's just, well, disputable at best," I said.

"I see," she said.

"Are you even... What is that in your hands?"

"A stamp."

"From where?" I said, leaning over her shoulder to have a better look.

"India, to mark the independence."

The tatty piece of paper had the tricolour of saffron, white and green flying high in the Bharat[56] sky. How strange it must've been for her to see the queen's head replaced, to have had this sense of Empire and watch it all fall apart. She peered above the rim of her reading specs.

"For you," she said, putting the stamp in an envelope and hesitantly giving it to me with both hands as if she was Lord Mountbatten himself handing back the deeds of the subcontinent to its rightful owners (thank you Trina for the Bengali history lesson).

"For us? I mean, for me?" I said.

Mrs Finch knows shedloads about India, which she talks about fondly and with a certain air of superiority. It never bothered me before, but since getting back from Sylhet some of her opinions get right under my skin. How can you like someone who doesn't see you as equal, who shows such contempt for

56   Sanskrit name for India.

your ancestors, your race, and your culture? What makes her any different to the Mill Crew?

"It's an original."

"Did you live in India?"

"After the war, dear."

"Was Mr Finch posted there?"

She poured herself some tea in a floral design cup with four interlocking Ds on the bottom. She's the only person I know who actually drinks out of bone china. In any Asian house that stuff would take pride of place in the sitting room showcase.

"Do you know, I heard on the radio the other day that countries who import tea by land call it cha, or some variation. Isn't that fascinating?" she said.

"Fascinating," I said, letting her wriggle out of my question.

"Apparently, the word tea is from coastal China. It travelled to Europe through the Dutch East India company by sea. Tea exported on the Silk Road came from inland China where it was called cha. That's why we Brits call it tea, and you Indians call it cha."

"I'm English!"

"So you keep saying," she said, pouring some tea from the cup into the saucer. "Now, the book. That word you used. Disputable?"

"To put it lightly, yes," I said.

"Back in the days when Forster wrote this novel there wasn't a proper education system in India; no good health care or fair laws, no railways; you had no means to mine and utilise your natural resources. The leaders squabbled amongst each other like animals and paid little regard to the welfare of their people."

"But who's to say that we wouldn't have developed our own systems, just as good if not better if you hadn't colonised us?" I said.

"You?" she said. "I thought you said you were British?"

"I am."

"Apparently not.

"I can be both, if I want to."

"Then on whose side would you have fought? Gandhi's?" she said. "Conflicts demand you to choose, you can't be on both sides of the question like a Spanish interrogation mark!"

"I'd have fought for freedom, regardless of sides," I said.

"Freedom is relative, dear. You think the people in India are free, or the boys hanging around on the street corners of Shaleton are free? People will always be ruled by one system or another.

"Well, anyway, I didn't like the book. I just didn't."

"Not everything inspirational has to be aspirational," she said, grabbing a blanket from the side table, wrapping it around her body till she was almost head to toe in tartan and then snuggling up in her armchair.

"Now then, my little cocoa bean. I want to hear all about your trip back home to Bangladesh. Where did you say your father was from, near Assam somewhere?"

"Yes, Sylhet."

I told her everything that happened that night; how Dadhi found my tampons, how I'd agreed to marry someone twice my age and how the chaiwala saved Meghna's life in the cow shed. She didn't seem surprised. I hesitated from time to time, I didn't want to feed her prejudice any more than Forster had done already, but something about the way she sipped her tea from the saucer now, like Meghna does when it's too hot, gave me hope that she could change.

"So, when's the big day?" she said.

"My eighteenth," I replied.

"And I suppose you haven't seen the man, spoke to him?"

"No. And don't want to either."

"Ee, I don't know. Why do they marry the girls off so young?" she said, setting the saucer down on the tea table.

"Meghna says the older the girls get the harder it is for the husband to mould them into what he wants, so the dowry gets higher," I said, trying my best to keep it together.

She listened with patience and handed out love, Earl Grey and tissues at the appropriate times. A little before tea, I rekindled the fire and got ready to leave our lovely, racist neighbour and go back to the misery of our house.

"Oh, Sakthi," she called as I went to the back door.

"Yes, Mrs Finch?"

"Wash under your oxters, dear."

Meghna has been spoiling her own cooking to get Father back for his cruelty in Bangladesh. She overcooks the rice and makes his favourite curries too spicy – and when more violence doesn't work, he sends me out to pick up takeaway from the restaurant. With nothing to do but clean after Dadhi, despite all the grief she gives her, she zaps and naps her way through the day. She's lost tonnes of weight since we got back, and she's stopped wearing saris, choosing instead to stay in her nightgown or to put on a loose-fitting salwar kamiz to hide her body and her bruises.

This afternoon, as I was doing my laces up to go and get some food, she began to stir on the sofa where she now sleeps. I made us both a cuppa and sat next to her.

I had the most wonderful dream, Sakthi, she said.

"'bout what, Amma?"

It was long before the Great Storm. The sky was red and gold, and the trees were bursting with fruit, mangoes, coconuts, jams, papaya, jackfruit, all begging to be made into bortas.

"Yer makin' us 'ungry, sounds like heaven."

The river was calm. Small fishing boats drifted out with their coloured sails into the delta. In the distance, the Hindus were banging drums and racing their noukas.[57]

"And what were you doin'?"

---

57 A Bengali wooden boat.

Sitting on the veranda with Amma, enjoying the cool air, waiting for Baba to come in with the day's catch. We'd sort the hilsa from the rest of the fish as they were too expensive to eat. Then we'd make a fire in the open and smoke whatever was left. I was about your age, running around the fields, chasing the chickens around the house, as free as the breeze, she said.

I snuggled up close to her and linked arms, but she seemed distant and uncomfortable with the intimacy. Her ribs pressed against my forearm, her shoulder no longer the soft cushion it used to be for my head.

Have you forgiven your amma, for making you wear the burka? she said.

"You were lookin' out for us, I get that now," I replied.

Thik ache, but I should have told you.

"I should've seen it comin' like, I just din't wanna believe it. Anyway, he threatened ya, Amma."

Nje, still, it's my fault you're in this engagement.

"Please, stop sayin' that," I said, looking at her tortured soul. Meghna has aged years in the few weeks since we returned from Bangladesh. The roots of her hair have greyed, and her skin has lost its glow. Her eyes, at one time burning coals, are now nothing but the dying embers of a campfire waiting for someone to piss on them.

You must hate me? she said.

"Na, Amma, but I don't get why ya protect Abba?" I asked, a long shot.

She went into the kitchen and made herself a plate, but the rice was way too soft and turned to mush between her fingers and the tuna cakes were burnt black on one side. She didn't even bother to turn them over so they at least looked nice. Not even the Naga pepper cheered her up as it sat there half eaten next to an equally melancholy slice of lemon and a tiny mound of salt. I rolled my sleeves up, made a little ball, and tried to feed her like Padma Aunty did in Bangladesh.

"Amma, ya need to eat," I said, but she turned her head away. "*Accha*, I need to get dinner from the Bismillah. Is there owt you'd like, I could ask Mr Shah?"

I'm not hungry, she said.

"I saved me bus fare, maybe I could buy some shutki?" I said.

Dukkito moina, sorry, I don't feel like cooking.

"But ya love cookin', Amma."

I'm tired, I'll go back to sleep.

When she sinks into these lows, I have to say or do something to snap her out of it, to stop the train going off track, but it's hard always having to be there, to be the signaller. She's depressed, that's obvious from her abuse of the telly, and the sleeping in the day, especially when Father is home. I don't blame her for it, but what about me? I'm the one whose life has been turned upside down, yet here I am looking after her. It's selfish, I know, and I can't believe I'm writing this, but I'm too ashamed to tell anyone. It just makes me angry. And I'm scared to even put down these thoughts, because how can time heal, if the pain is cryogenically frozen within these pages?

When I finished the washing up, I put on a niqab (I no longer need to hide my maturing body, but now Father insists I cover my face), closed the door a little harder than I should've and headed out.

The Bismillah was heaving. Dast has turned the business around. The menu has changed, and now the double doors of the kitchen, the beating heart of the restaurant, open and close like a bicuspid valve pumping curry into the foyer. Waiters, all from the Black Paws of course, dressed in jeans and cheeky smiles, carried out trays of food pre-fashioned on plates instead of being presented on bulk in serving pots. And behind the bar, Dast was making a whole new range of non-alcoholic tropical cocktails.

"Wow!" I said.

"'ad to change summat, or we'd go under," said Dast.

"*Shabash*, man, well done! Proper mental in 'ere."

"We charge everyone a fiver at door now, and then they only 'ave to cough up the real cost of makin' their order."

"*Accha*, so, if I ordered a chicken bhuna, I'd just pay for the cost of the chicken, the spices, the oil and so on to make that dish?"

"*Haan*, an' the drinks. But that's if we still made chicken bhuna," he said. His brown eyes held my gaze through the veil a little longer than comfortable.

"And what ya makin' now?" I said.

"Guava 'n' tonic, wanna try? Take a seat," he said.

I put the straw behind my veil and took a sip.

"What d'ya reckon?" he said.

"*Bari moja*! It means very tasty in Bangla," I said.

"Cuts through the spice like a beer *yaar*," he said, holding his index finger up against his pink, full lips.

I picked up the menu. Inside, all the traditional British curries, the rogan joshes, jalfrezis, kormas and whatnot were given exotic twists. Ganges hilsa fish on a seabed of basmati rice, Kashmiri mutton with mountain pickles.

"'ow the hell are Shaletonites gonna know what they're orderin'?"

"*Arre yaar*, that's just it, innit?

"What is, Dast?"

"*Suno*, listen. Folk come in 'ere and ask for a chicken tikka or some shite like that and if they like it, they Google it and make it for 'emselves. So we end up losin' them customers. Well, now they can't coz we in't callin' our food like that no more, d'ya know what I mean?"

He put a lychee crush and tamarind fizz cocktail on a tray and told one of the boys to take it over to table 39. I scratched the top of my head trying to figure out the business model.

"Right, so the curries are now exclusive to The Bismillah?" I said.

"*Theek*. And for the pub next door it's a finger up the—"

"Proverbial!"

"That's the word I were lookin' for," he said with a cheeky smile. I cocked my head to one side and rested it on my hands.

"What?" he said.

"Dunno, guess ya surprised us," I said, petrified of complimenting him in case Father overheard us. Didn't matter, Dast wasn't the modest type.

"Not just a pretty face, innit."

"If I do say so myself."

While he shook the cocktail makers, I wondered why I hadn't noticed those bold, Pakistani features before. His deep-set eyes, his angular jaw – Daniel Radcliffe, with South Asian tweaks to his genome. He's a good egg too, saving all his pennies to put a deposit down on a new house for him and his mam. And there was that time when some random woman dropped her shopping in the middle of the road because the bitter gourd had ripped through those thin placky bags you get in Asian shops. Dast, superhero-in-waiting, jumped off the wall and raced over to pick everything up. It's like he's put himself on community service to make up for being such a radge the rest of the time! When the curry was ready, Dast brought it over.

"Ee ar," he said, giving me the bag and stroking the back of my hand with his thumb.

"What ya doin', you?" I said, alarmed, delighted.

"Shh, or yer father'll chuck us int' tandoor," he said. Never mind the tandoor, I was burning up inside. And just like on the rickshaw in Bangladesh, I couldn't take my hand away.

"Will ya go out with us?" he said, under his breath.

"You 'avin' a laugh? Let go ya silly bugger or you'll get us both done!" I said.

"I'm bein' serious like."

"Yeah, me too."

"Is it coz you're seein' that ginger *gora*, what's he called again?"

"Tone? *Na*! And don't call him *gora*."

"Then why won't ya go out with us like? See, ya do like him. I can't believe it. Is he gonna come save ya, yer knight in shinin' armour? He gonna learn ya to bend it like Beckham, is he?" he said, big smirk across his face.

"Gi's me hand back before Abba lays one on ya."

"He wouldn't 'urt a fly, yer ol' man."

"Who you tryin' to kid?"

"Dastgir, *jaldi beta*, Dadhi will be hungry," Father shouted over from the swinging doors. I ripped my hands out of his and shoved them in my pockets.

"*Jee*, Uncle," he said, giving me a wink.

A young man raised his arm up to grab his attention. No more shouting, whistling, finger clicking. As he printed off the bill, I saw a healthy jar of tips behind the till. I was chuffed to bits for him, he's finally put his brains to use. Touched and a little red, confused but content, I slipped out and made my way home.

Potatoes are the greatest

Nature shapes the folk that live under her grace, that's my theory anyway. In Shaleton, even though Winter beautifies the frozen landscapes around, she has the opposite effect on the people, who look pale and vinegary. And her beauty and perpetuity stand in stark contrast to the crumbling houses and litter-strewn streets of the old mill town. So, when the northerlies blow fierce over the narrow cobbles, I wonder why Father left the tea gardens to settle thousands of miles away in this dreary place.

Nobody comes here but the odd news crew reporting on some pre-teen scrag up the duff, or a lottery winner who no longer needs to queue at food banks. And now and then, a magnum of champagne socialists take a guided tour of England's industrial age with some filly dressed in factory overalls. She uses the simple past to talk about the squalor the honest labourers lived in. But what she ought to use is the present perfect, for it was anything but perfect in the present.

For the lads hanging around in parks and on street corners, Shaleton's where dreams come to die. With nothing to do and nowhere to go, they sniff glue and swig Special Brew, then crush the cans to play cuppies in the alleys to stay warm. When boredom sets in, frustration boils over into violence. At least, that's the story I got from Tone over the months we walked to school through the blistering cold.

Today, I met him in our usual spot at the end of the ginnel. He's shot up in height since last summer and when he takes his blazer off he cuts quite an athletic figure. Seeing his sunny face in the morning always makes me smile. I'd never tell him, but I miss him when he isn't at the bus stop because he has to cover for his dad at the market stall, or he has to take his mam to accident and emergency to have her stomach pumped. He's my wonderwall. Yet somehow, I can't bring myself to tell him my darkest secret – I'm engaged. What am I afraid of? A friend would never reject me, so did that make us more than mates, or less?

"Ya reyt, Sakthi?" he said, making a rollie with one hand and scrolling through his phone with the other. Quite the talent!

"Reyt. Hey, how d'ya know it's us under this niqab?" I said.

"Coz o' way ya walk. Ya kinda, like, glide. And when ya stand still, ya got that 'and on your hip, 'an't you, like yer gonna bring the whole house down," he said.

"Humph."

"Ee ar, got summat for ye," he said, giving me the headphone from his left ear. For a moment we stood connected by a metre length of white cord. We were practically holding hands.

"What is it?" I said.

"Noah ant' Whale," he said.

"Who?"

"Just listen," he said, but before he could play the damn thing, we both got jolted back by a pull on the cord from behind.

"Dast!" I said. "What d'ya do that for?"

"Why ya 'angin' out with that *gora*, thought ya said ya weren't seein' him?" said Dast.

"Who you callin' g—" said Tone, his sentence interrupted by a shove.

"*Arre, screw deela na ki?* 'ave ya lost the plot?" I said to Dast.

"I thought we were together," he said, putting his arms around my hips and pulling me in to his chest. His coat was warm and soft, his skin smelled like Nivea.

"And why d'ya think that?" I said.

"Well, ya 'eld me hand t'other day int' restaurant."

"*Na-to*, I din't. You took mine."

"But ya din't take 'em away, did ya? Just like now." I looked into them big, brown eyes again and he slowly started to take my veil off.

"*Amake chere dao*, let go of me!!" I said.

"You what?" he said, squeezing my arm tight.

"You don't own us Dast, I can do what I want," I said, and pushed him away.

"Well, it in't f'kin' right, he in't one of us," he spat. Did he mean Muslim, or Asian, or human? It wasn't totally clear.

"*Accha?* God, I thought you were different. More fool me," I said.

"Slappa! And you, ya ginger twat. Piss off back to daddy 'n' stay away from our girls or we'll f'kin' 'ave ya," said Dast, and got a big cheer from the Black Paws on the opposite side of the road as he pushed Tone to the ground. Tone squared up to him and got a bloody nose for his troubles. Dast tore the headphones and chucked them back in his face before joining his posse. I swore down there and then never to let him into my head again.

"Well, actually, he is me boyfriend," I shouted after Dast, hoping the words would catch up and slap him in the face. I turned to Tone who had his head between his knees trying to stem the nosebleed with the bottom of his school shirt.

"What ya doin', ya daft 'apeth?" I said.

"Defendin' yer 'onour!" he replied.

"Oh, you too? I can defend myself thanks very much, Ivanhoe."

"Ivan who?"

"Ivan... Never mind."

"Were ya bein' serious like, ya know, 'bout you and me?" said Tone.

"You and me? 'ave all men in me life lost their flippin' minds all of a sudden? I were just sayin' that to 'urt him," I said, a little ashamed after seeing Tone's head sink.

"F'kin' puff. Wouldn't 'ave done owt without his gang," he said, picking up the torn headphones from the floor.

"You jokin'? Seen muscles on him? He'd 'ave pasted ya."

"So ya do fancy him then."

"No, I don't."

"What's it ya said, 'I thought you were different?' And what's that secret language ya speak between you?"

"I don't fancy him, and it's not a secret language... we just share some of the same words in Bangla and Urdu. Tone. Tone, wait up," I said, and chased after him, holding my robe around my waist so I didn't trip over it. I caught him up at the junction where he stood repeatedly pressing the button on the pelican crossing.

"Is it true like, that yer ol' man gives food away to the gang?"

"You make it sound like a crime," he said.

"Soz, I din't mean it like that. I think it's amazin'," I said, pulling his untucked shirt down at the bottom so he came slightly closer. He resisted at first, but when the lights still hadn't changed, he talked.

"Dad grew up in some council estate in Glasgow when all that shite between Celtic and Rangers were goin' down. But 'alf the time, it had nowt to do with religion he said, it were coz folk were poor as fuck and couldn't feed their families," he said.

"Right," I said.

"So, when he came t'England to get away from all the trouble, he wanted to be a grocer, so he could help his mates out if they couldn't eat. He reckons food ont' plate is 'alf the battle to keepin' kids out of trouble, so that's what he does. And the gang leave us alone," he said.

"Well, it in't the only reason why the gang leaves ya alone. Yer smart, yer funny, caring, ya make people feel good when they're around ya. There's more to Anthony Drummond than meets the eye," I said, linking arms and pulling him close.

"In't ya scared of gettin' caught?"

"Nah, who's gonna know it's me?!"

When we reached the school gates, Mr Belton told Tone to tuck his shirt in and waved me through with a smirk. Such an arsehole! We walked past the quadrant of sinners and made our way straight to assembly in the canteen. It's the only time in the day we have together. In September, the whole year was separated into sets, and Tone, who's in a lower set, spends most of his breaks in group detention with the Mill Crew. They never grass on each other, so the teachers punish all of them whenever any one of them does anything wrong. Last week they had to serve time for rubbing cod-liver oil on the supply teacher's chair, so she spent the whole day walking around the corridors stinking of fish.

At exactly 9am, Mr Belton came in from the gates and stood at the front of the hall. Behind him were two sliding doors, which open up on Mondays and Thursdays to reveal an altar and an enormous white cross. He took a booklet from on top of the piano, drew his belly in and bellowed so loud the kids at the back might've questioned if our physics teacher was right when he wrote up the inverse square law for sound.

"Turn to page forty-three in your hymn books," he said, and we all groaned.

"Third time this month," whispered Tone, as we stood up to sing *Give me oil in my lamp*.

"Rather that than *Onward Christian soldiers*," I said.

"Gawd, anythin' but that."

"Besides, I quite like this 'un. It's catchy."

Mr Jackson, the scrawny, eccentric piano teacher started off with eight verses of improvisation before he came down on all the keys at once to signal the vocal cue. I love belting my lungs out. And out on those words, hidden amongst the quavers and crotchets, comes all the pain and frustration of growing up in our house. We don't really have music at home, only Meghna singing whilst making curries and those old records she brought over to England from Bangladesh. And so, in assembly I sing, savouring every note. It must be quite the sight for my classmates to see a girl in a full veil sing hymns with such gusto. But I don't care, a tune is a tune.

At the end of assembly, Tone's name was called out alongside the rest of the Mill Crew, again. They were put on litter duty because they'd substituted 'give me joy in my heart keep me loving' in the second verse with 'give me wood in my cock keep me fucking.' Tone, on this occasion, guilty as charged.

Mondays, I love Mondays! First class is English. I lap up everything like a plate of dhal and then regurgitate it to Mrs Finch, who kindly sorts the literary vomit into strands of intelligent thought. Ms Cocker, legend that she is, wants me to audition for the part of Puck in the school play. But fat chance Father will let me dress up as a sprite and prance around stage making people laugh.

"Fairies can wear burkas, it's post 9/11 avant-garde," I told the costume designer.

"That old chestnut," she replied with a wry smile, so I had to settle as a prompter for Kelly. That sucks, though admittedly, she does suit the part.

After morning break, we have maths. And if I have to learn one more simultaneous equation, I hate to think what I might do. Kelly shares the pain, and when she kept on writing y down as the answer for everything in algebra, Mr Shepherd finally clicked that she wasn't being stupid, she was simply asking a question – why? Still, I tried my hardest so that come parent's evening Father would see that I could run admin in the restaurant. That I could be the son that he wanted so bad, if only he'd let me, if only he'd give me a chance.

At dinner time I sold my lunch vouchers to a prefect for half the price making a tidy sum of one pound fifty, which, when added to my bus fare both ways came to a grand total of two pounds eighty. If I can pull that off every day, I'm in for just shy of 15 large ones a week. I've been saving up to buy some normal clothes after Meghna chucked everything, and Kelly says she doesn't mind going to the shop for me.

After lunch, we went back to our form rooms for wet break and sat on the radiator by the window for a gossip. School is like my social network since I can't have a phone or internet at home. So, whilst Kelly can't wait for the day to end, I dread it. I cherish dinner time, talking to who I want about what I want. As we sat there watching the rain pour down, a couple of fifth formers went out into the middle of the rugby field and started snogging each other – a dare we presumed. The whole class was up against the window. For those who could see that far it was quite the sight, tongues racing to taste every cavity in every molar as Mr Belton's stocky figure came trundling over to untie the unholy union. It took him ages to get there, and when he finally did, he grabbed them under their arms and guided them to the headmaster's office.

I wonder what it feels like to be so into someone, to let them in like that, and for some reason I've now got Dast in my head (I know, I promised I wouldn't let him in). Kelly finds it disgusting. She can't get round the idea of something going in her mouth, never mind her 'vajayjay', as she likes to call it (why can't we girls say it? Vagina. Vagina. VA-GI-NA). Anyway, when I think about it, it does sound quite frightening, the thought of you-know-what, yet here we are, humanity, mushrooming. I'll have to ask Trina about it. She'll know, she's married now.

That afternoon it tipped it down so bad Tone convinced me to take the bus instead of brave the downpour. The 923 is a microcosm of Shaleton. On the top deck are the chavs. Tone fits right in there, and this is where the Mill Crew sit. Near them their protégés, who aspire to be dropouts one day. The lower deck is crammed with goody two shoes. On the back seat are the fifth formers, cool prefects, whose mams cheer at footy matches and dads go to parents evening. And in front of them their sidekicks. Apart from these prestigious seats, the rest is a free-for-all.

The top deck was packed because of the rain, so I came downstairs with Tone and stood by the second set of double doors. Some of the wide-boys followed us and pushed their way towards the back. That's when it all kicked off.

"Ey up, here's one of 'em black moving objects," I could hear one of them say, brushing his flies against me as he squeezed past. Could he have helped that? There's no way of knowing.

"Hey Fatima, get yer tits out for lads," his mate shouted.

God, I get more attention dressed head to toe in these sheets than I ever did with my skirt pulled halfway up my thighs. The jeers hurt, and for all the protection the veil gives against the unwanted leering of men, it isn't soundproof.

"Aloo Akbar!" the first boy shouted, shooting air bullets.

"That's Kev, ignore 'im, he's jus' messin', tryin' to get up int' gang," said Tone.

Some of my friends seemed embarrassed, others joined in the laughter. They have every right to. I don't think twice when they rip the piss out of their own religion or dress codes. Still, it felt personal, and because they couldn't see my face, my pain, they treated me like an object with no feelings. Nobody stuck up for me, and why would they? Slagging off Muslims like this was normal round our way. But the reaction of the other Muslim girls on the bus was more disheartening. A couple of them wore burkas, and they cowered at the front near the driver, who offered some protection. But the others who wore headscarves, and not the full veil, joined in the mockery. Things have moved so far over to the right that even our own have difficulty finding the line.

My chest tightened and my mouth felt dry. My throat closed up like someone had me in a chokehold; this has happened a few times since I got back from Bangladesh. I wished Dast and the Black Paws were here. I hated them, their possessiveness, their self-righteous belief they were somehow morally better than the Mill Crew, but they brought a sense of security to the Asian community.

Tone shifted his weight from one foot to the other. With one word he could've stopped it, these boys knew how much his family helped them and respected him for it. But I'd browbeaten him into silence earlier today and he wasn't getting his fingers burnt again.

"You can defend yerself, right?" he said.

"Hard as nails, me," I replied, and took a deep breath.

There was a moment of reckoning. Think, Sakthi, I said to myself, what would Trina have done? She'd have smashed seven shades of shit out of them! No, that wasn't going to work. From Tone, I knew the seat Kev was sitting on meant he didn't think himself tough enough to take on the fifth formers. So, I planned my attack hoping the prefects would come in when I needed them.

Think sharp, witty, play to the crowd, this is your turf, I thought as I walked to the back. It went quiet, with only the murmur of the engine below.

"What ya starin' at, Bin Laden?" Kev said. I looked at him, but he couldn't make eye contact. His mates who had been shouting with him stared out of the window or giggled into their rucksacks.

"Aloo Akbar?" I asked him.

"Yeah, in't that what you terrorists say?" He fist-bumped his mates and then made a pistol with his hands and pretended to shoot me in the head.

"Kev, right?"

"What's it to you?"

"Well, Kev. It's Allahu Akbar, not Aloo Akbar. You've jus' been chantin' 'potatoes are the greatest,' ya tuber-loving Neanderthal," I said and, right on cue, the prefects burst into laughter.

"Slappa," said Kev, and went back upstairs with his mates.

One of the prefects, the one I sold my lunch vouchers to, invited me to sit at the back with them. I'd won the respect of the lower deck, and in doing so, had won it for the other Muslim girls too; the two girls wearing burkas thanked me when I got off. At the ginnel by our house I cracked up laughing.

"What's so funny?" said Tone.

"Slappa? Second time today," I said.

"And yer wearin' a bleedin' burka!" he said.

"Thanks, for bein' there for us," I said.

"Nah, ya did it on yer own... ya slappa," he said, jabbing me in the ribs. But truth be told, I'd never have worked up the balls if he wasn't by my side. In a way, his silent support attracted me so much more than his chivalry earlier today. I gave him a big hug, and we went our separate ways.

Trapped

Trina's electric blue sari and sparkling tiara lit up the red brick terraces of Shaleton. The neighbours all came out of their houses to catch a glimpse of the new bride, skipping along the road on a rainbow of love with gulap jams and rosho gula for all. After she'd walked into our house, I blocked off the door for the groom, Akaash, as is Bengali tradition. I placed a small sign on a ribbon across the entrance with the amount he'd have to pay if he wanted to have his wife back – three camels and a sherbet fountain! Short, a little tubby (as every man should be according to Meghna), dirty skin colour, yet friendly (again Meghna's words), he stood outside trying to barter his way into the family.

"*Ish*, look at 'em clouds Dulabhai[58]," I said, perfectly willing to settle for just the sherbet, but he wasn't to know that.

"You drive a hard bargain, sister," he said, Queen's English.

Three camels are nothing, pay up you scoundrel! said Trina.

Thik ache, I'll pay! For both your love, and your temper,* he said.

Two wives for the price of one, she said, and he took out his wallet and pulled out a clump of dark pink bills. Dadhi glared at me, I wasn't meant to take them all. Father came downstairs to welcome the guests.

"*Slamalaikum*," said Trina and Akaash in unison.

"*Wa'alaikum assalam wa rahmatullahi wa barakatuh*," said Father.

---

58   Elder sister's husband.

116

I took down the barrier and showed them to the sitting room. Meghna brought out a tray with shemai[59], and tea to be served in the cups and saucers from the showcase – the royal treatment. After the hellos and superficial background checks, Father and Akaash began on the enthralling topic of business tax for small and medium enterprises. When the men were sufficiently in love with the sound of their own voices, Meghna took Dadhi up to bed for a nap, and Trina and I went out for a walk around the neighbourhood.

"*Accha*, Trina Apa, spill the beans, what is he like?" I said to her the moment we turned the corner.

"Oh, I love him too much," she said.

"So much," I corrected her.

"So much... I love him so much," she replied with a smile.

Trina painted a different picture to the one I had in my head of the man that had told her he'd driven Maradonna around Manchester. Akaash worked hard, saved money, and invested in England, not in Bangladesh. He wanted just two kids, a cinch she said, as easy as making a mamlette[60]. And he told her they could be whatever they wanted to be as long as it made them happy.

"As long as it made them happy?" I said. Perhaps he isn't aware of how Bengali pensions work? Have kids. Let wife and free education system bring them up. Make them choose medicine, accountancy, engineering, law, or anything else that pays well i.e., not art. Take all the credit. Send kids on a no expenses paid guilt trip. Draw family pension. I think there are a couple more steps, but let's not labour the point.

"On the Qur'an, Sakthi, that's what she told me," she said.

"*He* told me, not she," I said.

"He, sorry, my English is too bad... sorry... so bad."

I walked into the corner shop and tried to pay for the sherbet fountain with the fifty-pound notes Dulabhai had given me,

59 A milk and vermicelli dessert.
60 Bengali slang for omelette.

117

but the shop keeper seemed unimpressed. Trina added a bottle of water and smiled. How does she do that? Make everyone turn to putty. The shopkeeper took the money and examined it very closely before placing it under the float and giving me the change. Trina tried the sherbet, and then quickly drank some water to wash away the taste.

"*Accha*, Sakthi, and you? There must be so many – is that right, so many – Londoni boys to choose from here," she said looking at all the brown faces, driving around in their Mercedes Benz. "I cannot believe beautiful girl like you does not attention."

"*Na*, not really, they are all Pakistani, and errr, hello, niqab!" I said.

"Nobody interested in treasure chest, everyone wants what inside," she said.

"Treasure chest! Me, I am more like Pandora's box!" I said, recoiling momentarily from the sour kick of the sherbet.

"*Arre beti*, come on, I saw how you looked at rishkawallah, nobody aksed you?"

"You swap your s with your k all the time. Rickshaw, not rishka, asked, not aksed. You never say a and the, and you miss the helper verbs like to have and to be."

"You *are* avoiding *the* question!" she said.

"I am spoken for, remember?" I replied.

Sharing secrets in the Bengali community is a risky game, especially if they can be used to shame your family back 'home'. Information about boys, eating pork and drinking alcohol has to be exchanged on the basis of mutual destruction, and I hadn't anything on Trina yet – she was, as far as I could see, an absolute angel.

Accha, have you heard anything about who it is?* she said, switching to Bengali.

Nje, a man from the neighbouring village, Abdul Sarkar,* I said.

Abdul Sarkar Ripon? she said.

Father calls him Ripon, I said.

Ish, Sakthi, I wish I could give you half of my happiness,* she said, wiping a tear from her eyes.

"Trina, *Apa*, what's wrong?" I said.

We sat down on the swings in the playground where we rocked in silence. On the opposite side of the park the Mill Crew were playing keepy-uppies and drinking from the bottle every time the ball hit the ground. Trina felt in her bag and pulled out a packet of lights, lit a cigarette and took three long drags before throwing it on the ground and putting it out with her sandals. She looked at me knowingly. The smoking, it wasn't much, but it was a token of trust, and I took it with both hands.

Sakthi, the man you're betrothed to, I know him.

"Oh, and? Tall, dark and handsome, is he?"

*He was quite a few years above me in school. But everyone knew him. A mean boy, always picking on girls. He was expelled for eve-teasing, so his abba put him in a restaurant."

"Eve-teasing?" I said.

Nje, when boys compliment girls, you know, but sometimes a bit too much. *Accha*, how can I explain this? Have you seen the old Bengali movie *Dost Dushmon*? Maybe Meghna got it on Bangla TV?* she said.

"*Nje*, I know the one," I said.

*There's this scene where the lead actor is singing *Chumki Choleche*,* she said. She took her smartphone out and showed me the video. *It's a classic. Four lakh[61] views, three thousand likes, and just 180 unlikes. That's eve-teasing,* she said.

"That is horrific! Ugh, how can people like this clip?" I took a deep breath. In the video, the man is pretty much manhandling the girl that he purports to love, despite her making it abundantly clear that she doesn't want him near her.

"Sometimes, so bad, girls suicide themselves," she said.

"Kill themselves!?" I said.

61 Counting unit in South Asia, which is equivalent to 100,000.

Nje, because of shame. So, when he was younger, he... oh, it's just rumour,* said Trina.

"Tell me, I have a right to know."

Accha, he took pictures of this girl, naked. A week or so later, he asked her for money and said that if she didn't give it to him, he would send the photos to her classmates."

"How did he get her naked?" I asked.

That's not the point, Sakthi! she said.

"Sorry, sorry, of course, you're right. Sorry. And? Did she pay him?"

*She didn't have the money and couldn't ask family for shame."

"So, what happened?"

The next day a fisherman found her body in the Surma Nadi.

It fell quiet for a tick, a long tick, one seemingly without a tock. The wind rushed past my ears. My head felt heavy. The horizon got narrower, like the curtains coming down after a play. And then it went black. When I came round, I could see the Mill Crew, who were sat on a memorial bench drinking beer, falling about the place with laughter. Trina helped me up, brushed the dirt off my robe, and we walked back to prepare supper.

The absence of sound in a Bengali home is unsettling. The telly was on mute, and those sepia images of Uttam Kumar calling out to his Juliet in *Chhadmabeshi* were playing. The first call had dropped. Meghna sat on the couch all on her own, counting prayer beads. Akaash stood in the doorway and Father was hovering over the phone. At last it rang and he picked up.

"*Inna lillahi wa inna* something or other," he said.

"What does that mean?" I whispered to Trina.

That's what we say in Arabic when we hear someone has died. It means we are for Allah and to Him we will return, she replied. In the corner Meghna started to weep, softly. Tears upon tears streaming down her face, like she had saved them all for this moment. And soon after, her body started shaking and the crying became louder.

"*Ya Allah*, Amma, who died? Abba?" I said.

"Your khala,"[62] Father replied.

"Surma? Kushiyara?" I said, but the nod didn't come. Meghna, heart shattered into a thousand pieces, leant forward and carried on serving tea and nimki.[63] Just three months ago they were in each other's arms, laughing like schoolgirls, reliving those moments when they were young and free and safe and loved. The way she told her stories, I could taste the sea salt in the air, smell the achar on their fingers, and when she hugged me, I wished that she'd never let go.

"Padma Aunty?" I said quietly, hoping that if nobody could hear me, nobody could answer the question. "What happened?"

Father took me into the kitchen. It was a road accident. And the driver, petrified of being lynched to death by the public, fled the scene leaving her lying there as roadkill. I took the money I had extorted from Akaash earlier in the day and asked him to put it towards repatriating her with Nana and the funeral back in Bangladesh. He took it and beckoned Trina, who had been comforting Meghna, to join him. She bent down to touch Meghna's feet and then gave her a kiss on her cheek. She came over and held me tight in her arms.

"Come and visit, sister, in happier times. Manchester not far as Sylhet," she said.

Through the window netting I could see Akaash open the passenger door for his wife. After she'd got in, he gently closed it, raced to the driver's side and drove off. Father picked up his prayer mat and went off into the bedroom. Meghna went into

62 Aunty on mother's side.
63 A salty snack.

121

the kitchen to sort through her spices. Why won't she come to me, I thought. Why won't she hold me, or look at me?

"Amma, 'ow can ya cook at a time like this?" I said.

How else can I mourn? she snapped.

I spent most of the half term holidays with Trina in Manchester just to get out of the house. She's learned to drive, so every day she picks me up early and drops me off late. Father never lets me stay overnight in the house of a non-blood-related man in case he brings shame upon the household. That is, the woman's household, not the man's. As it happens, Akaash is the nicest person ever. Trina has proper lucked out (though I admit, when she told me she cried with love cooking curries for him, I almost hurled in my niqab).

In the mornings, we made the food for the day and we swapped recipes. Trina has already made quite a name for herself in the neighbourhood as a pakharajuni[64], and Akaash promised to help her set up an all-women-run cafe. When he returned around lunch time, he washed up all the dishes that we had used to cook, ate and took a nap before the long evening shift. In the afternoons, we went for long walks in the Dark Peaks and talked about our childhoods, me in the present tense, she in the past.

I confessed to her all my sins; that my best mate was a white boy from the other side of the tracks, that I craved sausage barm cakes, I used tampons and smoked rollies.

Arre buka, silly. Do you think girls at Dhaka University are walking around with diapers between their legs, or that they've never had a smoke? she said to me in utter bewilderment.

"Yeah, I guess," I said.

64 An amazing cook.

Bangladesh is moving on, but the diaspora live in the past, she said.

"What do you mean?" I said.

My teacher at school says culture is a river. In the centre is the fastest part, but as you move to the edges, the river slows down. Sometimes, the water moves so slow it deposits sediment and changes course. That's the diaspora.

"*Thik ache*, but what about the village elder, he is traditional," I said.

Every village has an old man holding on to power, she said.

"*Accha*, so why did you have an arranged marriage?" I asked her again.

"*Nje*, arranged, but not forced," she said. "It's no different to meeting someone online."

I loved that week together, cruising around in her banged-up Beetle. She's going to fix it up herself she said, and I believed her. She went through the gears, effortless, confident, and pushed down on the accelerator as we reached the quieter A-roads around the lakeside. I stood up and leaned on the windshield, took off my niqab and let the wind run through my hair. For a moment, I was back in the tea estates, riding on the back of that rickshaw – the last time I'd felt freedom, tasted it.

"How's Jyothi?" I asked her, sitting back down. When I looked in the vanity mirror to fasten my veil, for some bizarre reason I saw him, his infectious smile.

"Still making seven-layered tea, but he has lost weight," she said.

"Even more? He was already a bag of bones," I said.

"Some people naturally thin, sorry, *are* naturally thin. Do you miss him, miss Bangladesh?" she said, indicated to the right and put her whole weight in turning the wheel to take a sharp corner.

"Why did you take me to see him, Trina?" I said.

You know, because he makes seven-layered tea, she said.

"*Na, asholei*, seriously like, why him? There are others all over Sylhet."

"Because he is best, and view is—"

"Stop playing silly buggers, will you? When I was with Meghna in the cattle shed, she looked at him like she knew him from another life or something. What is going on Trina, come on, fess up, tell me?"

"*Accha*, but promise do not tell to Meghna Aunty. Promise?"

"Cross my heart," I said.

Trina pulled into one of the roadside parking spots along the lake and turned the engine off. She took a tiffin box out of the boot, and we sat on the bonnet of her car, eating lamb samosas and drinking in the view.

"Yummy, these are gorgeous," I said.

Chinese pastry, more thinner, so you really taste filling, she said.

"So?" I said, taking a bite from one of the immaculately turned corners of the pastry, browned to perfection.

Accha, about five or six years ago I got a call from Meghna Aunty asking for a favour. Anything, I said, I'll do it. She said that there was a chaiwala on the lake that she wanted to know about, and whether I'd go and find out how he was doing.*

"Jyothi, *thik*?"

Nje, Jyothi. Be discreet she said. So I went to the stall, and I had a cup of tea. I was the only one there. He was struggling, so I told him about seven layered tea, and how it was all the rage in the tea gardens. He said he didn't have the money to set up a business like that. I told Meghna, and she's been sending him what little money she could get her hands on, 500 taka here, 1000 taka there.*

"Meghna is sending money back to Bangladesh as well?" I said.

So, I gave the money to Jyothi and helped him set up his tea stall business, you know, made flyers, brought my friends there. We got to know each other a bit, and I liked him, and I was so proud of what we managed to achieve. It was my own vanity, that's why I wanted you to see it, she said.

"So, what's his relation to Meghna? I do not get that part," I said.

I don't know, on the Qur'an, Sakthi, I honestly don't know. You'll have to ask Meghna Aunty yourself, she said.

"She says she cannot remember anything of that night," I said. "And yes, I miss Bangladesh; the people, the flavours, the colours, the sounds... not so much the smells though! And do you remember those men at the shingara stand?" I said.

Trina laughed and held my hand. I look up to her, and not just because she's older. She walks with a spring in her step and a quiet confidence rare amongst Asian women in our community. She is neither first generation immigrant, tied down by tradition and religion, nor second generation, carrying the burden of integration on their shoulders. She is unashamed to be Bengali, and proud to be British. But that was to change.

One evening, she dropped me off at the gate of our house. When I got out the car, my head got jarred backwards and I fell to the ground. My niqab had been ripped off and then someone threw liquid over my face.

Ya Ghafoor, Sakthi, are you alright? said Trina.

"Get some water, run, quick," I screamed.

My face was burning, my head spinning from hitting the ground. I scrunched my eyelids to save my sight and wiped off as much as I could with my robe. Trina came with a bucket of water from the house, which I dunked my head in until the stinging stopped. I slowly opened my eyes.

On the other side of the street stood the culprits, laughing their heads off. I recognised the older of the two boys from the school bus. He wore those chonging white trainers that somehow managed to stay clean even in the filthy back alleys of Shaleton. Three red lines ran along the length of his tracksuit legs, a chav's tuxedo, and a football anorak about ten sizes too big swamped his weedy frame. That diabolical face, eyes alight and teeth clenched tight was capped with a hat of the same tartan Mrs Finch often wore as a shawl. In his hand he held an upside-down bottle of water.

"Kev, ya moron!" I said.

"Pakis fuck off 'ome, next time it'll be acid," he shouted, and walked off chanting 'Pakis out' with his mate.

"You know those boys?" said Trina, helping me with my veil.

"They are in Tone's gang," I said.

"Your Tone?" she said, eyebrows raised.

"*Nje*, messed up, right?"

"*Accha*, and why he did call us Pakis?" said Trina, clearly shaken.

"They think we are all the same," I said.

But we are independent, we fight the Pakista—

"Yeah, well, welcome to Britain," I said.

I don't know what hit her harder, the fact that Kev thought she was an outsider, or that he couldn't distinguish her from the next brown face on the road. Nothing hurts pride as much as indifference and, despite her openness to other cultures, Trina is a proud Bengali. After tea she called her hubby to swing by with the car so she could follow him home. They drove off together. At the end of the road, Akaash stopped his car and jumped into hers. As the interior light faded, he leaned over and gave her a passionate kiss. I blushed and ran into the house.

Beethoven's nymph

In the early hours of Easter morning, Shaleton looked at peace. The powder snow on the rooftops glazed the terraces till they looked like a lemon drizzle cake stretching the length of the street. In Mrs Finch's garden, autumnal plants have long given way to dogwood and witch hazel, peeking their heads above the white quilt. Winter jasmine was scaling the walls by the door, where a green wreath hung around the bronze knocker. As I entered her house, I could see a Christingle sat on the mantelpiece, its single flame flickering in the draught of the chimney. On the table, was a huge box of fresh vegetables and a couple of containers of homemade soup. Mrs Finch was pottering in the kitchen, she'd asked me to come over as she needed a favour.

"Now, the secret to the perfect Simnel cake is in the marzipan," she said, setting the sugary almond balls into Tupperware and closing the lid tight, which required almost all her strength.

"Why are there eleven balls," I said.

"For the apostles," she said, and if she was about seventy years younger, she would have followed that with 'duh'. Still, my head wasn't fully screwed on, so I went on to embarrass myself further.

"Shouldn't there be..." I said. Mrs Finch tutted and looked up at the sky. "Oh yes, Judas, persona non grata."

She slid the festive treat into the oven at gas mark three, which she found by turning the knob all the way to max, and then back halfway. I gave her my arm and helped her to the armchair.

"Are you expecting guests?" I said, taking off my veil and head scarf.

"The only guests I have come to me in my prayers, but they tend not to eat much... How do you see through those things?" she asked, pointing at the veil.

"Would you like to try it on?" I said.

"Me? Oh my, I couldn't possibly, it wouldn't be right disrespecting your religion like that... May I?" she said.

"Don't see why not," I said, and put the niqab over Mrs Finch's head. Her eyes flashed with intrigue through the gap.

"There, how does it feel?" I said.

"A little claustrophobic, nice and warm though," she replied.

"Yeah, it's snowing, in April, what the hell's going on?"

"Mind your p's and q's young lady!" Mrs Finch reached over to the table and lifted the teacup and saucer to her mouth to have a sip.

"Ah, a design fault," she said.

"Blame God," I said.

"I'll tell him when my time comes." She took off the veil and breathed a sigh of relief. I could see her lips pressed tight, her nose twitching to make some ludicrous remark about Islam, but she refrained, and came up with a milder comment.

"Good for reading books, keeps you focussed," she said.

"Yes, I suppose it does... Are you religious, Mrs Finch?" I asked.

"Yes, I am. You?" she said.

"I don't know. I suppose I should be, then when so many bad things happen, how could there be a god? It just doesn't make sense that he would arbitrarily punish people like that," I said.

"People like you?" she said.

"Well, I was thinking of Meghna. She's been through so much, and then her sister died a month ago, and she's been in this depression ever since. No matter what I say or do, I can't get her out."

"Yes, I've noticed. Can she see someone about it?"

"Father says it'll bring shame on the family, and that's that. She won't go because she doesn't want to upset him. Especially now that Aunty Padma has passed, he's the only one supporting my grandad and two younger aunties back in Bangladesh."

"And what about you, chuck, do you have someone to talk to?"

"Me? Nah, I don't need to talk. Besides, who's going to understand what I am going through right now?" I said, making sure the sleeves of my robe were fully down and covered my wrists.

"There must be lots of girls in your shoes. What about that thing the youngsters use to chat, what's it called again?" she said.

"I can't get online at home though," I said.

"Can't you go to the local library?"

"It's shutting down."

"Oh, that's right. What a shame... And what about that boy you're into, Tone, right?"

"Tone? I'm not into Tone!"

"No? So why is it that since you got back from Bangladesh you can't sit still for two minutes, and you're busy looking out of the window all the time. I might be half blind, but some things I can see."

I made a fire to avoid the conversation. After the kindling caught, I formed a tepee-like structure with three hefty logs. I could feel the heat on my face as well as Mrs Finch's stare. Under my veil, I'd forgotten how to hide my emotions, and now she could read me like an open book.

"You're blushing," she said. "You do like him."

"I'm not blushing, Mrs Finch. It's the fire," I said, blowing at the base until the logs set alight. Mrs Finch raised her eyebrows in a knowing way and smiled.

"Ask him out," she said.

"No! He wouldn't want to go out with me. Look at the state of me," I said, pulling at the robe material. "Besides, I don't fancy him, remember?"

Mrs Finch got out of her armchair and walked over to the gramophone, took out a record from the sleeve and placed it on the turntable. She wound the lever, lifted the needle, and let it drop around two-thirds the way into the vinyl.

"Listen, Beethoven," she said.

"I've heard this on some advert on the telly," I said, thrilled that I recognised a piece of classical music.

"Never mind the telly, how does it make you feel?" she said, and we both stood in silence for a while.

"The first part, what is it, that instrument? A violin? It's all alone, quite sad sounding, calling for help almost," I said.

"Faint cello, but more double bass. And then?"

"And then, ah, they're the violins, right?"

"Yes, go on, close your eyes and feel, Sakthi."

"It's like the violins have found the double bass and they're lifting it out of its sadness, and it makes me feel, dunno, I'd say optimistic, but that word doesn't fit right. It makes me feel happy, no, that's not right either. It makes me feel like I can do anything I... oh, wait, I see what you're trying to do... very clever. But there's a difference between real life and a piece of classical music," I said.

"Oh, yes?" she said, raising her eyebrows (she does that a lot).

"Well, it's repetitive for a start. Life doesn't give you so many chances, at least not from where I'm standing," I said.

"What if I told you that Beethoven wrote that last section completely deaf, with only faith in his own abilities? That his father had beaten him as a child, disappointed that he was not as good as Mozart? That he put the music out to a hall of people waiting for him to fail, and when he didn't, he couldn't even hear their applause?" she said.

"He was deaf?" I said, and she took my hands in hers. Her eyes met mine, the wrinkles radiated back towards her ears, the tips reddened by the warmth from the fire.

"You have to take a leap of faith. Tell him, tell Tone you love him."

Sometimes I wonder if she's living her own fantasies through me. She makes it sound so easy, but the thought alone was terrifying. Little old me go and tell Tone that I want him. Comedy sketch of the year. That'll get some laughs from the Mill Crew. In any case, I changed the subject.

"Happy birthday, Mrs Finch," I said, and gave her a present I bought from the second-hand stall using the money I saved from selling lunch coupons to prefects.

"Oh, how did you know?" she said.

"It's written on the inside cover of Ulysses, a birthday gift you got from Mr Finch ages ago. I was reading it," I said.

"What is it?" she said.

"A book, in Braille, so you can read on your own. It's good to be prepared," I said.

"On my own, did you say?"

"What's the matter? Don't you like it?"

"Yes, yes, I do chuck, it's not that... Thank you," she said, and the bell rang for the oven, so we went into the kitchen.

"So, what's the favour you need?" I said.

"Would you take this cake over to forty-four Bridge Street tomorrow morning? The roads are too icy for me and my walking stick. It's for an old friend of mine who helps me with the groceries," she said.

"Of course," I said, and washed up the teacups.

"It has to cool, and you need to finish it," she said as she hobbled over to the oven and peeked in through the door with one hand on her back. The sweet smell of almond and honey was coming out of the vents.

"Wonderful, he is risen," she joked.

"He is risen, indeed," I said.

Early in the morning, I went over to Mrs Finch's and took the tea towel off the Simnel cake she had left to cool on the kitchen table. She was fast asleep, so I quietly opened the storeroom door, took out the apricot jam, and spread a thin layer over the top of the cake. I rolled out some more marzipan and cut a circle into it using the cake as a template, and then placed it on top and crimped the edges. I took out the Tupperware. I wondered if I should leave a space where the twelfth apostle should be, just to drive the message home, but opted in the end to place the balls evenly around the edge, given I didn't know the recipient. I beat an egg and brushed it over the surface before putting it under the grill. When it had caramelised, I took the cake out and placed it in a tin, making sure to wrap it up to protect it from the cold.

Bridge Street is on the other side of the crossroads. The houses aren't so different to the ones where we live, but their prices have gone down because of the soaring crime. Shops have their windows boarded. The nearby park serves as a meeting place for junkies and drunks, and the drains are blocked with fast food bags and cans of pop. Urban blight has set in like tooth decay, and the whites want root canal surgery. The only real option though is extraction, and when they sell up, it is increasingly an Asian family that moves in.

The garden at number forty-four was paved with concrete slabs, and outside was a white van. I opened the gate, then slammed it shut at the sound of barking dogs scratching their paws against the inside of the front door. A tall, red-haired man opened it and the boxers raced towards me, standing up on their hind legs trying to get at the cake.

"Dinnie mind them, they'll dae ye nae harm," said the man, ordering the dogs back into the house.

"It's Sakthi, Mrs Finch sent us."

"Aye, I ken who you are lass. The boy doesn't stop bletherin' on about youse."

"The boy?"

"Sakthi," a familiar voice called out of the first-floor window. It was Tone! Mrs Finch! I'd been tricked by a nonagenarian.

"Well, aren't you going to stay?" said the man, Tone's dad I presumed from the likeness.

"No, I... I can't, I really mustn't," I said.

"Sakthi, wait up!" said Tone.

Mr Drummond put the dogs on a leash and welcomed me into the house. I walked in to find a woman setting the table for dinner. Her chin almost hit the floor when she saw me standing there in a niqab. Tone raced down the stairs and came in a few seconds after.

"Mum, Dad, this is Sakthi," he said.

"Happy Easter," I said.

"Tek that bleedin' thing off yer 'ead. Can't understand a f'kin' thing yer sayin'."

"Mum!" said Tone.

"Happy Easter, Sakthi. Sit yourself down by the fire lass, where it's nice and warm," said Mr Drummond.

"Thanks."

"Would you like a wee tipple, a glass of wine?"

"Dad!" said Tone.

"Aye, of course, sorry Sakthi," said Mr Drummond.

"Don't worry. D'ya go to service then?" I said.

"Aye it was good, but I prefer the midnight mass. The atmosphere, the candlelit service, the lack of organs in the evening make it so much more personal, more rustic," said Mr Drummond.

"Well, if ya like rustic, then you'll like this," I said, handing him the cake.

"Wow, still warm. Good ol' Mrs Finch, utterly dependable," he said.

"Nobody eats Simnel cake on Easter Sunday," said his wife, swirling her gin around in her glass in the corner of the room.

"Some do. Anyway, it's the thought that counts," he said.

I took a seat by the fire and looked around the room. It's simple enough. The walls are bare, the table and the chairs are solid wood and appear to have been rescued from a skip. The sofa, like the one in our house, can unfold into a bed, and on the shelf above it is a little alarm clock and Tone's glasses.

"And hoe dae the Muslims celebrate their religious festival, Eid, did I say it right Sakthi?" said Mr Drummond.

"Yeah, that's right. Well, we don't really sing," I said.

"Isn't it all a bit drab without a wee sing song?" he said.

"S'pose it is," I said.

"Jesus came 'n' gave us wine 'n' song, bleedin' Mohammed came 'n' took it away. No wonder yer all blowin' each other up in yer miserable faith," said Mrs Drummond.

Mr Drummond stood up and apologised. His wife stumbled across the room and swayed in front of me, steadying herself on the mantelpiece.

"So, you're her, hey? The one," she said to me.

"What d'ya mean?" I said.

She came right up close to my face; her breath stank of gin.

"I won't let a f'kin' Paki take away our lad," she said.

"Marie! Stop with your haverin' and leave the poor lass alone!" said Mr Drummond. He grabbed her arm and led her out of the room. Tone left too, leaving me all alone with the sleeping boxers and the fire as company. I searched the flames for comfort, long and hard. What was I thinking? That I could waltz in here and expect them to treat me like their own? And why should they? Tone would be out on his ear if he ever dared come round to ours. I walked as quick as I could to the front door.

"Come back! I were only f'kin' jokin'," said Mrs Drummond, shouting over from the kitchen.

"Sakthi, wait!" said Tone.

I ran down the street, and Tone came after me. The sun lay low over the snow-topped terraces, the sky, that blue you get in holiday brochures, crisp and clean. Mrs Finch had opened the door to these feelings inside, and now they came rushing like the plumes of smoke from the chimneys. I turned to face him under the rail bridge, trembling with cold, with fear. With love? This felt much more than friendship. But how could I love him, given who he is and where he comes from?

"Yer coat, ya forgot yer coat," he said, panting, hands on knees.

"Thanks," I said, and forced myself to walk away.

"Wait! Jus' gi's a sec. I got ya summat," he said, pulling out of his pocket a really old Walkman that played cassette tapes.

"Wow! That is a relic," I said.

"I found it int' attic. It works good like, but it eats batteries," he said, caressing my arm.

"Tone... we can't be—"

"Me mam, she says stuff, she in't all there," he said.

"Sorry, I din't know. And the black eyes, I always thought it were yer dad," I said.

"Me mam. But listen. Come back. Me nan's comin' for lunch in a bit. She's dyin' to meet ya."

"I'll only be trouble," I said.

"I'll be there, by your side, like ont' bus," he said, shivering, goose bumps on his pale skin, hair standing on end like snowdrops on the frozen ground, ears pink from the cold. The morning sun shone through his hair, making it glow like melting copper around the edges.

Tell him, Sakthi. Mrs Finch was banging around in my head. *Tell him you love him.* I summoned up all my strength, clenching my fists in prep for the response.

"I..." I said.

"Yeah?" he said.

Tone stood up straight and took a step towards me. I wanted to hold him in my arms so bad. He went to touch my arm and I pulled back a little, but then the smell of roast and gravy wafted across the street and wrapped us together in a blanket of cosiness. He came closer, I felt his tummy rumbling, his steely abs pressed up against my rice belly. God, how embarrassing. Too many curries! I tucked it in and took a deep breath.

"I..., I, erm... have you ever heard Beethoven's Ninth?"

"Ninth what?"

"Ninth symph—"

A train passed overhead, the sound echoing off the stone walls so we couldn't hear each other. I looked at him stood there in his trainers and tracky bottoms, freezing his nads off. All he needed was his hoody and there'd be little separating him from Kev. The thought terrified me, that I could fall for a chav. By the time the train passed, I'd bottled it.

"Beethoven's nymph?" said Tone.

"Never mind, it'd never work," I said with a frown.

"I'm only messin'. In't that the one they play before all the footy matches? And what'd never work?" he said.

"Nowt, see ya back at school," I said.

"Sakthi? Sakthi, at least listen to t' tape," he called after me.

I left him stood underneath the archway. I turned around, hoping like in the films that he would turn around too, and we would rush into each other's arms. He didn't. He ran off, arms folded, back home. The snow started once more, like powder, that stuff you find inside glass balls. Fine, so fine each flake floated, refracting and reflecting the light from the sun, a million rainbows suspended all around me. I thought about Mrs Finch huddled by the fire – she has a lot to answer for.

Leg before wicket

Three simple words, subject verb object, but placing these three together is as hard as marrying the same poles of two magnets. For weeks I've practiced in front of the mirror, I love you, I love you, I love you, but the words weigh heavy on my tongue. Have I ever loved anyone? At least, I've never told anyone, not even Meghna. After a while, I gave up, and took solace in that mix-tape, 'Now Sakthi', curated just for me. I played it over again, and today the magnetic strip wore so thin it finally snapped. I repaired it with Sellotape, like Trina does with those old Linguaphone cassettes she picked up at the Salvation Army store for free. And batteries for the Walkman, I rob them from around the house to feed my addiction. Father almost smashed the alarm clock that calls out the adhan in frustration when it stretched out one of the Arabic syllables a bit too long for lack of power.

I love the physical side of holding this brick in my hands, the mechanical buttons which make a nice click when they're set into place and the hum of the motor. Through a little window I can see the wheels turning, like I'm looking inside the soul of the person who made the tape. Tone has opened his heart, copied it down and put it in my hands. And in my most escapist of moments, fully submerged in the melodies kissing my earlobes, it's as if I'm holding him. Some days, on the way to school, I want to push him up against the stone walls of the A627 and snog his face off in front of the streaming traffic. Most days though I just bite out chunks from the inside of my cheeks in mortified silence. I still haven't told him about my engagement; it would spell the end of whatever we have for sure.

"D'ya wanna go see cricket with us?" Tone asked me this morning on the way to school as I was flipping the cassette over to the B-side.

I carried on like I hadn't heard him, or at least in my mind, I thought that maybe I hadn't heard him right. That it was a figment of my imagination, and I heard what I wanted to hear, but actually he was just updating me on the cricket scores. But his face gave him away, pained like he was waiting on that third lottery number that would pay off the nine tickets he'd bought previously.

"Tone, there's summat I gotta tell ya," I said, thinking that now was the time to explain what had happened in Bangladesh, but he couldn't see the look on my face, so he kept talking driven by his nerves.

"Just say yeah," he said, taking my hands in his.

"OK, yeah," I said, the words coming out of my mouth before they could be hounded back by reality. What was I thinking? I don't know. I guess somewhere deep inside I thought that this might be my only chance to love, and even if it isn't requited, it's a feeling I desperately wanted to taste, especially after listening to Trina talk about Akaash.

"Yeah?" he said. "Really? You in't 'avin' us on?"

"Yeah, really," I said, and we walked to school the rest of the way in our usual silence. I had butterflies in my stomach, a lightness in my step and this overwhelming feeling that I belonged somewhere, with someone. Perhaps Mrs Finch was right after all.

Six hundred and twenty-four hours (not that I'm counting). That is how long since I agreed to go and see a dozen-odd men standing on a field polishing their balls, occasionally jerking into action like they've got posh Tourette's. Trina dropped me and Tone off outside the grounds at Old Trafford. She offered to cover for me (I'd spent loads of time with her since she arrived, and Father would never suspect anything) on one condition: that I tell her all the gossip.

Aww, look at you two lovebirds. Shouldn't I have taken you to, what's that place Akaash was telling me about, Gretna Green? she said handing me the tickets. Tone got the gist and blushed a whole spectrum of reds before he returned to his normal colour, pasty enamel. I, well, it didn't matter what colour I became, nobody could see.

"Thanks Trina Apa," I said.

"You are welcome," she said, and we arranged to meet at the bus stop a little after the match.

It was a northern summer's day, and we sat more or less halfway up the terraces of the Brian Statham End. Tone brought lunch. He opened a small box about eight slices deep in bread and a placky bottle filled to the brim with Vimto.

"Tell a lot 'bout a man by how he makes cucumber sarnies," I said.

"Yeah? What do they say 'bout us?" he said and gave me one. I took it and held it up as a jeweller might a precious stone.

"Christ, it's not a diamond," he said.

"You're right, there in't no carats in this sandwich," I said. He got it, and he laughed. What an amazing feeling! Ice duly broken, I squinted at the gastronomic construction.

"Let's see, yeah, just what I thought."

"Go on, let's 'ave it then chef."

"White, square bread, crusts removed with a sharp knife, divided diagonally into four quarters. Inside, hmm, interesting. A light spread of butter and cucumber slices made with a cheese slicer, not aforementioned sharp knife, so each piece is exactly the same width. Impressive," I said in a posh accent.

"Why, I thank you, your grace," he replied with a mock courtesy.

I bit into the sandwich.

"Crisp, not at all soggy, a result of either deseeding, which isn't the case, or freshly made cucumbers that have been salted and left to stand to help drain the water content. No mint, presumably as it may overpower the delicate flavour," I said.

"Very observant," he said.

"Meghna would also be impressed," I said.

"Why d'ya call yer mam that, Meghna?"

"Well, I call her Amma, which means mum in Bengali, when I'm talkin' to her. But, when I'm talkin' 'bout her, I call her by her name coz sayin' 'me mam' sounds like I own her or summat."

"Fair enough," he said, and took a bite of his sarnie, the corner I noticed, not straight from the middle.

"Besides, she's more than just me mam, she's her own person like, and ya lose that when don't call her by her name. D'ya know what I mean?"

"Kinda, I guess," he said.

"Anyway, this allows me to conclude two things," I said.

"Go on Sherlock," he said.

"Either, one: you're anal about cucumber sandwiches."

"Please don't use anal 'n' food int' same sentence."

"Soz. Point taken."

"And two?" he said.

"That ya want some of this burka-clad booty," I said. OMG, what utter trash talk. Had I lost the plot, left my dignity at the turnstiles? If that's what happens when you're into someone, I'm not sure I want to go there.

Tone looked at me deadpan, for ages, and then split his sides. I breathed a sigh of relief. He moved the sandwich box to one side and held me tight in his arms. For the rest of the afternoon, a smile stretched across his face like he'd put a banana sideways in his mouth. I felt safe, happy. I drifted off into my own little world until a loud noise shattered the bliss.

"'Ows'aaaaaaaat?" Tone shouted, bending both knees and sticking his hands up in the air.

"What?" I said.

"Soz, leg before wicket. When the batsman—"

"I know LBW ya muppet, but what d'ya scream?"

"How's that? Except, ya gotta stretch out the second part for dramatic effect. 'Ows'aaaaaaaat?"

"Raaaaaight," I said, and he sat back down. I could've stayed like that the whole day wrapped in his arms, but the last wicket fell before the tea break. When the crowds had gone, he led me down the terraces.

"Where ya tekkin' us?" I said.

"Close yer eyes, 'n' careful not to trip ont' boundary rope," he replied.

"In't we gonna get done for this?"

"Yeah, probably!" he said as we walked onto the cricket field. After a while, the ground hardened under my flats.

"You can open 'em now," he said.

"Wow! That's well far!" I said, looking down the wicket.

"Twenty-two yards. So, if ya made a ton on singles then you'll 'ave to 'ave sprinted almost a mile with all that gear on. Mad hey? If ya watch it ont' telly, it looks like a couple of fat gits runnin' to chippy, but they're proper athletes."

"Steady on, man."

Tone talked non-stop, but his nervous banter only made me want him more. He told me all about the speed of the pitch and fast bowlers, about wedging and about the Duckworth-Lewis method for scoring when rain stops play. I was enchanted by his enthusiasm, his passion. If he could love a game so much, then he could love a girl. A girl like me. My desire grew with the length of his sentences. I looked around the grounds. The wicket was like a raft on a sea of green, and we were drifting, just me and him with nobody around to tell us no. I took his hands in mine and drew a deep breath.

"Now your turn, go on, close 'em," I said.

I unfastened the veil and pushed back the headscarf, letting it fall on my shoulders. Pressing the back of his right hand on my cheek, I leant in towards him and rested my head against his chest. His breath licked the back of my neck, his heart raced. He caressed my face, examining every feature with tenderness.

"It's like Braille, you're smilin'. No... cryin'?"

I stood on tiptoes, right foot curled around my ankle and fluttered my wet eyelashes on his neck. His breathing grew deeper, his Adam's apple bobbing up and down as he took a long, hard gulp. He placed his left hand on my hips. I thought he'd be more confident, more sure, but he trembled as much as I did. I stayed still, frightened even the slightest movement might snap us out of this bliss. I placed my palms on his shoulders and softly blew on his eyelids.

"Open 'em," I said.

"I daren't," he replied.

"What ya afraid of?"

"Dunno."

"Then I'll close mine too."

I pressed my mouth against his like I'd read in all those teenage magazines. Trina had shown me too at her home in Manchester using a mango, but mangoes don't kiss back. He pulled me in closer, tighter. His glistening lips tasted of cucumbers and ash, of rebellion. Delicious. My heart, usually slow and steady like the bass drum of an indie rock song now raced along with the frenetic beat of grime. Tone opened his eyes and looked into mine.

"I...eh," I began.

"What is it, Sakthi?" he said. Violins raced up and down the major scale all around me, it was time to say goodbye to the minor.

"I'm in like with you," I said. "Does that sound weird?"

"No. And I'm truly, madly, deeply in like with you," he said.

An old man wearing overalls came marching over from the stands, head shaking, fingers pointing, making all kinds of grunts and guttural sounds. Tone grabbed my hand, and we ran across the field, dizzy as you like, until we got to the turnstile where we burst out in laughter. He touched his lips, red and swollen, pulled me in and kissed me again.

When we left the ground, Father not Trina, waited for us at the bus stop. The hairs on my neck stood on end, I could hear my pulse in my eardrums. Hands, moments before locked in ecstasy, now in the grip of fear. My sweaty palms slipped out of Tone's. I folded my arms tight across my chest to control the trembling. Father casually scanned the timetable for the next bus. He took a long, hard draw from his cigarette and then squished the butt end against the shelter till it crumpled under the force of his thumb.

"There I am getting my hair cut, and the barber puts on the cricket. He's a Pakistani fellow who likes to watch in between clients. All of a sudden, he laughs out really loud. 'I never thought I would see a burka at a cricket ground,' he said. Then the burka starts walking, 'gliding' is how he described it. Now who walks like that, I thought. Still, I wasn't convinced until I saw your ginger hair," said Father, glaring at Tone.

Tone's head sank into his parka, and he fiddled in his pocket.

"How's that? Isn't that what they say?" Father said.

We sat waiting for the 273, Tone at one end of the shelter and me at the other, with Father in the middle. Tone lit a fag with the end of the previous one.

"She's getting married, you know?" said Father.

Tone's eyes turned to me; the sweet kiss we shared had a bitter aftertaste. Damn it, why didn't I tell him?! My lie will have hurt him much more than Father's truth. But he took it on the chin.

"I know, but I still love her," said Tone.

"Love? What do the British know about love when half of your marriages end in divorce? Love is a commitment," said Father, irritated that the blow didn't land. The bus pulled up, and we left Tone to get the next one back to Shaleton.

"You can't keep us apart," he said, as we stepped on.

"If you *love* her, you'll keep yourself apart," said Father.

When we got home, Father went up to the bedroom and came down with a bamboo cane, about a metre long. He stood at the bottom of the stairs, calm and composed. Just looking at the stick brought me to tears, the pain manifesting itself before the first blow. I begged him, said sorry a million times, kissed his feet. Meghna came out of the kitchen when she heard all the fuss.

"'I can't keep you apart'. Isn't it?" he said. He slipped his jacket off and placed it on the end of the banister, rolled his sleeves up and took a swipe. It struck above my hips and sent a stinging pain up the side.

"O ma go, please Abba, I won't do it again," I cried.

"*Na?* Let me make sure," he said, and took another swing.

Ya Allah! What did she do wrong?* asked Meghna.

"Why don't you ask your daughter?" he said.

The next blow landed so hard on my back it smashed the bamboo right down the middle. Meghna looked on in horror, powerless to stop him. Father went into the kitchen. I could hear him chuck the stick in the bin and rummage through the utensil drawer.

Jao, run moina,* whispered Meghna. I ran up to the bathroom and locked myself in. I could hear his footsteps come slowly up the stairs.

"Open this door at once," he said. "I will break it down, if I have to."

I held fast, he wouldn't, would he? Father battered the door. Meghna reasoned with him, but to no avail. Eventually, the doorframe came away. I curled up under the sink, but he pulled me out and the blows started again, harder, and more frequent than before.

"*Shor-er baitcha*[65]!" he said, wielding a wooden cooking spoon.

Ya Maboud, stop striking her body, she's only a child,* said Meghna, and tried to wrestle the spoon away.

"Shut your mouth, it's your fault she has become like this."

Accha, even a farmer doesn't hit his cow in this way!*

"I have to teach her a lesson."

Not the bone! said Meghna. She put herself between us and took the blows, which I felt every time she flinched her torso. Father, tired from all the violence, left the room leaving me sobbing in Meghna's arms.

Ish moina, when did you become such a rebel?* she said, putting pressure on the bruises like she wanted to squeeze out the hurt.

"Sorry, Amma. Forgive me, for everything," I said.

Shhhhh, said Meghna, and she held me tight in her arms.

After a while, we went down to the kitchen. Meghna made me a plate of rice with some shutki borta, a lemon, and fresh coriander leaves. For a moment, I forgot everything, the chilli doing its intended job. She sat down opposite and watched me eat in loving silence like in the days before we got that stupid letter from Bangladesh. Father was upstairs talking to the imam on the phone. I heard him say my name a couple of times, but I couldn't make out what he was saying as Meghna started asking me questions about all kinds of random stuff. Then she offered to buy me some clothes to wear under my robe, and when I finished eating, she even washed up my dish. We went into the living room where she laid my head on her lap and stroked my hair while we watched *Saat Bhai Champa* on the Bangla Channel. Father came down the stairs in his longi with the brochure of Mycombe Girls in his hands. He looked at Meghna and then he turned to me.

"It's the only way to protect you before marriage," he said.

---

65 Child of a pig – a strong insult in Bengali.

"Protect me, from who?" I said.

"From yourself!" he replied.

"You said he couldn't afford it, Amma. I would never 'ave... You told me he couldn't afford it!" I said and ran upstairs to my bedroom.

₡. CURRY & CHIPS

Mycombe Girls

First day at God School, and Father made sure to drop me off, recorded delivery. The taxi pulled up at the front gates of this grand building. The entrance has six Greek-looking columns supporting a balustrade that goes across the top of a flat roof. On either side, huge square towers give it a medievally castle feel. We went up the marble steps and through a heavy set of double doors into a hall with a ginormous chandelier. An older student in a hijab bolted past, her bare heels pounding the parquet floor, her chador[66] fluttering behind.

"'Scuse me, where's registration?" I said.

"Back down the stairs, sister, into the small side entrance. It's marked, sorry, got to run, I have to do the adhan," she said.

"Which way is east?" Father called after her, and she pointed to our left before legging it up one of the towers.

When the call to prayer started, Father put my bags to one side, rolled up his shirt sleeves and trouser legs, and got ready to pray on the spot where we were standing. I stood behind him and went through the motions. Knees locking and unlocking till I was prostrate on the ground, lips moving to reproduce the shapes for Arabic sound, but mind somewhere different altogether, with Tone, floating on that sea of green.

When we finished, we went back out as the girl had said. Registration took place in a small room with just a table, a chair and a woman dressed in a burka frantically filling in forms. A couple of girls with their parents stood ahead of us

66   A shawl.

in the queue. I sat down and read a small brochure on the building, the same one I saw on our kitchen table a few months back. Mycombe Court had been a jewel of the Regency period until a kitchen fire burned the place down. After hundreds of years in the family, its English owners didn't have the dosh to restore it, so they pawned it off to some religious funders in the Middle East. Now it has a new purpose – to 'prepare our young, talented, Muslim women to be future leaders'. Apparently, Islam in the West needs a softer, female face. But judging by the woman behind the desk, this may not be the answer.

"*Slamalai—*"

"What is your name?" she said, giving me a form to fill.

"Sakthi," I said.

"Your Islamic name, child!" she said.

"It's Farzana, her name is Farzana," Father replied.

All the pens on her desk were aligned, parallel or perpendicular to the table edges. When I finished with the form, I deliberately put the biro down askew and watched her veil move faster and faster with each draw of her breath.

"Write the Islamic year!" she said, returning the form and straightening up the pen.

"1436," Father whispered in my ear. I corrected the year and placed the pen back down skew-whiff, which she then moved through a whole three degrees until all was again in perfect, rectangular harmony.

After the paperwork was done, she barked at me to follow her. I didn't say goodbye to Father. He could go hang himself for all I cared. I lugged my suitcase up the stairs and followed her to the dorm room, dropped my bags at the foot of the wooden, mattress-less bunk and sat down.

"No time to rest, you're already late for the first lesson."

"First lesson? It's gone midday!"

"Islamic school eight till lunch, kuffar[67] school one till five. Now run, you heathen, I've heard all about you," she said, shooing me out of the room.

I walked down a flight of white stone stairs with a green runner down the middle. The small alcoves, where busts of cherubs or statues of Venus might have once stood, were either left empty, or if the space was too conspicuous, filled with ceramic vases decorated with Arabic calligraphy. In the corridors, the walls were draped with floral tapestries. At the bottom of the stairs, some girls appeared to be polishing the brass banisters, and they pointed me in the direction of the school.

The classrooms ran along both sides of a long corridor. The rooms to my left were bare except for low-standing lecterns to hold the Qur'an. Inside, students dressed in black hijabs rocked backwards and forwards, rote-learning the sacred text. Some looked possessed, others glazed over. The rooms opposite had desks, chairs, a long wooden table, and a smart board – Kuffar school as Mrs Kazi so elegantly put it. I knocked quietly on the door and tried to sneak in.

"What makes a hero, or a heroine?" said the teacher, holding a marker in her hand like she was wielding a sword.

Honest. Caring. Brave. Handsome. One by one the girls took the pen and wrote their thoughts up on the board and returned to their seats. The tables were set up in groups of four, not single, forward-facing desks like in the other classes. Miss Qureshi, whose name was written on the board, walked around listening, not delivering her lessons like a sermon. Heads were shaking, hands gesturing, and the noise was even louder than the hum of Arabic from across the way. I sat down next to the only black girl, who had her name tag on her chest – Beydaan, a name as pretty as herself. The teacher glided to the front, her

67 A disbeliever.

robe tangoing around her legs. She clapped her hands once and the students went quiet.

"Which heroic traits do you have?" she asked the class.

"Miss, I'm bare modest, Miss," said one girl.

"Miss Qureshi, you can't call yourself modest," said another.

"Zaineb's comment was tongue-in-cheek, Fatima," said Miss Qureshi.

"Allow it, Fart-ima," said another girl, who looked the spit of Zaineb; twins I presumed.

"It's Fatima, Miss, tell her!"

"Thank you, Aaliyah, that'll be enough."

"I was bein' serious, blud," Zaineb loud-whispered to her sister.

"Meet our roommates," said Beydaan, shaking her head.

Miss Qureshi was a tall, slender figure with light skin and big brown eyes, almost cartoonish. She was young too, and rocking the Malala look, headscarf worn loosely showing her frizzy black hair.

"*Assalamu'alaikum*," she said to me when there was a natural silence. It caught me off guard. In Bengali culture, the younger greets the elder first as a mark of respect.

"*Slamalaikum*," I replied, which got a laugh from the class.

"*Wa'alaikum as-salam*. The reply is *wa alaikum as salam*," said Fatima, making no attempt to hide her disdain.

"Farzana, what do you think makes a hero?" said Miss Qureshi.

"Honour, Miss," shouted Fatima.

"Honour!?" I said.

"Stand up," muttered Beydaan, giving me a nudge.

"No, ya mad?" I said, but some hard-wired cultural reflex zapped me, and I got to my feet.

"Miss, a good Muslim should be honourable at all times," said Fatima.

"What 'bout honour killings?" I said to Fatima.

"Miss, girls who shame their families should be punished," she said to the teacher, and got applause from half the class.

"Nobody 'as the right to take life," I said to her, and got a cheer from the other half.

The argument spread through the classroom like a disease, passed on through anger and intolerance, until the discussion descended into a brainless row no better than Prime Minister's Questions in the House of Commons. Miss Qureshi, perched upon her desk, watched in silence, and took notes. When the bell rang, she clapped her hands, and again the room fell silent in an instant.

"Don't forget to acquaint yourself with the library. Next lesson, tragic heroes – King Lear."

Outside the class, Fatima brushed past me and mouthed a word.

"What d'ya say?" I said, but she ignored me.

"Be careful, she is nothing but trouble," said Beydaan.

It took a good few days to settle down into any kind of rhythm, given that classes and breaks have to fit around the prayer times. After Asr prayers, I took a stroll around the school building. In some places the work isn't finished. Soot stains the stone walls, and the burnt skeleton of the old house stands hauntingly like gallows up against the sky. It gives a sense of transience, of what was, but no longer is. I wondered if the board left it like that on purpose, to show how Victorian luxury has been replaced by a madrasa in the heart of England.

At the back, as you come down the main steps, there's a fountain, and after that a grassy hill with two stone gazebos at the top. I sat down under the canopy of the western gazebo, which gives its visitors stunning views of the surrounding countryside. I loosened my headscarf and let the rays warm the back of my neck. Trina would love it here, the summer breeze, the rolling hills. I pictured her sitting on the bench opposite undoing the latches of her tiffin box. Out here, the movement of the sun and the moon bring a certain joy, a certain certainty that as the day began, it will end, and so will my time in this place.

But inside, if we stick to celestial metaphors, there is not a moment's rest, yet time somehow stands still, like I'm on the Jupiterian equator travelling faster, even though the days are longer. Even making an entry in my journal takes forever. Is it because I'm putting more thought into my words, or because I'm unconsciously writing slower to fill the void? Inside, I lose all concept of time, and life is a fevered dream, like I've fallen down a rabbit hole. If only I could find a hookah-smoking caterpillar to help me get out.

Thankfully, I have my room mates. Beydaan is always counting her prayer beads – a nicotine patch for God addicts. I get the sense that she just tolerates me, but I'll take that for now. And the twins, Aaliyah and Zaineb, who despite their physical appearance could not be further apart in character. They form the perfect comedy double-act and have helped me get over that initial urge to slam doors on a few occasions. They're a good bunch, and I'm glad I don't have to share a room with Fatima.

After a while, I headed back down the hill in search of the library. It's a small room hidden in the East Wing, with a few tables and chairs and at best ten shelves of books. Mrs Finch has more in her lounge, and those are only for herself to enjoy. It isn't hard to find a copy of King Lear – the only Shakespeare they have – and it fills up an entire shelf alone. The shelf below is taken by Oliver Twist. And that is the entire English syllabus. There is quite a large section on maths and science, and on history and geography, but the largest section is home economics, which takes up at least a quarter of the total shelf space. Preparing Muslim women leaders for the future? Hmm, how would King Lear's Fool put it? 'My arse'!

"'ow can ya stand it 'ere?" I said, as I walked into the dorm room. Aaliyah and Zaineb were ironing their hijabs; Beydaan was, well, take a guess.

"Wha's eatin' you, fam?" said Zaineb.

"This effin' place, from the inside," I said.

Zaineb pulled up a stool right in front of me, her face inches from mine. Her jaws worked away at the gum in her mouth and when she was ready, she pursed her lips and blew a pink bubble that popped millimetres from the tip of my nose.

"Tell us then, stop bein' such a miserable git!"

"It's nowt, forget 'bout it."

"Wallahi man just tell us, it ain' that deep," she said, blowing another bubble.

"Can ya not see what they're doin'? They in't preparin' us to be leaders, they want us to be the honourable wives of leaders. They want us all to be like Fatima."

"Gyal really pissed ya off, innit," said Aaliyah.

"Way she talks through the teacher like she's above us. I could strangle the little... arghh."

"That'll be bare hard. She's proper in wif God," said Aaliyah.

"Anyway, how d'ya deal with it? Knowin' yer bein' fattened up like a qurbani cow[68], and when the right man comes along with the right price, yer off," I said.

"Wha' d'ya mean?" said Aaliyah.

"Well, 'ave ya seen the library?" I said.

"Yeah. And?"

"And? It's this eensy-winsy, cold, dark, damp room int' arse end of nowhere. And the books, well, in English literature ya 'ave a choice between Oliver frickin' Twist and King bleedin' Lear."

"Standard, but so wha'?"

"So what?"

"Got yer whole life to read, innit?"

68 A cow that is sacrificed on Eid.

"Fair, but that in't the point. Libraries in't just where books are kept like, they're meant to be inspirational," I said.

"Right, so wha' we gonna do? Exactly, nothin', so why ya gettin' vexed, why ya even bothered, man?" said Aaliyah.

"Fam, who needs libraries anyway?" said Zainab.

"Who needs libraries?" I said.

"My books, my inspiration – it's all up here, innit," said Zaineb, pointing to her temple.

"Alie!" said her sister.

I held my head in my hands. Zaineb took a laundry basket from the corner and put it in the middle of the room. She swung her arms up in the air and circled it. Aaliyah joined her, and together they pulled me up and we went round and round enacting a grime adaptation of Macbeth, somewhere on the outskirts of Islamabad.

"When shall we three meet again?" said Zainab.

"In thunder, lightning, monsoon rains," said Aaliyah.

"O'er a pot of biryani rice," said Zainab.

"Cooked in chilli, cumin, spice," said Aaliyah.

"Where the place, fam?" said Zainab.

"Upon the tilla, innit" said Aaliyah.

"There to meet with MacHusein," said Zainab.

"Double, double, toil and trouble, fire burn and cauldron bubble," they said together.

"Come on Sakthi, spit some bars," said Zaineb, as we circled the basket, twisting, turning, holding our hands together in an unholy trinity.

"Shh, we are going to get into trouble," said Beydaan from her bed.

"Thrice the Ganges python hath hissed," I said.

"Thrice the lips of death she'd kissed,

"The hijras cry – 'tis time, 'tis time,

"Round about the cauldron go;"

"In the dirty washing throw," rejoined Aaliyah.

"Lacy knickers, stiletto heels,

"Infidel's tongue, bacon meals,"

"Hearts of lovers, diseased with lust," I said.

"Boil thou first i' our pot of rust!"

"Double, double toil and trouble, fire burn, and cauldron bubble," we screamed, grabbing Beydaan and dragging her into the circle.

"We are going straight to hell," said Beydaan.

"We're witches, we're from hell!" said Aaliyah.

The door burst open and that narky old bint from registration stood there and screeched so loud she might've been auditioning for a part. Comically, we froze in our theatrical stances.

"*Astaghfirullah!* All four of you, in the mufti's office now."

"But Mrs Kazi—" said Beydaan.

"And you, wait till I tell your father. You are here free of charge thanks to the goodness of the imam. He'll be so disappointed."

"Please, Mrs—"

"Enough! Run!"

The mufti's room isn't at all what I expected. It's small for starters, smaller than what it should be for someone holding her office. And it's spartan, with only her desk, some chairs and a sofa set in the corner. One entire wall is covered with books in Arabic, and opposite, resting on the windowsill, stands an array of plants even Mrs Finch would be proud of. She offered us a seat and poured us all a lovely cup of tea from a samovar. Mrs Kazi was standing by the side of the mufti's desk, eyes bulging, hands clenching and unclenching. The door opened and Miss Qureshi walked in and stood behind us.

"Mrs Kazi says you were chanting like witches," said the mufti, but the girls all took the fifth. The mufti sat on her chair and sipped her tea, waiting, looking for cracks in our defence.

"May I at least ask what went into this cauldron?" she said.

"Lizards' tails, raven's beak, cumin, chilli and coriander, the usual stuff," said Zaineb. Aaliyah jabbed her sister in the ribs before she could incriminate us any further.

"Were you making a spell, or a newt jalfrezi?" said the mufti, and just like that she opened us up.

"Basically, yeah, it's the library, Miss," said Zaineb, looking over at me to take the baton.

"I wouldn't call it a library, it hardly has any books," I said, looking out of the window.

"It has everything you need for your exams," said the mufti.

"Everything for the mind, but nothing for the soul," I said.

"I told you she was trouble," said Mrs Kazi, shifting her weight from one foot to the other, unable to bear the dearth of right angles on the mufti's table.

I giggled.

"Eyes to the ground, show some re—"

"Thank you, Mrs Kazi. I'll take it from here," said the mufti. She walked over to the flowers, sprayed them with water and gently wiped down each individual leaf. She picked up the hibiscus, clearly her pride and joy, and turned the pot around so the back had an equal share of the sun. She poured the left over from her tea into the soil.

"I understand your frustration with the library, but that doesn't mean you can break the school rules, no matter how light-hearted it was. Because even if it's a joke for you, for others it can be offensive, and hurtful," she said, looking at Beydaan.

"What rule? No really, what rule?" I said.

"Heresy!" said Mrs Kazi.

"No need to be quite so dramatic!" said the mufti, making eye contact with Miss Qureshi and revealing the faintest of smiles. "Mrs Kazi, what punishment suits this heinous crime?"

"Ten thousand repetitions of the name of Allah. They can join me after the evening prayers," she said.

"Aww, Miss, that's bare tight, that is!" protested Zaineb.

"You'd like more?" said Mrs Kazi, and Zaineb folded her arms, crossed her legs and got herself into such a state she'd have fallen off the chair had it not been for Miss Qureshi's steadying hand behind her.

"And as their pastoral tutor, Miss Qureshi. What do you suggest?"

"One rhyming couplet in iambic pentameter, each girl, on what it means to be a Muslim woman."

"But Miss, how d'ya fit all that in two lines?" said Aaliyah.

"Perhaps you'd prefer to write an entire sonnet?" said Miss Qureshi.

"No, Miss."

The mufti stood up and walked around to the front of her desk.

"Stand up, girls," said Miss Qureshi.

"Ladies, ten thousand repetitions this evening, and one rhyming couplet on my desk first thing. Otherwise, you join the girls on banister polishing duty for the rest of the week."

We excused ourselves and headed back to the dorm. That night, after we'd done our chores for God, I stayed up to help Beydaan with the rhyming couplet until my eyelids could no longer stay open. I fell asleep as soon as I put my head down on the pillow, and barely noticed the rock-hard bed.

Alif, ba, ta

A couple of months have passed, but the morning adhan still jangles every cell in my body like God's playing a glissando on my DNA, especially the ones that code for lie-ins. The days are getting shorter, and colder, and the girls do the Fajr prayer double time and run back to bed before school starts. I envy them, I can never get back to sleep. So, when the rebels on polishing duty, half-drunk with tiredness, open the doors to do their chores at around five, I go for a walk around the grounds.

The surrounding countryside makes me think of St John's, and in many ways, Mycombe Girls is not so different. Both have uniforms, both are guided by religious values, and both have unhealthy scepticism for all things *other*. I still remember that day when Mo in my class stood up and said he wanted to be an imam when he grew up. The week after he was banged on the Prevent Scheme, his parents hauled in before the cops, and his home turned upside down. I wonder what would happen if I told Mrs Kazi I wanted to grow up to be a priest?

Breakfast is at seven. And after milk and cereal, quiet as mice the girls file into school for Islamic education. Every morning there are seminars that teach tafseer,[69] the Hadith and Sharia, but the day always starts with reciting the Qur'an.

"*Alif, ba, ta*, read it again," shouted Mrs Kazi, like Mr Belton on a cocktail of Red Bull and Tabasco, before moving on to instruct another student.

---

69 Exegesis of the Qur'an.

Some girls know all eight thousand odd lines of the holy book off by heart. Like robots they'd rote learned the sacred algorithms to guide them through life on Earth and prepare them for the glory of God. Their humming was hypnotic, and if it wasn't for Beydaan's rumbling stomach (she was fasting) I'd have been deep into a trance. Mrs Kazi came round to make extra sure that didn't happen.

"Come on heathen, *alif, ba, ta, tha, jhim…* repeat!"

My lips formed the letters, but my brain was someplace else, invariably, and inconveniently, with Tone. He comes to me between surahs and ayahs, on every mim and mu'aanaqah[70], even in the teeniest fractions of time, indivisible by God or the instruments of modern science. The cucumber, the smoke, that first gunpowder kiss. Bang! Mrs Kazi's bamboo cane slammed the top of my wooden lectern and split in two halfway up its length. The chastening sound sent shivers down my spine and reminded me of Father.

"*Alif, bi, te, say, gin, kha,*" I said.

Fatima and the Jihadi Massive who followed her broke out into barely restrained laughter, which Mrs Kazi allowed just long enough to make the point and then put an end to it with her trademark shriek.

"*Alif, ba, ta, tha, jhim, hah…* say it louder!" she shouted.

"No wonder they call Islam a violent religion," I said.

"What do you know about Islam? You can't tell me the first ten letters of the Arabic alphabet! But you've read their bible I've been told, you sing their songs. I suppose you're going to tell me the Old Testament is all about peace and love? Well child?" she said, leaning forward and growling, her foul breath sticking on my cheeks. Somebody should buy her some mouthwash, with alcohol, it might lighten her mood.

My mind went blank. I cursed myself for not knowing, for not being able to defend my argument.

70 Stop signs in Qur'anic script.

"Ignorance is as big a sin as zina,[71] but Allah be my witness, I will get the whore out of you before you leave this school," she said.

The girls gasped. My secret was out. I looked around at the faces. No. They already knew. Fatima mouthed the word she had said to me outside the classroom again. Mrs Kazi whacked the cane on some other unsuspecting slacker and reading recommenced, even louder.

Beydaan's grumbling tummy was soon making me hungry, and lunch couldn't come fast enough. On Thursdays, the school's board of governors are invited, so the girls have to swap their hijabs for burkas to cover everything. We ran up to the dorms to get changed and then to the dinner hall, set up with four lines of tables, just like in Hogwarts (if only this was Hogwarts!). The board, all men, took their seats at a long table on an elevated platform at the far end of the hall. The mufti stood up to address the school on the achievements of the week (misdemeanours were dealt with discreetly in her office, as I knew only too well) and then took her seat on the very left of the table. The imam then gave a long sermon before saying the magic words our famished ears wanted to hear.

"*Bismillah al-Rahman al-Rahim*," he said. The girls duly repeated, Zaineb finishing the last syllable with a French fry pressing against her lips.

"What does that even mean?" I asked Beydaan, who sat with us at lunch to increase her suffering, such a martyr.

"In the name of God, most Gracious, most Compassionate," she said, apparently shocked by my ignorance. "Did you not grow up in a Muslim family?"

"Yeah, but just coz we read the Qur'an don't mean we know what any of it actually means," I said.

On the menu today, curry and chips, a favourite of the board. When potential funders came, as they often did from the

71   Extra-marital and pre-marital fornication.

Middle East, this exquisite meal (and the use of cutlery) was the most tangible example of how the school has been integrating seamlessly into British society.

The Messrs at the top table were eating something different though. Two South-Asian-looking men were pouring water with napkins over their arms, while another two were attempting to serve spuds with a silver spoon and a fork using only one hand. A baby potato slipped out of the spoon and rolled all the way down the table to the mufti, who caught it with her hands as it nosedived off the edge. She gently put it on her plate and got up to help the struggling waiters. Years of cultural programming, the same knee jerk reaction to when I stood up to speak to the teacher, now manifesting itself in the role of the sexes.

"Ya gotta be proper bad-ass to sit up there wif all those men," said Zaineb, prodding a piece of chicken with her fork.

"Fuck, Zaineb, how many times, fam? Hold that fork wif the left hand," said Aaliyah.

"I thought we weren't allowed to eat wif our left hand," replied Zaineb, and the two sisters went into a silent stand-off.

"I reckon she can 'old 'er own," I said, as I watched the mufti sit down after all the men had been served. When the waiters approached her, she moved her chair slightly to the side and gently nodded her head as a gesture of thanks. There's an air that surrounds the mufti, like she's at peace with herself, her role in this school, and her vision of life, and that protects her from all the misogyny.

"Yeah, d'ya see how she roasted Mrs Kazi," said Aaliyah.

"Nah, I feel bad for her, man. It's be bare lonely tryin'a be a boss bitch round all them men," said Zaineb.

"Why is she not sat in the middle?" said Aaliyah.

"Women will never take centre stage in our religion, not as long as men like Orange Beard are in power," I said.

"D'ya know him?" said Zaineb.

"Yeah, he's the imam at our local mosque. He's the one that got my father to send me to this god-awful place," I said.

"Sakthi, you are too hard on Islam. It is not to blame for all the ills of society. The imam, he is traditional, but he means well," said Beydaan.

"Soz, 'scuse me while I throw up!" I said.

"Everywhere you see problems, I see answers," she said, and excused herself from the table. Zaineb looked at her sister and put her arms around my shoulders.

"What?" I said.

"Ya know we all chose to be here don't ya?" Zaineb replied.

"Yer windin' me up, right?" I said.

"It's got some of the best grades in the country, and at least we ain' havin' to hide who we are, and ain' nobody callin' us Pakis or terrorists," she said.

"Don't 'ave to hide who we are! What d'ya call this then?" I said, pinching the material of the burka.

"Yeah, fam, I get it. Ya gotta read Arabic, dress like this and learn about Islamic culture, but how is that meant to be different from learnin' French and about the French revolution?"

"The difference... the difference is I 'ave a choice," I said.

"A choice? Of a handful of European languages from over a gazillion in the world! There's more varieties of bubblegum, innit?" said Zaineb.

I pushed my plate away and waited for everyone to finish. When the board had left the room, the students all got up at once and made their way out. I arranged to meet the twins outside as I first needed a bit of time to get my head around what I'd just heard. That someone would voluntarily subject themselves to this hell. As I reached the exit, I could hear a couple of girls giggling.

"Whore," someone said, but I couldn't make out where it came from because everyone was wearing a burka.

"Who said that?" I asked.

"Said what?" said Fatima, with that condescending tone.

"Nowt, must've been in me head," I said.

After lunch I went up to my usual spot at the top of hill where Zaineb, Aaliyah, Beydaan and some other girls were gathered. The older student who I saw sprinting through the entrance hall was there with a stopwatch in her hand, and a pen and pad. She took out a piece of chalk from her bag and made a line on the ground.

"Sakthi, perfect timing. New students' challenge," she said.

"What challenge?" I said to Aaliyah.

"See that thing runnin' along the top of the school where ya do the adhan?" she said.

"The balustrade?" I said.

"Yeah fam, ya gotta get there in time for Dhuhra,"[72] she said.

"That's 'ardly a challenge," I said.

"Fam, that's not the hard part," said Aaliyah. "Ya have to have enough breath left in ya to make the call for prayer, innit."

"Last newbie couldn't even make it past the first syllable," said Zaineb. I thought of the alarm clock on our mantelpiece after I'd swapped the batteries for dead ones.

"But I don't know 'ow to call the adhan," I said.

"I'll help you," said Fatima, coming up the hill and taking off her shoes. "Come on, it'll be like Chariots of Fire."

I looked at Beydaan who was shaking her head and counting her prayer beads at about triple the normal speed, but my pride was too big to back down. I gave Aaliyah my coat and shoes to hold on to, and Zaineb started counselling me on race tactics and how to negotiate the different terrain. Apparently, it was all about who got to the bottom of the tower first. At precisely two minutes to Dhuhr, the girl in the chador called marks, lowered her hand, and we set off down the hill.

72 The midday prayer.

I took the longer route away from the trees to avoid the pine-needles on the ground, but Fatima went straight through making a bee line for the fountain. We got there at about the same time, with me perhaps a whisker ahead. I could feel her breath on the back of my neck. I ran around the edge on the solid flag stones, but Fatima jumped over the fountain wall and waded through the ice-cold water. When she came out the other side, she was a good few metres in front. I made one last push to get to the bottom of the tower first, but she was too far ahead.

Fatima took the outside of the spiral staircase, holding on to the rails and I trailed behind her. Her burka had soaked up half the water in the fountain, so instead of hiding her figure, it stuck to her long, slim legs. Halfway up she began to tire, fighting the weight of the material as it tangled around her ankles. I took a deep breath, pulled my burka up to my thighs and raced past her on the inside, precariously balancing on the thinnest part of the step with barely enough space for my big toe. Just as we reached the top, I felt a knock on my ankles and tripped headlong onto the roof. Fatima clambered over the top of me and onto the ridge, putting both her hands in the air to the cheer of the girls on the hill. She turned round and came back to me, panting on my hands and knees.

"Have you worked it out yet?" she said, drawing in a lungful of air.

"What?" I said, feeling the bump on my head.

"What I said to you outside the classroom," she said, pulling the pine needles out of the bloody soles of her feet. How's that for passion?

"I don't care," I said, pathetically in retrospect.

"Wow, you look like you want to have a swing," she said as she walked over to a drain to wring out the water from her clothes. I stood up and brushed myself down, wrists and elbows sore from breaking the fall. The scab had ripped off one of the cuts on my forearm and it stung every time the sleeve touched it.

"I've seen too much violence in my life already to hit a fellow—"

"What, Muslim? Don't make me laugh!"

"No," I said. "Woman."

"Pff," she said, and made her way back down the stairs.

"What 'bout the adhan?" I shouted after her, but she ignored me.

I stood there on the roof, a pile of nerves, dry hurling into the breeze instead of calling everyone to prayer. The girls at the top of the hill started to make their way to the mosque after Mrs Kazi went out to shepherd them back in, their black robes contrasting beautifully with that pastoral green backdrop.

Have I missed a trick? I thought about Kev, that time on the bus, and in front of our house. Mrs Finch, her comments on Forster, and the way Mr Belton looked at me when I rolled my skirt up. And then there's Tone's plain-talking mum, to put it nicely. The list went on, little misgivings that I'd put away under 'paranoia', they all came back as a knot in my stomach. Were the girls right? Is this my safehouse, the place where I can grow, learn? And what about love? Surely that yearning to touch someone can't be put on hold. As she headed back into the school, Mrs Kazi looked up at me and shook her head.

When we finished the Dhuhr prayer, we filed back into the classrooms for normal classes. All the lessons have their own Islamic twist; history classes revolve around the life of the prophet, art centres on calligraphy, floral designs and architecture, and maths and science are taught with vigour. However, biology books are devoid of penises and vaginas, their pages stapled together if they showed the human form or talked about sex. Home economics has the same weight as economics, music and drama are deemed to be un-Islamic, and even though the school has wicked sports facilities, there's no P.E. teacher. Instead, we have sewing, craftwork and cooking workshops. And when the girls get bored of knitting socks, hats and jumpers, their minds wander into unholy pastures. More than once Aaliyah and Zaineb have been put on polishing duty for making nipple tassels and willy warmers (Zaineb insists 'it was the size what did it').

Miss Qureshi pushes the envelope in her English classes. She has certain freedoms because, as a Cambridge-educated Muslim woman, she is the presentable face of the school. During tabloid or Ofsted visits, it is she who shows them round. That aside, the imam has a hard spot for her. His eyes twinkle when she places her hands on her sides, revealing the slimness of her waist in perfect classical ratio to the width of her hips. This afternoon, Miss Qureshi seized every inch of her freedom and walked out the front gates with the whole class in tow.

"Where we goin', Miss?" I said.

"The Peak District," she replied.

"Are we allowed to do this, Miss?" said Beydaan.

"Easier to ask for forgiveness than permission," said Mrs Waseh, the geography teacher, who had jumped on the chance to turn her lesson into a field trip.

The private school coach dropped us off at Hathersage in the heart of the Dark Peaks. The fresh air and the hilltop views across the moors were liberating. Some of the girls made sketches, while those less talented took rubbings of rocks and tree barks. Some talked. Thinkers, like Beydaan, marvelled at the beauty of the world. Even Fatima seemed to be at peace. The twins gambled polishing duties with twig races in the clear valley streams. I collected wildflowers, pressing them in between the pages of my notebook.

"Who are they for?" asked Miss Qureshi.

"My neighbour," I said.

"The one you have to read to?"

"Yes, Mrs Finch."

At almost every turn my eyes fell on something new: the fluffy texture of the clouds within reaching distance, the boulders and overhangs of Stannage Edge. And Mrs Waseh opened up like Wikipedia to quench our thirst for knowledge. Meanwhile, Miss Qureshi reeled off lines of Byron and Shaw, elevating the scientific descriptions of nature into an ethereal landscape. On hearing her quote Wuthering Heights, my head dropped.

"What's wrong, Sakthi?" said Miss Qureshi.

"She's actin' all emo about the library, Miss," said Aaliyah.

"So, I've been thinking about this since that time in the mufti's office," said Miss Qureshi. "Can't you make your own library?"

The girls laughed. The same laugh I heard in Bangladesh when I said women should be running the restaurants down the Curry Mile, not men. A laugh that should've been a cry.

"We ain' got no wonga, Miss," said Aaliyah.

"There must be lots of people holding onto old books they don't read. I'm sure they'd donate to a worthwhile charity?" said Miss Qureshi.

"We could convert the Red Room," said Zaineb.

"Fam, they're dickheads, they're too peak to let us chill in Red Room, tha's where they do all their fancy shit," said Aaliyah.

"But they only use it one hour a week," said Zaineb.

"What 'bout one of the old rooms damaged in the fire?" I said.

"Yeah, quick lick of paint and the north stables be looking like Bodleian Library," said Aaliyah.

"Come on, it'll be fun," I said.

"They'll never let us," said Aaliyah. "And what about the mufti? She'll have a heart attack, she hardly deserves that."

"Nah, she seems sympathetic," said Zaineb.

"Sympathy is a great Russian novel; it demands a lot of its reader. But empathy is a short story that outlives its life on the page and stirs people to action," said Miss Qureshi.

"Miss, that's deep, Miss. What's it mean?" said Zaineb.

"How can you frame your argument so that she can feel your loss like it's her own?" said Miss Qureshi.

"The mufti's book collection," I said, and Miss Qureshi smiled.

We got back to school in time for the Maghrib prayers. Beydaan came up last from the mosque and said Miss Qureshi had sent for me, so I went to find her in her room. She insisted on staying with the girls of the lower school, instead of living in the more spacious eastern wing where the other teachers resided during term time. In her room there was a narrow single bed with the covers ironed and tucked in around the corners. A metal wardrobe stood by the door and a desk below the window was stacked with books about three feet high.

"You got a rough deal, Miss," I said.

"The school day starts early, too early to enjoy the sunrise, but the sunset... From this window, I can watch her paint the evening sky on a canvas of hope," she said.

"Watch out, you'll get done for sun worshipping," I said. "And is the sun feminine?"

"Isn't she?" said Miss Qureshi, offering me a seat by her desk.

"Then you might say the same about G—"

"Yes, you might," she said, before I could articulate my blasphemous thoughts. Miss Qureshi sat down on a hard, long-backed wooden chair, ruffled through some papers on her desk and then took out a folder. Her face hardened as she glanced inside.

"This is a report from your French teacher at St Johns. It says you have a rare talent for language, that you became semi-fluent in a couple of years," said Miss Qureshi.

"Can I?" I said, and she passed me the folder. I brushed my fingers over the St John's coat of arms on the sleeve of the report. Eyes closed, I pictured walking through the fields, the ripe smell from the neighbouring farm wafting up my nostrils like I'd fallen face first in steaming pile of cow shit. You miss the funniest things when they are taken away. Miss Qureshi poured me a cup of tea, and I flicked through the pages.

"Interesting, no?" she said.

"I guess," I replied.

"So, how is it a bright young student with an immense talent for language, can't get past the first ten letters in Arabic?"

I shrugged. More reports followed, this time from the teachers at Mycombe Girls, each talking about unfilled potential, a life wasted. These were the reports I imagined Dast would get, not me. I flicked through the pages faster and faster, treating them with growing contempt.

"So, you're with them?" I said.

"You feel wronged, you want to lash out and bring the whole house down. I understand," she said, putting a plate of *makroudh* biscuits and a box of tissues on the table.

"How could you know how I feel? You don't know me."

"Because you're not the only one," she said, looking at my fingers clenched around my sleeves. "I know it might not feel like it right now, but it'll get better, I promise. I'm on your side."

My lips quivered.

"Sakthi, listen. These are the years which determine how far you go in life. Now you can fight through the pain and make the best of it, or you can let your hatred consume you," she said.

"But it hurts, Miss."

"I know, Sakthi."

"I hate him. He took away everything, everyone I love, and I want him to pay."

"By sabotaging your future? You're stronger than that, you have so much more to give the world than vengeance. And what about your mum, don't you owe it to her?"

I put the tea down on the table and ran out.

"Sakthi," Miss Qureshi shouted after me. "Sorry, I shouldn't have..."

Back in the dormitory, Zaineb was hanging up her robe to let out the creases, Aaliyah was carefully placing the Qur'an back on the shelf and Beydaan, as usual, was counting prayer beads. Avoiding all eye contact, I took my clothes off, threw them on the floor and crashed into bed, chest heavy, shoulders heaving. The lights went out and the girls fell asleep. I turned onto my back, put my Walkman on and thought of Tone.

The Library

Over Christmas, Father ordered the Black Paws, his zero hours Gestapo, to keep me and Tone apart. A couple of times, just before Maghrib prayers when the back alleys were quiet, I heard the tapping sound of pebbles on my bedroom window. And when I opened the curtains, I saw Tone stood there blowing kisses like the cheese ball that he is! He's grown a beard! Bless. How I wished I could rub my cheek against his. It was agonising to have him so close, and not be able to hold him. But our twilight rendezvous were cut short on both occasions. The first time, the Black Paws roughed him up a little, more bark than bite really, but the second he got such a kicking that Dast had to step in to stop him being hospitalised. He dragged Tone to his feet and looked up at me like he was doing me a favour. I didn't know whether to hug him or punch him, I just wanted to be with Tone, to nurse his cuts and bruises, my 'white knight', so fucking what? Eventually, Tone got the message, and I didn't see him for the rest of the holidays.

Mrs Finch, my usual sanctuary when the walls are closing in, was in hospital with a throat infection, and Trina was banned from visiting for her part in the elopement to Old Trafford. That left Meghna, who slouched around on the couch with Dadhi watching Bangla TV till it was time to eat, pray or sleep. The first day I was back she cooked up a feast; black tiger prawn bhuna, aubergine borta, and sabji bhaji. The smell of Bengali five spice frying in the pan made my heart break. I'd shut her out of my mind the whole term, my own mother, but her love never wilted, never waned. I

172

didn't dare look in her eyes in case she worked it out. And when the hurt was too much to keep inside, I bit into a Naga chilli to defer the pain.

Cooking aside though, we had little to say, so I spent most of the time at home reading. Miss Qureshi lent me *Anna Karenina* (Tolstoy must have known there were thousands of women in nineteenth century Russia with time to read his gazillion page love stories). Poor Anna, she reminds me of my own ludicrous situation, the helplessness of it all, the waiting. And if time stands still at Mycombe Girls, it goes into reverse in Shaleton. I thought of everything that got me to where I am now, especially about what Miss Qureshi had said. Should I buckle down? Having returned to Shaleton, I've come to realise I want more than what this old town can offer.

When I walked back through the school gates in the new year, I stood outside the front entrance for a moment and breathed in the countryside; free-range beats the hell out of battery reared. I dropped my bags off in the dorm and ran over to Miss Qureshi's room. Before the winter break, we had written to hundreds of people about our library project, scouring the phone directory for posh-sounding double-barrel surnames that could part with a book or two. But nothing came of it and Miss Qureshi, who'd been so lifted by our newfound sense of empowerment, seemed to be contemplating how to best prepare us for failure. But a couple of days after term started, on a crisp January morning, her slim silhouette raced down the steps of the south portico and over to the fountain in the parterre where the girls stood getting some fresh air.

"Farzana, a letter," she shouted. The girls huddled round as I clumsily opened the envelope with my cold hands. I skimmed through the first few lines before reading it aloud.

"It's from Mrs Finch," I said.

"Who?" said Zaineb.

"Tha' old woman, her neighbour," said Aaliyah.

"Well, wha's it say?" said Zaineb.

"Says she's been ill... she got my letter... says she called the council about the closure of Shaleton Library and whether we could have the books... and the answer is... 'yes'."

"That's amazing," said Miss Qureshi.

"Wait, and she's enclosed a cheque to help pay for re-painting the north stables and buying new chairs and tables."

"No way!" said Aaliyah and snatched the letter from my hand. A thin, rectangular piece of paper dropped to the floor like a sycamore leaf. I picked it up and read it, my hands shaking, eyes all watery.

"What is it, Farzana?" said Miss Qureshi.

I passed it over to her. Zaineb jumped up onto the fountain wall and tapped her thighs. The others linked arms in a semi-circle around us and waited with bated breath.

"Drumroll," said Zaineb.

Miss Qureshi took a look at the cheque, and then just before she was about to tell us the amount, she took another look, raised her hands to the sky and whispered a few words to God (I presume).

"Twenty," she said.

"Twenty quid?" said Aaliyah. "Tha's not even enough to get us a—"

"Thousand," said Miss Qureshi, under her breath.

I sat down on the edge of the fountain to steady myself. I looked around at the girls. Aaliyah was lifting Beydaan off the ground in a bear hug, and Zaineb was running around screaming and shouting like a woman possessed. All those tired hands will be rewarded not in the afterlife, but here on Earth. And if we could do this, what else could we do if we put our minds to it? As the girls celebrated, though, I read back the letter. Mrs Finch was not at all well, and a part of me wanted to be with her. I'd hate it if we never got to say goodbye.

In the cerebral distance, I could hear the girls talk about what books we might get. Zaineb wanted the entire Harry Potter series, Aaliyah wanted Shakespeare, and Beydaan more on Islam. We all huddled around in a circle, arms around each other's waists. But there was something missing, or rather someone, and by the time I'd turned around to thank Miss Qureshi, she'd left.

When the books arrived from Shaleton Library in early February, there were so many we had to stock half in the south stables till we could get round to sorting them. And by we, I mean the girls, the four from our dorm and around half a dozen others, who gave every waking second they had to the cause. With Mrs Finch's donation, we managed to get an all-women construction company to plaster the walls and replace the floorboards. What we had left we used to buy long study desks and lamps.

"I thought I might find you in here, the all-conquering," said Miss Qureshi, grinning from ear to ear, bursting with pride.

"We did it, Miss We really did it," said Zaineb.

"Well, we still gotta sort 'em fam, otherwise it's just meaningless masses of information," said Aaliyah.

"Right, so I were thinkin' 'bout this the other day, 'n' the fact that we don't 'ave computers like, why not use the old library card and Dewey Decimal system?" I said.

"Dewy wha'? Wha' the hell is tha'?" said Zaineb.

"Dewey Decimal system, it's named after the man who came up with it," said Aaliyah.

"There's someone called Mr Decimal?" said Zaineb.

"Nah, Dewey ya moron," said Aaliyah.

"Jokin' bruv!" said Zaineb.

"Nah ya weren't, man," said Aaliyah.

"Mrs Finch told us 'ow it works. It's all 'bout relative indexin', so no matter which library ya go to in the world, ya can find books just by knowin' where the subject lies in the Dewey Decimal system. In't that right, Miss Qureshi?" I said.

"Yes, exactly," she said.

"So, wait. If I went to some random library and looked under 234 in the system, I might find 'God, the Rod, and Your Child's Bod: The Art of Loving Correction for Christian Parents'?" said Aaliyah, holding up one of the books in our new collection, and the girls split their sides.

"How about this one: 'Enlargement is thrilling?'" said Zaineb.

"*Astaghfirullah!* That's haram!" said Aaliyah.

"Nah fam, this ain' porn, it's on photography, innit," said Zaineb, all innocent like.

I gave the girls a photocopy of the classifications that I had printed out with the help of Miss Qureshi beforehand. I could see Zaineb's perfectly plucked eyebrows formulating a question way before the words left her mouth.

"Eh? I don' get this," said Zaineb. "The numbers 200-299 are on religion, but numbers 220-289 are all on Christianity."

"So, what, Islam has numbers 200-220?" said Aaliyah.

"Nah," said Zaineb.

"Numbers 290-299 then?" I said, looking at Miss Qureshi. She smiled and urged Zaineb to continue with her thought process.

"Islam, wif over 1.5 billion worshippers around the world, has the number 297," she said.

"Gimme tha," said Aaliyah, and took the sheet out of Zaineb's hand. "Well, Parish government and administration has its own number, but the entire religion of Islam has only one number."

"Seriously?" I said.

"Buddhism doesn' even get an integer. It's relegated to right of the decimal point!" she said.

"Bloody hell, I wonder what Beydaan would make of all this?" I said.

"Where is Beydaan, by the way?" said Miss Qureshi.

"Gettin' books from the south stables, Miss," said Aaliyah.

"She's brave, it's dark down there," said Miss Qureshi.

"Shall I go and get her?" I said.

"No need, it's you I came to see. I got this letter in the post, but I can't make head nor tail of it," she said. Miss Qureshi gave Aaliyah an envelope and the girls all gathered round to see what it was inside. Aaliyah took out a piece of paper and put it up to the light.

"There ain' no writin' or anythin', just these weird kinda holes, like some ol' biddy's used it as a pin cushion," she said, and passed the letter over to me.

"It's Braille!" I said, running my fingers over the signature. I couldn't read it, but there were four letters, each painstakingly punctured into a sheet of vellum.

"It's from him, innit? That boy Mrs Kazi talked about in class," said Zaineb.

"Tone," I whispered.

Miss Qureshi smiled, reminded us that it was Thursday, so the Board would be in school and we were to change into our burkas, and glided out the room.

"Braille, genius!" said Zaineb. She blew a big bubble from her mouth and pulled up a carton of books to sit on.

"Hey, no chuddy int' library," I said.

"Must've taken ages fam, hand prickin' each dot like tha'," said Aaliyah.

"Read it out, Juliet," cried Zaineb.

"I can't read Braille very well."

"Not so fuckin' genius after all," said Aaliyah.

"Alie!" said Zaineb.

I placed my fingers on the raised dots. I'd had some practice at Mrs Finch's house after I'd bought that book for her birthday, but not much.

"It'll take donkey's years, I can't remember all the letters," I said.

"Fam, it'll be like hangman, innit?" said Zaineb.

I sat down on one of the desks and together with the girls managed to decipher the letter, letter by letter.

Dear Sakthi,

*I'm not so good with words. Writing in English is
as foreign to me as writing in Bengali, but at least
I have Mrs Finch here to help.*

"Wait, your nonagenarian neighbour helped your boyfriend
write a love letter to you... in Braille?" said Aaliyah.

"Apparently," I said.

"Legend," said Zaineb.

"Yeah, she's wicked like, and a little nosey it seems," I said.

"Come on, get on with it. I'm dyin' here," said Aaliyah.

*How's the new school? I hope you have managed
to find a cool new set of friends to form your
Muslim girl group The Black Moving Objects.
Seems such a long time ago that incident on the
bus, how well you handled it, I was amazed, and
scared to be honest.*

"What incident?" said Zaineb.

"Never mind, get to the juicy bits," said Aaliyah.

*On my side, apart from mum, all is good. I have
left The Mill Crew after a number of the gang
were arrested. Some Muslim guy had rolled
down his window to pay them for washing his
windscreen at the traffic lights, and they threw a
bucket of acid all over his face.*

"God, horrific!" said Zaineb.

"Country's gone mad, all these politicians stirrin' up hate,"
I said.

*It has been months now since I last touched your
face on the cricket green at Old Trafford before we
were so cruelly ripped apart.*

"Here we go," said Aaliyah, rubbing her hands together.

"Old Trafford! Is tha' where ya went on a date?" said Zaineb.

"Shh," said Aaliyah.

"D'ya wanna listen or what?" I said.

> *Not a day has gone by since that I haven't thought about you. My fingertips on your face, seeing your smile after it had been hidden away for so long.*

"And the rest is for me to know, an' you never to find out."

"Nah bruv, ya can't do this to us. Come on, this is the only romance we'll get the whole term, please," said Aaliyah.

"There's a box of Jane Austen over there," I said.

"Aw, she's blushin'," said Zaineb. "Ya gonna write back?"

"I'll write to him after we're done here," I said, folding the letter and putting it in my pocket.

We decided in the end that we'd file the books under subject matter, though as Zaineb pointed out, that still left us with the same ethical conundrum as Mr Decimal – where to place subjects within the library according to their importance. I personally suspect there was no such moral discussion two centuries ago when the white man was colonising the world, so I begged to move the motion that literature should be front and centre. I was voted down unanimously, and we put Islam by the entrance to appease Orange Beard whilst placing all the romantic novels well out of view like they were jazz mags.

We returned to the dorm before Isha[73] prayers to find Beydaan all on her own in the dark. Legs crossed, one arm folded across her chest and the other dragging a brush through her wet hair, she sat naked and shaking on the edge of her bed. Her robe, a towel and her underwear lay in a scrumpled mess on the

---

73 The late evening/night prayer, usually done before midnight.

ground. Her misbaha was ripped, the prayer beads scattered all over the floor.

"*Ya Allah*, what happened?" said Aaliyah, picking up the towel and wrapping it around her.

"Sister, wha's wrong?" said Zaineb, collecting the beads.

I sat next to Beydaan to comfort her but, before I could put my arm around her shoulders, she got up to dress herself. She threw on a robe, put her hair in a ponytail and tied a cotton scarf around her head.

"You were right, Sakthi. Hope you are happy now," she said, and ran out the room.

"Right 'bout what?" I asked the twins, but they just shrugged.

Beydaan spent the whole night in the mosque. When we saw her again at Fajr prayers the next morning she was a wreck, a ghost ship sailing aimlessly about a vast ocean. After prayers she let me keep her company. We sat shivering by the frozen fountain waiting for the sun to come up. That hour was pure torture. In my head I went through a whole bunch of worst-case scenarios: a death in the family, or perhaps her asylum status had been repealed. I kept my trap shut and sat there till she was ready to talk.

"I have to leave," she said, finally.

"Leave! Why?" I said, but she wouldn't utter another word.

When the sun had risen, we made our way back to the main building, but instead of turning left towards the dorms, Beydaan went to the right towards the entrance hall.

"Where ya goin'?" I said.

"Father will meet me at the gates," she said.

"What 'bout all yer stuff like, yer calligraphy?"

"It does not matter."

"So that's it, yer just gonna go without sayin' goodbye?"

Beydaan walked off into the entrance hall and up the stairs the muezzins take to call the adhan. That's not the way to the gates, I thought.

"Beydaan? Beydaan, wait!"

Her long Somali legs carried her up three steps at once. My Bengali stumps were a blur trying to keep up, bare feet stumbling on the cold, stone floor. When I got to the top she was on the balustrade, looking out over the wintry hills to the west.

"Leave me alone, Sakthi," she said, gasping for breath.

"What happened, Beydaan?" I asked, trying to get her talking, to let the adrenaline subside, to buy Fear some more time.

"I'm a stain on this world… a shame to my family," she said, as she looked down and took a big gulp.

"You? Yer like the first in line for 'eaven," I said.

"Stay back, I'll jump," she said, and she inched forward till her toes wiggled over the edge with anticipation, a taste of eternal freedom before committing the rest of her body to the set meal.

"No fuckin' way. You in't leaving us 'ere with Orange Beard 'n' Mrs Set-Square. I'm comin' too," I said, and stepped out onto the ledge.

We stood there, the two of us, quiet, our robes fluttering in the morning breeze. A layer of low-lying mist stretched out all the way across the pastures and we were above the haze, in the house of God, blue skies all around, gorgeous sunshine on our backs. Way below us, a car pulled up in the driveway.

"I am serious, Sakthi. I am going to jump."

"Me too. I in't got owt to lose."

"You always want to play the hero," she said.

"What did I ever do to ya, Beydaan? Tell us, I'll take it back, I'll count a million prayer beads," I said.

"More jokes! You cannot help yourself. Well, it does not matter anymore," she said. She closed her eyes and balanced with one foot on the ledge and the other floating mid-air. I grabbed her hand.

"You go, I go."

"Sakthi, please."

"We can fix you, Beydaan."

"Allah hafiz, Sak—"

"I'm gettin' married," I said, as a last resort, and she put her foot back down on the balustrade.

"To whom?" she asked.

"To a mean man fifteen years older," I said. "So ya see, I'm not so different to anyone else 'ere. And you jumpin' off the edge takin' us with ya, suits just fine."

"Why have you not told anyone? How can I believe you?"

I pushed up my sleeves to show her the cut marks on my arms. She looked at me, lips trembling, eyes streaming. Below, the car door opened and a girl with a doll in her hands stepped out.

"My sister," whispered Beydaan.

"Come off the ledge, nobody needs to know 'bout this," I said, and she edged her feet back and stepped onto the roof.

"Oh God, I thought I'd lost you," I said, and hugged her like I'd never let her go. She looked into my eyes, all welled up, squeezed my hands and ran down the steps to her family.

I stood there on the roof and watched the car drive off. My heart was racing, pounding like it wanted out, and after a minute or so had passed I let out a huge breath and fell to my knees. I wanted to scream, to curse God. Beydaan, the immaculate student, who reads her prayers five times a day, who's practically memorised the Qur'an. If she's a blotch on society, what hope is there for the rest? Tomorrow, it could be Zaineb, Aaliyah, or any one of us making an unseemly mess on that gravel below. Cold and exhausted, I pulled myself up off the floor and stumbled back down the stairwell to get ready for recitals.

The Sublime

I stayed at Mycombe Girls over half-term instead of returning to Shaleton. It was nice to have some time and space to myself, to read, to think, to go for walks, though admittedly much of it was spent listening to Tone's mixtape in the gazebo on top of the hill. From there, the white stone of the school building glowed in the low, wintery sun, melting into this most English of dreamscapes. And as all but a handful of teachers and students had gone home, in the afternoons I took my headscarf off, pulled my robe up past my knees and bathed in the gorgeous light. My skin tingled with the warmth of the rays, and as I ran my fingers up my thighs there was the faintest of resistance from unshaven skin. How strange it was not to have to do my legs every other day like the girls waiting for the bus to St Johns, how blissfully liberating.

In the evenings, I did up the new library, sorted boxes, made lending cards, and strategically placed books out of view that might draw the ire of Mrs Kazi and the imam. When I was arranging the section on Islam, I thought about that last evening with Beydaan. I wondered how she's doing and even more about why she had to leave suddenly like that.

Towards the end of the holidays, as I walked back to the dormitory late one afternoon, I passed a tall, decorated vase placed halfway up the stairs in one of the alcoves. The ceramic was this deep, reflective blue; the colour the sky turns when you're having a moment, and running through it were these intricate gold, floral patterns.

"The Fatimid period," said the mufti from the bottom of the stairs.

"Funny, I never noticed it before," I said.

"Sometimes, only when you look at something from a certain angle, can you really appreciate its beauty," she said.

"How did they..."

"Lustre," she replied. "It's a technique developed by Muslim craftsmen in 300 A.H to give the pottery this metallic look. But that's a replica."

"A.H.?" I said.

"In Christianity they use Anno Domini – In the year of our Lord. In Islam, we use Anno Hegirae – In the year of the Hijra. That's the year that the prophet had to flee his hometown of Mecca to set up his new religion in Medina with just a handful of followers," she said.

"So, why not the birth year of the prophet?"

"We believe in God, and the revelations in the Qur'an, so the founding of the religion is important, the message, not the messenger himself," she said.

"Right, so if in Islam we don't idolatrise Mohammed—"

"*Sall Allahu alayhi wa salam*," she said.

· "Sorry, yes, peace be upon him. So, if we don't idolatrise, then why do people get so het up when the prophet is drawn in a cartoon?" I asked.

"That's to do more with politics than religion. Muslims see an attack on the prophet as an attack on their identity," she said.

"But why get so worked up about it?" I said.

"Imagine if someone burned the Union Flag. Would people in your hometown – Shaleton, right? – would Shaletonites accept that? It is after all only a pattern on a piece of material. Or would they perceive it as an attack on British identity? Indeed, in the US, most Americans support amending the constitution to ban flag burning."

"But by that logic, that turns the prophet into a symbol, which we just said he is not," I said, and the mufti looked at me with this proud smile.

"Ah, but there's a difference between being a symbol, and being an idol," she said. "Come to my office tomorrow, I have just the book for you... I think it's in English."

"Thanks, I will," I said, as the adhan sounded for Asr.

"Shall we pray together?" she asked.

"Yes, I'd like that," I said, surprising myself. I thought about asking her why Beydaan had left, but it didn't seem like the right time, so we walked to the mosque talking about the Fatimids.

Before she began the prayer, the mufti asked me to stand by her side, and not behind as was usual when the imam led the prayer. I said the niyyah[74], and together we lifted our hands to our ears. She said Allahu akbar, before reciting the surah Al-Fatihah, the first verse of the Qur'an. We did four rak'ah[75], and at the end of the last one we sat kneeling on the floor, hands open like a book, offering du'a[76] to the Almighty. Did God exist? Was he a man? In that moment it didn't seem to matter. I was overcome by a sense of calm and togetherness, and of a reason to live, to work, to actually give a fuck.

Term started again, and after breakfast the mufti asked if I could come by her office. To my surprise, when I walked in, I saw Father and the imam on the sofa. I gave them my salaam and sat opposite where Miss Qureshi came to join me. Father perched on the edge of his seat brooding, knees open, his bulging forearms resting on his thighs, poised like a rattlesnake ready to strike. The imam was going for that chillaxed fundamentalist look that so many before him have tried and failed to pull off. He

74 A declaration of the intention in one's heart to do an act for God.
75 A single iteration of prescribed movements and supplications performed by Muslims as part of the prescribed obligatory prayer known as salah.
76 A prayer of invocation, supplication, or request, even asking help or assistance from God.

had on this long, white tunic with matching Nike trainers. His beard was freshly dyed with henna, and I could swear he had eyeliner on. He poured Miss Qureshi a cup of tea and offered her one of the mufti's sand biscuits. Whenever he got a chance, he looked at her just a second too long, and then crossed his legs tightly, to control his feelings shall we say. The mufti shut the door, picked up some papers from her desk and sat on a chair in between the two sofas.

"Farzana, as you must know by now, school regulations require that you pass both the Islamic component as well as the national curriculum component to progress into the next year," said the mufti.

"Yes, miss," I said. Couldn't she have warned me about this meeting last week? She must've known.

I reached down into my pocket and brushed my fingertips over Tone's letter. The dots were soothing. I read the Braille and thought about our time on the cricket ground, the freckles on his face, his breath on the back of my neck. It was worth it, every single second with him that day. Opposite, Father's fists were clenched and next to me Miss Qureshi had her hands clasped together.

"So, it saddens me to ask such a bright student to repeat the year," said the mufti.

"Miss, please, I can chan—"

"Silence! Show some respect," said Father.

"Miss Qureshi, do you agree in this course of action?" the mufti asked, almost like she was inviting opposition.

"I would," said Miss Qureshi, refusing to look at me.

The mufti opened a folder, took out a piece of paper and slid it in front of Father, who signed it and then passed it over to me. I took the pen from his hand and signed too. The nib, heavy with anger, left a canyon in its wake.

"I'll ask Mrs Kazi to reassign you to another dorm with the fresh intake of students," the mufti said.

"That's not f—"

"Silence! And take your hands out of your pockets," shouted Father, raising his hand before realising where he was. At this stage, the imam casually put his teacup down and wiped his beard with his sleeve.

"As her sponsor at this school, I feel responsible for the welfare of this young, talented student, so let me make a suggestion," he said, edging forward on his seat.

Ugh, chunder.

"Farzana has spent a lot of time this year in building up the school library and given how much the girls appear to be benefitting, it might be a bit heavy to hand her such a harsh penalty," he said, looking at Miss Qureshi for acknowledgement.

I pinched myself, like proper hard.

"Perhaps if she spent the same time in the mosque instead, she might improve her grades. I can ask Mrs Kazi to provide her additional support so she can catch up. When she has, we can grant her access to the library again," he said.

"You want to ban me from library?" I said.

"Ban is too strong a word, and it would only be temporary, till her grades are at the level we would expect of a student of her calibre," he said to the mufti.

"You can't do that, the library is all I've got! Miss Qureshi?" I said.

"It's better than having to repeat the whole year, isn't it?" he said.

"Yes, I suppose," said Miss Qureshi. "Though I am scep—"

"Well, then, it's decided," said the imam.

"I cannot thank you enough," Father said to the mufti before turning to the imam. "And you brother, we owe, I, I owe everything to you. Even after being tried and tested by this little minx you still have the forgiveness to give her a second chance."

"I see her like my own daughter," replied the imam.

The mufti got up to see me out whilst Miss Qureshi was left with the unenviable task of entertaining Orange Beard and Father. She picked up a book from her table on Islamic pottery, and as she opened the door she spoke quietly in my ear.

"I don't want you to change, I want you to learn, to think, to grow," she said, placing the book in my hands, but I shoved it back at her and made my way to Mrs Kazi's class.

In the evening, Miss Qureshi sent for me. When I knocked on the door, she asked me to come in and offered me some rooibos, which I declined. I stood by the door, raging, still raw from this morning's stinging exchanges with the imam. There are not many mirrors in Mycombe Girls, but I imagine I looked quite the little terror. Miss Qureshi must've drunk half a pot of tea before mustering up the courage to speak.

"You're upset, Farzana," she said finally and tried to hold me, but I pushed her away and pressed my palms tightly against the side of my head to stop it from exploding.

"You hung me out to dry," I replied.

"I couldn't..."

"You said you were on my side."

"I had to think of all the other girls, who work every waking hour of the day to get the grades."

"He played you like a fiddle, the imam," I said.

"It's not about me!" she said, raising her voice. "I tried to tell you not to waste your talent, to work hard on your Arabic, but you wouldn't listen. You're your own worst enemy."

"So, it's all my fault, is it? All this shit that's happened to me over the last year, I fucking deserved it, is that what you're saying?"

"No, that's not—"

"I suppose same happened to Beydaan, she forgot to count a prayer bead or something, and next thing she's on the... never mind," I said.

"I don't know anything about Beydaan, but Farzana, listen—"

"All these walks in the Peaks, the library, why do we do it? What's the point if you're not there for each other when it really matters? I needed you to stick up for me in front of Father. I wanted him to see how good I am, how good I can be, but your silence was even more damning," I said.

"Come here," she said.

"No," I replied.

"Sakthi, come here," she said, and I tried to push her away again, but this time she fought me, wrapped her arms around my shoulders, and rested my head against her bosom.

After a while she stood me up straight and wiped a tear from my eyes. She walked over to the almery, and from a locked drawer took out an object covered in a dark, blue cloth and gave it to me. I removed the fabric to find a side-by-side translation of the Qur'an, the right sheet in Arabic, the left in English. I closed the book and put it down on the table, perhaps a little too disrespectfully.

"Look closer, the first page, what do you notice?" said Miss Qureshi, encouraging me to pick it up again.

I reluctantly took it in my hands. There was just the title and the name of the author, all pretty nondescript. The type was Times Roman, set on slightly off-white paper that felt nice to the touch. I looked at Miss Qureshi hoping she might let on, but she seemed curiously excited to see if I'd get there.

"The translator," I said at last. "It's a woman."

"Precisely," she said.

"Can I?" I poured myself a cup and sat down on the chair by her desk, flicking through the original text and checking the translations.

"So, you do know Arabic," she said.

"I can get the gist."

"What verse are you reading?"

"An-Nisa 4:34," I said, and Miss Qureshi recited the entire section without looking.

"You're a *hafiz*! You've memorised the Qur'an," I said.

"Well, my mother tongue is Arabic, it helps," she said with a smile. "Why did you turn to that verse?"

"Father," I said, and felt my voice go. "He says this line over and over."

"Does he..."

"Meghna gets it mostly. And now she's all on her own," I said.

"You can still help her, by learning and getting a degree, a job, by using your time here to get ahead in life, and then perhaps you'll find a way to support her in the future," she said.

"I've not been sent here to learn, Miss."

"What do you mean, Sakthi?"

"Never mind."

"Sakthi, there isn't much you can do about the gender you're born with, but there are things you can control," she said.

"Like what?"

"What does the translation say?"

"But those [wives] from whom you fear arrogance – [first] advise them; [then if they persist], forsake them in bed; and [finally], go away from them." I said.

"Go on," she said, her eyes sparkling with anticipation.

"The Qur'an... it doesn't say beat your wives," I said.

"No, not according to this translation," she said.

"So, it's open to—" I said.

"Interpretation," we said together. I could feel my brain grow in those moments.

"In most books written, especially older ones, texts translated are by men. That means there is a male bias, conscious or unconscious, on everything that we read. It's important that you, that all women understand what it really says, so that you may interpret it for yourself in the modern world."

"And what good'll that do? Men'll still beat women," I said.

"Yes, but they cannot use religion, as many do now, as an affirmation of their right to do so. Once you take that 'moral' justification away, everything else has to follow," she said.

"You want to reform Islam?" I said.

"Not the religion, the practice."

"Good luck with that."

"It's already happening. We hope women growing up in your generation and the next will be able to live as equal to men. Imagine that world, Sakthi."

"We?" I said.

"Yes, we. Why do you think the mufti has tolerated all your rebellions with such minor punishments, and not kicked you out? She sees you could be a great ambassador for Islam, she sees you as the future," she said.

"The mufti is in on this?"

"And the girls, do you really think a bunch of 15-year-olds are so into books that they want to devote all their time to the library? They're doing it for you, for what you believe in, what you stand for."

"Well, and they're bored!"

"Pay attention in your Arabic class and next time you read the Qur'an; a whole new world will open up to you. There's so much you can take from it, to learn from it," she said.

I thanked her for the tea and headed back to the dorm, passing that Fatimid era vase. I tilted it a little and looked inside, and there on the base was an image of a man and a woman together, hidden out of plain sight. That's what the mufti meant when she was talking about looking at things from different angles. And the image meant that figures must not have been banned by the Qur'an, just interpreted by someone in that way, apparently centuries later.

When I opened the door to the dorm, I found that book on Islamic pottery on my pillow. The girls were already in bed as Mrs Kazi had called lights out. It felt strange, lying there in the dark without hearing the rhythmic clicking of Beydaan's prayer beads and the faintest aspirations as she repeated the name of God. It had helped me fall asleep, a reassuring blanket of sound in the still country nights. And now without that religious metronome, I lay awake thinking about what Miss Qureshi had said. Across the room in the bunk bed Aaliyah was reading something with a Maglite.

"Aaliyah, have you heard of The Sublime Qur'an?" I whispered.

"No," she said.

"And have you got any spare AA batteries?"

New Musliminahs

Book clubs, study groups, debates, we even have a line-up of guest speakers. The library has taken on a life of its own and become a place we can come for peace, solace, and inspiration. Even the Jihadi Massive has been caught in the literature section, Fatima hiding a copy of The Philosopher's Stone in the folds of her robe. Only, I'm still banned, so I've been lending books from the gazebo on top of the hill like some exiled political leader. And whilst I've been away, Miss Qureshi has helped me improve my Arabic enough that I can understand large passages of the Qur'an unaided by translations. I never thought I'd say this, but Tafseer classes have become the highlight of my day, fighting tooth and nail with Lady Right Angle about the right interpretations.

"Surah an-Nur, Ayat 31. Fatima. Read," instructed Mrs Kazi in the class this morning.

Fatima sang the verse, each syllable weighted or drawn out perfectly, operatic in its delivery. The whole class was mesmerised by the beauty of her pitch and tone. Oh my, if this is the way angels speak, then who wouldn't believe in heaven.

"Make sure you don't recite it like that in front of the funders when they visit next term, else you lead them astray," said Mrs Kazi.

"Yes, miss, sorry miss," said Fatima.

"And what does this ayat mean?" she asked the class. Aaliyah and Zaineb raised their hands, but the teacher ignored them and chose the girl sat next to Fatima.

"Correct. A Muslim woman must cover her face, her head, her bosom in the presence of a man, so as not to tempt him," she said.

I'd talked about this with Miss Qureshi a lot over the past few weeks and it was clear, least in our heads, that women were not bound to cover their faces, or even their hair. I wanted to raise my arm but given how she completely ignored the twins; I chose another tack. I slowly untied my headscarf and let it fall around my neck.

"Farzana, put your hijab back on."

"Why, Mrs Kazi?"

"Why? Are you deaf? Did you not hear the verse? It's Thursday, the school's board of directors will be walking around."

"Yeah, but where's it say we have to wear a hijab, or cover our faces?"

Aaliyah mee-mawed across the room telling me to stand down, but I'd had this itch for a long time. Most of the class stopped reading, with only a handful of students so absorbed by the script that they carried on in their own little world.

"I won't take the bait," said Mrs Kazi.

"Just saying like, I wouldn't interpret it like that," I said.

"So, for more than one thousand years, the great scholars of Islam have misinterpreted the surah an-Nur? According to you," she said, and drew some level of satisfaction from the snickering.

"No, how you've interpreted it isn't right," I replied, which was met by a bunch of internalised fist bumps. You can always tell when the twins are behind you, they've got this kind of sharp, micro-aggressive nod that I've only ever seen in Tone when he's listening to cricket.

"And what's your... interpretation?" she said in air quotes. God, I can't stand people who do that.

"Well, it doesn't say we should cover our faces for a start," I said. "But also, why doesn't anybody ever talk about the hijab of the eyes? That men too shouldn't perve on women."

194

"There's a hijab for men?" said Zaineb.

"Silence!" said Mrs Kazi.

"Why, why should we women have to cover ourselves? Why not tell people to be respectful of each other, like it does in the Qur'an? Why not emphasise that lesson instead?" I said to the class.

I could almost hear Mrs Kazi's blood bubbling, like those prehistoric swamps you see in the movies. She becomes a caricature of herself if you press the right buttons, such a sight to see. One more button I thought, and she'll erupt, but which?

"So, you're the one? Sent to liberate all of us oppressed Muslim women. My my, how those books have gone to your head," Mrs Kazi said, barely able to contain her disdain.

"Why does the imam get away with letching over women, when if we so much as smile at another man we're labelled as whores?" I said and braced myself for the repercussions.

"That's enough! Insolent child, to the mufti's office right now. The rest of you, read surah Al-Nisa, ayat 34," she said, grabbing my ear between her index finger and thumb and marching me off down the corridor on a leash of pain.

I sat outside the mufti's room massaging my ear until I heard my name called through the door. When I entered, the mufti was sat behind her desk with Mrs Kazi, eyes bulging, stood by her side.

"Will that be all, Mrs Kazi?" the mufti said, and the old bint nodded and made her way towards the door.

"Kuffar, you'll burn in hell," she said to me as she left the room.

"Funda-f'kin'-mentalist, see you there," I replied.

"That's enough, both of you," the mufti intervened.

Mrs Kazi slammed the door as much as respect would allow. The mufti poured two cups of tea from a small pot and invited me to sit down with her on the couch. She added some boiling water from the samovar, and a dollop of honey, and stirred it without the spoon making a single sound.

"Opinions are like tea, they can be too strong; you have to add water, and sugar to make them palatable," said the mufti, opening my file. "It seems you have made excellent progress in your Islamic studies."

"Thank you, Miss," I said, a little surprised that Mrs Kazi would have given me such good grades with the level of torture I subject her to on a daily basis.

"So, what is it this time?" she said.

"We were reading the surah An-Nur, and I was trying to say it doesn't necessarily mean women should wear a veil, and that men use religion to keep women down. I mean, why else are we forced to cover up?"

"A woman might do out of choice," said the mufti.

"Out of choice?"

"A symbol of her faith, or a reaction against the fashion industry; even, some have argued, to liberate herself."

"Is that why you wear the hijab, Miss?"

"A bit of all of that really, but mostly I just feel comfortable in it," she said. "Now, let's get to why you're here."

"Yes, Miss."

"It's true there may be other interpretations of the Qur'an, and it's right we should discuss them. But did you want to contribute to scholarly debate, or did you want to undermine Mrs Kazi? I take issue with the latter. Mrs Kazi is not the enemy."

"I'm sorry," I said, looking down at the ground, her gentle words even more brutal than the cane.

"Yes, well, we live and learn. At least, that's the aim. We'll let this one slip. Just get your head down and think more carefully about what you say," the mufti said.

"Yes, thank you, Miss."

"Oh, Sakthi, before you go. Have you heard of the Persian philosopher Rumi?"

"No, Miss."

"He said before you speak, let your words pass through three gates. At the first gate, ask yourself, is it true? At the second gate ask, is it necessary? At the third gate ask, is it kind? Remember that."

"I will, Miss."

After the Dhuhr prayers, Miss Qureshi gave me a letter from Beydaan. She wanted to meet, so I arranged to see her on the weekend at Stannage Edge when the girls would go for a walk. On Sunday, the coach dropped me off at the Plantation, and from there Beydaan and I took the path up the side of the rock face and followed the trail northwest along the ridge towards High Neb. The first hour we spent in silence, accompanied only by the sound of the breeze rolling over the heather. When we reached the summit, the countryside unfolded before us, silver-white clouds racing over the green hills that so define this land. I was a little overwhelmed by my own sense of belonging, how England could have such a pull on my heart.

"Near my village, there is a similar ridge, but when we look out into the horizon, all we see is desert," said Beydaan.

"D'ya miss it?" I said.

"This country has given me back my life, so I owe it everything, but… it will never be home."

I took out a tiffin box with some food I'd filched from the canteen and Beydaan poured us both some tea. She told me about her life back in Somalia, about making sabaayad flat bread and sambosas with her mother to sell at their village stall.

"The ladies would gather around in the evenings, eat and talk about village matters," she said, laughing to herself as if she had been transported back to that happy moment. "They got more done in a few hours than the men in an entire month."

Her father steered clear of politics and kept two dozen or so goats, but when her brother was wounded in a fight with the neighbouring tribe, they had to sell the entire herd to pay for the medical bills. After the operation, they struggled to get day jobs on the farms around their village because of the drought. When more communal violence broke out, the whole family decided to run, first to Mogadishu, and then to the UK where they sought asylum.

As the afternoon wore on, we moved towards the cairns at Crow Chin before doubling back to our starting point. At that time, I couldn't help but think that Beydaan was holding something back. I mean, why would she give up her scholarship, a once-in-a-lifetime opportunity and just up and leave like that given what she'd told me about fleeing Somalia. It didn't make sense. But just as I turned to ask her, she drew a deep breath and exhaled.

"He touched me," she whispered.

"Who did, Beydaan?" I said.

"The imam," she said, covering her face with her hands.

"He's such a perv," I said. "The other day he tried to squeeze past Miss Qureshi in the doorway when he could have easily waited. She got the fright of her life as his crotch brushed her leg."

"No Sakthi." Beydaan looked into my eyes. "He *touched* me."

"Are ya alright?" I said. Such a dumb question, of course she wasn't, but I didn't know what else to say. It's at times like this I wonder if there is some defect in my personality, whether I'm becoming a sycophant, a Bond villain. A numbness spread across my body. And instead of giving her a hug like any normal person would, I went straight into facts. "When? Where did this happen?"

"In the south stables, when I went to get the books," she said, disappointed, I guess, with my emotionless reaction. Has Father's abuse driven out any sense of pain? Is that why Meghna never ever cries?

"That's why ya took so long?" I said.

"Yes," she said.

"Are ya gonna report it? The mufti, I'm sure she'd know what to do."

"Oh, I should never have come here. There is nothing to be done. You must not tell anyone, Sakthi, promise me."

"Of course, I promise, Beydaan. But, if ya don't then he'll get away with it. He might be abusin' other girls too, so if ya speak out ya might be able to help 'em."

"I can't," she said, shaking her head.

"Why can't you?" I said, tearing the wild heather from the ground.

"I'm not like you!" She sprang to her feet and walked up to the edge of the outcrop. For an instant, I thought she'd jump, but I didn't stop her this time. I couldn't be there for her every waking second of the day. She had to be able to fight her own demons.

"Because I'm circumcised," said Beydaan, turning around and moving away from the edge. "My grandmother, she found someone to do it in England."

"Why dint ya tell someone?" I said.

"Why did you not tell anyone you were being forced to marry?" she said. "I felt so ashamed, they'd have put granny away. I could not do that to her, she meant no harm. And she is my flesh and blood. Where I come from, that is all you have," said Beydaan.

"OK, so... Sorry, tryin' to get me head around all this. What 'bout the imam like, how does he fit in?"

"The imam found out that I'd been sewn up, so—"

"Sewn up! Sorry. Go on," I said, clearing my throat.

"So, if I report him..."

"He'll tell on yer gran."

"And everybody would know I'd been..."

"Circumcised."

"No, worse than that... tarnished," said Beydaan. "I do not have your bravery, or Aaliyah's brains. I do not have Zaineb's humour, nor Miss Qureshi's upbringing. I have nothing, I am

199

nothing. And my family is my only route to happiness. Their honour the only currency, so if that is devalued, there is no hope for me."

"Yer stronger than ya think," I said, taking her arm in mine.

"Thanks, Sakthi," she said, and dried her eyes.

We walked half an hour or so longer until we reached Robin Hood's Cave and sat on one of the old grindstones, waiting for the other girls who had taken another route. When they saw us, Aaliyah and Zaineb ran towards Beydaan and lifted her off the ground. For a moment, we were a family again, singing, dancing, belly laughing like we did that day reciting Shakespeare around the laundry basket. We headed towards Upper Burbage Bridge, hand in hand, where Miss Qureshi had asked the coach driver to pick us up. Beydaan hugged everybody and got off at the bus station in Hathersage and we headed back to the school in time for the afternoon prayers.

And that's when it came, the shortness of breath, the stabbing in my chest as it finally sank in what Beydaan had said on the ridge. I rested my head between the seat and the window, eyelids heavy with sorrow. God, why can't you have given us two hearts as you have two lungs, I thought. In a life as messed up as this, you must've known hearts would break. Yet somehow, Beydaan's pain, this shared injustice amongst women acted like an analgesic against my own grief. Her struggle, my struggle; my struggle hers. I drew strength from it, if that makes sense, and it made me even more resolute to join Miss Qureshi and the mufti in the fight to change things, their feminist jihad. But first, I shut my eyes and let the hum of the engine put me to sleep.

The bus dropped us off at the back entrance. As we walked in through the gates, one of the girls from the lower school ran down the steps of the south portico and raced along the path towards the fountain.

"Is tha' Fartima? Runnin'?" said Aaliyah.

"Didn't she come wif us, barely noticed!" said Zaineb.

"Sakthi!" she shouted. Just as she reached us, her legs got all tangled in the folds of her robe and she crashed to the ground head-first and passed out. I ran to her and put some water over her forehead till she eventually came round.

"You'll have a nice bruise on tha' noggin. Why ya runnin' like a mad woman," said Aaliyah.

"The library," she said. Miss Qureshi and the other girls quickly gathered around Fatima. "They're ripping everything up."

"Who is?" I said.

"The imam, and a dozen or so other men who I don't know. They've locked the doors, and they're tearing pages out of all the books."

The girls sprinted back up the steps and through the corridors before arriving at the doors of the library. They were shut and shored up by a couple of heavy desks. Through the door glass I could see the imam at the centre of the room next to another man who was smartly dressed. They seemed to be reading off a list, and directing the others which books to remove, and what pages to rip out. I smacked the door with the base of my fist and the carnage stopped, momentarily, as the men turned around.

"Abba? Abba. Abba. No! Stop, please stop. I beg you, please."

He ignored me and they got back to work. I pathetically tried to force the door, but the door was equal to the challenge. I got a nice bruise on my shoulder to show for it, only this time Father didn't even raise a hand.

Miss Qureshi arrived from the mufti's office.

"Can she stop them?" I asked, but she shook her head.

"Don't let them see you like this," said Miss Qureshi, pulling me up off the ground.

"How can he get away with this?" I said.

"I don't know," she replied.

We met Aaliyah and all the girls from the upper and lower years in the main entrance hall. As I went to climb the steps, my legs gave way and I collapsed in a big heap on the floor. Mrs Kazi, who had to break her prayers because of all the commotion, stood above me. She picked me up and swung my arm over her shoulder. Fatima took my other arm and they both helped me up towards the dorm. I looked around the faces, the expressions of solidarity. With this one savage act, Father and the imam had brought the girls together, and sowed the seeds for rebellion.

The Stoning

At the beginning of the summer term the library was reopened, and my ban was lifted. On the surface, nothing much changed. Each book was in its rightful place, only now the sweet, sickening scent of attar wafted around the room replacing that musty, educational odour of old books that makes you feel clever before you've read a single word.

"Educational odour?" said Aaliyah.

"Yeah, d'ya know what I mean?" I said.

"You've gone doolally from all that time in the mosque," she said.

"What'll ya read first, Sakthi?" said Zaineb.

I scanned the shelves, searching for a title that caught my eyes or a spine that hasn't been broken. God, how I missed this place: stepping on that little three-wheeled footstool to reach the top shelf; reading the date stamps in those old library books that have been taken out of circulation; analysing the notes that others have made in the margins; was Heathcliff born evil, or was he made so by his unforgiving environment? This is what makes my world turn, not the febrile politics of hate.

"How about this one? 'The Essential Guide to Being a Good Muslim Woman," said Aaliyah.

"Library's grown," I said.

"And shrunk," said Zaineb from the back of the room, pointing out that the entire Harry Potter series has been removed.

"We'll get them again," said her sister, giving her a hug.

But it's not just Harry who's been banished by the imam, Father, and their bandits. Loads of the books have large chunks torn out leaving just a handful of pages hanging by a single thread to their bindings – empty carcasses of knowledge.

"This is all my fault," said Fatima, standing by the double doors.

"You, Fatima... how?" I said.

She covered her face with her hands and sobbed. Aaliyah and Zaineb gestured to each other to give her a hug, but neither did. I asked her to come and sit next to me and held her hand.

"What 'appened?" I said.

"Remember that fight you had with Mrs Kazi on covering up?" she said.

"Yeah, me ears are still 'urtin'," I said.

"Well, after that day she told me and a bunch of other girls that we had to go down to the library and make a note of all the books that might be un-Islamic," said Fatima.

"Wha' d'ya mean ya had to?" said Zaineb.

"She said she'd mark down our coursework if we didn't," said Fatima.

"OK, let's all take a deep breath," I said.

"Ya spied on us? She fuckin' spied on us, man! I'm gonna rip ya apart ya little—" said Zaineb, throwing herself at Fatima.

"Hey, hey! Stop this right now!" I said.

"She fuckin' dobbed us in. All tha' hard work, gone, coz of her," said Zaineb. Part of me wanted to see seven shades of shit beaten out of that self-righteous suck-up, but Fatima seemed proper upset. I split the two up and asked them to sit on opposite sides of the desk. Aaliyah glared at Fatima whilst comforting her sister.

"We've gotta stop fightin' amongst ourselves," I said.

"So why ya tellin' us now?" said Aaliyah.

"I'm getting married," said Fatima.

"Good luck to the poor wanker tha' gets you," said Zaineb.

"Married? Bit out the blue, in't it?" I said, fetching her a cup of tea and some biscuits. Aaliyah pushed herself to get Fatima a box of tissues, and even that seemed quite the achievement.

"Remember what you were saying in class? So, I told my dad the imam was looking at girls a bit funny, and that some of the girls in the upper school have been promised to the men that come every year from the Middle East."

"The funders tha' are comin' this week?" said Aaliyah.

"Yeah, their sons and whatnot," said Fatima.

"Tha' can't be, tha' can't be fam," said Aaliyah.

"Tha's scandalous, man!" said Zaineb.

"Next thing, he's on the phone arranging my engagement to my cousin in Karachi," she said, eyes red and swollen, tears streaming down her cheeks. "He says it's the only way to protect me and get me through the school, and I know he's right, but still…"

"Hey, it's OK, come here," I said, reluctantly putting my arms around her shoulders.

"Nah bruv, she's lyin'! That shit only happens in the Daily Mail," said Zaineb, ready to pounce again.

"I'm sorry Sakthi, I didn't know who else to go to," said Fatima.

"Listen, Fatima. Talk to the mufti, she'll know what to do," I said.

"Hold up, just hold the fuck up! Wha' d'ya mean the imam was lookin' at girls funny?" said Aaliyah, pacing up and down the room.

Fatima spent the next hour describing in detail all the incidents of abuse the girls suffered at the hands of the imam during his school inspections on Thursdays. They went from lewd comments and staring to touching a girl's hand or stroking her back. But those were just the girls that came out. None of them knew what happened to Beydaan.

"Fuckin' perve, I knew it," said Aaliyah.

"Ya don' expect an imam to… ya know," said Zaineb.

"Is that why Mrs Kazi 'elped us up at bottom of the stairs?" I said.

"Yeah, I'd just told her," said Fatima.

I remembered what Trina said at the mela in Bangladesh: 'give them an inch, they'll take a mile'. The imam certainly took a mile, even though nobody had given him an inch to begin with. Something had to be done. Over the next hour we went through a good few packets of jammy dodgers and custard creams, all united in finding a way to stop this creep. In the end, Fatima came up with the plan. So, we agreed that Thursday in the canteen, when the funders sat down for lunch, we would make a stand.

We woke up on Thursday to the sound of gunshots. The guests had arrived, and the board members welcomed them with some deer stalking before breakfast. I mean, as if you do. For the rest of the morning, Fatima and a select group of girls had been asked to give them the guided tour. The men walked around the school in their white gowns, red and white chequered ghutrahs and black iqals, with the burka-clad girls in tow. After the Dhuhr prayers, the girls filed into the canteen, orderly and in silence, like we had planned. The mufti, sat to one side of all the men, rose to address the hall. The girls stood up to give their salaam.

"*Walaikum as-salaam*," she replied. "Firstly, I'd like you to give a warm welcome to our guests, without whom we would never be able to have such a wonderful school," she said.

The girls applauded politely.

"Ya sure ya trust Fatima?" Aaliyah whispered.

"It's a trap, fam," said Zaineb.

The mufti went through the points of the week as she always does on Thursdays.

"There is a small group of girls amongst you that has brought the school attention."

"That's it, she screwed us," said Zaineb.

"They have been brave and, under the guidance of Miss Qureshi, have shown the world outside that the students at Mycombe Girls are as capable as anyone, and can do anything. So, please give a round of applause to our very own hikers. Today you conquered Stannage Edge, tomorrow the world." she said.

The hall broke out into raucous applause, and cheers, which raised the roof as well as a couple of eyebrows on the head table.

"I'm sure," I said to Aaliyah and Zaineb.

The mufti waved her hands and called for quiet.

"Haji Syed Khan, who has been so helpful in setting up this school for the girls, would like to say a few words before lunch is served," she said, and Orange Beard took the stage. Don't even want to call him that, it trivialises his sins, turns him into some fictional pantomime villain, but to call him an imam is still a little hard to stomach.

"Books, wonderful things, aren't they?" he said.

"Here we go," I said.

"Newton can tell you how to work out the mass of the world, using your brains as scales, and the poetry of Blake, or Byron can elevate your soul into the stratosphere so you may feel like you're in the company of God himself."

I'll bet one of Meghna's lamb samosas that he's never read a word of Byron. He stopped, paused for dramatic effect, and held up the Qur'an. Quite the show he put on for the guests.

"But books can never replace the word of God!" he said, and the visitors nodded in agreement. He had them eating out of his hands. I completely underestimated our enemy, passed him off to be some village fool.

"Knowledge corrupts, and absolute knowledge corrupts absolutely," he bellowed out across the canteen. "From today, your Islamic teachers will guide your learning, so that *insha'Allah*, one day you may become good Muslims, an example to girls all around the world."

My brain was in tumult, my heart an intifada. I mean, the nerve, to lecture us on being good Muslims after the things that he's done. Rumi's gates were frantically opening and closing in my mind, but Rumi was not a woman, he never had to put up with this shit. I rose to my feet as we'd agreed, covered head to toe in my burka like the rest of the girls and walked up the central aisle until I faced the imam head on.

"Sit down dear, don't be disrespectful," said the soft-voiced mufti.

"Surah An-Nur, Ayat 30... Tell the believing men—"

"I know Surah An-Nur, child," said the imam, to the laughter of the visitors.

"Tell the believing men to lower their gaze and to be mindful of their chastity: this will be most conducive to their purity. And verily, God is aware of all that they do," I said to him, loud enough so the whole hall could hear me.

"What's your name?!" said the imam, looking at the mufti, who shrugged and asked me to sit down again.

"You're a pig," I said.

The imam jumped off the stage. He grabbed my arm with one hand and tried to lift my veil with the other, but I wriggled free and pushed him back.

"Pig," I said louder, my voice trembling. The imam raised his hand as if to strike me, the mufti rose out of her chair and rushed to stop him.

"Pig," said Aaliyah, stepping forward to stand by me.

"Pig," said Zaineb, and stood on my other shoulder.

"Sit down, you impudent sprites, you'll go straight—" he said.

"You should be ashamed," I said.

"Reveal yourself!" he said.

"Shame," I said.

Miss Qureshi rushed to my side and whispered in my ear, but this time I wasn't going stop, not after what he'd done to Beydaan.

"Shame," I said, over again, louder each time.

"Shame," joined in Aaliyah and Zaineb in stereo.

"Shame," shouted Fatima, finally, to my great relief. She signalled to the other girls until the dissent spread from one dinner table to the next and the whole room chanted together in a chorus of rebellion. The guests sat there, mouths open, digesting the scene before they'd tasted a single morsel. The upper and lower schools circled around the imam, linking arms to form a mass of bodies like a granuloma.

"Stop, you will stop immediately!" shouted the imam.

The chanting carried on, building up to a crescendo. A few of the girls had taken off their sandals to hurl at him, but it wasn't necessary. The words were equally painful. They fell on him like stones, each one heavier than the one before, till he cowered on the ground with his head tucked between his knees.

Then the fire alarm sounded, and the sprinklers came on. Our burkas were drenched with cold water. The girls scattered and ran back to their dormitories, still incognito behind their veils. As I left the dinner hall, I looked back to see the visitors circling the imam.

The next day, the board summoned me to a meeting in the Red Room. It is the only space in the school where the original artwork has not been touched, and the indulgence of the period shines through as bright as the sun through the massive, arched windows. Some of the men had undone their collars and loosened their ties. A few had even rolled up their sleeves. I turned up without my burka, just a loose piece of cloth to cover my hair and neck. A few turned away in horror, but in others I saw a flicker of a smile. Miss Qureshi was chatting to the mufti in the corner where I joined them, and they pointed out who was who. The meeting started bang on time – seventeen minutes past eleven thirty.

"That's quite a stunt you pulled," said the General Secretary.

"What makes you think it was me?" I replied.

"Some girls say they recognised your voice," he said.

"Yet others will say the contrary," I replied. He acknowledged the stalemate.

"Very well, Miss... Haque, isn't it? Let's not beat around the bush. What is it that you want?" he said. I looked at Miss Qureshi and the mufti. Nobody has ever called me by my surname before.

"Sorry, what? Me? What do I want?" I said.

"We are aware of the information you hold. Miss Qureshi tells us you are a hard-working, talented student with a bright future. The mufti would be happy to write a glowing reference if you wish to move on to a private college to prepare you for university. Oxford, isn't it, to study law? We'll even pay your tuition."

"Information?" I said.

"Yes, you know..."

"Oh, about the imam?" I said, and he cringed.

"Why are you laughing?" he asked.

"I thought I was going to get... Never mind," I said.

"I suppose you're entitled to enjoy this moment."

"Trust me, I take no enjoyment from what has happened in this school, under your watch. And now you want to buy my silence with freedom. Freedom that should've been mine in the first place."

"Well? he said.

"Well... no. No thanks," I replied.

"No, Miss Haque?"

"Nope."

"Then what do you want?" he said, pouring his tea into a saucer.

"Beydaan, we'd like you to re-admit her in time for the exams. And that the imam's place on the board be replaced by a female imam, and two additional places be created to be filled by girls from the upper and lower schools," I said.

"We?" said the General Secretary.

"We," I replied, full of pride.

"You wish to stay at the school?" he said looking around the room.

"Yes... I do." I said.

"Allah have mercy upon us," he said with a smile.

I gave the board my salaam and walked towards the door, turning round at the last moment. "One other thing, we'd like to take this room as a common room."

The mufti asked me to wait outside. I left the door ever so slightly ajar so I could make out what was being said from the hall. Another man now spoke in a malefic tone.

"It's impressive what you have achieved with these girls, the hiking, the library, the incredible sense of empowerment, but what kind of message does it send if you teach them to defy their leaders, or their elders?" he said.

"In my opinion, it shows the children that they can achieve anything they want if they put their minds to it," Miss Qureshi replied in a strong and confident voice.

"Yes, your opinion, well, we'll come to that later. Surely, Miss Qureshi, it is not lost on you that we are an Islamic girls' school? There are certain values parents entrust us to instil in their daughters at this delicate age."

"I doubt parents would object to a library."

"How wrong you are, Miss Qureshi. On the contrary, my inbox is cluttered with complaints from parents that their girls are reading Romeo and Juliet."

The General Secretary took over, gentler in his approach.

"Miss Qureshi, the board has made a decision about your future at this school, which you may appeal," he said.

"I understand," said Miss Qureshi.

"You may find it comforting to know the vote was not unanimous," he said, shutting the door firmly.

Miss Qureshi came out of the boardroom a few moments later and gave me a wink and a smile.

Later that day, we read the evening prayers together, which took much longer than usual as she spent a good twenty minutes extra in *du'a*, and then we went our separate ways up to our rooms. She didn't come down for dinner that evening. In the morning when we all gathered for prayers, we realised she'd gone.

৬. MANGO KHATTA

The indefinite article

I came home for the summer on the day of the by-election, the first in over fifty years. A humongous Saint George's flag draped around a closed-down factory chimney dominated the terraced skyline. And high above the cobbled stones, banners of 'independence' fluttered in the breeze. England has always been a proud nation in the football stands, but not in the run-down streets of Shaleton. Father didn't hang around to welcome me. Suited and booted in a dark blue three piece, a Union flag bow tie and black cab cufflinks, he was off to throw a party at the Bismillah and cash in on the novel patriotism. Curry, after all, is a British invention some would have you believe. What a pile of shit! I gave him my salaam, which he half returned and bolted out the door. Meghna was in the kitchen experimenting with Bramley apple slices marinated in cumin-flavoured yoghurt. When she saw me, she dropped everything and ran towards me arms open wide.

"*Assalamu'alaikum*," I said, and crouched down to touch her feet.

"*Wa'alaikum as-salam*, moina" she said, squeezing me tight.

I let down my hijab.

Every day more beautiful, she said, stroking my cheeks with the outside of her fingers. She put the dessert in the fridge, pulled out all the curries from the oven and heated them up on the stove.

"Amma! It's—"

Nje, Ramadan, I know, you're supposed to be fasting.

"Where's Dadhi?"

214

Sleeping, shhh. Meghna set the table and served the curries in her nicest bowls as I sat there awkwardly, a guest in my own house! On the left, pan-fried tilapia, skin crisp like crackling. On the right, spinach, left to melt in a culinary sauna with garlic, chilli and coriander, topped off with grilled king prawns. And in the middle, Ganges river-sprat simmered in a sour rhubarb sauce.

"*Accha*, in't there any shutki?" I said, ungratefully now I think about it. Must've taken her the whole morning to make all that food.

Na moina, Trina said she has a new recipe she wanted to show me when she comes here later, she said.

I sat down at the table, put a spoonful of rice and spinach on my plate and ate, while she sat next to me and caressed my hair. When I finished, I glugged down a glass of water and put the dirty dish in the sink.

"Amma, can I go see Mrs Finch now?" I said.

But you haven't touched anything, what about the khatta[77]? It's your favourite, I made it especially for you, said Meghna.

"I'll 'ave it later like, int' evening, I promise."

Technically, I was still under house arrest. But the reservation for the restaurant was so big, Father had reassigned the Black Paws to washing dishes, cutting onions, and serving customers, and that left the coast clear.

Thik ache, jao, but don't get caught! she said.

"Thanks, Amma," I said, washed my hands and ran out the back.

"It's a historic day," I said, slipping my shoes off in the kitchen before coming through into the living room.

77 A tangy fish dish.

Mrs Finch, as she herself likes to say, was on the crapper. It sounded like the climax of the 1812 overture (most likely one of Meghna's fusion dishes). As I sat down on a pile of old almanacs waiting for her to finish the fourth movement, so to speak, I saw something catch the light of the glowing fire. Peeking out from underneath a copy of The Telegraph, was the key she usually has hanging round her neck day and night.

I tried to fight the temptation, but the imp in my head was doing Arabian double somersaults with curiosity. I ummed and ahhed for ages and then finally mustered the courage to open the door.

"An historic," said Mrs Finch, coming out of the bogs.

I scrambled to put the key back but forgot to lock the door. Such an idiot! Mrs Finch sat down on her armchair, gave me the newspaper to read aloud and placed the key back round her neck. Should I have told her? I dread the thought of disappointing her, of betraying her trust.

"An," she said again.

"Why an?" I asked.

"It depends on how you say a word dear, not just on how you spell it. When I was a lass, people used to say historic without pronouncing the h," she said.

"What, so people would say 'istoric?" I said.

"Precisely, so it started with a vowel," she said.

"Yeah but, we don't talk like that no more Mrs Finch," I said teasingly. I enjoyed bringing the old lady to within a heartbeat of a grammatically induced cardiovascular infarction, and then helping her recover with a cheeky smile.

"Ee, I tell you, we're losing our language," she said, taking a deep breath and reclining into her chair.

I poured her a cuppa.

"Did you get my letters? I wrote bigger so you wouldn't have to strain your eyes," I said.

"I did dear, thank you. I was happy to read you managed to get the library project off the ground," she said.

I wondered whether I should tell her that Father and the imam had destroyed all the hard work that we'd done. But I didn't want to cause her unnecessary heartache, so I kept schtum.

"And this Miss Crikey, your English teacher, sounds like just the person you need on your team."

"Miss Qureshi. But yeah, Miss Crikey might be a better name given how rebellious she is with the school board."

"And she speaks good English, despite being... you know?"

"A foreigner? Yes, she speaks the Queen's English. Oh, you'd love to meet her Mrs Finch, she's a breath of fresh air, a real inspiration to all the girls at the school."

"And she likes literature. English literature. Is that right?"

"Yes, so she has this amazing memory, I think from learning the whole Qur'an off by heart, so during walks out in the Peaks she can recite whole passages from Dickens, or Austen."

My eyes welled up, and I couldn't keep it in anymore. I told Mrs Finch what happened to the library, and to Miss Qureshi after the visitors arrived from the Middle East. But she was anything but disappointed. Every penny she'd donated, was a penny well spent she said, if it meant that the girls who'd come face to face with adversity came out stronger.

"And they thought they could keep you down," she said, with a smile.

"What were they thinking," I said, taking the teacups back into the kitchen and washing them up.

"Bring me that letter from the kitchen table, will you chuck?" Mrs Finch called over.

"The one from the council?" I said.

"Yes, that's the one. Open it," she said.

I took out a few sheets of paper. One was a set of instructions, and the second, a thicker piece of card, quite large, had a list of political parties and their candidates.

"Pick someone," she said, like I was shopping for ripe mangos at the local Asian store.

"It's your vote Mrs Finch," I replied.

She leaned forward and took my hand, her wrinkled skin rough in my smooth palms, her grip weak in my fingers. She seemed frail, much more than when I left for Mycombe Girls.

"No, dear. The future belongs to you, not a bitter, old woman like me," she said, handing me a biro.

I looked at the piece of card. Mrs Finch watched, poker face, as the pen hovered above the names.

"It's too hard, what do I know about politics?" I said.

"Politics isn't just about knowing, it's about feeling," she said. Her eyes flickered with excitement, some sense of fulfilment that she'd found in this gesture. "Is today going to be a historic day, or *an* historic one?"

I took the biro and put the cross neatly in the box, placed the card back into the envelope and carefully closed it. I was shaking from this simple act; that I could have a say in my own future. Mrs Finch seemed content and got comfortable in her chair.

"Run along now dear, the postal vote deadline is 5pm."

Outside, it was balmy. A tension hung around the town as thick as the muggy air. Folk walked around without making eye contact, like they'd short-changed you. Whilst others, a small minority, went out of their way to be friendly. Kevin was on his bike, pulling along an advertisement for an anti-immigration hotline, highlighting the new Tory drive to rid the country of illegals. He smirked as he rode past, humming 'Hitler has only got one ball'. It bugged me at first, but then, anything that kept him off the corners... I slipped the envelope into the letter box and went home.

In the evening, Trina dropped by to say hello. If it wasn't for her visits while I was at school, Meghna would've gone round the bend with just Morose and Incontinence for company. They'd decided to learn English together and spent hours every day tasting each other's dishes and practicing the imperative, so they could write down cooking instructions.

"Where have you been?" said Trina.

"You are not going to be believe this." I told her of Mrs Finch's generosity, and we talked about how we'd voted until Meghna served up her experimental dessert. She dolloped it on a quarter plate and waited patiently for the verdict.

"Yuck... it's disgustin', Amma," I said, spitting it out in the sink.

Accha, in theory, the ingredients work,* said Trina.

Nje, perhaps the cumin was a bad idea?* said Meghna, looking to Trina for a nod of encouragement.

"I 'ope ya in't gonna give that to poor Mrs Finch. I 'eard the result of the last dish ya sent over," I said.

Her tongue liked it, just not her bum, said Meghna.

The two of them fell about each other, giggling like schoolgirls. Trina turned the heat down on the main hob, took a spoonful of shutki and blew on it to cool it down. She squirted some lemon juice on it, planted a stalk of coriander as garnish and fed it to Meghna like she was the maharaja's wife.

Ya Allah, Sakthi, come taste. Isn't this the best shutki bhuna you've ever had?* said Meghna.

I scraped some out of the pan with my pinkie. Oh, wow, it was to die for. Somehow, she managed to combine the heat of the chilli, without compromising the smokiness of the dried fish in the least.

"Yeah, it's OK," I said, and sat in the corner, arms folded, making myself as small as possible.

Ish, your mother must be so proud of you, happily married, expecting your first child and a pakharajuni[78], yet still so young. She'll be telling the whole village,* said Meghna.

"Pregnant? Nobody tells us anythin' these days!" I said.

78 Amazing home cook.

Well, an aunt is as good as a mother, said Trina.

Meghna kissed her forehead. Trina washed up the dish that I had left in the sink earlier and mopped the floor whilst Meghna put the shutki back into the oven for storage.

"*Accha*, and you Meghna Aunty, how you did bote?" asked Trina.

"Your uncle took my bote," replied Meghna. In English!

"It's vote, not bote," I said.

Na, Sakthi, bote is the Bengali word for vote. You don't hear us telling the English that pyjama should be pronounced *paijama*!* said Trina.

The two of them had a right good chinwag about politics and the rise of anti-Islamic sentiment in The North, which my Bengali was not good enough to follow. In that instance, it dawned on me that Meghna and I always talk about household chores. We talk through touch, smell, and taste, but spices can only communicate so much – anger, love, happiness; they certainly can't express in-depth political argument. Have I missed a trick again? Have I pushed her away? All because I couldn't be bothered to speak back to her in Bangla. Meghna went up for Isha prayers and left us girls to catch up in the kitchen.

Arre beti, why do you look so sad? She loves you more than anything else in the world if that's what you're sulking about?* said Trina.

"All this time I have been running off to Mrs Finch to read those stupid books, when Meghna..."

A mother's love—

"*Thik ache*, but that is what all mothers say. It is not just her love I need though, it is her blessing. And blessings must be earned," I said.

She's learning English, Sakthi, not just because she wants to fit in, which she can't by the way because of Uncle, but because she wants to be able to talk to you, write to you, her beloved daughter who she misses so much, she said.

"*Nje*, about what?" I said.

I don't know, politics, literature. She grew up within a stone's throw of Lalon Shah, one of the greatest poets in Bengali history, it runs in her blood, in your blood… Why else do you have such good Bangla pronunciation. Where else did you get your intelligence from? Trina said.

"Father, I thought," I said.

"*Kenno*, why? Because he is a man?" she said.

At around midnight, me, Trina and Meghna prepared some narkel-er meeta for seheri[79]. I grated the coconut flesh and ground the cashew nuts in a mortar and pestle. Meghna took the ingredients, put them in a bowl and mixed in sugar, eggs, condensed milk and ghee. Trina added saffron to make it look pretty, and sprinkled pistachios and almonds on top of the mixture before placing it on the stove. When it was done, I let it cool in the fridge and turned on the telly.

We watched the result come in. We lost, I lost. So much for that newfound sense of empowerment. And what would this mean for us, our community? I laid half-awake with a queasy feeling in my gut, like I was watching the tranquil ocean rapidly drawing back, knowing full well that moments later a tsunami would crash down upon us and drown us all in its dark, briny waters.

79 A pre-dawn meal before a fasting day.

The burka

When the Islamic channels broadcast the news that the hilal[80] had been spotted high up in the Arabian sky, my stomach rejoiced. The summer days had been long, nothing had changed there. But in recent years Father had forbidden us from binge eating in the night during Ramadan so we could feel the real hunger of the downtrodden. "Just think about those poor Afghan refugees who have been re-settled in Lapland, imagine how long their days are," he said, and he was right, but my hunger was well beyond the help of moralisation.

A little after sunrise, Father got up to wash for Eid prayers. He'd left his bedroom door ajar, and through the crack I could see him getting undressed. Lungi fastened tight round the waist; he slipped his pants off underneath almost like he was disgusted by the sight of his own penis. When he pulled his t-shirt above his head, I could see a bunch of dark lines running across his back from each shoulder blade to the bottom of his spine. I must've been half asleep still, but I could swear right then, his back twisted and morphed into this phantom, sharp teeth baring, bloodied eyes enlarged, and growled so loud the whole world must've shit a brick, another moon. I ran to the kitchen and held Meghna tight for comfort.

Dast arrived a little before seven o'clock in a panjabi that reached down to his ankles. He's grown a thick beard that makes him look namazee[81], which he accessorised with a deadly serious face.

80 The crescent moon.
81 Pious.

"Ya reyt, Dast?" I said.

"*Assalamu'alaikum*," he replied.

"*Wa'alaikum as-salam.* All good at the resto? I 'eard yer strugglin' to cope with the workload from all the extra business."

"Everythin'll be fine, *insha'Allah.* I 'eard ya aced yer Arabic, top of the class yer ol' man said. Says you'll stay there to do yer A-levels 'n' all."

"Yeah, it in't that bad after all."

"*Mash'allah.*"

I haven't heard that many Arabic words come out of his mouth in all this time I've known him, and now they're in every other sentence. I looked at him, hands on my hips, head tilted like a question mark, but he waited in the lounge in silence, eyes turned down to the ground. When Father was ready, the two of them left together to the mosque.

"What's with him?" I asked Meghna.

It happens to all the boys. They have their fun, then they start getting serious when they have to get married, she said.

"Married? *Na*," I said.

Nje, moina. It's not just the girls who are arranged.

"But he in't the marryin' type, Amma."

Thik ache, you'll see.

Meghna and I prepared the food for the day. Bhajis and bhunas, the house was overrun by spices, floating in the air, stinging your eyes and itching your nostrils till you sneezed that blissful sneeze of ecstasy. Meghna took the thick cut aubergine circles we had marinated with turmeric, cumin, and chilli. She placed them tenderly in the oil, turning them from side to side as a mother does a suckling infant, from one breast to the other. At the same time, she added the green mangoes into the hilsa khatta and kept an eye on the tandoori.

I hovered around her impatiently. When the aubergines had softened and browned, I lifted them straight out the pan and bit into them, tearing away at the purple, crumply skin and relishing that soft, succulent core. The taste of that first, delicious morsel of food, the tickle on the back of the throat, sent me to seventh heaven. Mouth-watering, the salt, the spice, endorphins flooded my brain and I floated round the house all morning on a chilli high.

At lunch time, the men returned from the mosque for a quick bite with the imam, who despite his shameful expulsion from the school board, continued to lecture all around him on how to be good Muslims. Father still wasn't aware of his reputation, and despite the urge to scream his crimes to the entire world, I kept my lips sealed to honour the promise I'd made to Beydaan. I brought out a bowl of water with a lemon so they could wash their hands and eat in the lounge.

"Sakthi has become quite the A-grade student," the imam began.

"Thank you. I can't thank you enough for the way you single-handedly pulled her out of the gutter," said Father.

"We were lucky, caught her just in time, we've got Allah to thank for that. You know, it's so easy to lose the path," he said, looking at Father.

"Yes, brother," said Father, rubbing his sleeve.

"But we'll change things one by one if we have to, right Dastgir?" he said, placing his hands on his knee.

"Thank you for showin' us Allah's will," said Dast.

God's will? What about yours, you daft 'apeth? I looked at him in bewilderment. He's lost something. He smiled at me, but not like before, you know, that ear-to-ear grin that was so contagious you couldn't help but smile back.

"*Alhamdu lillah*," said the imam.

"Farzana, tell your mother to serve the food," said Father. But Meghna, the good hostess that she is, was already on her way out the kitchen with tandoori chicken, samosas and sheesh kebabs alongside some naan, raita, mango chutney and satkora pickle.

The imam, as usual, stuffed his fat little face. I wanted to garotte him with his own beard but resisted the temptation.

Instead, when they finished eating, I again brought out a bowl full of water and lemon so they could wash their hands. This time I made the water a little too hot, just a small dig at the imam, so he recoiled when he dipped his hands in. He smiled at me to acknowledge where the power now lay.

When we had fed the men, Meghna and I finished the curries that were left from yesterday. They always taste better when they've been left to stew overnight. After, we went upstairs to listen to some of her old Bengali records which she'd brought over from Bangladesh when she first arrived in London.

Early in the afternoon, a little after the Dhuhr prayers, there was an unexpected knock on the door. A bit groggy, I got up from my afternoon nap to answer it. Three women dressed in black burkas stood outside in the baking sun.

"*Assalamu'alaikum wa rahmatullahi wa barakatuh,*" said one woman.

"*Wa'alaikum as-salam,*" I replied, trying to work out who the hell they were when a familiar giggle gave them away.

"Zaineb?" I said.

"*Eid Mubarak*, Sakthi," she said.

"Zaineb! Aaliyah, Beydaan. *Eid Mubarak!*" I invited them in and introduced them to Meghna, who was charmed by the wit of the twins. Beydaan didn't speak a word and just nodded or shook her head.

"Lost her voice, innit," said Zaineb.

We went upstairs to my room as Dadhi was dozing on the couch. The girls lifted their veils, except Beydaan who was adamant she didn't want to take hers up, presumably in case Father walked in. I didn't think to question it, perhaps it was the norm in her culture.

Meghna brought in a half plate of samosas and some tea to tide us over until dinner. The witches on the tilla[82], reunited in our insanity, laughed about the year that had passed, and wept when we thought about school without Miss Qureshi. But it wasn't long before we turned to gossip.

"Ya seen him yet, your hubz?" asked Aaliyah.

"Seen, yeah, but the Black Paws won't let him near us," I said.

"On whose orders?" said Aaliyah.

"Take a guess," I said.

"He's a piece," said Zaineb.

"Innit tho," said Aaliyah.

"God, I miss him. That smile, his red hair, them freckles, the Manc lilt," I said.

"'Better to have loved, right, loved and lost, then never to have loved at all'. Innit what Shakespeare said?" said Zaineb.

"Fam, you think Shakespeare said everythin'! It was Beyoncé," said Aaliyah.

"That's what they say to comfort the broken 'arted. I reckon love's like chilli, once you've 'ad a taste, the whole world seems bland without it," I said.

"So, what, ya love him, right? Love," said Aaliyah.

I sighed. How can you know if it's love the first time? Without any previous experience, without any frame of reference.

Beydaan excused herself to go to the loo, which without the use of her voice she did in quite an unbecoming manner. She had a strange smell about her as she walked past, familiar, but I couldn't quite put my finger on the perfume. I asked the twins why she was being so quiet, but they insisted Beydaan was doing just fine, and I shouldn't worry my little head over her. When she returned, we tucked into the samosas.

"These are bare yum," said Zaineb.

"And spicy. God, you Bengalis like it hot," said Aaliyah.

82 A small hill.

"Swapped the birds eye chilli for Bengali Naga. Gives it an extra 'f-you'!" I said.

Beydaan hiccoughed. I gave her a glass of water, but she seemed at a complete loss on how to drink it under her veil.

"I've seen ya smash down hot chillies before, Beydaan," I said.

"D'ya know, Dorset Naga is one of the hottest chillies in the world, scientifically speakin'?" said Aaliyah.

"Is it really?" said Zaineb.

"It's 923,000 Scoville heat units, two hundred times hotter than tabasco sauce," said Aaliyah.

"Beast, man," said Zaineb.

Beydaan hiccoughed again.

"Y'alright, Beydaan?" I said.

"D'ya know, the longest episode lasted sixty-eight years? Some poor man in Iowa. First few decades he hiccoughed forty times a minute," said Aaliyah.

"That's mad, fam," said Zaineb.

Beydaan let out a burp, and then a giggle, deep in tone.

"Who is this?" I said.

She breathed heavily, her chest and broad shoulders inhaled and exhaled trying to control the hiccoughs. I looked through the mesh and slowly lifted up her veil to reveal a pair of blue, water-filled eyes.

"What the—? Tone!" I screamed.

"Shh, you'll give him away," said Aaliyah.

"But 'ow the 'ell d'ya find him?" I said.

"Duh, there ain' that many gingers sellin' vegetables down the local market in Shaleton."

"It's a soft g, like a j," Tone said, a little sensitive about his hair colour.

I wrapped my arms around him, and if it wasn't for the hiccoughs, I could've stayed like that forever. Oh Love, how I doubted you. Love, that singularity hidden so deep inside my heart now exploded in a big bang and filled me with warmth and light.

"Why the bleedin' hell 'ave you been hidin' all this time like?" I said.

"Ya never told the poor bastard ya love him. He wanted to hear it straight from the horse's mouth, innit," said Zaineb.

"Fam, ya dum? D'ya not get all the hints we dropped?" said Aaliyah.

"I love you, ya silly bugger, I love ya with all me heart," I said. We kissed, our arms entwined like the roots of a banyan tree.

"Err, do you two want some time alone?" said Aaliyah.

She went to keep Meghna company in the kitchen, while Zaineb sat by Dadhi to make sure neither would walk in on us. Father was in the toilet next door, so I spoke to Tone in whispers till he went back down to the living room.

Tone looked a picture, more a Picasso than a Monet. His face was covered in cuts, his body in bruises, tender to the touch. His hands wandered, I let them. I kissed his face to heal the wounds, our lips edging closer together until finally they locked. And after some time of looking longingly into each other's eyes, Tone's face became a little serious.

"Sakthi, there's summat I need to tell ya," he said. I prepared myself for the worst. I'd already said to myself that it was fine if he'd been with another girl. It'd be unreasonable to expect him to be faithful to a ghost.

"It's OK, ya don't 'ave to tell us," I said.

"No, I really should," he said.

"OK, if it 'elps ya," I said.

"What d'ya mean if it 'elps us?" he said.

"You know, if you've been with another girl, then that's fine by me. I'm just sayin' ya shouldn't feel obliged to tell us," I said.

"No, silly, it's not that at all," he said.

"It's not?" I said, slightly embarrassed.

"Sakthi, listen. Shaleton's changed a lot since you've been away," he said, with the same distressed face.

"Is that it, ya daft sod? I 'an't seen ya in ages, 'n' you wanna talk 'bout Shaleton?" I said, playfully wrestling with him.

"I'm bein' serious like."

"Ok. Jesus. Soz. 'ow d'ya mean Shaleton's changed?"

"The Mill Crew. The older boys 'ave left for the city, are in prison or 'ave jobs 'ere and there. There's a new lot comin' through, and they're well fuckin' radge."

"And you? You still int' gang?"

"Nah, fell out with one of the young'uns. Kev, remember, the kid ont' bus? Well, he in't a kid no more. Goes around calling himself Acid K!"

"Yeah, said he'd chuck acid on me face not long ago."

"See, they've taken it to a new level."

"Why is that?"

"Dad reckons this new government has given 'em courage. I hear 'em goin' round sayin' they want Muslims out," he said.

"And what d'ya fall out over?" I asked him. Tone looked away. "Me?"

"Nah, wanted out anyway."

I gave him a big, wet kiss, tongues and all like those kids on the rugby field at St John's. It felt amazing, Kelly was so wrong about that one. But our bliss was interrupted by that creaky floorboard on the staircase. I quickly let down Tone's veil and sat on my bed, pretending to eat samosas. The door opened. Father came in and told us that Meghna had been shouting for me to come and help set the table for dinner. Of course, I didn't hear a single thing, I was so transfixed by those gorgeous freckles and blue eyes. Aaliyah arrived, out of breath, only to see Father had already beaten her to it. He ushered us all out of the room and followed us down the stairs.

When we got to the kitchen, Tone sat down on the opposite end of the table to where Father usually sits. Meghna put all the curries out in her best crockery, and I set out the plates and water tumblers with the help of Aaliyah and Zaineb, brushing past Tone's body on every opportunity. Father came in with Dadhi, we all said the basmala[83] and tucked into the feast. Meghna served Tone with a few pieces of lamb bhuna, a spoonful of rice and some tomato and cucumber salad.

"Is everything alright?" Father asked, looking at Tone.

"She's lost her voice, innit," said Zaineb.

"And how does that stop her from eating?" said Father.

"Erm, sore throat," said Zaineb, flashing a look at me across the table.

"Gloves, he can't take his gloves off, it'll give him away," Aaliyah whispered in my ear.

"What's that?" said Father.

"Maybe Beydaan'd like some cutlery?" I said and ran over to the kitchen drawer and brought over a spoon and fork.

"Don't you use hands to eat in Somalia?" said Father.

"She's lost her voice," said Zaineb.

"So you said," he growled.

We had dinner in silence. Father watched us all eat with intense scrutiny. Tone, mortified that he was going to get sprung, managed no more than a couple of bites. Every time he lifted the fork towards his mouth, his hands shook so bad that half the pilau wobbled off and back onto his plate. Father cleared his throat and took a sip of water.

"Funny things are humans," he said, asking Meghna to pass over a bowl of hot water and soap.

"What d'ya mean?" said Zaineb, who presumably received a kick in the shin under the table from her sister judging by her expression.

"We're creatures of habit, aren't we?" he said. Zaineb twitched to answer, but thankfully on this one occasion she kept her trap firmly shut.

83 Islamic phrase meaning 'In the name of God, the Most Gracious, the Most Merciful'.

Father has something of the Italian mafia about him. The fitted suit, the well-kept beard. He speaks softly, like one of the characters out of The Sopranos, who'd make some astute, intellectual observation about life, before casually lobbing some poor bugger's head clean off their shoulders with an obscure weapon. He stroked his beard and looked directly at Tone.

"Yes, creatures of habit," he said again, standing up and taking a meat cleaver out of the kitchen drawer, his little armoury.

Tone clenched his fork sensing the impending danger.

"You see, you haven't said a word since you've entered this house—"

"She's lost her v—"

"Shut up," he said.

He walked behind Tone and slammed the cleaver into the dinner table, missing Tone's right arm by a few millimetres, but catching the sleeve of the burka so he couldn't move. Tone tried to pull out the knife with his weaker hand, but the blade was lodged deep in the wood. Father came back around and sat down on his seat, lit a cigarette, and took a large draw.

"Smoke? Or do you prefer rollies?" he asked Tone, offering him a fag. He blew the smoke all the way across the table. My legs were restless and by some defensive instinct I grabbed the saltshaker in my hand.

"The fork, you see. No Asian or African would have gone for the fork over the spoon to eat rice. So, I thought you must be a westerner. And then there was that thing you did with your hands before dinner, what was that? A cross?" said Father, stubbing the cigarette on a slice of lemon. He stood up and walked over to the kitchen drawer again, but this time he took out a fruit knife.

"Abba, I can—"

"*Haramjadi, bho,* sit down! So, you're not Asian or African, you're not a Muslim, so who are you? And then I thought about the final part of the puzzle. What girl leaves up the toilet seat? Other than those sinful hijras," he said, looking at me.

Oh God, I thought, would that be our undoing, a lousy toilet seat?

"So, you see. Like I said. Creatures of habit," said Father as he slowly walked behind Tone and put the knife to his throat. The twins let out a shriek. I got up to intervene, but Meghna silently pulled me back down on the chair.

Sakthi's Abba, come sit down, dinner is getting cold, said Meghna.

"Now, I can only think of one white, Christian, man, who would be dumb enough to come into my house, to cavort with my daughter, under my own bloody nose."

Accha, I don't understand. If you knew all this time, then why didn't you say something? Why play such games? And you, Sakthi, have you lost your senses?* said Meghna.

"Lift up your veil," he said, pressing the edge of the blade against his throat. Tone put his hand between Father's arm and his neck, but it was useless fighting against Father's strength. Aaliyah began to weep and held her sister's hand.

"You can't make her, it's not right," said Zaineb, defiant to the last.

Father laughed. And with one sudden movement he ripped off the veil, revealing Tone's face, pale as a ghost. Dadhi shook her head in disgust, Meghna gasped before showing her disappointment. Father lifted his arm to strike him but stopped at the last minute. He dislodged the cleaver from the table and used it to point to the door.

"*Shor-er baitcha.* Get out!" he said.

"Please, I'll do anythin'... I'll convert," said Tone.

"Next time I see you with her, I'll kill you," he snarled.

Father grabbed Tone by the scruff of the neck and showed him out. He slammed the door and picked up the first object his eyes fell on to beat me. Meghna and the twins could only stand and watch.

Vimto

Officer Iqbal introduced himself like a good old-fashioned English bobby, hat under his arm, big smile across his face. Over his radio, a voice crackled that the back has been secured. His partner came round the front of the house. Officer Smith was leaner than his colleague and wore a scowl like it was standard kit issued alongside handcuffs and batons. The two men stood shoulder to shoulder blocking the front door.

"Probably best if we come in," said Officer Iqbal.

I led the officers into the lounge and went to tell Meghna. She quickly dressed and ran down to the kitchen. Five minutes later she entered the living room with a tray full of tea and biscuits. Iqbal thanked Meghna about a million times, almost embarrassed by her kindness. His partner turned down the tea and walked around the room looking for something, his manners I imagined.

"Just a few questions and we'll be on our way," said Iqbal, to which Meghna replied in Urdu. "Sorry Aunty, my Urdu is terrible, to my dad's dismay."

"What is this about, Officer?" I said.

"I'm afraid there was an immigration raid on your father's restaurant last night after an anonymous tip-off. We found three men working without papers, and there was one other hiding upstairs who managed to get away. We're just trying to find—"

"Who sleeps here?" said Officer Smith, interrupting.

"Nobody," said Meghna, blushing.

"So why is there a pillow, a blanket and an alarm clock? Are you hiding someone in your house?" he said.

"Hiding? *Na-to*," said Meghna.

"Speak English, we're not in Pakistan!" said Officer Smith.

"Excuse me, Officer. Why are you searching the house? Don't you need a warrant for that?" I said.

"So, you're the smart one? Know your rights, do you?" he said, making air quotes. Smith found a copy of the Qur'an on the mantelpiece. Even the soft brushing of his fingers over the page riled me, like nails scraping down a blackboard. He took the book in his unwashed hands and pretended to recite the text.

"Allahu Akbar," he said in a mock Arabic accent before Meghna snatched the book away. He laughed and pointed at the picture of the Kaaba on the wall.

"Are you going to be GI Jane or Jihadi Jane when you grow up? Maybe you'd like to join the Islamic State?" he said to me.

"I think that's all we need for now," said Iqbal, springing to his feet.

"You can watch your dad go down on the afternoon news," said Smith, and left the house.

Iqbal apologised for his partner's behaviour and left his card in case we had any more information on the missing man or wanted to file a complaint. Meghna took the card politely and closed the door gently behind him.

"Let me call HQ Amma, it in't right the way he behaved," I said.

What good would it do? she said, putting the Qur'an back.

I switched on the local news and sat there frozen with disbelief at what I saw. The media was in on the sting, they caught everything on film! Immigration officers surrounded the Bismillah, blocking every exit like they were busting some Colombian drug cartel. The cameras followed the officers as they sneaked into the premises. When they got into the main dining area, I could see Dast in the background drop some cocktail glasses and run towards the kitchen.

"Cops!" he said, as loud as he could, before he was grabbed by one of the officers and put in handcuffs.

"I in't done owt wrong," he shouted.

But the more he struggled the more aggressive the officer became and finally he slammed Dast to the ground and knelt on his back to keep him down. Meghna drew a sharp breath.

Ya Ghafoor! Are they allowed to do that in England?* she said.

Po-faced customers made their way out whilst the rest of the staff were rounded up and told to sit up against one wall. Father came through from the back office clutching a whole bunch of papers. One by one they took the cuffs off all the staff leaving three, including Mr Shah the tandoor chef, who seemed close to tears. What'd happen to his little girls now if he got sent back to Bangladesh? The camera zoomed in on the officer speaking to Father.

"It's my duty to inform you that you are in breach of Section 15 of the Immigration, Asylum and Nationality Act 2006, and you will be issued a penalty notice within the next few weeks," said the officer.

"You can't do this, we'll go bust, we'll all be out of jobs," said Dast, spluttering with rage. "It's all we got!"

Ish, he's just put down the deposit for a new house for his amma,* said Meghna.

"Shut up," said the officer holding him down, and pushed his head against the floor. There was a deep cut above his right eye.

"Hey, in't that Officer Smith," I said to Meghna, who wiped a tear from her eyes.

The producer cut to the news presenter in the studio who gave some background to the situation. She then turned to a spokesperson from the Home Office.

"Is the government trying to send a message?" the presenter asked.

"Illegal labour cheats hard-working taxpayers, honest businesses and legitimate job seekers from employment opportunities," he said.

"The conservatives took a big hit in the election. Is the Prime Minister now trying to be tough on immigration?" asked the presenter.

"We are living in dangerous times and there is a grave risk posed to public safety by illegal immigrants in the UK," said the spokesperson.

"Is the Prime Minister pandering to the wishes of the Far Right?"

"Listen, there are no winners when it comes to illegal labour, not even the workers, many of whom have been trafficked and exploited by criminal groups. This has nothing to do with politics, and everything to do with the safety and security of our Great Britain, which the Conservative Party deeply care about, and the Labour Party will tear apart."

The presenter thanked the Home Office spokesperson and turned to a live stream from a reporter on the ground who'd been chatting with customers of the Bismillah.

"So, what do you make of all this?" the reporter asked.

"Such a pity, we love India, and we love curries, and I wish there was a way we could work something out," said one woman.

"Well, it's just another example of Muslims doin' what they want, makin' up their own rules. Won't be long before the whole country is under Sharia," said a man standing next to her.

"What does Sharia have to do with this?" said the reporter.

"Well, they're dilutin' our culture," he said.

"Think of it like Vimto, sometimes culture needs a little diluting, don't you think?" said the woman.

"They should all be sent back if you ask me. Thanks for the curry, thanks, but no thanks to the fundamentalism," he said.

"Shameful," she said, shaking her head.

"Why is it?" he said. "I just hope I get my money back."

"So hateful, so divisive," she said.

"Britain for the Brits," he said, and walked off before anybody could further question his beliefs.

I turned the TV off and sank back into the sofa.

Trina and Akaash came over as soon as they'd heard the news, but it wasn't till late in the afternoon that Father showed up having spent the night wandering the streets. Meghna made him a plate of saag and dhal, he ate and then went to his bedroom where he stayed till the Maghrib prayers. At around nine in the evening when we sat down to have supper, Father told Akaash what had happened. Apparently, Dast had turned the business around, but the kitchen couldn't cope with the demand. Recruiting onion cutters and dish washers to work long, hard hours was nigh-on impossible, so he gave the jobs to anyone who'd work. Dast offered them cash-in-hand and free meals. Father didn't ask any questions.

"How did they find out about the workers?" said Akaash.

"Some bloody bastard snitch," said Father.

Kev, I thought. It must be. Tone said they were up to something. Father paced around the confines of our living room, turning in tighter and tighter circles, winding himself up till he snapped.

"Desi sweat, blood, built this country. Pakistanis, Indians. Bangladeshis! The bloody commonwealth!" he shouted, thumping his fist on the mantelpiece. "Does that not mean anything to anyone anymore?"

God, first Meghna, and now Father with all this pent-up politics. But I preferred it much more when the ladies talked. Less chest banging, more empathy, that's what we need right now, that's what this whole world needs – a big dollop of empathy, like a spoonful of raita over a burning hot biryani.

"The Irish had it, the Jews, the Blacks, and now it's the turn of the Muslims. Tolerance is an illusion in this country, there's always someone to hate," said Father.

Uncle, what did they fine you? asked Trina.

"Twenty thousand for every illegal," said Father.

"*Ya Maboud*, sixty! You'll go bankrupt," said Akaash.

"*Na*, they'll reduce it for a first-time offence, but money isn't the biggest problem," said Father, his thumb and fingers massaging his temples.

"No?" said Akaash.

"I don't have a tandoor chef!" Father screamed.

"But Uncle, there must be hundreds out there," said Akaash.

"The good ones have opened up their own restaurants, the bad ones have opened up fast food joints. Others drive taxis. It's easier, better pay and more flexible hours."

Why don't you do the same, Uncle? said Trina.

"A glorified rickshawala? I'm a businessman!" said Father. Akaash twitched in his chair.

"Can't you get a chef from Bangladesh?" said Akaash.

"The bloody Tories. They passed a law, so workers coming from South Asia have to earn a minimum of thirty-odd thousand pounds to work in a British restaurant. No curry chef earns that, we'd all go bust!"

"Why don't you train up the locals?"

"*Arre beta*, we look after our own!" said Father. "Besides, you can't teach taste buds over months what they usually learn over decades."

Father has become a victim of his own success, or rather Dast's. His customers, for the most part, no longer stuff their faces with baltis of cheap, bland curry or complain of Delhi belly. They come from far and wide to discuss whether the coriander is overpowering the cumin. They don't pay with loose change no more, but credit cards. And now Father has had a taste of real money, every penny of which he sends back to build the mosque in Bangladesh, he doesn't want to go back to the days of mopping up puke from outside the shop window.

"*Aitcha*, I don't get it, how are the others surviving if they can't get visas for their kitchen staff?" said Akaash, stroking his goatee.

Trina put her hand on his arm. Meghna sighed. The room went quiet, with only the sound of spoons stirring sugary tea rattling in their cups. Father went back upstairs. We all knew the consequences of the raid. My marriage is the only way to pay off the fines and keep the restaurant running. It's no longer a matter of if, but when. And I pray that *when* is a day far, far away.

Live, and Let Live

Father still hasn't got over the humiliation of the raid. In the weeks that have passed, he's barely uttered a single word other than those he offers in prayer. The kitchen staff at the Bismillah have been doing their best to keep the place ticking over, but without Mr Shah, the restaurant is all but doomed. Dast called him our USP to sound all clever, and he was right. Since he was taken, Father has been doing the Z-reads way before any of the pubs rang for last orders.

Our own people turned against him, petrified of guilt by association, as did his hard-earned white customers, who tut-tutted as they walked by in the street. Sadder still, the locals turned against each other. Our differences should've brought us closer together, the intrigue, the natural human state of inquiry, but instead we treat each other with increasing fear and suspicion. More than once, Father has come home stinking of paint stripper rather than fenugreek after scrubbing anti-Islamic graffiti off the brand new metal shutters that protect the restaurant windows.

With all the media attention Father has become a tinder box of race-hate, and last Sunday the fuse was well and truly lit. It was, fair to say, the worst day of my life. After the Charity Shield cup final, the kids were out late in the evening kicking about placky bottles and small rocks to recreate all the goals. I was sat by my window playing red hands with Meghna, waiting for Father to come home so we could eat. But then Kevin stumbled down the alley, pissed out of his skull after the match.

What's he doing here? asked Meghna.

"Don't know," I replied.

When they saw him, the kids ran off home and he climbed up onto an old washing machine left out to rust, swigged his beer, and shovelled down a bag of chips drenched in tomato sauce. Out the corner of my eye, I could see Father in the fading light, head down, trudging down the alley. He walked past Kevin and took his key out.

"Muslims, out!" shouted Kevin, raising his right arm.

Father paused for a moment, his huge frame heaved a sigh, and then he opened the gate.

"You should fuck off back to yer own country if ya know what's good for ya, ya Paki bastard," said Kevin.

"Can't afford to eat well, but you can drink?" said Father.

"What d'ya say? Oi, Paki!" said Kevin.

"I've heard it all before," said Father.

Now a fully-fledged hooligan, with tattoos and shaved head, Kevin set his fish supper on top of the washer, glugged down the dregs of his Special Brew and walked right up to Father. They were the same height, but he was no match for Father in strength. Any sober person would've stepped down, but pride and beer forced him to stay. I ran down the stairs and called Tone from the landline (Dast would've made things much worse out of his loyalty to Father).

"Abba, come inside," I shouted from the back door, a little taken aback by my sense of care for this man who had caused nothing but pain over the last couple of years. He ignored me, and the two of them circled each other for an age like dogs in a fighting ring, their faces inches apart, bellies growling.

"Yeah, well I bet ya in't 'eard this. It was me that called the pigs on ya," said Kevin, spitting on Father's shoes. Father blew a puff of smoke into Kevin's face.

"What did you say?" said Father.

"You 'eard us, Paki," replied Kevin.

Father went to grab Kevin by the collar of his football shirt, but Kevin deflected his arm and the house keys fell to the ground. As Father bent over to pick them up, Kevin smashed the beer bottle over his head, sending him crashing to the floor. The drunk swayed a little and steadied himself on the dustbins. I ran out the door, shouting for Meghna.

As I reached the back gates, Father was crawling on his hands and knees, wiping the blood off his face. Tone arrived a couple of minutes later, my knight in shining armour, in his jammies and armed with a toothbrush.

"What ya gonna do with that like? We're fighting fascism, not tooth decay," I said.

"Sakthi, close the gate," said Tone, unimpressed.

"But Father?"

"I got yer dad."

Meghna joined me and begged Father to come in, but again he refused.

"Kev, put the bottle down, mate," said Tone.

"Shut the fuck up, Paki lover," Kevin replied.

"Yer mam needs ya, ya can't help her from behind bars."

"Just listen to yerself, 'yer mam needs ya', blah blah. You were one of us, but you've changed since ya got yourself some of that tight Islamic pussy. I bet Mr Jihad in't so happy yer bangin' his girl," he said.

Meghna looked at me disapprovingly. I did my best to tell her with my facial expressions that we hadn't had sex, I was far too embarrassed to say those words out loud.

"Yer drunk Kev, go home," said Tone.

"Come with us, Tone, ya belong in't Mill Crew."

"I don't wanna be part of that no more, Kev."

"You'll never be one of 'em, d'ya not get that? It don't matter 'ow much ya fuck that little Paki girl, 'ow much curry ya eat, yer white trash, you'll always be white trash, just like us."

"Right, that's enough like. You better fuck off right now before I twat ya one."

"You? Twat me? For this Paki?" said Kev, bending over in a fit of laughter. "If ya in't part of the crew anymore, we'll fuck ya up if ya lay a finger on anyone of us. Now, to sort out this sorry little cunt."

"Kev, come on mate, one last chance. It's not too late, no one needs to know this 'appened," said Tone.

Kevin grabbed Father, still a little worse for wear, by the back of his shirt collar. He gripped the neck of the bottle, his thumb over the lip, and went to bore the jagged glass into Father's crown.

"Abba!" I screamed.

"Kev, no. Stop!" said Tone.

Tone threw the toothbrush at Kevin to distract him and then jumped in to dislodge the bottle from his hand. The two boys fell to the ground and wriggled around in the urine-drenched alley. Kevin threw a few drunk punches, but most whistled past Tone's ear. One landed, bringing a groan from Tone, who lifted his fist to strike him, but stopped at the last moment. He pinned Kevin to the ground, chest heaving.

"Hit us ya fuckin' pussy! That's it, come on, yer just like us after all, in't ya?" said Kevin.

"I in't nothin' like you," said Tone, grasping Kevin's footy jersey so that he was a few centimetres off the ground. He let go and turned to check that Father was OK. But as he lifted his hand to wipe away the sweat from his eyes, Kevin reached down into his tracksuit bottoms, pulled out a knife and drove the blade in one swift motion straight into Tone's stomach. Tone collapsed to the floor.

"Tone!" I screamed.

"Sakthi, no!" said Meghna.

I ran out and pressed my palms round the blade to keep the blood in. Kevin lost himself for a second, some horrific realisation no doubt that blood runs red, not white, not brown, not black, not yellow, but red, bright red in this instance as it dried on his shaking hands, under his fingernails. As Kevin's future behind bars played out in his mind, Father picked up the broken bottle from the floor and slashed at his assailant's face, leaving a deep cut from the corner of his mouth up to the lobe of his ear. Kevin yelped with pain.

"You'll pay for this ya Paki cunt! We're gonna fuck up every motherfuckin' last one of ya," he said and stumbled off effing and blinding down the alley.

Father threw the bottle down on the ground and looked at Tone, who lay on his back, PJs drenched in blood.

"Hang in there, Tone. Abba, do something," I cried.

Father bent down on one knee, leaned in, and whispered something in his ear. Tone's eyes widened, and he looked at me and mouthed 'I love you' before closing them tight. Before I knew what was happening, Father placed his hands around the knife handle and pulled out the blade from his stomach, opening the wound. The blood came gushing out.

"Abba, no!" I screamed. "Amma *bachao*, help!"

Call an ambulance, Father said to Meghna.

"You bastard, ya did that on purpose. You bastard, I hate ya. I fuckin' hate ya," I said, desperately trying to stop the blood from spraying out. I could picture a knife clear in front of me, as clear as Macbeth saw the bloody dagger. I'd grasp it with my right hand and thrust the blade straight into his bastard heart, but I wouldn't pull it out. I'd push it farther in, look in his eyes and twist it so he'd feel the pain until he let out one, last pathetic breath.

"And who'll take care of your amma and her family then? You?" he said, wiped his hands on the napkins that Kevin had left on the washer along with his takeout, lit a cigarette and waited in silence.

It took forever for the ambulance to arrive. When it did, the pool of blood around Tone had encircled him and he was slipping in and out of consciousness. One by one the lights in the windows came on, and now, the spectators who'd watched the fight from afar clambered over each other to get front row seats for the main show – a Bengali girl weeping in the arms of her white lover. What a scandal! I felt a tap on my shoulder and watched in a daze as the paramedics stretchered him away.

The sound of crashing glass snapped me back to reality. Dast came sprinting down the back alley and stopped by Father, panting, hands on his knees.

"Round the front..." he said, gasping for air. "What 'appened here!?"

"Never mind. What going on?" said Father.

"It's the Mill Crew. They're smashing up all the windows along the main road," he said. Dast clasped his hands together and blew into them to make a hooting sound. And within seconds the Black Paws were clambering over the back walls and standing by his side.

Father got up to volunteer.

"*Nahin*, not you, Uncle. Yer hurt," said Dast, and ran off with the boys grabbing whatever they could use as makeshift weapons along the way.

I ran up to the bathroom but couldn't lock the door because the inside latch had been removed. I searched everywhere for some nail scissors, razors, anything I could use, but all the drawers and cupboards were empty save for sanitary pads and some bars of soap. Meghna opened the door and found me shaking underneath the sink. She gently pulled my sleeve up and ran her fingers along the scars on my forearm. It was soothing, not only her touch on my skin, but knowing that she knew. After a while, she picked me up, carried me to her bed and rested my head against her bosom while she counted prayer beads.

That night Shaleton went back in time. Burning tyres lay strewn across the streets, their rubber lungs billowing smoke that took on the shape of demons. Broken bottles, small rocks, old furniture, anything that could be hurled by furious arms littered the streets. In amongst the debris, phantom-esque figures wrapped in the England flag taunted and tormented the Asians then disappeared into thin air. When the red and blue lights finally came, there was only an angry mob of brown faces who redirected their rage towards them.

Accha, why are they arresting our boys?* asked Meghna. I went to the window to join her. *Why don't they run too?*

From Meghna's bedroom, we watched the long arm of the law face a hail of petrol bombs. They moved fast, fencing off the road to stop the riots spreading, and then held tight for reinforcements. There was a minute or so of silence as the youths restocked on makeshift ammunition, and the coppers, shell-shocked, took the time to regroup. When the missiles started again, they banged their batons on their shields, hoping to intimidate the mob. But instead, it was like a klaxon call and the number of rioters swelled to the hundreds.

One officer caught a brick on his helmet. He shook off the knock, and in a fit of rage broke the line and charged, baton raised high and shield in front, towards the rioters like a Teutonic knight. About ten metres from the barricades, he was smacked by another brick that smashed his face from the side. He lost his balance, tripped over some garbage on the road and tumbled to the ground. Then, a milk bottle bomb exploded a few feet away, spraying fuel all over his body armour. He lay there burning as the other officers stood and watched, outnumbered, and terrified.

Where are you going? said Meghna.

"Be right back," I said.

Sakthi? Sakthi, come back! You'll get hurt. Moina!

"There in't owt left to live for Amma. Might as well do the little good I can with what freedom I got before it's taken away," I said, running past Father as he was climbing up to the attic.

As I stepped out the door, I could hear bottles smashing on the ground and the loud crackling of a bonfire. In the distance, some white vans had been torched, their corpses smouldering in the evening breeze. Fireworks zipped inches above the ground and exploded metres in front of the riot police, a kaleidoscope as the lights reflected off their shields. I found the battle alluring, and the fact that my life had been torn apart minutes before made me even more reckless in the face of danger. The fallen officer's radio crackled, as he rolled helplessly on the ground. "Mike, there's a girl approaching. She's unarmed."

I prayed that one of those projectiles would hit me square on my head, that the decision to live or die could be taken out of my hands. No luck. Even Tragedy has it in for me. Out the corner of my eye I could see Dast signal to the others to hang fire and let me help the wounded man. I took my hijab off and wrapped it around him to smother the flames. God, I'll never hear the end of that. His knee was badly hurt from the fall. I helped him get up and he leaned on me for support as he limped back to his unit.

"Fuckin' cowards, the lot of you," he shouted, as we passed the line.

As soon as I was safe, the riot recommenced with added fury. I looked around the faces of the frightened officers, men and women, who hours earlier were tucking their children in bed and curling up in front of the TV with a cuppa, or a book. They looked on in stunned silence. How did it ever get so bad?

"Where's the back-up, chief?" I heard one man say.

"There ain't none, we've called in everyone. It's spread across all the northern towns. We have to sit tight till the army get here," she replied.

On the back of the ambulance, the paramedics carefully removed the stricken officer's helmet, revealing some nasty burns around his neck. Dried blood stuck like treacle on his cheeks, sweat-drenched blonde hair clung to his face, his eyes stared into the distance, his body shivered with adrenaline. It was that Officer Smith, from the raid.

"Will have to buy another, if I'm gonna join I.S.," I said to him, pointing at the singed hijab on the floor. He slid off the back of the ambulance and walked away without saying a word. I picked up the hijab and folded it neatly on the top of a police car.

"What you did was stupid, and brave. Thank you," said Officer Iqbal as he walked over.

"God, don't you sleep?" I said.

"It's all hands on deck at the moment," he said.

I looked down the road at the Asian youths who had swelled in numbers again, all angry, all chanting that the police were racist. How hopeless they must feel if they think that even the law is against them. What hope is there for them if they can't feel safe and secure in their own homes? And while I write this, I notice my shameful use of the possessive, because them, also includes me.

"All this..." I said with a sigh.

"This is how we lose them," he said.

Officer Iqbal offered me somewhere to wait till the violence died down, but I assured him I was perfectly safe to walk back home. The rioters stopped throwing their projectiles till I reached the house, where instead I got a barrage of abuse from Meghna. She slapped me hard across my cheeks and then hugged me tight. Father had already started taking down the suitcases for Bangladesh from the attic. But marriage was the last thing on my mind, even if it was my own. I sat on my bed, shattered, not knowing whether Tone was dead or alive.

Out the Frying Pan

Father used up three-quarters of the space in my suitcase with gifts for the groom's family, leaving hardly any room for my own clothes. 'Don't worry,' he said. 'You'll get so many beautiful saris on your wedding day, just take the essentials.' With that he set off to the restaurant to hand over the safe keys to Dast. Trina passed him at the front door, her melodic voice gave her salaam before she wandered into the kitchen, where Meghna was making snacks to tide us over on the eleven-hour flight to Sylhet. I waited for her anxiously at the top of the stairs and when she got there, I quickly pulled her into my room and shut the door.

He's alive, she said, putting a half-plate of piping hot lamb samosas on the dressing counter.

"Oh, thank God," I said, and hugged her.

But Sakthi, he's in intensive care, it's still touch and go. You need to be prepared for the worst, she said, and I nodded, tears streaming down my cheeks.

"Oh, ah... *ya Ghafoor!*" Trina's calf seized up. I laid her down on the bed and pushed her toes towards her head to stretch the muscles. She's almost in her third term and loving every minute of her pregnancy, except the excruciating leg cramps.

"Why are ya—"

"Oh God, your tears, they tickle when they fall on my feet," she said, bursting with laughter.

When the pain subsided, she stood up and without any warning tipped out all the designer shirts and trousers Father had put in my suitcase and chucked in my hijabs and robes, some toiletries, and told me to get my passport.

"Have you gone mad?" I said.

"*Taratari*, Sakthi. Hurry!" She closed the half empty case, took it downstairs and placed it in the hall next to a dozen others, bulging with goodies for family back home.

"OK, the joke is over. Come on, we got to get this stuff back in the case. Father will be back soon," I said, coming down after her.

"You are not going to Bangladesh," said Trina.

"What?" I said.

"You are not going to get married."

"Yeah, right."

Meghna came running into the hall from the kitchen with an oil sieve in her hands. She held me against her chest with her forearms and then looked into my eyes.

"Sakthi, moina, listen to me," she said.

"What's goin' on, Amma?" I said.

"You are going to run away," she said.

"Right. First. Can you two stop startin' ev'ry bleedin' sentence with 'you are going to'? I get it, you've mastered the future tense, nice one, but it's drivin' us nuts. Second, more important, marginally mind, I in't runnin' away!"

You can't stay here anymore Sakthi, it's not safe, said Trina.

"Abba'll go apeshit, ya know what he's like, Amma. We've still got bruises from last time," I said.

Meghna touched her ribs and winced as all the memories came back. She'd asked him if she could work as a seamstress and send money home to her father, who was struggling to look after her two younger sisters. He lost the plot, and if I hadn't been around for the school holidays, who knows, she might've made the red tops.

"*Accha*, and you Amma, what'll you do?" I said

I'll stay here with him, she said.

"He'll beat you."

Ish, he'll beat me anyway.

"Na, na, na! That in't good enough," I said.

Sakthi, I know it's hard to leave your mum, trust me, I've done it. But get an education, a good job, and then come back to get Meghna Aunty, said Trina.

"That'll take a decade, it's a death sentence for her," I said.

Well, then we both lose, said Meghna.

"And what 'bout yer family, Amma? What 'appens if he stops sendin' money, to punish ya? What'll 'appen to Nana? And Surma and Kushiyara, will they not 'ave to 'ave an early marriage? Why should they suffer, and not me?" I said.

They will find a way, insha'Allah, said Meghna.

"Insha'Allah!" I cried.

"Chol Sakthi. Come on, we do not have time," said Trina.

How can you weigh one person's hopes and dreams against another's, to see happiness as a zero-sum game? As I stood there frozen with indecision, the front door opened.

"I forgot the safe keys," Father said, picked them up from the shelf and left. The three of us held our breath, and as we exhaled in relief the door opened once more and Father stepped back into the house.

"You know when you get the sense that something isn't quite right, but you can't put your finger on it? But when I saw the half empty suitcase my curiosity got the better of me," he said.

Meghna and I looked at each other, Trina turned sideways on and covered her tummy with her hands instinctively. Father crouched down to unzip my bag. He stood up slowly, and then punched the wall so hard his fist left a dent in the plaster, and a framed picture of the Mecca Sharif jumped off its peg and smashed on the floor.

"Going somewhere?" he said.

It was my idea, said Meghna, voice catching in her throat.

Mouth, shut! he said in Bangla.

"I in't gettin' married, Abba," I said, and I held Trina's hand as tight as that day on the rickshaw. Perhaps he'd understand, there was nothing left to lose.

"*Aitcha*?" Father slipped off his shoes and rolled up his sleeves with the usual calmness that passes over him before moments of gratuitous violence.

Maf kore dao, forgive us,* cried Meghna.

"I work night and day to put a roof over their heads and this is how they show their respect," he said to a third party that nobody but he could see. God, I presumed.

"I in't gettin' married! Not to that monster," I said.

"You will marry whomever I choose before you disgrace this family," he said.

"You can't make us, it's illegal," I said.

"I don't care about the bloody law," he said, walked into the kitchen and came back with his weapon of choice. He hit me as hard as he could, and when the wooden spoon became dislodged from his grip because of the force of the beating, he used his palms to clout me around the head. My ears rang with the blows, my cut lips stung from the salty tears.

"I don't care if ya kill us," I shouted.

*Sakthi, *jao*, get out of here,* said Meghna, pulling at Father from behind until he started lashing out at her.

I scrambled up the stairs and into my room where I sat with my back pushed hard against the door waiting for him. I lifted my sleeves, and where the spoon had struck my arm were long, raised bruises like stigmata. But he never came. There was a moment's silence and then a shriek of pain. I ran back down the stairs just in time to see Father dragging Meghna into the kitchen by her hair. He slammed the door behind him. Trina stood shaking, one hand up against the wall and the other holding her orna back as she dry-retched in the corner.

"What the hell is goin' on... Trina?" I said, but her quivering lips weren't ever going to form any of the shapes you need for speech.

"Sakthi!" Father roared from the kitchen. I put my ear up against the door. The next time he shouted the sound went through the wood like it was a film of soap.

I opened the door to see Father standing by the cooker holding Meghna by her neck. He lit the stove and put the pan of oil Meghna had used to deep fry the samosas back on the heat. The blue flame, turned up to the max, licked the sides of the wok as the left-over pastry burned to a crisp. The oil bubbled and foamed, and when the rapeseed started to smoke, Father took the wok and held it a few inches above Meghna's head.

"You monster, you call yourself a Muslim," I said.

"Now, say it again, say you won't marry," he said.

"Swear down, I'll call the cops," I said, reaching for the house phone.

"You wouldn't dare," he replied.

Father pulled Meghna's head back by the hair to reveal the bare skin around the V-neck of her blouse. Her breathing grew deeper, her bosom rose and fell. She scrunched her eyelids tight and gritted her teeth. She'd been here before, the point of no return, where words only added fuel to the fire. Father turned towards me, and without looking away he poured the boiling oil over her breasts. Meghna wailed, arms and legs flailing, body writhing on the kitchen floor. Father tightened his grip, spreading his legs further apart to steady himself as the oil rolled around the pan.

"Stop, please stop!" I cried.

"Put the phone down, now, or it's the face," he said.

Trina came into the kitchen with Dadhi, and Father loosened his grip and put the pan back down on the stove. The old lady walked over to him and placed her hand on his arm.

Son, said Dadhi.

You stand up for her, but what about me? Where were you when I needed you all those years back in Bangladesh? he said. Father shed one, solitary tear, evidence of a beating heart. The tear fell into the pan and made a loud hissing noise that startled him. He quickly regained his composure, and waved Dadhi away.

"You've shamed this family, Sakthi!" he said.

He picked up the pan from the stove again and placed it directly above Meghna's face, tilted, poised to spill its piping-hot contents with the slightest twist of the wrist. Now fully acquainted with the pain, her eyes rolled back in their sockets and her body went limp. Father let go and she keeled over on the tiles.

"I'll marry him, stop, please stop," I said, getting on my hands and knees and kissing his feet for forgiveness.

"Sakthi means strength. You're not worthy of that name," he said, put the pan back on the stove and went upstairs.

I undressed Meghna and poured cold water from the sink over her burns, red and blistered, whilst Trina went to fetch the car so we could take her to hospital. She closed her eyes to cope with the pain and lay shivering in my arms. How could he do this to her, his own wife? Are there no bounds, no limits to the price of honour? And what misfortune could he have suffered to push him to this level of barbarity? I fought every hate-filled impulse to call the cops. I had to be strong despite what Father said, for Meghna, for the sake of her family back in Bangladesh.

"Sorry, moina," said Meghna, her eyes searching for forgiveness.

"It'll be alright, Amma," I said.

9. ROSH MOLAI

Yes, yes... yes

Turmeric, musky in the rural swelter, brought me round from a deep sleep like smelling salts. Father has banned the gaye holud[84], it's a Hindu tradition he said. But the village women insisted I sleep with a holud mix on overnight to brighten up my dark skin before the wedding. At midday, when I got up, the monsoon heat was suffocating. Beads of sweat ran off my forehead gathering the spice and dust from my cheeks. They wet my parched lips, sweet as earth, bitter as the sea. The gamcha[85] was stained bright yellow, soon it'd be red.

After lunch, I took a bucket bath with the cold water from the well to wash off the body mask, and the henna paste from my hands. Meghna, my aunties and cousins, as well as a handful of womenfolk from the neighbouring houses came to get me ready for the ceremony. Everyone gave their tuppenceworth on the colour of the lipstick, the hairstyle, or the number of bangles (which I had already put on to cover the scars). Everyone wanted a golden bride, who, when paraded in the evening sun would glow like Sonar Bangla in its mellow, slumbering rays.

Whilst the ladies gossiped, I slipped off into the peace and quiet of my own mind until the voices around sounded muffled, like I was underwater in the lily-covered fushkonis of Sylhet. Every so often, I came up for snippets of air, and conversation.

84 A ritual in Bengali wedding ceremonies.
85 A traditional thin, coarse cotton towel, often with a checked design.

She would've brought shame on the whole family with that white crow. We would never be able to marry off our own daughters, said my aunty, Father's elder sister.

I held my breath and went under.

What was I thinking? That Tone would be welcomed, open arms into my family? Even Meghna was holding out for me to get hitched to a 'nice, Bengali boy'. Marriages in our culture are between two families, as much as two individuals, how could I not get that? I pictured Meghna having a cup of tea with Tone's mum around our kitchen table as Mrs Drummond secretly topped up her brew with gin and threw random, racist insults. I mean, what planet am I living on?

More air, more conversation.

A parent has the child's best interest at heart and knows what's right for them, often better than the child knows what's right for themselves, said another woman.

I dived below.

It's true that I owed a lot to Father. I had a roof over my head, I never went a day hungry, apart from when we were saving for that first trip to Bangladesh, and I went to a good school. He'd done this much for me, so why wouldn't he also make a good choice of husband? Except, it isn't for me, is it? It's for himself and some dark secret that I swear to God I'm going to find out.

At least he's a Sylheti, said one of the village women, prompting some of the older generation to nod in silent agreement.

I went under again.

What was Father thinking? That I'd not set my eyes on anyone else? He should never have brought me up in England, if he wasn't ready to gamble that I might go for a white boy. Did he really think I'd fight evolutionary instinct and choose my mate from a limited gene pool of British-Bangladeshis? While under, I found Tone floating around with me, equally lost. Would he still love me after everything that's about to happen? I must keep faith, that there is a reason to live beyond all this pain. That wrongs might yet be righted. That I might yet still live to control my own fate and somehow, someday break free. For what is the Future, if not the rambunctious companion of Hope?

One last gasp.

She's just a child! snapped my other aunt, Trina's mam, so loud that she dragged me back into full consciousness.

I looked in the mirror. They'd shaved off my moustache and plucked my eyebrows into two thin lines, so my default expression was that of inordinate, perpetual surprise. I barely recognised myself after being pasted with layer upon layer of makeup – a Bengali geisha.

"Take it off, take it all off," I said.

But brides should be beautiful, protested one of the village women.

Meghna asked everyone to leave the room and finished dressing me alone. She gently pulled the comb through my hair and then tied it into one neat ponytail, ready for the hairdresser. She lifted up the heavy wedding sari around me, ensuring that the folds fell correctly and the gold embroidery sat prominently around my neck and shoulders.

Sakthi, moina, I may not have you alone again. There will come a time in the next few days where you will have to lay together with your new husband, said Meghna.

I remained silent.

Accha, in Bangla we have an expression. We say, 'whoever kills the cat on the first night, rules the marriage'. Do you understand what that means?

"*Na*, Amma, no idea," I said.

In the olden days, the Raja got married to his Rani with a mighty feast. After the celebrations, when the newlyweds entered the bridal chamber, the Rani's pussy cat meowed. And the Raja said 'one'. When the Raja took a seat on the bed to take off his shoes, the pussy cat meowed again, so the Raja said 'two'. When a conversation began between the Raja and his wife, the cat meowed once more, but this time the Raja pulled out his sword and cut the poor pussy's head off.

"Right."

In the morning, when the Raja requested a glass of water and the Rani told him she was tired, he counted again, 'one', and the glass of water came within a matter of seconds.

"And 'ow is that meant to help us, Amma?"

Don't give up your chastity on the first night, or he'll treat you like a housemaid for the rest of your life. And there are other consequences for a young woman, she said, looking at me in the mirror.

"And 'ow am I gonna do that?"

You're gifted with language, use your words to protect you. If he's a good man, he'll listen, he'll wait.

"And if he in't?"

Then forgive your amma for bringing you into this world.

The whole village turned up for the wedding, everyone from the elder to the backstreet dentist. The architect was in the corner nervously tugging on a bidi, trying his best to show Father he was there, yet avoiding any direct confrontation. The servants walked around behind their masters, fanning away flies and heat with large bamboo pakhas[86]. I looked around for Jyothi, the chaiwala, but he was nowhere to be seen. Perhaps he couldn't get away from his stall? Maybe the hijras had duffed him up? They didn't look the sort who just wanted a cup of tea.

In the courtyard they were putting the final touches to the marquee for the feast, fairy lights the colours of the Bangladesh flag hanging down off the side of the walls like the branches of a

86 Hand-held fans often made of wicker.

weeping willow. Then someone shouted that the barjatri[87] could be seen at the bottom of the hill.

The damand is coming, block the gates! shouted one of the servants from halfway down the coconut-strewn path.

The cousins leapt into action, barricading the door with colourful ribbons. I tried to steal a glance, but they were too far away to make out faces. When they got to the front gates, I could hear this nasal voice bartering to enter the house. God how I wished it wasn't symbolic, that we could set the amount so high they would have no choice but to turn around and go back home.

What will you give, damand? my cousins asked the groom.

Five thousand taka, he said.

That's not enough for such a young bride, and such an old man like yourself, they teased.

Then how much? he asked.

Ten thousand taka for every year that separates your birthdays. And they all burst out in laughter.

How about a round, one thousand taka for each of you, he said. What a cheapskate! And how could such a trivial custom get under my skin so bad? Father ordered them to let the groom's family in. After everyone had freshened up, they sat down for the nikah[88], men with the groom and women with the bride in separate rooms. The maulana[89] came up to me with Father, the groom's father, and the village elder as a witness.

"Abdul Sarkar Ripon of Howpara, Sylhet District would like to marry you. Do you consent?" said the maulana, a little surprised when he saw my face for the first time. He looked at the village elder, who signalled for him to continue. The maulana twitched uncomfortably and dried the sweat from his forehead.

"Ma, think how happy it would make your Amma and her family in Bangladesh to see you married," said Father holding my hand, tight, like a vice.

87 The groom's wedding party.
88 The Islamic marriage contract of the Bengali wedding.
89 A Muslim man revered for his piety.

"Yes," I said, looking at Meghna weeping besides me.

He repeated the question three times before the men went off to ask the groom if he accepted me to be his wife. We signed the marriage certificates and the groom's family used my wedding ring as the den mohor[90]. In return, Father had offered him a British passport, and a share of the restaurant as a dowry – some Hindu traditions it would seem were allowed.

The groom walked up to the dais where I sat. I covered my face with my sari, as all good Bengali brides should, and he took his place beside me as the maulana recited a few verses from the Qur'an. He looked at my husband sternly, as if directing his words to him. The words were gorgeous, and for the one I love, I'd have received them with a servant's heart, ready to dutifully carry out the command. But for a man I've never met? It was a tall order.

The maulana asked the groom to place the ring on my finger. My new husband grabbed my hand and yanked it towards him. My body twisted uncomfortably to face him, and as he forced the band over my knuckles, I saw his face for the first time since that picture he'd sent Father a couple of years back. Photoshop was kind to him. My stomach turned at the thought of being in his arms, of having him between my legs. After the Islamic ceremony came the Bengali customs. Meghna spent all of this period bawling her eyes out like she was crying for both of us.

One of my cousins took the pallu of my sari and draped it over both me and the husband so we were wrapped together in a cocoon of stifling, bling-laced georgette. She placed a mirror in front of him so he could see my reflection.

What do you see, dolobhai[91]? she said.

I have seen the moon, he said. I hurled in my mouth but managed to swallow the vomit.

The groom placed a garland over my head, but when I refused to put one over his he seemed hurt. Even ogres have

90 A set amount of money, property given to the bride by the groom.
91 Affectionate term for brother-in-law.

261

a heart, I suppose. Trina's mam approached with a tray full of sweets and a glass of milk. She put the glass in my hands and moved my hands with hers so that I lifted the glass up to his lips, apparently to increase our love for each other.

The western idea of marriage is baffling. If you tie the knot at the peak of your love, the only natural way to go from there is down, isn't it? she whispered in my ear.

He took a sip and wiped his mouth with his sleeve. But when he brought the glass to my lips, I turned my head away. It lit a fire within him, the desired effect.

You won't make a fool out of me, he said tenderly, giving everyone the impression that he was whispering sweet nothings in my ear.

He took a spoonful of rosh malai from the sweets tray and placed it by my mouth, but I pressed my lips tight. He raged. He held my chin between his forefinger and thumb, digging his fingertips into my jaw to force open my mouth, but I bit down even harder. Finally, he pried my teeth apart with the metal spoon.

Not so rough, such a young bride needs to be treated gently, nurtured, she's your responsibility. Treat her with love and respect, and she'll love you back, my aunt told him.

Who was she kidding?

Now, darling, be a good wife, don't embarrass your damand, she said, imploring me to listen on this one occasion. I opened my mouth and swallowed down the milky sweet together with any shred of dignity that remained.

Outside in the sandy courtyard under the marquee, the wedding guests took their seats for the feast. The baburchis[92] had

92 Chef and caterers.

prepared an enormous meal of richly spiced curries and piles of saffron-coloured rice. They raced around the tables, serving food, and clearing plates in shifts so everyone got a chance to sit and eat – even the chancers who pretended to know the bride and groom. There was still no sign of Jyothi though. Does he know, I wondered. He must, everyone knew. Even the guy picking wax out of people's ears with metal hairpins was here handing out his phone number.

I should've been like a typical bride, gutted to leave my mother's arms, sobbing into the folds of my sari, head down contemplating the pain that awaited me on my wedding bed. But I couldn't help but look around. Meghna stayed by my side, whilst Father went off to check on the centre table, reserved for the closest family members. He'd ordered a feast of fried hilsa, prawns as big as your hand and a whole spit-roasted goat stuffed with a grilled chicken stuffed with a boiled egg. It made me want to become a vegetarian.

Some travelling Baul[93] singers swung by on the promise of free food. They mesmerised the guests with their Lalon songs, though a substantial religious minority frowned and moved as far away from the music as they could. The hijras came too, dressed to the nines in sparkle and shine. They swayed their straight hips and glared at people, like the women that Picasso drew from Avignon. Angular chins and wide shoulders, their big feet traipsed along the sand as they twisted and turned before collecting their money and blessing the home.

A photographer set the stage around us for the compulsory photo shoot. One by one the guests sat next to the newlyweds. The shutter opened and closed, and between every flash, I got a few more glimpses of my husband, till I could put them all together to make a Dadaist collage of his face. He is fat, not grotesquely, but enough for a substantial double chin. He is old, and just where his turban meets his temple, I could make out a

93 A musician that follows the teachings of the Bengali mystic Lalon Shah.

receding hairline. It didn't take long before my head sank, and I assumed the default bridal position.

You should be happy, today you'll become a woman, teased the photographer, a young man, a little older than me. He used the future tense, and I regretted the things I'd done in the marriage ceremony.

Towards the end of the line of aunties and uncles I never knew I had, finally I saw Jyothi. I wanted to leap out of my chair and run over to give him a great big hug, and one from Trina, but that would have been most unseemly for a Bengali bride. Besides, I didn't know if I'd even be able to stand with the weight of all that gold around my neck and the embroidery on my sari. When the room was almost empty and guests were all eating, he approached the stage.

Jyothi Bhai! I said, instinctively referring to him as family.

Sakthi, he said, in a gentle Sylheti lilt, placing his hand flat on his chest as way of offering his salaam. Somehow, from somewhere, he'd managed to rustle together a suit and tie, which despite fitting him in length, hung off his body like the skin of a baked aubergine. The waist of his trousers was all scrunched up and held up by a belt buckled through a self-made slit a few inches further in than the last hole. His shirt, without the fat and muscle to keep it in place, untucked itself.

Bap-re bap, taratari bouwka, come on, there won't be anything left if we carry on at this rate,* said the photographer, keen to get to the banquet before the grilled pheasant had all been eaten.

Jyothi stepped up onto the stage and kneeled beside me. His eyes were sunken, his jaws, his teeth skeletal. His skin was pale, and he had this terrible cough that bothered him enough that on occasions he bent over double in pain. Meghna suggested he fill his belly with biryani and come back after he'd been fed, but Jyothi insisted he wasn't hungry.

Aitcha, are you a relative? the photographer asked him.

Na, I'm the chaiwala. said Jyothi.

*The chaiwala! Is there anyone else, perhaps the fisherman, or the rickshawala?" he huffed. Meghna looked at him sternly. *Tik asse*, please sit on the groom's side.*

Father returned from the food tent and before he could get a handle on what was happening Jyothi collapsed. Father caught him like he would a fragile vase, and in that moment of contact when they locked gazes, I swear I saw a connection. Father's eyes widened like he'd downloaded a heap of lost photos from a memory stick. But when everyone's glares turned on him, he let him fall to the ground and shatter into a million pieces.

Baba[94], forgive me, he said, looking in Father's eyes, arm extended as much as his strength would allow.

You shouldn't have come, said Father, his hand easily fitting around Jyothi's biceps. He led him out the door.

Meghna urged me to keep calm. On so many occasions she'd been right, and I hadn't listened. This time I gave her the benefit of the doubt. But when Father came back, I couldn't help but protest.

"Why? Abba, why can't he stay?" I said.

"He wasn't invited," said Father, rubbing his sleeve.

"And why d'ya always do that with yer arm?" I said.

"Enough!" he said and walked away.

94 Honorific word used to address an older man, but also means father.

The Bridal Rack

The mattress had been made up immaculately for the phul shojja[95]. Pink and lilac petals lay scattered across the ironed, white sheets, tucked in tightly around the edges like one of Father's restaurant tables. Hurricane lamps flickered by the feet of the four-poster bed. Their paraffin overwhelmed the scent of the rose and lavender, giving the sensation I was on a funeral pyre, not my marriage bed. God how I wished those flames would engulf me, to end things here and now. I lay there still, arms folded, legs crossed, the bridal gown and the gold weighing me down till I sank into this sea of despair and self-pity. I thought of Meghna, of the millions of others who'd gone through this as a rite of passage. What made me so special? What gave me the right to moan?

Opposite was a dressing table with a large mirror. I looked into the glass. In the reflection I saw Meghna, I heard her screams.

"Is this how I was conceived, Amma?"

A blood tear rolled down her cheek. She reached out to me. I got up and reached out to her, but the illusion was shattered by the surface of the cold, hard mirror.

The room was bare. In the low light the peeling paint, the cracked ceiling and the damp that had risen up the walls were hard to make out. Perhaps that's why Meghna insisted on the lanterns, so I couldn't see the face of my tormentor.

95 Consummation of the marriage.

266

The doorknob turned. I sat bolt upright in bed. The rusty hinges creaked as the door opened. My husband's silhouette took up the frame, backlit by the strip light in the landing. He is short, and despite the pot belly, he has wide shoulders and muscular arms. He got into bed and watched me in the mirror, his back against the headboard. I felt naked under his lustful gaze. I could see he was touching himself under the sheets.

Take your clothes off, he said, twitching, choking as he jerked off harder, faster.

He crawled forward and sat right behind me on his haunches. I felt his breath on the back of my neck. I froze as he unravelled my sari, starting at the top and then releasing the folds from around my hips. He worked his sweaty palms around my waist and then up my stomach. He seized my breasts with both hands and pulled me back, so I lay flat on the bed. Resting his weight on one elbow, he ran his fat thumb under the hooks of my blouse and pushed my bra up till it sat around my neck like a noose. He lifted up his longi and placed both his knees between my legs. I felt the tickle of a bead of sweat trickle onto my collarbone, where it stayed in the divot, unable to escape his slithering tongue as it worked its way up my body.

I could taste the garlic as he tried to give me a Frenchie. With one hand, he held down my right arm above me so I couldn't turn my head. The other hand slid up my left thigh and moved my undies to the side. I could feel him, hard, throbbing. His eyes met mine in one last try to get an emotional response, but my mind was elsewhere. In the Dark Peaks to be precise. I had planned it all out, my first time with Tone. We'd sneak away to Stannage Edge, watch the sunrise, and then make love in Robin Hood's Cave. 'It's Baltic like,' he'll have said, but I'd keep him warm in my arms. A tear rolled sideways down my cheek and into my ear.

His penis was pressed against my labia now. I gritted my teeth and tensed my body as he got ready to enter. Meghna was still there, watching in the mirror. I remembered what she had told me before the wedding ceremony. With my free arm, I made a V shape with my fingers and slid them around his penis to control the depth of the penetration. And then I spoke to him, gently.

We don't have to do this tonight, I said, but he took my arm and lifted it up to join the other one above my head.

I'll do what I want, when I want, he said.

Wouldn't it be so much nicer once we got to know each other a bit better. It would mean so much more.

Mouth, shut, it puts me off.

"*Na, na, na,* I don't want to."

Slap! And as quick as I could feel the sting on my cheek, I was back in Shaleton, head up against the door, listening to Meghna's cries. He lifted his knees off the bed and supported his weight on the mounds of his toes, but just as he was about to push, I whispered in his ear a lie that'd hurt me as much as I wanted it to hurt him.

"You're not the first," I said.

His eyes lit up and he fell back on his knees. He flipped me over onto my stomach before he put his hand on the back of my head and pushed my face into the pillow so I could barely breathe. I passed out, I think. When I came round, I just remembered the motion of him above me, and that icky feeling of penetration. I lay there, limp, which pissed him off, but I didn't want to get hurt from resisting. And no, a woman in such a position can't just close her eyes and think of England. When he finished, I wished I were dead.

I woke up alone, dirty, degraded, right on the edge of the bed. My bare legs had been up against the mosquito net, and they bit through the mesh, so my ankles were all itchy and swollen. Still, something inside me stopped me from moving to the middle, even in his absence. I stayed there curled up like a foetus. My lips were dry, despite the humidity, and I could taste salt on the corners of my mouth. I pressed my hands down there. No blood, they told me there would be. Did it happen at all? Was this just a bad dream? I turned to lay flat, and an unfamiliar tenderness between my legs brought me back to reality.

Can I? said a faint voice behind the door. Meghna's.

I didn't reply.

She came in with a jug full of water from the well, as if that was going to wash away all the pain. I hated her, I hated everything around me. Pure hate, the kind you feel deep within in your bones. The cycle was complete. It was now my turn to hand down the suffering, the guilt, the shame, to the next generation like it was syphilis, passed on mother to child.

I've packed your bags, you'll go and stay with your in-laws for a few days, and then we'll all fly back to England. Your husband will join us as soon as we get his passport, she said.

Meghna pushed up the mosquito net, so it hung neatly over the bed posts. She sat down on the edge of the mattress and brushed her fingertips along the creased, sweat-drenched sheets till she reached me, and then she placed her hand on my arm. I flinched, and she got the message. We stayed like that for a while, in total silence. Meghna collected the paraffin lamps and set them to one side of the room. She picked up the few petals that were left on the bed, opened up the shutters and threw them out of the window.

"Just ask us, damn it."

She tried to speak, but no words came out. Meghna climbed up onto the bed and caressed my forehead like she did when I was a child. She lay down by my side and rested her head on my chest. I could feel her tears fall on my skin.

Dukkito Sakthi, I'm sorry.*

"Pray it's a boy."

Meghna held my hand in her trembling hands. She said a few lines of prayer under her breath and then took something out from a knot she had made with her sari. At the centre of her mehndi covered palm, just about where the fate line crosses the head and heart lines, sat a small, white pill with the numbers 009 engraved on it. It glowed brightly in the morning light that came flooding through the barred windows. Meghna placed a pillow against the headboard and asked me to sit up. She took a glass from the counter and poured some water from the jug.

For the headache moina; if you want it to go away.

"But I don't hav—"

Shh, just in case.

The Needle

Of the dozen suitcases we took to Bangladesh, we returned with just half. One had Meghna and Father's clothes, two cases were packed with wedding saris and gifts and the other three crammed full of food and spices. My aunties packed everything from homemade wild orange and Naga achar to rolls of sundried jujube and mango pulp. Meghna also packed a tub of dried Bombay duck, wrapped in five layers of cling film to lock in the stench in case customs thought we were smuggling a festering corpse.

When we got home, Father went straight to the restaurant to check Dast hadn't committed any crimes, Dadhi went to sleep, and Meghna put all the food away, her belly rumbling with anticipation. From the kitchen window, she watched me go out to the back of the garden with a trowel. I rolled my sleeves up and I dug, the deepest hole I could, till I couldn't lift my arms anymore. I stood up, and Meghna joined me in a moment of contemplative silence. I slid the wedding ring off my finger, threw it into the pit, kicked the soil back and then stamped over it to flatten the ground so as not to arouse Father's suspicions. "I don't ever want to talk about what happened that night," I said. I went back inside and wrote in my journal.

Some days later, Meghna asked me if I wanted to go out for some fresh air, the novelty of which forced me to accept the invitation. Light on her feet and in high spirits, she looked at everything as if she were setting eyes on it for the first time. She picked dahlias, chrysanthemum, and black-eyed Susan, smelled their petals, then crushed each one in her fingertips to see how the colours bled out. She greeted every passing stranger, no matter how sour their faces. And questions, she had so many questions. Why are those chimneys so tall? Where have all the white folk gone? Do flowers really have feelings? Her new-found zest drove me up the wall, given the bleakness of my own future. But I was glad she could finally see what the world has to offer, instead of lying there on that sofa in her usual gloom.

We strolled up to the top of the hill to my old school, St John's. I thought of Tone and the number of times we'd done that walk together, rain or shine. Has he come out of hospital? Should I share my pain with him? How would he react? Apparently, I had quite a few questions myself. Mrs Finch would know what's best, she was a good agony aunt. Meghna looked out over the hills, dark clouds slaloming round their moody peaks. A tear rolled down her cheek.

Ish, ki shundor. It's beautiful, she said.

"Han't ya been up 'ere before, Amma?" She shook her head.

In the distance a fat band of rain lashed down on the neighbouring town, and bolts of lightning danced through the clouds, striking the mill chimneys all around. Even this enthralled her. I wondered what might happen if she read some poetry, God, if anybody ever reads poetry these days. I'm sure the world would be a better place.

By the time we got home, we were sogging wet. Meghna changed into her favourite sari, the one her mam had on when they found her body after the Great Flood washed her up on some paddy field miles away. It was tattered and discoloured, but she wore it in such a way that all the blemishes were hidden in the folds. Meghna went into her bedroom and came back with another sari, the one I ripped that day she gave me the burka.

My abba gave it to me the day I left for London. It belonged to my amma. If you...? she said and helped me to put it on. It fit perfectly.

We went into the kitchen where Meghna sliced up some onions and put them in the blender, added the Bombay duck and chili powder and mixed them until they had become a red-hot paste. She served it on a metal plate full of rice, like they would do in the village. We sat down on the kitchen floor, cross-legged, and she watched me stuff my face, just like she had done when I was a child. God, when did I stop being a child? Life certainly feels heavier, that's for sure.

"In't ya eatin' Amma? You 'an't 'ad owt all day. Remember, the doctor warned ya shouldn't let yer blood sugar level drop so low again," I said.

Na, moina. Watching you eat fills me with so much joy, I have no room left for anything else, she said with a big smile.

"Amma, yer so cheesy sometimes."

Cheesy? she said, and then burst out laughing as I cried with joy and pain at the heat of the borta.

When we finished, Meghna opened the spice cupboard. From behind the turmeric pot, she took out a book and gave it to me. At first, I thought it might be the Qur'an, but when I opened it, I saw it was a notebook, handwritten in English.

"A cookbook," I said.

Nje, mostly my amma's recipes, but also some of mine, she said.

"Aww, thanks Amma. And the cumin and apple dessert?"

I used Bramley when I should have used Granny Smiths.

"Eureka!"

The letters were so painstakingly written, sitting perfectly within the guidelines that she rubbed out after. She decorated it with all kinds of food colourings, flower petals and scents. And there was a sidebar on every page with all her secrets. Put the rice under the quilt to make it extra fluffy. Add coriander leaves right at the end to ensure the scent is fresh and strong. Roast the garlic till it is charred so the mango borta has a smoky taste. And a little section at the back about all the achars and pickles, and which dishes they accompany.

"You wrote it in English... for me? That's what you've been doin' all this time with Trina?" I said, and she nodded.

273

We mustn't let the men in the restaurants wreck our cultural heritage, she said, half serious, half joking.

As I turned the pages, flicking from biryani to bhaji, borta to bhuna, recipes so scrumptious I could eat the paper they were written on, Meghna opened the fridge, took out a vial of insulin and drew it into a syringe. From the corner of my eye, I could see her pushing her sari to one side and finding the part of her body just above the hip that had become numb to the sharp pain from repeated injections. The needle caught my attention as it glistened in the afternoon sun streaming in through the window. A drop of fluid seductively rolled down its metallic surface. Her hands trembled.

"What's wrong, Amma?"

Na, kitchu na, it's nothing. I guess you never get used to the idea that you depend on this little tube of liquid to live,* she said, and promptly injected the insulin and discarded the needle in the sharps bin. I carried on flicking through my new customised cookbook.

We went to her bedroom to nap. In the corner of the room was an old gramophone that had come off some ocean liner, broken up by the ship wreckers in the port of Chittagong. It was given to her by her dad, and even Father didn't have the heart to sell it for cash or use it as firewood. Next to it stood a handful of records she'd managed to lug over in her suitcase when she first came to England.

Put on the Tagore record, Sakthi, she said, lying on the bed.

"*Accha*, which one is the Tagore?" I said.

It's got an old man with a long beard on the sleeve.

"This one?"

Bap-re bap, if you can't tell apart the beard of Lalon Shah and Rabindranath Tagore then I have failed as a Bengali, and as a mother!*

I placed the record on the turntable, pinched the dust off the stylus and gently set the needle on the vinyl. I wound up the gramophone and then lay down next to Meghna with my head on her chest. The hum of the accordion, the soft beating of the dhol, the twang of the ektara all came together. And then a man with a tender voice, one of the playback singers from the Golden Era of Bengali cinema, sang the lyrics. Meghna joined him.

After a while, her voice faded into my subconscious, the drum beat in perfect time with her heart and the accordion drew in and out with every breath. I dreamed I was on the bow of a sampan, wind in my sails, racing along the majestic Padma River. Meghna stood in the distance, 'Go, moina, don't be afraid,' she shouted from the quay, her size diminishing with the distance. Little fishing villages smoking their catch flashed by, their bare-footed children on the embankment waving, screaming as they watched me race along the silt-laden river. But before I knew it, I was all alone on the vast ocean, at the mercy of the waves. I opened my eyes, turned on my side and wrapped my arm tight around Meghna's waist. She pulled me in to her bosom, covered me with the pallu of her sari and I fell fast asleep.

When I woke, her drum had stopped beating.

PRESENT DAY

৮. DHAL BHAT

Gaol

Meghna lost in life; death was her consolation. She left it to me as a gift, like a book voucher, so the day after her funeral, wellies still caked in mud from her graveside, I went straight down to the police station to redeem it. I wasn't smiling any more but biting my lips. The officer sat me down in the interview room, made me a cuppa, and pressed Record. But when the time came to sign the statement on how Father had forced me to marry, my hands trembled like Meghna's when she was administering that last, fatal dose of insulin. My sweaty palms hovered over the dotted line. Just a tad of ink was all it'd take to put him away. But the ink came out like the scribblings of a mad person, erratic lines, or blots where the nib got stuck in some imaginary groove. A deep breath and it was done. But as I lifted the pen off the paper, I felt the glaring scowl of our society. For what child could turn against her parent like that? My heart yelped in pain, grudgingly pumping blood around this apostate body. No doubt I'll be subject to a life of sorrow, that sounds and colours will never be the same, true as a nightingale's song, pure as a northern rainbow.

"So, what happens now?" I asked the desk officer.

"Well, he'll be released on bail, and if what you said stands up in court, he'll go to prison for up to seven years, depends on what the judge decides," she said.

"And what about the men in Bangladesh?" I said.

"We'll pass on the details to the relevant authorities, and they'll deal with it under their national law, but there isn't much more we can do from here," she said.

"Can he still apply for a British passport… you know…?" I asked.

"He can, but I can't see the Home Office accepting the wedding papers given what you have just told me," she said. I breathed out and let my shoulders come down to where they ought to be.

"And seven years, is that it?" I said, shaking my head.

"I know love, I know, but that's the law. Let's take one step at a time, hey? Do you need to talk to somebody, you know?"

"What, like a psychologist? I'll be alright."

"And do you have a place to stay? I can't imagine you'll be going back home tonight if your father is still there," she said.

"I'm at boarding school, I'll be safe there," I said.

Trina picked me up from the station. I cried all the way to Mycombe Girls, thinking about what will happen to Meghna's family back in the Desh. But she assured me Akaash could spare the money to help Nana, Surma and Kushiyara, even if it meant delaying her women's restaurant. I felt ashamed. All that macho talk about taking one for the team, about happiness not being a zero-sum game. But I couldn't bear to think that Meghna died for nothing, that everything would just carry on as normal.

"What about Tone? How am I gonna tell him? And what about you? So sorry, I've been completely absorbed with myself. How are you doing?" I said.

First let's get you fixed. Did you read back through your journal? she said.

"Yes, and it only confirms what Father said at the funeral: that it's my fault she's dead."

It's not your fault, Sakthi. We're going to get you better, OK? she said. I nodded.

Outside the gates I gave Trina a big hug, thanked her for the ride and then watched her speed off in her little VW Beetle. I turned to look at the school. What now for me? Freedom, isn't that what I wanted? But what to do with it? I walked through the parterre and back to the dormitory.

"How'd it go... the funeral? Did they?" said Aaliyah.

"Had a quiet word with the imam like, an' he were... receptive to change shall we say. Says Islam don't, technically, forbid women attendin' funerals," I said.

"Is it?" said Zaineb.

"Yeah, but they still made us stand behind all men," I said.

"Oh my days, fam. I can't even. It's like bangin' your head against a brick wall, innit," said Aaliyah.

"Tell me 'bout it," I said.

"And your dad, d'ya bait him out to the Ol' Bill?" said Zaineb.

"Yeah, he'll get out on bail like, but the woman officer who took me statement says there's a pretty solid case against him," I said.

"That's bare mental, I'd never rat my dad out like that," said Zaineb, and got an elbow to her ribs from her sister.

"And what about your hubz?" said Aaliyah.

"He in't comin' no more," I said.

"They gonna nick him in Bangladesh? Ya know, for—"

Aaliyah hushed her sister up again, but this time I let out an involuntary laugh. Had I become immune to suffering, as Meghna had over all these years? Perhaps I was suppressing it. Perhaps the pain was in the post – the Bangladesh post – and it would arrive eventually, all messed up like that marriage proposal letter two years ago.

"Y' alright?" said Aaliyah.

"Yeah, yeah. Good to be back," I said.

I put my travel bag down on the bed and unpacked all my saris and salwar kamiz. One of the first rules the new woman-friendly board voted on was to axe the school uniform, and it passed unanimously on one proviso, that we could only wear clothes that would be acceptable back in our country of origin. It transformed the grounds into this throng of colour, and in my heart, I know that once the girls get accustomed to their freedom of dress, it is just a hop, skip and a jump before they can realise the freedom of their minds. Last of all, I took out the blue burka, the one that Meghna gave me the day after I had my first period. I folded it neatly and put it with the saris. I'll never wear it again, but strangely enough it gives me comfort.

"What 'bout you guys, did I miss owt from the board meetin'?" I said.

"Fam, we're finally gettin' a P.E teacher," said Aaliyah.

"No way, things movin' well fast 'ere like," I said.

"And he's peng blud!" said Zaineb.

"He?" I said.

"Only messin'! It's a woman, seems safe," said Zaineb.

"New school crest is up too, innit," said Aaliyah.

The three of us walked down the stairs and through the corridor towards the classrooms, and there, above the double doors where once the school rules stood, was a plaque. 'Question everything' it read.

The adhan belted out over the tannoy system.

"Hey, is that...?" I said.

We ran out onto the north parterre to see Beydaan at the top of the tower calling the adhan with Fatima by her side. Beydaan, whose voice was deeper, took the bass harmonies and Fatima the top, the two vocals interweaving around each other, calling everyone to prayer.

"Sick, fam," said Aaliyah.

"Alie!" said Zaineb.

I looked around at the old place and remembered that first day. The girl racing through the hall in her chador, the silver and gold shimmering all around. How far from home I felt, yet there I stood almost in the same position with a profound sense of belonging. Beydaan came down and gave me a hug, and we walked to the mosque with Aaliyah, Zaineb and the other girls for Dhuhr prayers.

I've been visiting Father in jail, partly due to some twisted sense of duty, and partly because I want to see the anguish in his face before he gets used to his new life behind bars. He showed no remorse during the court hearing, but maybe the cold, rat-infested, concrete cells of the prison would focus his mind.

From the south side, the two-hundred-foot minaret-like chimney of the compound is a prominent feature of the city's skyline. As you approach it, a Victorian gate house has thirty-foot high redbrick walls which extend from either side to form a barbed-wire-protected perimeter. Inside, the prison is like a brain cell, with a central nucleus and wings like dendrites. I sat in the visitor's room and watched people's faces, marvelling at the sheer variety of sentiment that could be expressed through just the eyes and mouth. After ten minutes a prison officer approached me.

"I'm sorry, there's been a mistake. Your father has been transferred to a more secure section of the prison. He's only allowed closed visits for now."

"Why is that, Officer?"

"He got into a bit of a scuffle."

The man brought me to a small white cubicle in which there was a single black telephone receiver, a three-legged stool and a small, square window that framed a similar room on the other side.

Father appeared in a white shirt with thin blue vertical stripes and dark blue denim trousers rolled up at the ankles. He's lost the rice belly that plagues all restaurateurs and his muscles have grown. His knuckles were scarred over on his right hand, and there were visible bruises on his face as well as a large cut that had been stitched up above his left eye. I felt bad for him. I guess when all is said and done, he's still my father, whether I like it or not.

"A bit of a scuffle?" I said to the guard.

"You should see the other guy," he replied.

We spent the first fifty minutes of the visit in a silent standoff. Father sat there aloof, phone receiver lodged between his ear and his shoulder. He examined his palms repeatedly tracing his index finger along all the major lines, checking for hairs on the back of his hands, anything but look at me. I had promised myself I wouldn't talk first, so I sat stubbornly on my chair texting Mr Drummond to set up a time I could visit Tone in hospital. Father caved in first, and with five minutes left on the clock he skipped the pleasantries and went on the attack.

"So, this is my lot in life? After everything, this is how you repay your father, by locking him up with thieves and murderers?" he said.

"That Christabel Pankhurst did time in 'ere pains me, but you? You deserve it as much as the man int' next cell," I said.

The barb went over his head. This isn't a fight for the intellect, I thought. I need to dig deep and scrap it out with the base instruments of psychological warfare, in which he is more battle-hardened. I readied myself, burying my emotions as far deep inside me as I could. And then I stuck it in him.

"*Accha*, what 'ave ya ever done for us, for Meghna? Other Bangladeshis from your generation are doctors, lawyers, even MPs, an' you... ya call yerself a businessman, but yer just a glorified onion cutter—"

"Ungrateful child! I was the one who brought you to the bilat[96]. You have no idea what I went through to set up a life in this country."

"Oh, ya reckon *I* owe *you*?"

"Well?"

"*Na, na, na*. You chose to 'ave me!"

"I wanted a boy!"

Even from behind the glass he can get under my skin. Poor Meghna for having to put up with his bullshit all these years.

---

96 Civilization, i.e., London.

"So, ya think you've done nowt wrong?" I said. He swapped the receiver to his other ear and placed his hands into his pockets. Leaning back on his chair, he looked into my eyes.

"And what would be my crime? That I didn't want my daughter to grow up a whore? That I wanted to keep her on the straight and narrow? Then I plead guilty, with pride," he said.

"Pride? Pride, ya say? More like shame. You should be ashamed of the way ya treated Amma, ya fuckin' animal," I said, slamming the desk in front of me.

"*Ma*, don't get emotional," he said.

God damn it, he always used that line with Meghna to make her feel like she was over-reacting. Infuriatingly, it worked on her, and it was working on me. I pinched my forearm as hard as I could under the table. The pain snapped me out of my self-pity, and I questioned him again. His admission of wrong-doing would go a long way in resolving my feeling of guilt.

"Ya feel no remorse for what ya did?" I said.

"Your mother died because of you, not me," he replied.

"*Na*, Abba, you drove her to suicide."

"Allah will be my judge."

"God don't exist, Abba! Or me and you talkin' through a pane of glass coz ya beat an' raped me mam an' forced us to marry wouldn't be 'appenin'," I said, gripping the receiver so tight the blood left my fingers.

"*Astaghfirullah*, I'll pray for your forg—"

"I don't need to be forgiven!" I said and slammed the phone down. Fuck! I preferred his broody silence.

I'd wondered if prison would change him, if it'd soften him up, but Father is a survivor, that generation who lived through the independence war, suffered famines and floods, so he took his sentence as yet another test from the Almighty. It made him even more resolute in his beliefs. He won this brief exchange, but I still had one weapon left. I got up to leave a few minutes before time was up.

"Where are you going, it's not time? Farzana? Farzana! You come back here right now, you hear me, it's not time yet, it's not bloody time!" he screamed, kicking his chair as I walked out the room.

Wires, that's all I can think of from visiting Tone for the first time in the ICU at the Royal Infirmary. And tubes, clear plastic tubes dripping saline and antibiotics into his motionless body. His mam sat by his bed holding his hand, stroking his hair. She looked like death herself as she rubbed her puffy red eyes, yawned, and rested her head on the mattress. When she saw me at the door she squinted, like she didn't know who I was despite all the hate she'd hurled at me that Easter Sunday. But then, why would she recognise me, she's never seen my face.

When it sunk in who I must be, she jumped off her chair and raced towards me waving her finger from a distance. I had this strange sensation like her mouth was moving, but the words were arriving moments later, and all muffled. She slapped me square across my cheeks and unleashed a torrent of abuse with her usual grace.

"You did this, you, ya fuckin' Paki bitch," she screamed at the top of her lungs, phlegm flying through the air.

"I'm sorry," I said, using the flowers I'd bought for Tone as a shield.

"Get out, I don't want ya near him again."

"I tried to save him, Mrs Drummond, honest I did."

She clenched her fists and thumped me. I lifted my arms above my face as a boxer would and took the blows. I deserved them, I guess.

"Marie, no!" said Mr Drummond, returning with two cups of coffee and a stash of chocolate from the vending machine.

"Get this fuckin' bitch away from me, now," she screamed.

"She means nae harm," he said, embracing his wife and mee-mawing "canteen" over her shoulder.

"It's her fault, her fault he's in 'ere," she said, sobbing into his chest.

The hospital staff arrived with the doormen, but I left without force. In the canteen I ordered a plate of food, but I couldn't eat. I rolled the peas about the plate, looking for shapes in their formation. Mr Drummond joined me a quarter of an hour later and sat opposite.

"They're not renowned for their haute cuisine," he said, taking out his lunch box.

"I tried to save him, Mr Drummond, but the blood, the blood just wouldn't stop, it just kept comin'," I said.

"Aye, I know you did, lass. He's still alive in case you haven't noticed, and that's because of your quick thinking."

"But she's right, it's my fault he's 'ere."

"Well, that's one interpretation. But then, if he hadn't met you, chances are he'd still be in that gang, and who knows how long before he was in the slammer, or dead," he said, offering me a sandwich.

"He made the best cucumber sarnies," I said, taking a great big bite out of the corner.

"Hey, makes, he's still with us, and don't be daft, he bought them from Marks and Spencer before the game. Our Tone couldn't boil an egg to save his life," he said.

"You mean... what a chancer!"

"But it worked, and now he has you. It's like winning the lottery!"

Yeah, a tenner! And if he has any sense, he'll use it to buy a pack of lights and five more tickets instead of going all in on me.

"We've already lost one. That's why she's like that," said Mr Drummond, welling up.

"Tone told us. I'm sorry," I said.

"She just couldn't take it, the grief, and I couldn't be with her because I had to watch the stall, so she took to the bottle. Before I knew it, she was so far gone I couldn't bring her back."

"It's not your fault, ya did what ya 'ad to do."

"And now Tone, our wee boy, in here. And when the doctors told us he'd caught a hospital infection... I can't bear to lose another one, it'll be the end of me, Sakthi. Children are meant to out-live their parents, not the other way around," he said, brushing his hands through his hair.

God, why do I hurt everyone I care about? Miss Qureshi, fired, because of my stupid hang-up over the library. Tone, lying in hospital because of me. Father behind bars and beyond rescue because of me. Meghna in her grave, because of me. Now, loneliness stalks, and I'm in its crosshairs. Is this my punishment, an ultimatum from above? Come into the fold or live a life devoid of love and laughter.

Between Father, Tone and cleaning up Dadhi's shit-stained sheets, there's hardly enough time to visit Mrs Finch, whose health has taken a turn for the worse. She spends more time in bed these days than she does reading a book by the fire. She rarely gets out of her nightgown, and the small cough that set in a couple of weeks ago has become much more serious, staining her pillows with a currant-jelly-coloured splutter.

I checked on her the other day and brought her a bowlful of rice and dhal, which she's grown to love. I rang the doorbell before using the spare key to enter so as not to give her a fright, but to my surprise the door swung open. A plump woman in her early thirties wearing a pin-stripe suit and carrying a briefcase stepped out of the house.

"She's in the India room, I'd hurry," she said and walked off.

When I entered the lounge, I could see the door by the grandfather clock was ajar. A set of stairs led up to another door at the top, the attic I presumed. The room was like a shrine, covered in trinkets and the like from India. A musty smell hung in the air, so I pulled the blinds and opened the windows.

Mrs Finch has been in love too, though she's never talked about it. On her bedside table stood a framed black and white picture of her with a man wearing an army uniform. By his side was an Indian woman and a small child, a girl, with pale skin and blonde hair. The man was tall and handsome, and Mrs Finch was clinging on to his left arm very tight. His right arm, free of her grip, was placed gently around the Indian woman's hips. A lapse perhaps, or an unfamiliarity with the canny power of a photograph to capture a moment.

Mrs Finch was lying on her back, eyes closed and mouth wide open. The doctor told her to admit herself, but she refused and instead found a quiet place where she could rest alone like a cat that knows it's close to death. In between the fits of chill and fever, we managed small stints of conversation. She opened her eyes and looked at the photo in my hand.

"That's my little Emma, she died, cholera," she said.

"She was gorgeous," I said.

I looked at her, and she could see the question I wanted to ask. Mrs Finch took the photo from me and brushed her fingers over her husband's face. The uniform he had on, a white tunic with white trousers and a dark blue peaked cap, lay ironed on the divan in the corner of the room. Next to it, Mrs Finch had set out her wedding dress.

"When you marry an army officer, you marry his job as well," she said.

"You were posted in India, right?" I said.

"After independence, the most awful inter-religious fighting broke out. Hindus killing Muslims, Muslims killing Hindus, people left everything they owned and ran away in search of safety."

"God, how awful."

"The British Army was to be pulled out and reassigned to different stations, but Harry..." She coughed, and grimaced whilst holding her chest. I helped her sit up so she could have a sip of water. "Harry had fallen for this little Indian girl, the one in that photograph."

"Harry your husband, Mr Finch?" I said.

"Yes, dear," she said.

"So, what happened?" I asked.

"One morning, I woke up in an empty bed and found a letter on the pillow. He apologised for the pain we went through after we lost baby Emma, and that he found comfort in the arms of the ayah. They decided to run away to her village in Pakistan-administered Kashmir."

Is that why she is the way she is? Because she blames Muslims for taking her husband? She coughed again, and I told her to rest up, but she insisted on finishing the story.

"And have you heard from them since?" I said.

"A few days later, they found him dead on the streets of Hyderabad, caught in the crossfire between the religions."

"Oh, that's horrible."

"Yes, such rotten luck," she said, putting on a brave face.

She fell silent again. I took that moment almost like a confessional. Mostly I spoke about Tone, about his red hair and freckles, about the taste of cucumber when we first kissed. And now, about the way he lay there in intensive care, his life hanging by a thread. I wondered what it's like for him, for anyone close to death.

"Are you not scared, Mrs Finch?" I asked her.

"Scared, of what?" she said, turning her head to look at me. The fat and muscle had left her cheeks long before her spirit would. Her skin was translucent, which only drew more attention to the blue of her eyes that radiated intelligence.

"Of punishment?" she followed up in my silence.

"No, of disappointment. What if Helen Burns was wrong, that there is no God, no heaven? What if it all ends with ashes to ashes, dust to dust?" I sat by her bedside holding her hands. Green fingers that tended to so many blooms had withered away into skin and bones, like okra.

"You have to have faith, dear," she said.

"How can you have faith in something you've never seen or heard, never smelled, tasted or touched?" I asked.

"Hush now, what a wretched question to ask a dying woman," she said, reaching for the crucifix that lay by her pillow.

"I suppose there's one small consolation," I said.

"What's that?" said Mrs Finch.

"That God's wracking his brains asking himself the same question, whether there's some higher being that created him?" I said.

She smiled and rubbed her thumb over the palm of my hand before turning her head back up towards the ceiling and closing her eyes. Mrs Finch took a sharp breath and groaned. I reached for my mobile to call an ambulance, but she placed her hand on my arm to stop me.

"Goodbye, Sakthi."

"Goodbye, Mrs Finch."

Torn

When I woke up this morning, I opened the curtains and looked out at the rain falling on the terraces, and the soggy leaves decaying on the streets. I made myself a cup of tea and then went up into the attic to sort out all the stuff that had been chucked up there over all these years. Around midday, the landline rang, and a thick Sylheti accent rattled down the phone. Through the static and crackling, the voice on the other end was baritone, though the caller introduced herself as a woman. She had some urgent news for Father. When I told her he was spending time in the nick she sounded sympathetic, not the usual emotion Father evoked in people.

Tell him our good friend Kamrul is at long last with the angels, and his name was the last word to pass his lips, she said.

I wondered if she dialled the wrong number, or if there might have been an error in connection through all those miles of telegraph lines, or even the shorter distance between her brain cells – well, she had Father all wrong, that's for sure.

Accha, who is this? I asked.

We met at the tea stall, on Victory Day, she said.

That was almost two years ago now and so much has happened, so many people have come and gone. At the tea stall with Trina, I could picture the chaiwala, Jyothi, making that seven-layered tea. But who else? I remembered some people were asking for money and shouting at Jyothi for no apparent reason. Could it be one of them?

The hijras? I said.

Nje, we were his DOT supervisors, she said.

293

DOT, what's that?

We made sure he took his TB medicine.

TB? Who, the chaiwala?

Nje... Kamrul.

I thought he was called Jyothi?

Kamrul is his Islamic name, Jyothi is his Bengali nickname.

But I thought his mother was a Hindu?

She named him according to his father's religion.

Wait, Jyothi has died? Inna lillahi wa inna ilaihi raji'un, I said. The line broke, and I didn't hear from her again.

He was at the wedding, just a few feet away from me, before he got chucked out. If only I'd taken that chance, I could've said goodbye. But Father said he didn't know him, that he was just a vagrant. Why would he lie? Father is many things, but he isn't a fibber. Just then I remembered that photo of Mrs Finch's by her bedside, and the way that her husband was holding the nanny. It triggered something. I went back into the attic where I had been tidying up and sorting out paperwork.

In the far corner, behind all the suitcases, spare bed linen, and stacks of books on self-starting a business that Father had bought for knock-off prices at the local library, was a steel cabinet. I opened the top drawer and worked my way through all the papers. I spent the whole day looking, not knowing exactly what it was I was looking for, bills, invoices, letters, pictures and what not. Finally, I got to the last drawer, which held a collection of old clippings of Bengali language newspapers and lots of photos, some stuck together and faded in the corners where Father had placed his finger and thumb to flick through them. Each one was dated, stating where it had been taken and with whom.

The pictures were mostly of Father with his school friends. They were in chronological order, and as the years passed and the boys and girls became older, some disappeared, whilst new faces joined. Some grew farther apart, whilst others became closer. Most got married, leaving behind a happy hardcore of singletons. Towards the end of the pile, only Father and one other young woman in her late teens was left. I turned the photos over and read the names and places. Rohan and Shefali in Shillong, Bandarbans, Srimangal. Shefali, I thought. Isn't that the name of the tea stall Trina took me to during the mela?

In one picture, the two friends posed on a Honda motorcycle, with their cameras in hand, looking directly into the lens. Father looked exactly as Mrs Finch described him back in the days. Shefali had a full figure, long silky black hair down to her waist, glowing skin, and that same unmistakable smile that Jyothi has... sorry, had. She sat Amazon style on the back of the motorbike, but there was something about the way she leant her head on Father's back so that her cheek rested in between his shoulder blades. And the way she wrapped her arms around his waist, placing her hands tenderly on his hips. Isn't this the photo Jyothi said his mother held to her bosom as she took her last breath, I thought? Rohan and Shefali were close, perhaps even too close.

I grabbed everything and went to find Dadhi in the lounge who had just woken up from her afternoon nap.

Dadhi, would you help me translate some Bangla, I asked.

Tik asse, bring it here, she said, but having looked at the headlines she closed her eyes and said she needed to rest. I hovered my smartphone over the text and translated it online. 'Illegal Sharia court gives one hundred lashes to adulterous man.'

Is it Father they're writing about, Dadhi? I said, grabbing her arm.

I'm tired, she said, and pulled her sari over her head.

You did this, didn't you? You got him whipped! They were in love! How could you be so cruel? To your own son! Trina's amma was right... you turned him into a monster, you, I said, and went into the kitchen to calm down. I have a brother... I *had* a brother, someone to share this world with. Now I'm left with nothing but the bitter dregs of a seven-layered tea.

As for Father, what a hypocrite! I mean, the nerve to dress me down on my relationship with Tone when he himself was with an unmarried woman. Building the mosque in Bangladesh may ease his conscience, but I sure as hell am not going let him off the hook so easily. What he did to Meghna, to me. I can still smell the paraffin, I can't bear to look at rose petals. But I want him to tell me to my face, to feel the shame as the words leave his lips. A dark adrenaline runs through my veins. I'm shuddering with excitement; the taste of revenge, a marmite-covered razor blade sliding deliciously across my tongue.

I waited some weeks to get a letter from the prison with Father's new visiting terms. When it finally arrived, I promised myself that I'd be stronger, that I wouldn't let him get the better of me like he did the last time. Father appeared through the screen holding a Qur'an. There was the usual silence, but that look of indifference had gone, and instead he seemed to be peering into the abyss. He had a letter tucked in his shirt pocket. Had he got the news? I took the receiver from the wall.

"Pick up the phone," I mouthed to him through the screen, but he sat there motionless. How could I extract a confession if he plain refused to speak? I'd have to push him somehow, but how if he couldn't hear me? A whole bunch of schoolboy gestures sprang to mind, but instead I swiped the screen on my phone and opened a note-taking app.

"You were lashed for being with an unmarried woman, you hypocritical little fuck dick cunt bastard," I wrote, and then deleted the last part because it might lessen the blow of the primary clause.

Father took the letter out of his pocket and unfolded it. Inside were a couple of photos. He took the first and tore it in half, in half again and then once more for good measure before throwing it up in the air like confetti. He did the same with the second photo. An then he scrunched the letter into a tight ball and threw it at the glass. I flinched thinking it was going hit me. When I looked up, he was rubbing his sleeve with his right hand like he always does when we're talking about this period in his life, I've just realised. I deleted the message and wrote a new one.

"Abba, are you OK?" I held it up.

Father ripped the phone off the wall and slammed the reinforced glass. When the prison officers arrived, he floored the first with a punch and smashed the other around the head with his chair. He climbed up onto the desk and thumped his head against the glass till it bled, leaving a red smear across the pane. Another warder arrived and held a Taser up to Father's leg, and when the voltage passed through, he squirmed and fell to the ground. I fell off my chair and watched the prison officers drag his dazed body away, legs trailing along the floor.

An officer came in to help me to my feet and took me through to a room where I could gather myself. What have I signed up for, I thought? Can such brinkmanship result in anything but tragedy? Have I got the stomach to play on, the guts to up the stakes? Yes, I'm not giving in, this is all part of Father's games, but he isn't getting away with it this time.

Dr Fischer met me outside the front gates of the clinic where Father has been sectioned. She scanned her fingertips to open a set of double-locking doors and then we passed through a long, sterile walkway decorated with patients' art, everything from simple palm-prints to Kandinsky-esque brain vomit. One or two of the inmates are clearly gifted and painted remarkable portraits of their co-inhabitants. I looked at their tortured faces, their mad eyes following me down the corridor, and I prepared myself for the worst.

At the reception they issued me a visitor's badge. As I waited to sign in, I could see the patients on the closed-circuit television screens that were behind the desk.

"Where is he?" I asked.

"They're in creative group therapy at the moment," she said, pointing at Father at the end of a semi-circle of patients.

He sat perfectly still, wearing a hospital tunic and slippers. His thick, curly hair had been shaved, exaggerating his manic expression. I gasped at his appearance.

"What happened?" I asked the doctor, holding back the tears.

"He got this letter, and, well, you know the rest. They had to shave his hair off to stitch up his head," she said.

"What did the letter say?" I said.

"We don't know, it was written in Hindi, or something. But when he came around, he kept on saying 'he's gone'. Do you know who he might be referring to?" she said, opening the door to her office.

Jyothi, I thought, it must be. Dr Fischer offered me a cup of coffee, sat down behind her desk, and opened Father's file. She spoke with a strong German accent which, though off-putting at first, had an air of authority. Shrinks should all have German accents, don't you think?

"Your father has a fear of people looking at him, pointing, and he wants to get them before they can get him. He's delusional," she said.

"Is that why he attacked me in prison?" I said.

"Yes, quite possibly," she said.

"What's his diagnosis?" I said.

"It's hard to say at this stage. We'll have to keep him in here and do more observations before we can confirm anything."

"Right, so is he on meds?"

"Yes, risperidone."

"And what's the outlook?"

"Again, hard to know if we don't know the cause. But he's in an extremely vulnerable state and it's important that we be thorough to avoid any long-term psychological damage," she said.

"Vulnerable?" She nodded.

"There's something else," she said. "He keeps repeating the numbers 24, 2, 24, 4, 24, 5 in that exact order. Lottery numbers perhaps, a phone number, safe code? Do they mean anything to you?"

"No, sorry, I'll have a think. And the letter?" I said, getting up to leave.

"Oh yes, it's with his belongings," she said.

The Qur'an, the letter and the photos were in a clear, plastic bag. I took out the scrumpled up note, which was written in Bengali, so I neatly folded it and put it in my pocket. Trina will help. I pieced together the torn photos. The first was a copy of the one of Father and Shefali on that Honda motorbike – the one I saw in the attic. The second was a picture of Jyothi, beaming behind his rickety tea stall. What a sweet soul! I opened the Qur'an to make sure nothing was wedged inside, and to my surprise I saw that a few pages were stapled together. I carefully took the staples out and read the script, surah 24, ayat 2 from the verse An-Nur. And the next leaf, surah 24, ayat 4 and 5. The numbers – Father was referencing verses from the Qur'an. And they all related to zina[97].

Here was the indisputable proof, my ammunition, locked and loaded, ready to be discharged with hate and fury. For the first time in my life, I have power over Father, I thought. How easy it would be to tip him over the edge now, to fill him with so much shame that he could not bear to live with himself. To pull out the knife as he had done with Tone. Wouldn't that be a more fitting punishment for his crimes rather than the pathetic sentence he was handed down by the judges?

"Can I see him... please?" I asked the warden, eagerly.

97   Islamic term that refers to illicit sexual relations.

"You'll have to be quick," he said.

I walked into the room where he was sitting with the rest of the patients, all in a semi-circle watching daytime television. Father was strapped into a chair with restraints. Even so, I had my guard up. With the slightest flick of his tongue, he could injure like a snake. Perhaps he too has a secret about me that I may not be able to deal with, I thought? What if he tells me that I'm not his daughter? The idea has crossed my mind.

As soon as he saw me, he started to fidget and wriggle. He gripped his chair over the ends of the armrests and locked his feet around the two front legs. When I got close enough, I could see his nostrils flaring and his teeth clenched tight. His smouldering eyes met mine, defiant to the very last. I put my hand inside my bag and pulled out his Qur'an and watched the colour drain from his face. I paused for a moment, to prolong his agony, but it worked against me.

No, no, no! I tried to shake off my conscience, but it kept on nagging. I read the texts again in my head, and anger gave way to sadness. Meghna knew, and despite everything, she still protected him. I looked at Father, a sitting duck. He is no different to me now, I thought. But the question is, am I any different to him? Do I really want to live a bitter life, cursed like Mrs Finch, unable to forgive? For surely forgiveness is the only cure for this insufferable pain. Forgiveness provides as much redemption for the victim, as it does relief for the assailant.

And just like that I was lost at sea again, on the boat, with nobody around. There was not a whisper of wind, and the ocean was like a mirror stretching out into the horizon. I looked over the edge to see an unrecognisable figure in the reflection, a demon, and recoiled back onto the deck with terror. I leant up against the mast, the boat swaying, when I heard someone. Meghna spoke to me, a faint voice from that distant quay.

"What would you do?" I whispered back.

৯. SEVEN-LAYERED TEA

Sakthi

The books lay in neat piles on the floor in Mrs Finch's living room, some in increasing heights where I'd used them as a staircase to reach the works of Austen, the Brontes, Carroll and Dickens on the top shelves. 'All the best English writers came from the front of the alphabet,' she'd say. I set the house keys down on the tea table and looked around the room, which was anything but living. An eerie silence penetrated the walls without the sound of the swinging pendulum, the crackling fire, and the birds tweeting in the back garden as they jostled for position on the feeder.

I sank into her armchair, deeply satisfying, yet sacrilegious, and after a few seconds I sprang back out and sat down on the stack of pre-war almanacs I'd made my seat over the years. This wasn't her house, but her home. Everywhere I looked, my eyes fell on some trivial detail: the mousetrap baited with Gruyere, the baking paper she used for bookmarks, her walking stick with which she'd aggressively point at foreigners as they passed by, minding their own business. I put the kettle on, and the bell rang.

"Sakthi?" said a young woman in a suit, heeled shoes, and a leather satchel, lifting the tone of the second syllable.

"Yes, that's right," I said.

"Houghton, from Houghton and Sons... and daughters, now I come to think about it. Gosh, yes, must talk to the old man about that. Call me Penelope," she said, letting herself in.

"Tea?" I asked, opening the windows to let out the stale air.

"No thanks. Just need a few quick signatures and I'll be on my way. Looks like the old lady has left you everything, which includes this rather old gramophone, the grandfather clock, this armchair... gosh, is this really all the furniture?" she asked.

"There's all that stuff upstairs in the India room," I said.

"Well, don't look a gift horse and all that. If you sign here, here, here, here, here, and here, all that 'stuff' will be yours. You did read the copy of the will I sent you by post, right?" she said.

"Yes, I did," I said, signing the paper and then picking up some of the books that lay on the wooden table to return them to their rightful place on the shelf. She got up from the chair and made her way over to the front door.

"Oh yes, the books," she said, turning around.

"Oh, I think I'll give them all to Mycombe Girls. There must be a wealth of knowledge in those tattered pages," I said.

"That's an apt choice of words," she said. "Hmm, you really have no idea, do you?"

"About what?"

"What have you got in your hand now?"

"Ulysses."

"Turn to the credits on the first page, what does it say?"

"First edition. Shakespeare and Company, Paris, 1922. Signed... James Joyce," I said, and she quickly typed it into her smartphone with both thumbs. I looked at her again, raising one eyebrow above the other (I've only recently become aware that I do that).

"That book alone would pay for your degree, and some," she said.

"Sorry, what?!" I said.

She took off her heels and climbed up the book towers I'd made till she got to one dusty shelf of hardbacks in the centre of the wall. She pulled out each book one by one and looked at the first page before carefully putting it back in its place.

"That shelf there, that's worth more than the house," she said, and got down off the stack. She massaged her feet, put her heels back on and walked somewhat inelegantly back to her car. I wondered which book Mrs Finch sold to pay for the library.

"You're a lucky girl," she said. Debatable, I thought.

"Oh, just one question. Did she say why?" I said.

"No reasons, no provisos. Oh, just one more thing. You won't be able to touch a penny until you're eighteen!" she said out of the window and drove off.

Outside, the garden wall was gaining height as people left flowers, photos, and other tributes. Even the tramp we passed on the town square the day of Meghna's funeral stopped by to pay his respects. He set down a can of Special Brew on the wall, opened another, downed the contents, and then crushed the can in his hands, his face contorting like the metal between his fingers. How many people, how many lives has she touched? He put the empty beer can in my hands and gave me a drunken hug before stumbling off down the road. In the distance, I saw a woman in Islamic dress cross the street to avoid our friendly hobo. Her face was too far away to resolve, but her gait was unmistakable.

"Things that bad?" she said, looking at the tin of beer in my hands.

"The homeless man, he gave—"

"Yeah, yeah, pull the other one."

"I swear down, Miss. Anyways, how did you...?"

"The local paper, and stop calling me Miss. You've earned your right to be treated as an equal," said Miss Qureshi, giving me a great big hug.

I invited her in, and she took a seat in the armchair. I waited for that uncomfortable feeling, the one I had when I sat down, but it never came, so I sat next to her on the almanacs.

"Are you going to speak at the service?" she said.

"Tone's dad, who's organising it all, asked me to close the ceremony, but what am I meant to say? On the one hand she was this sweet, old lady, and I wanted to make her dhal and read her Jane Austen till she fell asleep on that old chair you're sat in. But then she had this racist streak which made me want to slip poison into her Earl Grey."

"Probably best to leave that last part out," she said.

"And as for the people at the funeral, half of them don't know me and the other half hate me, my colour, my culture, everything I stand for. How am I supposed to walk the line between ignorance and hatred?" I said.

"You have to be tolerant."

"I? *I* have to be tolerant?"

"Is it any different to Mycombe Girls, to bringing the girls together, the imam getting his comeuppance?" said Miss Qureshi. "Those students hated each other before you got there, but you even got Mrs Kazi on side, who'd have thought after tormenting her with her right angles for the best part of a year."

"She told you about that?" Miss Qureshi tilted her head and put her hands out. "In any case, what has it achieved? Mam is dead, boyfriend is in intensive care and Dad's in the slammer!"

"That's the first time I've heard you call him Dad," said Miss Qureshi.

"So?" I said, replying to a text Trina had sent wishing me well before the funeral.

"So? Don't you see, you're accepting him and his relationship to you. You've had this dark cloud over you for so long and it's finally lifting. You can pick up the pieces now, move on, be who you want to be."

"If you say so, Sigmund."

"Freud, no, he thinks the universe revolves around a phallus. But Jung..." she said, with her usual understatement. "Listen, Sakthi, when I met you, walking late into my English class, you were an angry, confused child. And now... you've come so far, and learned so much... you won, Sakthi. You were put through the wringer, and you came out swinging, so be the beacon of love and hope we all know you are. Trust in yourself, and your audience, and take a leap of faith, tell them how you feel."

"What did you just say?"

"Take a leap of faith, tell them how you feel. Why?"

"No, no reason," I said, and smiled. Mrs Finch appeared behind the armchair like an apparition. She took out her old tartan blanket and wrapped it snugly around Miss Qureshi and then gestured to offer a cup of tea.

"Nice and warm in here," said Miss Qureshi, with that thawing shiver you get when you've just come in from the cold. She picked up a book from the side table and began to read.

"Kettle's warm," I said.

The leaves spun hypnotically around the pot. No wonder those old fortune tellers thought they could see the future in this caffeinated merry-go-round. But what does the future hold for me, I thought.

"And the hijab?" said Miss Qureshi, walking over to the kitchen with a couple of teacups.

"Dunno, feels right. Don't get me wrong, I'm not going out clubbin' in this, but today it's comforting... sound weird?" I said.

"No, not at all, plus it's tartan! And good that you've let out the creases."

"Yeah, the poor hijab has been through the wringer too."

In the chapel, a dour pastor, livened only by the bold colours of his stole, nervously looked at his watch as the latecomers took their seats at the back of the stalls. The service was crammed into the twenty-minute slot allocated by the cemetery management. He raced through selected versus from John 14 and Romans 8 to let people say their part, and when everybody had done so I stood up to take the lectern.

"Me mam always said people are like wild rice, even the toughest grains eventually soften, ya just need patience. I didn't 'ave a clue what she meant like, not until I met Mrs Finch. She were 'ard, even cruel sometimes in her opinions, her observations on life, but she meant well. She asked me once o'er a cuppa tea whose side I'd be on, Gandhi, or Churchill?" I looked over at Aaliyah, Zaineb and Beydaan, all squashed up on the edge of a pew. Mr Drummond leaned over and whispered something to them, and they all smiled.

"I'll miss that, the directness, the courtesy. Nowadays, we go 'bout our business lookin' at each other with suspicion, and life feels like one big game of wink murder. Dunnit? I wonder what she'd 'ave made of this, Christians, Muslims, old 'n' young, right 'n' left, our ragbag little community all gathered here for her funeral. But for me, today, if only for an instant – like the mist off our breath, I feel like we're together, in it together. That's Mrs Finch's parting gift to us and we should honour her by rememberin' what we 'ave in common, the values we share."

The pastor followed with a brief sermon and finished the service with a benediction. A young girl from the local parish stood by the coffin. Her red locks fell upon her slender shoulders, her pale skin a tribute to the quilted snow that covered the graveyard outside. When the pallbearers lifted the casket onto their shoulders and made their way down the aisle, she sang Aye Fond Kiss in a heart-warming voice that took the nip out of the December day. As her chest expanded in the freezing chapel and her lungs expelled the icy air laden with melody, the men lowered the coffin into the grave.

"Do not be afraid. I am the first and the last, and I am the Living One. I was dead, and now I am alive for evermore," said the pastor.

"Go on lass, it's you." Mr Drummond gave me a nudge.

"You sure?" I said.

"It's what she would've wanted," he said.

"We have entrusted our sister Maeve Elspeth Finch to God's merciful keeping, we now commit her body to the ground, earth to earth, ashes to ashes, dust to dust," said the pastor.

I stepped up to the graveside with a handful of earth and threw the soil into the gaping hole. Mr Drummond put his arm around my shoulder after I walked back to stand with the rest of the mourners. When the pastor finished, we watched the gravediggers go about their work. After the burial the crowd took their leave of the departed and headed back up the hill for the funeral reception in the town centre.

In the distance a tall, dark figure cut a lonely path across the graveyard. He walked hurriedly towards Mrs Finch's grave, and when he was close enough, I could make out that it was one of the boys from the Black Paws.

"Dast! What you doin' 'ere? Bit nippy for hill walkin' int' Dark Peaks," I said, nodding at his backpack.

His eyes darted here and there, but mainly stayed fixed on the ground, ashamed, or embarrassed, or conflicted, the range of emotions were transient and hard to read upon his tormented face.

"Came to pay me respect, innit," he said.

"To Mrs Finch, for what?"

"*Haan*, 'member time feds were all up in our face like, ya know, the night of the riots? Well, I got nicked din't I, an' lo behold it's Mrs Finch who's come and paid the fine, *hamdulillah*."

"What?! Why? No wait, first what?" I said.

"I know *yaar*, mental, eh? Long story like, but I also wanna say sorry to you."

"To me, for what?"

"For callin' ya a slapper an' all... I just got upset coz I really liked ya, 'n' I took it out on ya. I shunt've. So sorry for that, coz you, Sakthi, yer like the one shinin' light int' community, ya deserved better, sister," he said.

"Aww bruv, that's sweet. Yer not so bad yerself like, though I'm findin' it quite 'ard to get used to ya with a beard. What 'appened?" I said.

"I found God, innit?" he said.

"*Accha*? Is that where you're off to now, greener pastures?"

"*Insha'Allah*, he's all I got left."

"Well, when ya see him, put in a good word for us, won't you." Dast forced a smile.

"*Suno* Sakthi, listen, I bought these flowers for Mrs Finch, and I in't got a clue which ones she'd like. Could ya choose and put 'em by her grave?"

"Sure, gi's 'em 'ere," I said.

"Keep rest for yerself like," he said.

"Second fiddle to a corpse! Thanks, Dast," I said.

He gave me a huge bunch of flowers before turning on his heels and lumbering off into town with that massive pack on his back. It took a while to untangle all the stalks and take out the ones she'd like the best. I laid the flowers down on the ground and headed over to the Muslim section to be with Meghna.

Winter came early in Shaleton with a covey of red-breasted robins. In the still air, neither evergreen nor holly rustled, and the virgin snow crumpled pleasingly under my feet. All around the cemetery the hoarfrost transformed the rusty railings into elegant, crystalline structures, whilst high above the rooftops the moon sailed across a sea of stars. My fingertips stung in the biting cold; I felt alive in the ghostly wilderness. What I'd do to share this moment, one more worldly second with Meghna. I wiped a tear from my cheek and knelt by her grave.

"Amma, I'm free."

Glossary

accha/aitcha	OK. Used to express assent or understanding; 'okay', 'all right'. Also used interrogatively, at the end of a statement, to prompt agreement, approval, or confirmation; 'is that so?', 'really?' Used to express surprise, doubt, anger, joy, etc.
arre	hey, come on, yo. Used to express a range of emotions and commands, esp. annoyance, surprise, or interest, or to attract someone's attention.
bap-re bap	oh my. Used to express amusement or slight annoyance.
beti/beta	woman/man
bhai/bhaisab	brother
bhabbi	sister-in-law
jaldi	quick
jao/zao	go
jee/jee-oi	yes (polite)
jee-na	no (polite)
haan	yes, informal (Urdu)

ish	exclamation of pain, surprise, dislike, sympathy...
na	no, informal
na-to	no, denial
nahin	no, informal (Urdu)
nje	yes, informal
taratari	quick
thik ache/tik asse	OK, alright, it's good.
yaar	friend, mate, dude (Urdu)
ya Maboud/ ya Ghafoor	Oh God!

 Taste all the mouth-watering traditional dishes mentioned in this story by scanning this QR code.

www.sakthi.mishahussain.com

Acknowledgements

Onek dhonobad to my family, especially to you Amma and Abba for giving me this amazing heritage: the Bengali language, the music, and most of all the food, despite being so far away from Bangladesh. I was embarrassed by my culture when I was younger, but now I see that it is central to who I am – what an incredible gift.

A big shout out to Beatrice, Arman, Joanna, Hannah, Gilles, Ananya, Clara, Sharon and Will for their patience, advice and motivation as well as Mikhail and Emily for the inspiration. Safe to say without *The Master and Margarita* or *Wuthering Heights*, Sakthi may never have been conceived.

Similarly, thanks to the CBC class of Aug 17 which has spawned so many talented writers, many of whom were beta-readers for this book. You bore the brunt of the first iterations of Sakthi, bless, your feedback was both helpful, and kind. Good to see so many of you on the bookshelves.

Caroline Ambrose at the Bath Novel Awards, you are a legend. No doubt that without the BNA Sakthi would have been dead in the water, and indeed, almost was had it not been for the heroic efforts of Helen Corner-Bryant and Kathryn Price at Cornerstones who dragged it out and gave it mouth-to-mouth. Many thanks to the small team at Manchester Voices who helped with the voice of Sakthi, Tone and Dast. Can't wait to read your research into northern English dialects – so important. Meanwhile, to Mohona who drew on her East London childhood to help voice Aaliyah and Zaineb I say *dhonobad, innit*.

Flora Rustamova – you make editing fun. Thanks for banging my thick skull against a wall whenever I wrote something dumb (quite often) and for giving me courage when I felt like I had pushed the boundary too far. As for Lin Webb, some of your editorial spots were so good I want to shout it out from the roof tops. Thanks for saving my (halal) bacon.

Go raibh míle maith agat, Fiachra McCarthy for the striking cover design – just fantabulous.

Accha, I could not have written this book without the countless women from around the globe who let me in to their life stories. It opened my eyes to the scale of inequity and inequality worldwide. I can't name you without giving away your identities, but suffice to say, I owe you all a great debt of gratitude. Thank you for placing your trust in me.

To Bangladesh, the country that I was born in, and the UK the country that raised me – thank you. Whether I walk in the tea gardens of Sylhet or the green pastures in the North, I feel at home. Your beauty inspires me in more ways than imaginable, and your peoples are closer in their values than meets the eye.

Finally, massive thanks to Kevin and Hetha Duffy at Bluemoose. Such a privilege to be published by an indie press based near where the novel is set and by peeps who live and breathe the context. It was bold to print *Sakthi* and I'm grateful for your conviction to tell the stories that matter.

Shobaike dhonobad, ebon' bhalo thaken.